ROAD TO GANNEIOUS

ROAD TO GANNEIOUS

by
Gerald Richardson Brown

AUTHOR'S NOTE: This is a story. It is not a true story, although it is based on documented facts. I have taken the times and places of lives lived, and drawn from them a narrative that is imaginary. My portrayal of character and behaviour is fiction.

Photos by the author. Front cover: Loyalist landing re-enactment, Adolphustown, 2010; Bierhaus, above Salzburg. Back cover: reconstructed blockhouse, Coteau-du-Lac; George Parliament Wagar, great grandson of Eberhardt Waeger; author as American rifle-man. Spine: replica of *Endeavour*, Cook's ship; map detail, *Historical Glimpses of Lennox and Addington*, County Council, 1964. Page xi: Spital am Drau; page 141: old channel (*rigolet*) to facilitate navigation of Coteau-du-Lac rapids.

Maps by the author.

Volume 1 of 2

Library and Archives Canada Cataloguing in Publication
Brown, Gerald Richardson, 1930-
    The road to Ganneious / Gerald Richardson Brown.
ISBN 978-1-894994-68-2 (v. 1)
    1. United Empire loyalists--Fiction. I. Title.
PS8603.R6836R62 2012   C813'.6   C2012-902321-3

RECYCLED
Paper made from
recycled material
FSC
www.fsc.org   FSC® C100212

Printed at Gauvin Press, Quebec

Conundrum Press
Greenwich, Nova Scotia, Canada
www.conundrumpress.com

Conundrum Press acknowledges the financial support of the Canada Council for the Arts and the Government of Canada through the Canada Book Fund toward its publishing activities.

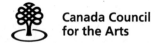

Canada Council   Conseil des Arts
for the Arts   du Canada

To all those who came before and to those who should know them:

Susan, Andrew, James, Milo, Mia, Angus.

"There are moments when we all, in one way or another,
have to go to a place that we have never seen,
and do what we have never done before."
— Karen Armstrong, *A Short History of Myth*

GANNEIOUS: Once an Indian village, later a French mission of the Sulpicians. Its exact location is not known, but thought to have been somewhere between the lower reaches of the Napanee River and the north shore of Lake Ontario. It was in this region the English called Cataraqui #3, that Johann Eberhardt Waeger, daughter Hanna, sons Thomas and Willem settled in 1784 as refugees of the American Revolution.

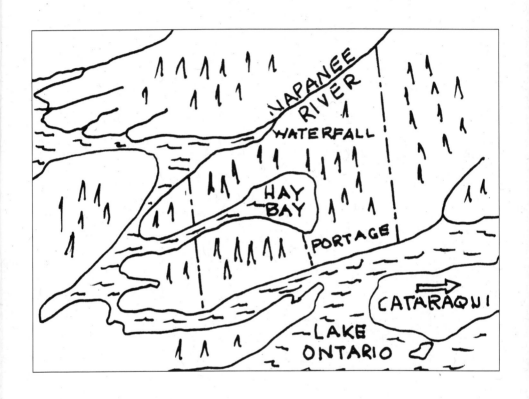

TABLE OF CONTENTS

BOOK ONE
THE PATHFINDERS

"I am Traveling to Heaven in the Chariot of Time,
I am Striving to Reach my True Home there."
— Mar Thoma Hymn

PROLOGUE

The rain from the night before had stopped, but the morning was wet with a cold wind blowing through the trees that formed a straight line across the churchyard. In spite of the rain, the last of the winter's snow covered the cemetery, except for the black hole in the hard earth that had been dug to receive his last remains. The few mourners that braved the elements had gone, leaving me to a final parting, surrounded by the ghosts of ancestors. The gravediggers appeared and took away the green cloth made to look like grass, which covered the pile of earth that soon would entomb my father.

As clumps of wet earth from the shovels of the gravediggers thumped down on the coffin lid, the hollow rhythm they made seemed to me like voices from the past. As I stood over the grave, the voices grew louder and more persistent until I became very agitated. I had come to mourn the passing of my father, but with the drumming of the dirt and stones on the lid of the coffin my sadness turned to regrets. I mourned not so much for my father but for his father, his father's father, and the lives of all the people that made the essence of this man being put into the ground to rot and be forgotten. It left me puzzled as I turned away from his last resting place to begin the journey home.

Suffused with thoughts of his life, and with regrets that I had not known him well, I hadn't noticed that I had been pulled to the very spot where his ancestors lay under the earth. At this very place they had made their first home in the wilderness. As I stood on the road under dark clouds I could see the black waters of the bay through the trees, the winter ice still clinging to the shoreline. The wind in the lofty pines whispered the story of the place, turning my thoughts inward, perhaps due to the recent passing of my father and a missing part of my life.

I fancied I saw a log cabin in a small clearing. From the stone chimney a plume of smoke curled into a heavy low-lying purple sky. Around one corner of the cabin I could just make out a small open-fronted shed intended to give the farm animals shelter from the snow. Beyond the shed a few stumps stuck their crudely cut tops above the snow and at the edge of the clearing a snake rail fence sat atop a pile of rocks.

A pair of snowshoes stood by the cabin door, and to the left of the cabin door a large iron kettle over a black fire pit told me of the recent scalding of a butchered pig.

The air was freezing cold and the wind off the bay whistled right through my clothes, giving me chills. A storm was on its way. I was about to leave when I spotted three men snowshoeing out of the woods.

The leader of this group was a man beyond middle age dressed in doeskins and fur, carrying a long gun under one arm and what appeared to be a dead rabbit in his hand. The other men, midway between boyhood and manhood, trudged behind the leader. It appeared he held the sole hunting prize, for there was no evidence that the younger men had bagged any game, although the oldest of the trio carried a gun. They had no pleasure in their faces, perhaps disappointed because their game bags were empty. Seeing me beside the road, the older man made a motion join them. Being very cold and not a little curious I welcomed his invitation.

The cabin was well and sturdily constructed, indicating a skilled builder. Inside, the air was tainted with smoke but very warm. A young woman stood beside the open hearth and turned a spit upon which roasted the carcass of a pig. She was in the full bloom of youth, her features flushed from the heat of the fire. When the men entered the room she abandoned her chore to greet them. The oldest man and the youngest must have been her father and her brother, for she passed them over without a glance and went to the man whom I presumed to be her loved one. She helped him remove his outer garments.

The father was short in stature and somewhat bent with hard physical work. He had rough features with a strong nose and pointed chin mostly hidden by a bushy beard. Unruly wiry hair, almost completely grey, fell in a sloping wave across his forehead. His blue eyes were still bright under dark brows and seemed to confirm my impression that he was younger in years than his appearance and bearing would indicate. He gave his name as Eberhardt, and from his manner I could swear he knew who I was and had expected me to visit his home. I was introduced to his daughter, Hanna, his son, Willem, and to James, Hanna's young man. I was told an older son Thomas had a farm "over on the river." Hanna explained that her mother had taken the other children to live with her family in Poughquag when the rebels confiscated their farm, and that after the war Lena had decided not to come to Canada.

I was invited to stay for supper, although my host apologized for the simplicity of his offering, as the roast pig was not yet ready. I accepted with all the grace I could muster while thinking I should leave before the storm broke.

Hanna served a meal of stew made of rabbit, fish, potatoes, squash, and preserved cranberry juice, which I was told was a delicate luxury of the St. Regis Indians. This was followed by Hanna's freshly baked bread soaked in maple syrup.

The company was pleasant and the atmosphere warm and welcoming, almost as if James and I were members of this motherless family.

After supper, Eberhardt retired to a chair in a corner beside the fire with his pipe. He told me of the hardships of his life, what with the crop failure and the ever-present danger from the starving Indians. But nothing was as bad as the war. Getting old, he felt his time was soon to come and he wanted to get something off his mind, something that was making him acutely anxious. The storm was now raging outside, forcing me to give up any thoughts of leaving, so I relaxed, prepared to learn something of Eberhardt's life and times. He began his story by telling of a visit from an Indian elder from the area.

"We had been settled in this place for about five years after the American war had ended, when one night a starving Indian came to my door and asked for food. He looked very thin and ragged but was of a tall and dignified stature. He wore a dirty blanket over his skins, pulled up to his nose against the cold, but the part of his face between his fur hat and the blanket was near frozen; a deep purple colour, the colour of the sky off to the east. A heavy storm was brewing.

"The Indian gave his name as *Deyohyogo*, which he said meant, 'touches the sky.' His condition in such weather moved my heart to pity for a fellow human out in the cold and snow begging for food on such a night, but while my heart was soft, my head was hard. It was a year of famine for both the settlers and Indians, with the crops failing and forage for the wild animals drying up in the ground. The deer and moose were dying from hunger and starving wolves. We had no money to buy molasses, sugar, or salt. The crops had failed that summer from drought. There was very little to eat for anyone. We had barely enough food to keep ourselves alive through the harsh winter, let alone feed the Indians.

"I was about to turn the Indian away from my door when Hanna came up to me and implored me to have him sup with us. Her young man was visiting and she had made a fish stew; enough, she said, for all. Looking again at the shivering figure at the door, I invited the Indian to share our simple meal. In spite of my worry that we would not have enough, Hanna served a fine supper.

"The brewing storm had turned into a roaring blizzard, but we were warm and safe, with a comforting fire in the grate. Since it was such a stormy night outside the cabin the Indian was reluctant to leave, so we retired from our supper and sat by the fire with a pipe. Full of food and good humour from the strong drink made by Hanna, the Indian seemed intent on telling the story of his homeland as his gift in exchange for our offering of food."

The ancient peoples of this place the Black Robes called Ganneious believed that Awehegowah, the great eagle, is the messenger of the Creator. She can see into the soul of man, and can fly higher than any other being. She lived with the Thunderbird, the bird of the wild storm. It is said her home was the birthplace of Hayehwata, who escaped death from his grandmother's anger and paddled his stone canoe across the lake the Cayuga people call Ganyadaiyo. Many eons ago when the earth was young, Awehegowah flew from the eagle mound to visit her hunting territory. Her keen eyes swept over the land below.

The soaring eagle saw below the sparkling great water fed by five rivers, in those olden days swollen with salmon and the wily pike. As she soared high above the pristine waters, the earth below the keen eye of the eagle was shaped like the ancient track of the Spirit Deer when she stepped into the primordial mud at the beginning of the world. The Spirit Deer left her presence at this place to last for all time. For many eons the waters rose as the ice retreated from the warmth of the South Wind, but the Spirit Deer's track was saved by the Spirit of the Woods so that man could hunt the animals and eat the fruits of the land, and at night dance with the oiled maidens shining in the light of many fires and driven to wild passion by the rhythm of the drums.

One summer day, a red man with an eagle feather in his hair dragged his canoe onto the beach. He was a warrior of the Gayogohono people from across the great water. He was Hehsot, my grandfather of the Cayuga people, which in the white man's words means 'People of the Great Swamp.'

At the place where grandfather beached his canoe, a stream flowed into the Great Lake of the Iroquois. Hehsot paddled his canoe upstream to its end, and carrying his canoe on his back, walked over the hill. There he could see blue water in the distance. He found the head of another stream flowing into the waters of a small lake. He paddled around the lake in his canoe, and saw it was a bay of the Great Lake, reached by a wide, crooked river. In the light of the campfire, he told his brothers of the land he had found. His brothers listened to his story, and for many years Hehsot and his kinfolk lived off the fruits of the land around the bay and fished in its bountiful blue waters.

I was confused by the Indian's description. I said to Eberhardt, "Was he speaking of the bay we see just yonder?"

"We call it Hay Bay because of the reeds at the east end. As near as I can tell, my cabin is close to the site of an old Indian village that the first American settlers knew as Ganneious. People hereabouts claim the village was at the waterfall on the Napanee River, where Clark's mills are situated, or at the mouth of the river. Others claim the village was beside the bay, or at the landing place by the lake. No one knows for sure, but there is an old woman with some learning that lives over by the river who tells pretty much the same yarn that the Indian *Deyohyogo* told me that stormy night."

The Cayuga people of the bay grew to be many, and hearing of the Great Spirit of the white man, sent a runner to ask the Black Robes to visit their village and speak of the ways of their Great Spirit. Many moons passed and no Black Robes came so the old chief journeyed to the east to see the great white chief at Cataraqui. The white-skinned chief listened to the runner and sent Father Fenlon, a Sulpician missionary, to Ganneious. Father Fenlon was welcomed to Ganneious with a feast of pumpkin fried in suet and bowls of corn and sunflower seeds. The maidens and young braves danced to the drums all night.

Father Fenlon and one other Black Robe told the people of Ganneious of the love their Great Spirit had for the Cayuga people. And they told them of the chief of all the Indians, who lived in Cataraqui. Many turning of the seasons passed in this way, and the Black Robes had their way with the people of Ganneious.

The soaring eagle that could see into the hearts of men knew that the great chief in Cataraqui was preparing for war against the People of the Longhouse who lived south of the Great Lake. With treachery in his heart, the great chief at Cataraqui sent runners out into the land to bring news of a great feast and passing of the pipe to be held at the fort of Cataraqui. Many chiefs and their families journeyed to the east to listen to the white man's chief and to pass the pipe. As soon as the Indians were assembled in the palisade of Cataraqui, they saw the treachery. The gates were shut and the soldiers came out of their hiding places with pointed guns. Able-bodied warriors were made galley slaves on French ships. Eighteen chiefs and sixty women and children were made slaves. In this way, Ganneious was no more. The people of Ganneious were forgotten.

Not everyone had been taken away by the great chief in Cataraqui; Grandfather Hehsot and his family were visiting cousins across the lake. His village was empty, but grandfather lived with a few survivors, old men and women that could not travel. Most soon died.

Tribes of the Algonquin came from the north, and after great wars with the Long-house people, began to settle along the north shore of the Great Lake. One of these tribes was the Mississauga, a tribe of the Ojibwa, enemies of the Cayuga. But, grandfather's sons and daughters were adopted by the Mississauga and lived with them in peace.

Eberhardt interrupted his story about the Indian by suddenly jumping up from his chair and anxiously pacing back and forth in front of me. At first I thought the heat of the fire and Hanna's strong drink had made him restless, but then I could see that he had become agitated by something in the Indian's story. After a few moments of pacing he sat again. His face showed pain, but regaining his composure, he said to me, "On that stormy night, listening to old Indian's love for what was lost to him, I wondered about my own lost heritage. I began to reflect upon my own life. *Deyohyogo* knew of his people, I know naught of mine. The Indian's tale whetted my appetite to learn something of my story. I remembered that Marga-retha, my mother, kept an old Bible that still exists after all these years, but her hope that I become lettered was a false hope. I dug potatoes and went to war instead.

"Hanna appeared to be gripped by the Indian's story and brought forth tarts that she had been saving for her intended. James had no ambition to face the storm so he did not move from his place beside my daughter. Hanna asked the Indian to continue his tale."

Many seasons passed before the Red Coats appeared in the country of the Indian and claimed it for themselves. At the end of their civil war that cut Indian lands apart, men were sent out by the great chief of the English to find Indian lands for the white men from across the Great Lake who refused to live with their brethren to the south or with the Black Robes. The great chief of the white man bartered with the Mississauga for a strip of their land as far back from the Great Lake as a man could travel in a day. For the use of their lands the Mississauga chiefs demanded that all their families be clothed and that those who did not have fusees should receive new ones, some powder, and balls for their winter hunting, as much coarse red cloth as will make about a dozen coats and as many laced hats. The agent of the great chief of the English reported the Mississauga chiefs appeared much satisfied that the white people were coming to live among them, except they showed uneasiness about talk that Mohawks would be living on their lands.

One day, when the woods were on fire with many colours, Awehegowah saw many canoes standing offshore with men of white faces and red coats. One canoe landed on the beach below a small meadow, beside which a stream flowed into the Great Lake. Finding the landing site a good one, all canoes came into the stream and the people gathered together. A man holding aloft a wooden cross read from the white man's Bible and prayed to his God. The sound of singing floated in the air over the clearing.

When the singing was done, their chief unrolled a large paper and men pulled small pieces of paper from the chief's hat. The new white tribe pushed their canoes upstream until they reached the old Indian carrying place that led to Ganneious. Here they settled on their new land and began to cut the trees and build wigwams from the trees. The great chief of the English promised provisions until the white tribe could provide for themselves. Some years the white people ate roots to stay alive.

One day, many seasons later, the eagle, soaring in the heavens looking for a scrap of food, saw a small clearing with a log cabin surrounded by tree stumps. No smoke came from the chimney, even though it was late in the season of growing. Awehegowah who can see into the hearts of men saw an old man lying on his bed, sick and alone, his dreams unfilled and his regrets torturing his fevered brain. He was still about this world, but his soul was dead.

"At this point the Indian finished his story. I thought he was a sorcerer and I wanted to see the back of him. Storm or no storm I wanted him to leave. He made me angry and depressed. Some of the words were the story of our landing in Fredericksburg, but they became frightening to me as I recognized myself in my last days. I could tell that Hanna was as agitated as me. She said to the Indian, 'What happens to the old man?' He said, *The future will be as it will be! When Awehegowah looks into the heart of the old man she sees only shadows.*

"With these words I noticed the Indian's pipe was cold and the fire was but a pile of embers. He got up from his place and prepared to leave, perhaps sensing my mental anguish. Having no bed for him, I was unable to insist that he stay for the night in any case, and since the storm had quieted some, I allowed that it was late. As he readied himself to leave my cabin, the Indian turned to me and said,

The eagle that can see in to the hearts of man cannot see into the heart of the old man in the cabin. She sees only shadows because the old man does not belong to this place. He is not made of the earth of this place. His ototeman, as the Ojibwa say, is somewhere else. Without the story of his tribe a man walks only as a shadow, he does not exist.

"The Indian was using words to deliberately anger me. I protested, 'I am only a poor farmer; nothing.' *Deyohyogo* looked at me with his black eyes full of sadness and spoke."

No man is nothing. A man may be as a drop of water in the stream that runs down the hill to the bay, but every drop helps fill the bay and makes it bountiful. As the water in the dipper you drink from carries the story of the stream, so earthly life carries the story of your tribe.

"After finding his blanket and hat, he prepared to leave my cabin and go out into the storm. Just as he was at the door he turned to me and said, *Hear my words!*

"When *Deyohyogo* walked from our cabin into the night I was muddled. Before that night I had no thought of where I came from, but that night it became very important to me. The Indian was correct, without a story I am but a shadow. I resolved to make an *ototeman* from my mother's Bible into which she had written things before I was born, the history of our tribe as it had come to her. It was a tattered old book bound in grey linen cloth, stained with age and her tears. It had been her most prized possession.

"One day near the end of the first summer in America, sitting in front of me on our rock, she took the book from a fold in her skirts and held it up in front of me. She said, 'Eberhardt, this is a book into which I tell the stories of your father's kinfolk. When I die, I want you to have it so that someday you will understand why your father left the old country and brought us to this God-forsaken wilderness. I hope one day you may get learning and make something of the story.'

"Mother's hope that I would be learned was not fulfilled, so I gave the Bible and her letters to Tom's wife, Mary."

Ancient grandfather Eberhardt had my attention. I knew he knew I was the source of his story. Being stuffed to the gills with knowledge, but by what transpired afterwards, evidently not much wisdom, I said, "Would you like me to take up the project?"

The sly old devil twisted in his chair and with a quizzical look, which I could see was affected, responded, "There's not much to go on. Do you really want to do this?"

Now hesitant, as I thought more about the work involved, I reluctantly, hooked by the old man's intensity, said, "Yes," and the deal was set. Foolishly, I promised to make a story from the words he had given me, along with Margaretha's Bible and

7

her letters.

"I hope you are true to my story, else I will forever be a shadow."

The storm increased in ferocity that night into a full-scale blizzard, with high winds blowing the snow into the clearing and piling it up in drifts wherever there was an obstruction to its wild fury. I was bound to stay the night, and much to my embarrassment and against my objection I was given Willem's bed in the loft, while poor Willem was told to sleep on the floor.

We were housebound in this fashion the next day.

During my visit, the old man told the story of his kinfolk, often boring his offspring who had heard some of the story before. I was enthralled at the revelations and determined to fix them to memory so that I could pass what I learned to his future generations.

The next morning I arose to a world of brilliant sunshine. With the sun came a release of the emotions of the past days. My inner world had been purged of sadness at the death of my father and instead filled with stories that drew aside one corner of the veil that had covered the deep essence of who he had been and the ancestral history that had moulded his life.

I thanked Eberhardt and Hanna for their hospitality and for something I could not then put into words. I bade them goodbye and stepped out of the cabin into the crisp winter air. I left with a very confused mind, but feeling that I had been given a gift that I needed to do something with. Fate had set me down on a road I could not leave until its end.

But fate was fickle. Mary, Eberhardt's daughter-in-law, was 240 years old, and was clearly not able to hand over Margaretha's Bible. After much searching of the minds and treasures of her descendants, fortune turned it up in the abandoned house of my grandmother. The house dated from the turn of the century, but had not been lived in since 1929 when my grandmother had sold it to a stranger. It was now a windowless shell, with many badly weathered clapboards missing, but it still stood, defiant against time, sun, rain, and wind.

It was in the disappearing house where my father was born that I found a dust-covered old trunk in a hidden room, which I had at first taken to be an abandoned cistern. In the bottom of the trunk, under a large number of pictures and letters, I found an object that on inspection turned out to be two books and some letters wrapped in oiled paper and tied with a faded blue ribbon. Beneath a packet of letters was a battered canvas covered ship's logbook, and an old Bible covered in grey linen cloth. With shaking hands I opened the Bible. It was written in German. Hardly believing my eyes, I flipped through the very yellowed pages, looking for personal writings. The last sheaves of the Bible contained several pages of barely legible handwritten notes and letters. It appeared to be a family tree. Going to a window for better light I peered at the first entry. There were many names that

I recognized from Eberhardt's story; *Kaspar, Ursula, Radenthein, Eva, Florian....* Skipping through the faint entries I looked for the word *Eberhardt* and close to the very end there it was; *Johann Eberhardt Waeger,...März 22,1732....*

In the cold reality of my world I had come to believe that the encounter with my ancient ancestor following my father's funeral was a vision, an illusion brought on by an overwrought son full of guilt. But now the truth of that vision was in my hands. Fate had delivered me to the road that would lead to the truth of my existence.

It took a journey to Salzburg to begin to cement the truth of my vision and the beginning of the story of Eberhardt, before he was born.

My wife and I were motoring north from a holiday in Florence. We left a day early to clear the Brenner Pass before the impending snowstorm in the mountains closed the road. Clearing the pass successfully, we bypassed Innsbruck, and since it was still early in the day we decided to drive to Salzburg where we found a delightful inn at the edge of that city.

The next day some inner voice urged me to go into the mountains to the south. Since we had made up a day we turned south towards Venice. After clearing the Katschberg Pass toll station we stopped at a lookout by the side of the road. On the slope of the mountain to our right clung a small house with chimney smoke wafting into the crisp, clear air. Looking down into a beautiful green and white valley we could see a town far below. The road sign pointing to the exit for this town read "Spital am Drau" and an arrow below pointed to "Radenthein." I was stunned. This homely road sign turned my spiritual experience into reality.

My thoughts sped back to an old man sitting beside a roasting pig on a spit over a smoldering fire, smoking Indian tobacco while a blizzard was roaring outside his cabin. Standing in this magical alpine wonderland I could distinctly hear his voice floating on the slight breeze coming over the peaks. The resonance of this place with the story the man told of his kin in those housebound days was so powerful that I now knew the truth of his tale. Silent in humility, I drove down the winding road and along the river to the place that harboured my beginnings.

1

JÖRG
The Warrior

In ancient times the Celts came up the rivers to mine salt. They called the region Noricum. Roman legions marched over the mountain passes to conquer the barbarian lands to the north and assimilated Noricum. Slavs came into the mountains by way of the Drava. They called the region Carantania. Bavarian armies brought German-speaking peoples into the valley of the River Drau and it became a region within the Holy Roman Empire. At the time of our story, the lands south of the alpine peaks were the Crown lands of the Hapsburg Emperor, Ferdinand II. One province was known as Carinthia.

From the Katschberg Pass on the road from Salzburg to Venice a traveller follows the Lieser River to where it joins the river Drau at Spital am Drau. About twelve miles to the east is the ancient town of Radenthein. It is here that our story begins, in the year 1620.

The drums and bells used to drive away winter were silent. The snow was mostly gone from the lower slopes, and soon it would be time to herd the sheep to the high meadows. Although the morning fog still hung over the cold mountain waters of the Kaningbach, the rising sun had found a notch in the eastern peaks and was sending its rays across the valleys to bathe the snowfields of the Nockberge in a pearl-like glow. In the shadow of the lofty Priedrof, the sun had not yet brought warmth to the brown fields, nor sparkle to the burbling

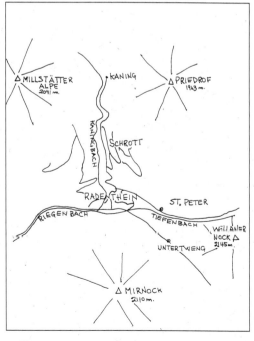

Kaningbach. A shroud-like mist hid the old hamlet of Radenthein.

Just above the mist, above Radenthein, on the lower slope of the Priedrof, a cluster of rustic farm buildings sat on a narrow plateau that clung precariously to the steep incline. Although it was late springtime, the snow was still deep in the wedge under the rock face, and in the shade of the buildings. The sun's rays had not yet reached the house of Jörg's father, still in shadow in spite of the brightening heavens above.

Two people stood in front of the small house made of saplings and clay daub. As Jörg walked on the path to the road below, the man and woman stood with slumped shoulders just outside the roughly-hewn door of the house. The worn and tired couple's eyes followed the slowly diminishing figure of their son as he moved down the path. He turned, threw his arm heavenward in a final farewell gesture, and disappeared around the slope of the hill, leaving the old man and woman to return to the work of the day.

He had not yet seen twenty-one seasons when Jörg left his home in the mountains to fight the Bohemians. In the early morning light he walked on the narrow cart path with the strong and precise strides of a hill man, bearing westward toward the crude road that would take him across the Kaningbach, and from there to the high mountain pass of the Katschberg. Jörg was short, even among his people. His face, visible beneath a green hat sporting a jaunty feather, was made from the rough features of the people that inhabited the region. Other than the colourful hat, his dress and manner were those of farm stock, from his brown coat and pantaloons to his heavy leather boots; boots that would take him along worn mountain trails through the upland valleys to the raucous Salzach River that flows northward out of the mountains.

To the south, beyond a cluster of hills, the river Drau gurgled as its glacial waters rushed down from the Tyrol to nurture the valleys of Upper Carinthia and beyond; a watery highway that had brought hardy miners and herders into these regions for hundreds of years. The alpine peoples that settled the valleys and hillsides and nurtured the thin land were a precarious human presence in the overall grandeur of nature.

The night before he left home, Jörg's brothers and his sister Eva came to his father's house for a gathering of the family. Florian and Balthauser came up from the mill that was just ending the winter season of timber sawing. Ursula prepared a feast of pork hocks, turnips, sausage, cheese, and his father's beer. Kaspar, Jörg's father, said a prayer over the meal and after the farewells, Florian and Balthauser left for the mill. Erasmus and Jörg's younger brother, Thoman, stayed until late evening when they went to spend the night with the sheep, which were threatened at that time of year by starving wolves.

Jörg said goodbye to his small son, Leonardt, who he was leaving to the care of his sister. Leonardt did not weep, not really knowing what was happening to him. He had already accepted Jörg's sister as his protector having lived with her almost since birth. Parting with his son, perhaps never to see him again, was difficult, but without a mother, Leonardt would do well with Eva and her husband Ambros.

Jörg had hoped to go without fanfare, but his mother, Ursula, had fussed over him as he was preparing to leave. She had stood in front of him in her broad apron, her brown hair streaked with grey wrapped in a bun. Holding back tears, she had gently bowed to him as she pressed a package of her special buns with unsalted butter and gooseberry jelly into his hands. She had also included cheese and a sausage. She wanted to preserve the dignity of the parting but she could not help scolding Jörg a little for leaving her. His father hung back until this loving scene was finished, then came forward just as Jörg was at the door, and without words, shook his son's hand. Jörg was startled since this was the first time his father had treated him as an equal. More than that, Kaspar had also been critical of Jörg's recent behaviour and as he held his father's callused and gnarled hand, Jörg waited for some sign of forgiveness. The touching of hands was his father's only blessing.

Close to the road, Jörg turned to look back at the house he was leaving. It was a cabin, really, tucked into the flank of the hill. Over the front entrance, carved into the roughly hewn lintel, was the family name, the letters so weathered they could no longer be read. The decaying lintel, the only distinguishing feature of the house, seemed to be a sign that it was right that he left before his own decay set in.

Jörg was leaving the home that had nurtured many generations of his family. His kinfolk had lived in these mountains and had overcome the alpine ruggedness, the religious conflicts and bloodshed that were the nature of the times. The stories that were told around the family's hearth after the day's work was done and before the children were sent to bed were about a battle-weary soldier named Jacobsgut des Unterweger, a Bavarian who came down the river to the Radenthein region and stayed. He built a shelter and a washhouse and then took the woman Gerda, who came to Jacobs from her father's house a distance away at Untertweng. Jacobs and Gerda coaxed sufficient abundance from the soil to raise children and prosper in a small way. A community grew around them, set on a narrow plateau between the road and the hills behind. In time it became known as Schrott. Others knew the several families who sprang from the flesh of Jacobs and Gerda as Unterwegers, and for many generations of war, pestilence, failures, and successes, they lived in the knowledge that God was looking down on them with favour.

But in Luther's time, talk of religious reform began to drift up the valleys like the voice of Satan. Trouble came when many learned reformers who could read the scriptures clashed with the authority of the Emperor. Soldiers of the Imperial army burned homes, and many people were banished from their homelands. It was a time of violent change. Jörg's grandfather Benedict, perhaps with an eye to the future for his family, began to use the shorter name Weger and proudly cut the letters into the lintel of the house he built for his bride, Ottilia. When Jörg was a small boy, Grandfather Benedict told him that the ground they had held for generations was changing hands thanks to the religious turmoil of the day.

Jörg's father told him the stories of the Schrott, Radenthein, and St. Peter settlements, and of the people that had settled the land, creating small farms on the rugged mountain slopes. As a young man, Kaspar had worked with his father and brothers caring for livestock, harvesting small crops, hunting for food, and cutting firewood for the winter. Kaspar had expected Jörg would assume the life of a farmer and herder but he had no taste for his father's life. Jörg's spirit was pushing him along a different path. He had taken to roaming the hills, using the river Drau to explore the world beyond the valley of the Kaningbach, wandering up and down the river from Lienz to Klagenfurt. Jörg's wandering became a problem for his father.

He fell in with rough men. Several were sent to jail for thieving and two were hanged. It was in Spital am Drau where he met the sister of one of his comrades, a fiery girl of seventeen. He was infatuated with her. Elizabetha was tall and thin with lustrous brown eyes and dark hair. Not particularly pretty, she was gay, determined, always seeking adventure bordering on the dangerous. She showed no inclination for a settled life, but in spite of being unfit for it she and Jörg were married. Kaspar and Ursula reluctantly honoured the marriage because Elizabetha came from his mother's village and she knew her parents to be "good people." It was a mistake.

He and Elizabetha had one stormy year together during which Jörg helped work the land of his father and grandfather along with his brothers. One year and two months after their marriage, Elizabetha died giving birth to a son. Jörg named his son Leonardt after Elizabetha's father. He brought the boy to his father's house and buried his bitterness in work. Ursula and Eva as well as Jörg's aunt looked for a wife for him, but they were not successful. He began to roam up and down the valley of the Drau again. His father was not pleased that Jörg spent so much time on the river, calling him a gypsy, "like the Hungarians." Kaspar was angry when word reached him that his son was drinking and carousing in Spital, but he knew Jörg was grieving so he said little. Another year passed in this way.

It was a year in which Jörg began to search out the destiny his grandfather had talked about. He saw changes coming. Religious conflict was raging between protesting reformers of the Church, and Ferdinand who was attempting to re-impose and maintain the authority of the traditional Church. The religious intrigues were blaspheming the beauty of Jörg's mountains and the peace of his valley.

Kaspar had met with some members of the reform movement that was sweeping up the valley, causing death and destruction to its adherents as the authorities responded with cruelty. Soldiers burned houses, destroyed churches, and dug up the dead from their resting places only to leave the coffins by the roadside. Desecrated bodies were fed to the pigs, holy books were burned, reform ministers and backers of the youth were cruelly tortured and banished, and many people were forced to flee the valley as the edict of Ferdinand's reform commission was zealously enforced. In the middle of the night soldiers broke into Jörg's uncle Adam's house, pulled his family out of their beds, and told them to leave the country. Then they locked the animals in the barn and set fire to the building. When Erasmus and Jörg went to see the damage the next day the smell of burnt flesh was still so strong they had to stand far away while they cursed the monstrous cruelty. Jörg knew it was only a matter of time before the Emperor, in the name of the Church, would root out all the reformers, and although his father was very secretive, Jörg felt he was taking a risk and urged him to go back to his Catholic roots. He had quarrelled with his father about this. Kaspar said Adam talked too much and had brought the tragedy upon himself.

'Besides," his father said to Jörg, "away to the north, past the mountains, reformers are giving Ferdinand much trouble. The Bohemians threw his envoys out a window of the palace, and have elected a new King, Elector Frederick of the Palatinate. He is a Calvinist and a leader of the protestors in the northern states. Ferdinand sent the Imperial army to put down the revolt, but so far he has not been successful."

In the midst of the turmoil in Carinthia a rumour was circulating that agents were recruiting for the army of the Catholic League under Duke Maximilian of Bavaria to help Ferdinand put down the insurrection in Prague mounted by the Bohemian Estates. Jörg had seen a notice, tacked to the door of the town hall in Spital, which gave the conditions and the rewards of service, which included an enlistment stipend, certain clothes and arms, and freedom to secure wealth by plunder. The Catholic League invited men between the ages of fifteen and forty to gather at Kruger Haus in the Katschberg Pass before the feast of St. Augustine.

It was at this time that Jörg began to think about being a soldier. Perhaps, he thought, after the war he could find a trade in one of the large towns in the north. He discussed the plan with his sister Eva, and she agreed to look after his child until Leonardt reached ten years of age. When Jörg approached his father with the decision to join Maximilian, Kaspar was furious that he wished to fight for the Pope, but in the end he gave his blessing, saying, "It might give you some self-discipline. Besides, I sense there is only future tragedy

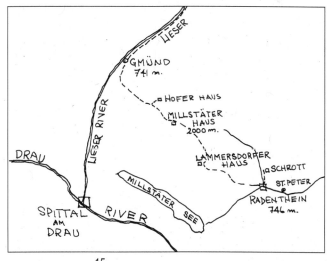

for you here."

So it was that a young mountain man set out on a path that would, after many generations, lead to a log cabin in the wilderness of North America.

The damp morning air was bone chilling, but it held the smell of warmth to come, and with the light breeze came a cacophony of sound from the small birds seeking their first meal of the day. The green earth was creeping up the hillsides, conquering the snow as it had done each spring of Jörg's life. Wildflowers were blooming, and patches of white in the greening meadows told of clover in bloom. It would soon be the time Jörg's brothers took the farm animals to the high mountain pastures for summer grazing as he had done many times. In his time as shepherd the mighty Priedrof that loomed over the valley had been his tutor and his joy. On the mountain he had learned the ways of the bears, the wolves, and their prey, his sheep. There he had learned from the crows that warned him against the wily mountain lions. Even the small creatures of the woods had pleased him, and from each he learned the joy of life and the tragedy of death. The miracle of wildflowers and stunted trees nourished by the tiniest patch of earth seemed akin to the struggles of his ancestors in the harsh climate of the mountains. In winter, wandering in the snowfields above earthbound life, the silence was so profound it had sharp edges. Jörg, in his heart, would miss his mountain more than his family.

But today he was leaving his beloved mountain, perhaps forever. He looked toward Radenthein, and toward his future. The road dropped into the mist that was still hanging over the valley and Jörg hesitated. He had made this journey countless times, but today the fog seemed like a cosmic curtain hiding the outside world; a world suddenly unknown and dangerous. The greyish cloud seemed like a final challenge to his departure, urging him to quietly accept the same role in life as his father and grandfather.

Casting guilt and doubt aside, he pushed on. The sunlight soon cleared away the moist cloud and Jörg walked with a livelier step. The sun began to warm his back as he crossed the bridge over the Kaningbach and headed north. The trail turned west toward Obermillstätt, a well-trodden and familiar route to Lammersdorfer Haus where he planned to spend the night. He would take the high country to Gmünd, preferring the warmth of the sun and soft snow of the alpine meadows to the darkly wooded creek trails, which would still be muddy and treacherous from the spring run-off. Besides, there was the danger of hungry bears roaming the valleys looking for fish in the swollen rivers.

Jörg climbed upward all morning through the thinning mist circling the small trees that still clung to the outcrops of rock. Sometimes he rested and faced the deep blue Millstätt See glistening in the green valley below and the thin, snakelike line of the river Drau stretching off to the east. By this time, Jörg was well above the lingering patches of mist, and as the sun approached its zenith the wide path he had been following ended at a small freshet. Someone had placed footstones across the rushing stream so that he was able to cross without getting wet. Here the trail narrowed as it penetrated the forest and began to rise steeply to the Millstätter Alpe. Before going on, he stopped in the clearing at the head of the creek and ate some sausage washed down with handfuls of cold, clear water. Across his back he carried bent wooden frames stretched over with animal skins he used for walking in deep soft snow. He removed the snow shoes and tied them to his feet. He began to climb.

He walked through the thinning trees all afternoon and as the sun was casting blue shadows over the slope, he came upon a small house half buried with snow. He knew this to be Lammersdorfer Haus. The door to the house was not locked, but it was unoccupied, the old man who lived there in the summertime had not yet left the comforts of the village below. The sleeping shed, a short distance up the hill, was also open. As night fell he built a small fire in the fire-pit, and after a brief supper of sausage and cheese, Jörg tramped through the snow to the sleeping shed where he wrapped himself in the blanket he carried. Exhausted from his first day on the trail, he was soon fast asleep on the platform built into the side of one wall of the shed.

It was in this manner that he crossed the Nockberge massif. He hiked along trails that had existed for many years, sometimes under the canopy of the thin forest, but mostly across snowfields where the sun warmed his bones after frigid nights in makeshift shelters at Millstätter Haus and on the Tschiernock at Hofer Haus. Here the elevation was almost 2100 metres, the highest point he would reach.

In the early afternoon of the fourth day, Jörg descended a trail beside a creek into the picturesque town of Gmünd on the river Lieser. He had an uncle in Gmünd but Jörg did not know the location of his uncle's house, and he had already decided to find his own shelter in order not to distract from his resolve to carry on to the Katschberg Pass as quickly as possible. For a few coins, he found food and shelter for the night at the alms-house attached to the church. During the meal, he enquired about the condition of the road to the pass from another young traveler, who told him that the river was high but the road was mostly dry.

Jörg left Gmünd at first light. The cart track was very rutted, but the footpath that ran beside it was indeed dry, and as the sun cleared the peaks it warmed the air. The river and the songs of birds attracted to the trees along its bank were his constant companions. He also greeted several fellow travellers, although his purpose did not allow him to tarry in conversation, but the birds and the few people on the road were a welcome change from the solitude of the previous days in the high country. The sun reached its zenith as he reached St. Nicolai, where he rested at a roadside inn. Food and beer were delivered by a pretty girl with black hair and eyes the faded blue colour of the sky seen from very high up in the mountains.

Refreshed, he set out to reach the meeting place at Kruger's before darkness set in.

After departing St. Nicolai, the Lieser became narrower and noisier and the road became more difficult. He spent that night at St. Georgen.

The following morning, in bright sunshine Jörg began the final hike to Kruger's with the snowy peaks of Großglockner soaring over his left shoulder. Jörg walked with powerful strides all day, gradually making height. The setting sun was beginning to flirt with the mountain peaks when he came upon Kruger's, a Bierhaus in the Katschberg Pass. He could not see anyone about as he approached.

This made Jörg anxious since he did not wish to be alone with Kruger and listen to his harangues, which would be inevitable when Kruger discovered he was going to join the Bavarian army. Kruger believed the Church had wronged him, and he did not hesitate in expressing his view of church people.

Jörg needn't have worried, since Kruger had left the business of the inn to his browbeaten spouse.

Frau Kruger laid some bread and sausage on a long table in the centre of the ground-floor room that had once been a stable. Jörg went to a shelf on the wall, took down a beer stein, and filled it to the brim. He had just started his meal when he heard shouts from outside the building. Peering through the small, dirty window beside the door, he saw a large group of young men, some riding in a cart and some walking. He counted eighteen, besides the grizzled driver of the cart. After all the men had retrieved their belongings from the cart, one officious fellow paid the driver, who then turned the cart around and urged the horses back down the road the way he had come. In a moment the men surrounded Jörg enquiring about his circumstances and his intent. Three of them he knew from Spital, and others looked familiar from his days on the river. One of the men he knew as Heinz told him the officious one was Günther, the recruiting agent.

Günther recognized Jörg as a new member of the group and approached him. Taking a small Bible from his shirt, Günther spoke the oath for new recruits. "Do you promise, on pain of damnation forever by God and the Church, to follow and uphold the standard of the house of Wittlesberg and Maximilian, the Duke of Bavaria, and to obey the orders of the officers and command of Count Tilly and those of the army of the Catholic League?" Jörg answered, "I do," and with these simple words the former alpine farmer and sheep herder became a fighting soldier for the Duke of Bavaria.

Günther's recruits were hungry and proceeded to order food. It was beyond Frau Kruger to keep order and before long it was chaotic, with each man helping himself to whatever he could find to eat or drink. The beer ran out and two large fellows, by this time quite drunk, made a noisy game of knocking the bung out of a second and then a third keg. By the time the men's hunger was met and their thirst slaked, the sun had long disappeared behind the rim of Großglockner, and Günther had decided that his men would stay put for the night. When Günther announced this decision, Kruger's wife promptly disappeared. Günther's announcement sparked another round of revelry, drinking, singing, and fighting that lasted until about midnight. The rowdies found places to sleep when they were exhausted, and eventually all was quiet.

T he next morning, at first light, the little band of tired and sick recruits crossed the Katschberg Pass on foot and began the descent to the Salzach River. There had been a sprinkle of snow overnight, but the sky was clear and the air crisp enough to make the snow crunch under leather boots with the hint of softness that comes with the warmth of spring. The group was mostly quiet. Some still suffered from the revelry of the night before, some appeared to accept their new life with serenity, some with obvious joy.

The road was wide enough to accommodate two abreast, which was a natural grouping. Jörg found himself walking beside a younger man who seemed too serious for the adventure opening up before him. He was taller than most of his compatriots and of lighter skin. He had yellow hair and blue eyes and he wore a foreign military coat. They walked in silence, neither man willing to open his life to scrutiny. But soon, curiosity overcame Jörg's reluctance and he ventured, "I am called Jörg." The tall one answered in a heavy accent, "I am called Jochenn. I am from Sweden." As they walked, Jörg learned that his tall partner was on his way from the south where the Duke of Savoy was raising an army to join with the northern armies to defeat the Emperor. Jörg wondered aloud why a Swede had joined an army of the Catholic League. Jochenn responded simply, "I am trying to get home. I have a favourable letter from Helga and I want to be with her." Jochenn was going home, Jörg was leaving home. The guilt came back at having left his son with sister Eva to pursue some unknown exploit in a far-away country.

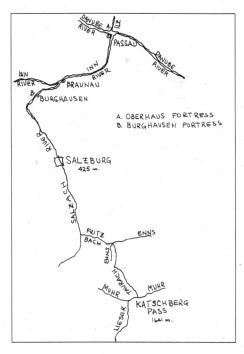

A shout from the front ranks announced the presence of a hamlet. A cluster of buildings took shape, dominated by a small but attractive church. Word spread in the ranks that it was the hamlet of Tweng. There were few citizens about. Some children watched the procession with curious eyes but did not approach the men. A few old men sat on a bench in front of the church re-telling oft-told stories. A priest came out from the church, and stood on the steps in a stance that left Jörg wondering whether he was welcoming them or guarding the church from invasion.

Günther announced a rest stop. The new recruits found suitable resting places and ate what rations they carried with them; some, it became clear, were well stocked with provisions that Frau Kruger had hidden from them the night before. As Jörg cut his sausage, he saw that Jochenn had nothing. This deepened his curiosity about Jochenn, and he considered offering him some of his rations, then hesitated about sharing his good fortune. In brutal times men had to shift for themselves.

He saw little of Jochenn throughout the rest of the day as they began climbing toward the Seekarspitze. Jörg found himself setting the pace with other men who grew up wandering over this type of terrain. By mid-afternoon they passed Obertauern lying above the road, and at dusk came to Untertauern. There were two inns here and to avoid a repeat of the chaos at Kruger's, Günther arranged for beds with the innkeepers by giving them credits that could be redeemed from the Imperial army resources. Although they were sceptical of this arrangement, the papers the agent carried looked in order and were properly sealed. Having a bed seemed to pacify the men and, except for two men who got very drunk, the scheme was a success for Günther, who needed the goodwill of the populace for further recruiting. Indeed, when Günther's authority became known, he was able to recruit four men at the Bierhaus that evening.

As they made their way down to the river Salzach each day followed a similar pattern. The men were gradually forming a cohesive unit and were beginning to anticipate reactions from each other, some discipline developing from a common understanding of each other's needs and aspirations. They left the snow behind and the air took on a sweet smell from the new growth that was just emerging beside the road. It was cold at night but the daytime temperature was warm. At the higher elevations, the strength of the sun was uncomfortable for some, but most of the men were already weather-beaten from years of living in the mountains.

When they reached the Salzach, the road to Salzburg followed the river. It was a well-trodden road that allowed easy walking and they arrived within sight of Salzburg in the late afternoon of the third day from Untertauern. Salzburg lay across the river about a league distant in the shadow of the Mönchsberg massif and the brooding Hohensalzburg fortress that guarded the approach. Here the river, which had kept them company for two days with its many moods, was now showing its strength as it shouldered its way between the Mönchsberg and Kapuzinerberg massifs, bathed in pink and orange from the setting sun.

Salzburg was something of a legend to Jörg. He was amazed at its large size, and as Günther's recruits got closer, he could see the citizens across the river preparing for the evening festivities. They came upon a small building at the side of the road, with a landing to the river's edge where a man and his three sons operated a bateau to take people and wagons across the river. Since night was fast approaching Günther was quick to arrange for the bateau and its rowers to ferry his men to

Salzburg. The recruits spilled into the boat with anticipation and anxiety because the river was running high and fast with the spring run-off from the mountains. One of the men, white with fright, said he had never been in such a vessel, but another man, apparently his friend, pushed him roughly into the boat and they were underway.

The bateau was about ten metres long with two giant sweeps, one on each end. There were places for four rowers athwart-ship. The prow and transom were square and slanted outboard from the keel to allow the boat to kiss the shore when loading and unloading vehicles. The deck could accommodate two carriages or one large baggage wagon using the ends of the boat as entry and exit ramps. This bateau had a short mast with six shrouds, which the crew could take down when transporting vehicles or a large number of farm animals. By holding the two sweeps at a certain angle to the current, much of the force needed to propel the vessel was taken from the river itself. The rowers also pulled with great gusto to avoid being swept below the town. In this way, they reached the legendary town of Salzburg just as night fell.

G ünther knew Salzburg well, having had recruited men from there, and in the gathering darkness led his new recruits about five hundred metres along the river bank to a small field abutting the cliff of the Mönchsberg. Wooden eaves, open at the front and partly cut into the rock face, covered somewhat rickety sleeping platforms. There were torches at each eave and a small fire in front of one of the platforms. On the north side of the field sat a small church and on the south side a large square building. The field was open to the river. Some of the sleeping platforms showed evidence of occupation, but Günther's men were able to find a sufficient number of unoccupied platforms for them to roll out their blankets.

Soon a fire was blazing from the supply of wood piled at one end of the platform, and a few troopers gathered around the fire. Jörg asked Günther who had built the shelters. Günther was pleased to be able to demonstrate his authority and replied, "During the first year of the war, troopers caused such chaos just trying to survive among the general population that the Emperor prevailed on the Church Bishops to provide facilities for his army in selected towns. For their part, the Bishops would receive, in perpetuity, portions of State land. An Italian order of nuns committed to the teachings of St. Ursula live in the square building yonder. There are two nuns in residence. They supply wood for fires in winter, but in return, they expect that we keep the place fit for others."

A surly voice came out of the shadows, beyond the light cast by the fire. "When do we get money to go into town?" Günther knew this was on the minds of his men, but he could not let the men loose here. He ignored the question and said, "We are here to arrange a bateau to Passau where part of Tilly's army has wintered and are mobilizing for the Bohemian campaign." After this, Günther abruptly disappeared.

The men began to grumble. They were almost out of provisions. A short, dark man that Jörg knew as Piet walked into the darkness of the town and returned shortly with a small pig that had expired from a slit throat. A spit was hastily built from tree boughs meant for firewood, wine emerged from pouches, and a feast got under way.

When the pig had been mostly consumed and the men were groggy from food and wine, Günther suddenly reappeared and began to distribute small amounts of money: by his calculation, too little to buy a woman's favours. He offered no explanation except to say that no more money would be theirs until reaching Passau. Some of the men went into the town to search for nocturnal adventure, and except for three of the men that were lost to Günther, no major incident disturbed the soundly sleeping troopers that night.

Early the next morning, two nuns appeared, each with a bucket of gruel. Jochenn spoke at some length to the short one, the one that carried an enormous weight. They spoke in the language of priests. Jörg was curious. It seemed as if Jochenn knew the fat nun, but before he could enquire of the situation, Jochenn walked away with the Sisters toward the Abbey church of St. Peter.

Frustrated by Jochenn's disappearance, he walked to the river where merchants were selling breads, fish, vegetables, and many varieties of sausages and cheese. Boatmen were sitting on the wharf beside their boats, waiting for suitable contracts for their services, and all looked as if they had encountered every charlatan known, and were capable of striking a very hard bargain indeed. Günther was there, talking and waving his arms in front of a whiskered old boatman, presumably trying to arrange transportation down river. Seeing nothing of Jochenn at the river, Jorg turned toward the centre of the town. He marvelled at the number of churches and taverns; it appeared as though Salzburg was populated by a large number of the faithful and just as many sinners.

The sun on the turrets of the Hohensalzburg Fortress, high above the town, reminded Jörg of the traditional ways of his people and of his duty to keep to those ways. The words of his father came to him, words of warning about the dangers of the city. Kaspar had extracted a promise that Jörg be careful of women and drink, and to show dignity at all times. Conscious of his father's words, he entered the Weinkeller Haus of the Benedictine monks, more from curiosity than from hunger or thirst. It was dark inside the room and before his eyes had adjusted to the lack of sunlight he heard his name. It was Jochenn with two other troopers; one he knew as Kurt, the other he only recognized. Jochenn shouted, "Here, join us!" Jörg could not refuse, even though he had no wish for their company this morning. The men were jovial from beer, but not rowdy. Jörg went to a spigot in the wall and filled a mug with brown liquid, then wove his way around drinkers to join Jochenn, Kurt and the third man, who he was told was called Gerhardt.

Kurt and Gerhardt were cousins, both from farms near Lienz. They had wanted to go north when the Imperial army won the battle against Mansfield's mercenaries at Sablat, but were persuaded by their fathers to stay on the farms through harvesting. Jörg, still pained about leaving his own father's farm, asked Kurt, "Why did you throw in with Günther?" Kurt's answer was direct, "One night three masked men from the countryside came into my uncle's church and killed him while at his prayers. They destroyed icons, stole a communion cup, then pulled uncle Karl across the stone floor trailing a line of blood the length of the nave and burned his dead body on a pile of hay. The next morning they hung the charred corpse in a tree beside the road for all to see. We heard later that the three masked men were brothers seeking vengeance for something the Jesuits had done to their family. Uncle Karl was just an innocent priest, going about his normal business and as far as we could learn was not involved in any violence against anyone. After that night my father begged me to leave, and the only way to get out of Lienz was to join the Bavarians. I want to get to Brandenburg, and it seemed possible with Maximilian. Gerhardt here wants to go to Sweden with Jochenn." Turning to Gerhardt he said, "Aren't that it cousin?" Gerhardt, not to be overshadowed by his more personable cousin, said, "Ja, that's it."

Jörg wondered aloud if Kurt knew the state of the war in the north. "Ferdinand was deposed last fall and Frederick is now the King of Bohemia. He's re-forming the Protestant armies and will make it hard for us. The fierce prince of Transylvania, Bethlen Gabor, has driven the Austrian army from Hungary; the way it looks now we should be on the other side. But it appears that Maximilian is putting together an army to fight with the Austrians."

After a few minutes, finding Kurt to be boastful about his exploits with women in Lienz, Jörg became restless and wished to leave. Jochenn, who had said very little during Kurt's graphic stories, was also frustrated with his friends, and as it was approaching the noon hour, said to Jörg, "Come!"

Jochenn led Jörg to the Benedictine cloisters of the Peterskirche. It took a few seconds to adjust to the gloom inside the Abbey but soon a very short, very round monk appeared, hustled up to Jochenn and beckoned to a small door in the rear of the church. After pushing a curtain aside, the two men followed the monk along a short, dark passage and entered a small kitchen. In the centre of the floor was a round table that covered almost the entire space of the room. Along one wall was a hearth with a steaming cauldron of red liquid, which by its smell was immediately recognizable as wine. There were two nuns sitting at the table on which had been placed quantities of cakes, cheese, and buns. Jochenn spoke to the nun with whom he had talked that morning, and explained to Jörg that the fat priest was Victor and the nuns were Sister Agatha and Sister Marie. The nuns were from the Ursuline order, sent from Lombardy to find a permanent home in Salzburg for their order. Having been in Salzburg for some time, they were anxious to hear the news of their sisters south of the mountains. Jörg learned that Jochenn had recently spent time in Verona and was the bearer of news. While Jochenn was talking, he began to believe his friend was something more that he was showing to the outside world. He was very comfortable in the company of the religious, and from what Jörg could make of the conversation was very familiar with the ways of the monk and the nuns.

Before Jörg could put his new knowledge of Jochenn together with what he already knew, Victor put a flagon of wine in front of him. Victor was hustling about, interjecting, joking in the Florentine dialect, and rushing back and forth to the wine kettle to make certain everyone was as happy as he was. After much food and wine, the nuns appeared to be bereft of questions to Jochenn, and with much pleasantness and dignity they ushered out the two men. They went back to their comrades quite drunk and stuffed with food. On the path back to camp, Jörg decided he must discover Jochenn's secret, but for now he needed sleep. He crawled under his blanket and slept until daybreak the next morning.

When Jörg was wakened, the word had already spread that Günther had hired a boat and they were leaving as soon as possible for Passau. The nuns brought the daily porridge, showing no recognition of the events of the day before. The men were preparing to leave even as they ate breakfast, and soon they were drawn up in pairs to walk to the wharf. The boat was similar to the one that had brought them across the river but longer, with more spaces for rowers. For the trip down-river there were only two crewmembers on board to help the owner, whom Günther called Herr Greiner. They stood by while the men boarded, and when all were aboard and settled the rowers pulled them to the middle of the river where the current took over.

During the day the current of the Salzach carried them past many half-deserted villages. As dusk approached, the river widened and the current slowed. Stretched along the horizon on their left was the fortress of Burghausen silhouetted on the ridge in the setting sun. The fortress was an object of some interest to the men so Herr Greiner told his passengers that it was built to protect the Bishop's salt boats.

Soon they came to the junction of the river Inn, which would be their watery highway for the rest of the journey to Passau. The men were told they would spend the night on the river because they were in enemy territory, and as the gloom deepened, Herr Greiner left his place at the stern sweep to one of his assistants and took up a position forward. He managed with some difficulty to light a torch that he used as an aid to see ahead, allowing him to steer the boat from danger with the forward sweep. Shortly, lights passing on their right indicated the presence of a town. It was Braunau, a Protestant stronghold and the reason they were passing the town at night. The recruits found comfortable positions to sleep.

The next morning Herr Greiner made it clear that his passengers were expected to help with the rowing because of the more sluggish current, so they drew lots and took turns, four at a time. Just before noon, on June 6, 1620, Günther's band of recruits reached the city of Passau.

Günther informed his men that they would not stop in the town, but would cross the Danube to the mouth of the Ilz River where they were to be billeted and learn the skills to kill other men. While passing the town, Jörg noticed the streets appeared to be deserted except for a few old women. Günther had no explanation for this since he thought there should be many people on the streets, it being noon on a bright sunny day. "Remember this, if you get drunk and create some mischief in the town where the army has no authority over you, Herr Schultheiß the *Bürgermeister* of Passau, will impose his authority on you as chief magistrate of the town, and he is very, very hard on carousers."

Rounding the point of land where the Inn met the Danube, the rowers bent to their oars more strongly to overcome the merging currents of the two rivers. On a high promontory across the Danube, the Oberhaus Fortress commanded the confluence of the three rivers. The red roofs and white walls of the fortress amongst the dense green forest was a rare sight, a beauty that seemed to mock the homely buildings of Jörg's youth. Observing Jörg's curiosity Jochenn explained, "The Oberhaus Fortress was built for the Bishop of Passau four hundred years ago as protection against the Turks and the townspeople who were seeking freedom from the weight of the Church. It is home for Bishops and serves as a military outpost and prison." He pointed to a similar fortress-like building at the water's edge. "That is the Niederhaus."

Just where the Ilz met the Danube, the rowers pulled into a landing place at the foot of the steep hill. There were several ferryboats and many small punts at the landing, causing Herr Greiner to curse while attempting to find a landing without bumping other boats. Disembarking from the boat that had brought them from Salzburg, the men were marched up the road to the Oberhaus, where they were to live and train for battle.

Günther and his band of recruits soon came to a gate house and encountered two guards dressed in long grey coats, pantaloons, and hats with long peacock feathers tucked into the bands. They carried long muskets. With a few words from Günther, the guards waved the men through. As the recruits came round a bend in the road in a somewhat haphazard march, it was clear why the town was deserted. The woods opened up into a large clearing in front of the Fortress. A large crowd of burghers had gathered under the north bastion to the right of the gate. Directly in front of the gates, a platoon of uniformed soldiers stood at attention below a limp regimental standard hanging in the hot, humid air. On a slight knoll, above the heads of the shouting and cheering mob, could be seen two gibbets with a dozen men about to be hanged. Suddenly the roll of drums was heard, and with the flash of an officer's sword the bodies began kicking; trying to find footing in the last moments of their agony, hoping desperately to prolong their existence on earth. The sword flashed again and one body disappeared from view, leaving a severed head hanging in the noose swaying to and fro from the heavy blow.

As the new recruits pushed through the surging crowd, they could see the man writing on the ground from the hopeless efforts he was making to preserve his life. Even before the bloody head in the tightly strung noose stopped its gruesome dance, some members of the crowd ran forward, intent on looting the dead bodies as soon as they were lowered. It was evident that some of the figures rushing toward the swaying bodies were women, distinguished by white bonnets bobbing in the bright sunlight of high noon. The dead were stripped of their boots even before they could be let down. Günther explained that the officers had taken any evidence of their bravery from the men to be hanged, but let them keep their boots to allow them to die with their boots on, as they would in battle. The mob had no such qualms, stripping the bodies of their boots and clothing.

Jörg noticed that Jochenn was very agitated, and once again he wondered what story his friend had to tell, what made him cringe from these hangings in an age when such violence was part of everyday life.

The crowd had begun to drift away from the gruesome scene, the lust for vengeance satisfied. Jochenn approached a woman who was carrying a pair of boots. She shied away from his advances as if he was intent on stealing her stolen boots, but when he extended his hands palms down as a sign of peace she stopped.

Jochenn spoke to the woman, "What reason for hanging those poor souls?" The woman showed no pity, "They defiled the *Bürgermeister's* daughter."

"All of them?"

"Two."

"What were the crimes of the others?"

"Thieves they were, imprisoned since winter. Herr Schultheiß told the Colonel he had to hang them by the neck or he would get the Bishop to clear out his soldiers. The one that owned these boots won't do any more thieving."

Brushing past Jochenn and heading down the hill she held up the boots and cackled, "He won't need these in his grave. God rest his thieving soul!"

Jochenn turned toward the gallows above and made the sign of the cross. Then he bowed his head and mumbled something in words Jörg could not understand.

Inside the Oberhaus, they met up with a sizable contingent of other new recruits who were also training for warfare. Günther turned his recruits over to Captain Harder, their field officer, a tall, thin man with blazing blue eyes and a hooked nose. He ordered a sergeant to take the men's names and other particulars, and having done so, the sergeant showed the men where they could sleep. Their quarters consisted of a large room with rows of beds placed against the walls, like a hospital. The sergeant took them through a door at one end of their sleeping quarters into an adjacent room where they could get food and beer.

The next morning, Günther's unit of sixteen men was ordered to line up in one corner of the yard where some men were carrying muskets and appeared to be learning how to shoot and load, while another unit was training with pikes. There was no cavalry; it was being trained outside the walls since the number of extra men and food animals inside the Fortress was already overburdening it. An officer stood in front of the unit and was sizing them up for either musketry or pike assignments. The Carinthians, although short in stature, were very strong in the chest, shoulders and thighs from their mountain bloodlines, and all but three would train to use the pike. Jochenn, the tall Swede, was among those who were to learn musketry. Jörg was to become a pike man.

The officer in charge of the pike men, a large, puffed-up, middle-aged former dragoon sergeant the men called Big Fritz, told them the characteristics of a strong pike and its relationship to an individual's strength and height. He then divided them into three rows of four and led them to the armoury to select their pikes. Jörg found a suitable pike and breastplate, and with the others re-assembled in the courtyard to start the training that would equip him to kill men.

In drills, Jörg learned precision in handling and marching with the pike, and the manoeuvres needed to defend the musketeers in battle. Accustomed to walking with long paces, he found it an effort to keep his paces as short as those ordered by Big Fritz. "Weger there! Shorter steps! Shorter steps! Eighty steps to the minute!" Big Fritz kept shouting at him until he was able to march as the rules demanded. After they became familiar with their weapons, the musketeers and the pike men were brought together in the regimental squares that formed the basic unit of Tilley's army, with pike men massed in a central square surrounded by musketeers and flanked by cavalry. The men formed into companies of 150 men, with four companies to a brigade and two brigades to a regiment, the latter consisting of 1200 men. The regimental squares were organized in the field as an inverted "T" formation with squares at the three points of the "T," flanked by ranks of cavalry to form a deep line. Jörg was assigned to the second rank of the square called *Anna Magdelena*, dedicated to the Duke's sister. *Anna Magdelena* formed the base of the "T," and was commanded by Captain Harder. To attack, the squares moved at a measured pace with the first ranks of the pikes used against enemy cavalry, as well as to protect the musketeers from enemy pikes. The role of the musketeers was to set up screen of cross-fired musket shot impenetrable by the enemy. It was important for the pike men to be highly disciplined so as not to get out in front of the line and get shot by one of their own men.

After drills, the men were free to do as they pleased. Many of the recruits left their quarters for taverns clustered at the river's edge to find female company, or just to drink and tell stories. The more adventurous went across the river to the town itself. Some got out of hand and ended up in the Fortress prison, a few for serious crimes of theft, assault, and rape. One of Günther's recruits, accused of spying for the Turks, was sentenced to be executed. All troopers were ordered to turn out for the execution.

Jochenn refused to go. No amount of bullying by his sergeant would budge him, and finally the angry sergeant, still muttering threats, left him to his own thoughts.

It was a cold angry day with black clouds overhead, and as soon as all the men and officers were assembled in the courtyard it began to rain. Anxious to get the execution done quickly because of the rain, the Colonel ordered the poor miscreant to be taken from his cell and tied to a hitching post in the centre of the courtyard. Two men dragged the prisoner into the rain and lashed him to the post. He showed no reaction, likely made comatose by alcoholic drink. With little ceremony, except for a priest who gave the last rites, the Colonel ran his sword through the man. He ordered an axe man to severe the head of the spy and put it on a stake near the gate. The Colonel wiped his bloody sword on the dead man's shirt, turned and marched from the scene, his gruesome duty accomplished. The men were dismissed.

When Jörg returned to quarters, he sought out Jochenn and asked him, "as his friend," why he was frightened of hangings. After a long painful pause, Jochenn told Jörg his story.

"When I was very young, I think about five, it was a time of civil strife brought on by Charles against the Catholic Sigismund. Some men from the town came to my father's house in Uppsala and held me and father while they broke our Catholic icons, and when my young and beautiful mother objected they ravished her, each in turn. Father screamed and fought with the men until they put a rope around his neck and hung him from a beam in our house. When they were finished with mother she lay in a pool of blood. As they were leaving, an officer casually severed father's head. He fell at my feet. The stiffness had begun to set in and his torso flopped onto my shoulder, covering me with blood. The men laughed at me as they left. I was so young at the time that some of the details are vague, but I carry always the nightmare of my father twisting on that thin rope.

"I sat with mother, weeping and frightened, and tried to get her to talk to me as she became cold and stiff. But after a while, as young as I was, I knew she was dead. I ran from the house, but no one came to answer my calls for fear of meeting the same end as my parents.

"Alone, I wandered for several days begging for food until I was taken in by Father Olaus, who adopted me. It was that day I became a Christian. Eventually, I was made a Deacon of the Domkyrka in Uppsala. I took the oath, and for six years was a faithful priest, but when I met Helga I knew I could no longer adhere to priestly virtue. At my confession, Father Olaus suggested I go to Rome saying he thought it would cure me of lustful desires, as he called them. I was robbed on the road to Verona and had to seek sanctuary from the clergy of the church of San Zeno. I was made a Verger, and stayed at that place for some months."

"Did you know Sister Agatha there?"

"She was of Brescia and had been sent to Verona to teach the girls of the Parish. We shared some duties."

"But now you are going back to the place of your childhood sadness?"

"Eventually I wrote to Helga. I received a favourable response, so, yes. I am trying to get home to Uppsala."

Jörg was curious why a man of the cloth would be a soldier. "What if you have to kill?"

"The military is for protection on the road. I don't intend to kill. I think I will run away if necessary."

"To be run through by an officer?"

Jochenn shrugged and answered with a note of finality in his voice, "If necessary."

All summer the recruits trained with the pike for several hours each day until Captain Harder was confident they could protect themselves and the musketeers. Jörg seldom went into the town. Suffering from the heat during the day in the enclosure, exhausted from the ever-present dampness at night, disgusted with the smells of offal from both men and animals, the proximity of his comrades, and their constant bickering amongst themselves, Jörg escaped to the countryside. So, after the day's training, instead of going to taverns, Jörg walked in the surrounding hills. The rugged beauty of the surroundings reminded him of Radenthein, with the Oberhaus a dominant presence in the woodlands covering the hills. But during his wanderings in the countryside he wished for the company of a woman. He seldom thought now of Elizabetha, and he found himself wanting to replace her in flesh rather than memory.

He had a minor entanglement with a brown-eyed girl named Zetta who worked in the bakery. She was not pretty and because of a lonely childhood she had found companionship with woodland creatures and was at home in the woods. She and Jörg roamed the countryside together. There was some danger from roving bands of soldiers of different armies looking for loot or to find a place of shelter, but the risk was minor. His rambles in the woods around the Fortress with Zetta provided some normality in his life, but she left him for a soldier in one of the new regiments that arrived at the Oberhaus. Without Zetta, Jörg's walks were no longer pleasant, and he became anxious to leave for the battleground.

He had not long to wait. One afternoon early in July they were told after drill to be ready to move out the next morning to join the main force of the army that was camped at a bulge in the river just east of Passau. Some of the men had formed pleasant liaisons with town women and were emotionally torn about leaving, but Jörg was eager to get out into the open country, no matter how dangerous.

At dawn, the men were drawn up in units, with brigade officers trying to mobilize their companies while the men said their last words to those they were leaving. Some of the town women had decided to go with their men and were waiting outside the gatehouse to follow the army. Eventually, the baggage wagons appeared with their iron wheels ringing on the stones of the courtyard, drawn by fully decorated teams of horses. The baggage was loaded and they were ready to leave. The portcullis was raised with much cursing and shouting by the gatekeepers, the gate was opened and the newly formed regiment marched out. The men were drawn up in the battle formation they had learned, with house standards still unrolled. Camp followers stood outside the gates waiting for the last man to march through.

Crossing the Ilz, the regiment met up with the main army that was camped beside the Danube. The cavalry was massed on a sloping field fronting the river, and the men and horses joined with the infantry into a single marching unit. The colours were unfurled, with the giant standards of the House of Wittelsbach and the eagle of the Duke of Bavaria floating in the breeze at the head of the column. It was a truly impressive sight; many thousands of armed men on the road for as far as Jörg could see, about half musketeers and half infantry, supported by cavalry and artillery. There were twelve large guns named after the apostles, drawn by teams of oxen. Tilly, on a large bay horse, rode at the head of this grand army in advance of the leading squares of pike men. Jörg carried the image of the impressive array into battle and reflected upon it later when everything seemed chaotic, ugly, and savage.

They crossed the Austrian frontier the next day and joined with the sick and dispirited Imperial army at Linz, and the two armies marched to Pilsen, now held by Mansfield's mercenaries. Mansfield had been told by Frederick to hold Pilsen for the Protestants, so the twelve apostles bombarded the town giving the pike men little to do during the siege. Jörg spent the time getting used to military life in the field. Count Tilly, known as "The Monk," had a reputation for being strict, but let his officers make the domestic arrangements for the men, so the camp showed little evidence of discipline. Outside the walls of the town, houses to quarter the soldiers were few in number, so soldiers had to find suitable places to sleep and relax as best they could. Married soldiers threw up shelters made from poles and waxed linen, well to the rear of the guns, and often couples had to curtain off the marriage bed from other members of the unit. Some men concluded that the siege was going to last and built permanent shelters. Others simply slept out at night, largely those who had to perform some duty at the walls, such as building ramparts to protect the artillery.

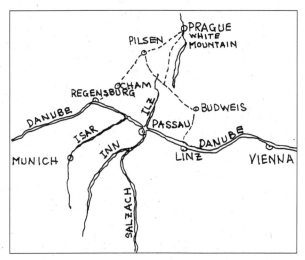

Jörg and two others from Carinthia found a stable about a mile from the town and Günther convinced the farmer to accept receipts for their billeting. Jörg and Karel, a boy from Spital with whom he had become friends, found a corner of the loft that proved to be quite comfortable. It was hot for sleep as it was under the roof of the stable, but it was dry. By early October it became clear that Mansfield was not going to surrender, so "The Monk" made an agreement with him to the effect that he would remain in the city with his army, allowing Tilly to safely turn towards Prague. Mansfield had no choice; in truth, he had no money. Tilly's army broke camp and marched toward Prague.

In mid-October the Catholic armies encountered the Bohemian force at Rokitzan, a two-day march from Prague. There they lay, facing each other for a fortnight. It was said the King himself was in the Bohemian camp trying to settle differences between the leaders of the Protestant army. The lack of action, and the fear for his life when the fighting would finally begin, made this a very anxious period for Jörg. It was getting late in the season, with cold and misty nights. The units took turns lying in their positions during the nights, in case of attack, which the men hoped would not come that winter. Indeed, it was common knowledge in the camp that The Duke and the Count of Bucquoy, commander of the Imperial army, did not agree on this; the Duke urging attack, and Bucquoy urging caution, mostly because of the poor condition of his troopers, some who had been in the field over two summers.

On November 5th, it appeared the waiting was over. Jörg had been sleeping in arms when the noise from the enemy camp indicated movement of some sort. The camp mobilized for a battle that was expected at dawn. While waiting, Jörg went from a state of utmost panic and fear to a calm acceptance of his fate. Indeed, he became coldly calculating about how he would act in the coming battle. Then word ran quickly through the ranks that the enemy was withdrawing. The men in arms began to relax, some given over to a cheer, but swiftly on the heels of this news, they prepared to march. It took most of another half day to decamp and load the wagons.

Then, for almost two days, the army marched parallel to the enemy with the Bohemians commanding the road, the Catholic armies the wooded hills. The countryside was ravaged and largely deserted. Burned crops, the carcasses of dead farm animals, some half-butchered, others starved, were strewn along their route. Hamlets were looted of everything that could be taken away in wagons. Houses were burned to the ground, many churches were desecrated and icons stolen. The people of the towns and countryside had fled from the armies.

On the second night, the enemy stopped, and by the fierce light of burning farmhouses to the northeast the Bohemian troopers were seen clearly preparing to take a stand along the ridge of a chalk promontory above a small stream. The lively figures seen straining to take up their positions against the fiercely blazing landscape behind was like a scene from hell and seemed to foretell the horror of the battle that Jörg felt in his weary bones was about to begin. They lay in arms all night, waiting.

Jörg woke in a panic, his heart racing. In an instant, he knew the Bohemians were getting ready to fight. All had been quiet in the night, but as dawn was breaking in a thin, jagged line of pink outlining the black mounds of the chalk hill, he heard movement from the direction of the enemy lines. Jörg knew in the dark part of his soul this was the day that would test his courage in spite of the rumours that the battle would be delayed for the winter. During the siege of Pilsen, his courage was tested, but not by killing a man in hand to hand combat. During the journey down from the mountains, his trip on the river and his subsequent training, he had feared the first moment of armed combat.

The battle for the white hill that protected the town of Prague was about to begin. Just as the day was dawning, the great mass of infantry waded into the stream and across the base of the hill under the guns of the Bohemians. The pike men stopped short of the enemy line. Jörg could see the mobilization of the Bohemians as they took up positions all along the crest of the white hill. The rising sun outlined infantry, cavalry, and guns stretched across the ridge. Word among the waiting troops was that Tilly and Bucquoy were arguing whether or not to attack. A Dominican monk could be seen hustling toward the council tent and a few moments later there was heard a fiery exhortation to the leaders to, "Put trust in God, and the righteousness of our cause and victory will be sure."

This seemed to settle the issue because suddenly the cavalry on the left of Jörg stormed a small breastwork below the hill commanded by the Bohemians. After a brief struggle they fell back, leaving many dying men and horses impossible to rescue. The shrieking of horses and moaning from the dying men lying in the mud of the stream bank sent shivers through the massed pike men as they awaited their orders. Suddenly the shout, "*Salve Regina*" went up from the rear of the lines and with a call to the Virgin "*Sancta Maria*" the heavy cannons in front and behind began to boom out and the line leaped forward with a savage roar. The musketeers began to fire. Jörg was in the second rank of pikes and anxious to engage the Bohemians, but the rank in front, disciplined to keep a tight formation for the protection of the square, kept him from making a headlong plunge at the enemy's line. As he tramped up the hill under the guns of the Bohemians, it was with abandon and a strange exhilaration. About half way up the hill he heard a great battle waging to his left, but it was strangely quiet on the right.

Then they were in amongst the enemy. At first, Jörg was aware only of the horrendous din; the grunts of effort, the praying of wounded and dying men, the sound of pikes being snapped, the screaming of dying horses and the far away boom of the guns. Soon smoke from the guns hid the battlefield. Then, out of the haze, a Bohemian pike man came charging straight at him through a bloody line of downed men and horses. He was able to focus his eyes on the tip of the grey iron point and suddenly felt very calm. He dropped and turned at the same instant. As the point followed him down, he drew his own pike back and across his body and plunged the butt across the oncoming shaft to direct it below him, then, with a shortened grasp, he brought the tip of his pike upward and aimed at the chest of his adversary. The momentum of his charge impaled the man.

He hardly felt the weight of the soldier move up his hands, his arms and his shoulders. The surprise in the Bohemian's eyes frightened Jörg. The soldier's body crashed into him with a spew of blood and vomit. Jörg's gut turned sour from the smell, but he fought his sickness and slithered out from under the hulk and retrieved his pike without looking at the dead soldier. He stumbled forward in a trance, instinctively raising his bloodied pike to protect himself from a second charge. It did not come. The Bohemians were running away. This brought a great whoop from his comrades, and emboldened, they ran after the retreating foe. Jörg charged with insane anger at the running enemy, thrusting his pike now covered in blood, at anything in his path. With the back of a man with a large curving feather in his cap in his sights he tripped over a groaning soldier and fell face forward into the wet, muddy earth. The fall and the cold earth of the battlefield sucked away his anger and he came to himself. He looked up to see Bohemian officers brandishing their swords, trying to make their own men fight, but with no success. Into this melee rode the wounded Bucquoy straight from his recent sickbed, with his standard-bearer and reserves. It was a rout. The Bohemian army was streaming across the river towards the city.

Jörg sank to his knees and thanked God for his deliverance. But in truth it was the strength of his arms and shoulders inherited from his alpine farming ancestor that had saved him.

Some fighting was still taking place on Jörg's left, below the hill. Some of the Bohemian army's Moravian soldiers were standing to the last man against Tilly's men. Soon the field belonged to Maximilian and Tilly. The battle took less than an hour, but the hill was soaked with the blood of thousands of Bohemian soldiers. One of Tilly's cavalry officers, blood seeping from a wounded leg, was riding up and down the line holding aloft the King of Bohemia's captured banner, cheered on by the shouts of the victorious Catholic army. Jörg searched for Jochenn after the battle, but could not locate him either among the living or the dead. He heard Karel calling his name. Finally they caught sight of one another and Karel came up to him, uninjured except for a limp received when a horse stepped on his foot. Karel had not seen Jochenn since before the battle when he had seemed agitated and fearful. Jörg said, "I bet he left the battlefield to take his chances with bandits to get home to his Helga."

That night the army encamped outside the city wall. The next day his Highness the Duke arranged the surrender of the city by the Bohemian Directorate in return for certain privileges for the Estates, including religious rights and protection from the Duke's soldiers. The next day, the army marched into Prague with all standards flying, both those of the conquered and the conquerors. The Duke offered the enemy soldiers the opportunity to leave, but for some time they refused because they had not received pay for their service. The King, in his haste leaving the city, had abandoned eight wagons of goods at the Hradschin gate, including silks, jewellery, firearms, and swords. Maximilian took one of the King's horses and left Prague to attend to political affairs. The loot the King left would gladden any mercenary's heart, and both the citizens and soldiers fell on the wagons and took away all that they could carry. The greed resulted in a few skirmishes among the soldiers before their officers could gain some control. In addition, to escape the marauding Hungarians of Bethlen Gabor, the people from the countryside had brought their farm animals to the city and herded them inside the walls, making the city a virtual storehouse to be plundered. The defeated Bohemian soldiers who were found in the city were slaughtered over the next few days. The dead from the battlefield were loaded onto wagons and brought to the field beside the main city gate and dumped there. The next day, Jörg searched through the dead for Jochenn, but did not find him, nor could he locate him at camp. A trooper who knew Jochenn said that he had deserted to make his way to the Saxon army at Bautzen.

All winter, citizens were accosted, houses looted, men robbed and beaten, women debauched. There was constant carousing and drunken revelry by the soldiers. Jörg took part in the looting, because there was no other source of food in the city or the countryside. Since killing the Bohemian soldier in the battle he was not able to fight when challenged by one of the men, nor could women arouse his passion.

The battle for the chalk hill and the cruelty and horror he had witnessed in the previous months was appalling. Jörg had always tried to live according to his innate sense of justice rather than through the emotion of religion, but the brutality he had witnessed exceeded his capacity to rationally understand his fellow man. Perhaps only God could judge after all. The satanic ugliness and savagery of life began to eat at his conscience, as acid eats the stomach. He carried around monumental guilt in the daylight, and at night suffered through nightmares in which he was swept along in a blood red river, with some netherworld force pulling him into the whirlpools while horned demons laughed and leered from the safety of the river's edge. On most nights that winter, he woke with his heart racing, and in a cold sweat.

One day, Jörg was exploring a section of the city north of the Cathedral looking for food that other soldiers may have missed. The streets were mostly deserted; former residents had left to escape the looting and raping by Bethlen Gabor's soldiers. He left the street through a small arch in a wall made of stone, and walked through an open gate into a small courtyard. Several of the doorways to the residences were standing open, some doors smashed and trampled over by looters. One door directly across from the entry gate stood closed. He knocked. He knocked again, and was about to smash the door when he heard a sound from the other side of the panel, and it opened a crack. He explained to the dark eyes behind the narrow opening that he had had no food that day. The crack widened, revealing a dark-haired girl about his age. She was frightened, but realized she had no choice but to open the door, certain that he would force his way into the house if she resisted. She walked to the back of the house, leaving the door ajar.

Jörg went into the bare main room of a small cottage that had been completely looted of all that was easy to carry, although some heavy furniture remained. The girl had disappeared and he could find no food. He found the girl in the street behind the house, standing on the pavement waiting for him to leave. He walked towards her. She watched his approach with fear in her eyes, but she did not move. She seemed to be less afraid of him in the open, with the road as an escape route. He talked to her from a distance, explaining that he would not hurt her and wished to have only food. She responded that she was also hungry. He recognized her as German, but he had some difficulty with her words. They stood apart, with nothing to say, but what he saw in her deep-set eyes caused him to linger. Although the eyes showed fear, they seemed also to be begging for contact. As they stood facing each other, a small flicker of a smile at their predicament touched her face. He asked if this was her home. She said, "No. It is that of my uncle."

Then the story came in a rush. "I am from the country. Father's farm was looted and Bethlen Gabor's soldiers burned the hay and buildings. They cut off father's head and roasted his torso in the fire at the farmhouse. I found his head later, half burned, with one eye staring at me." She shuddered at these last words, but continued with her story, showing emotion only by the wetness formed in her eyes. Jörg asked how she had escaped.

"I was in the fields when they came, and I hid in a root cellar that was in the shade of the trees at the edge of the woods behind the barn. The soldiers burned the barn, but they did not find me. I lived in the cellar for two days. I ate raw potatoes but I had no drink. When I came out of the cellar, father's farm was a ruin. I did not wish to live in the root cellar so I came to Prague where my uncle lived. My aunt and uncle are gone and I have not found what happened to them."

With nowhere else to go, she stayed in her uncle's house. Jörg told her to go back into the house and he would bring food. With this promise, he walked down the road backwards so as to keep her in his vision. He turned a corner at the end of the road and stopped to watch what she did. She stood fixed in the road for several minutes, but when he peeked around the corner for the third time, she was gone.

For a while after leaving the girl, Jörg was happy. To bring her food would make him feel like a man again, and help cleanse his soul of brutality. He had a cache of food at the camp, but it was a four-mile walk. He could steal food from the commissar's wagons at the Palace, but that was too dangerous. He decided to walk to camp for food and hoped she would be at the house of her uncle when he returned. He kept thinking of the girl's eyes, and his desire for female company after his year with Elizabetha now returned, but the responsibility he was undertaking posed a burden. The rumour in camp was that the army was leaving Prague to help the Spaniards in the Palatine, and he worried what he would do with the girl if she wanted him to stay.

He returned at dusk to the house where the girl lived, and they ate the food Jörg had brought back from his secret supply. From the light of the candle, he could observe her during the meal. She was strikingly beautiful, with dark brown eyes and short dark hair. She was a little taller than Jörg, but in spite of hunger, she was not thin. Her bare legs were shapely and her body exhibited the svelte fullness that comes with motherhood. This thought made Jörg curious enough to ask about it. At first, she was silent, not wanting to relive the events of the past, and not sure she could trust this foreign soldier, even though he was being kind to her. Then, while the two of them sat on the floor with the candle at their feet throwing its soft glow in a small circle, her face obscured by the gathering darkness, she told her story.

"I am Katarina. Father was a Government official in Graz, in the duchy of Styria. He was in charge of the records for land allocations to the subjects of the Emperor. He was a follower of the teachings of Luther, and had a small collection of translations of some of the Gospels of the Holy Book that he read to me each night. I loved the stories, but wondered what they meant. In the summertime he took me on excursions into the countryside, along the rivers, and the grain fields. Father was a kind man."

Jörg could not see her eyes, but he knew she was crying. With what seemed to him an act of courage, she went on.

"Mother made me acquainted with the society of Graz. She taught me all the skills I needed to know to be a good Christian woman. Mine was a happy childhood. Then, one day an official from the Palace came to our house in Graz with three men and they searched until they found father's collection of readings. They took father away and gave him the choice of going to the dungeon or leaving Styria. Shortly after, uncle Albrecht came with a wagon and we took what possessions we could carry to Bohemia, where father settled on a small farm outside Prague. About a year later, uncle Albrecht came also to Bohemia and lived in this house. Now uncle Albrecht and auntie are gone. I pray they are safe, somewhere.

"When I was old enough to marry I wed Benedict. We had a little girl Anna, but three years later, the plague took them both away, as well as my mother. I went to live with father, until Bethen Gabor's brutal soldiers killed him and burned him. I dug a hole in the ground under the big tree in our garden and buried his remains." She said it softly with a quiver in her voice. Jörg touched her arm in sympathy. She took his hand and gently removed it. She wished to grieve alone.

During the brief moments of her mourning, Jörg was able to put aside the brutality of the war and regain some of his faith.

When he was not in camp they stayed together in her uncle Albrecht's house during the weeks before the army of the Catholic League was due to go west to join the Spanish army. Those weeks passed in a gossamer cloud of happiness for Jörg. Katarina brought out in him feelings he had never experienced before. At first, she was hesitant to respond, due to the recent trauma of her life. She did not want to tarnish the love and memories of those she had lost, but she lived in harsh times and had learned to put the ugliness behind her to survive. Katarina found bedclothes and proceeded to make a sanctuary out of the old carved wooden bed left by her uncle and aunt. It was white and billowy like the clouds that floated over the green hills of Carinthia. The first week they were together they spent mostly in the old wooden bed, entwined in a rolling sea of white cotton. They both knew it could not last, and they took a lifetime of love from those brief weeks in Prague.

Jörg and Katarina spent that winter in Prague, in the abandoned house of her uncle. Her aunt and uncle did not return to their home, and Katarina came to assume they were dead, killed by soldiers or by thieves. It was a winter of vengeance by the Emperor against the Bohemian Estates for defying his authority. He wanted no less than the blood of the rebels and the elimination of the protest movement. On an otherwise fine spring day in June, Ferdinand took revenge with bloody executions in the square in front of the town hall, with the severed heads of the victims spitted on the Charles Bridge. Jörg and Katarina watched the executions with the crowd of citizens while hundreds of soldiers of the Imperial cavalry patrolled the streets. The scene led the couple to believe they should leave Prague as soon as it became possible.

The Catholic army was preparing to leave for the Oberpfälz. Prague was now bereft of its wealth, its future taken away by roving bands of soldiers and even its citizens raged against King Frederick and his Queen for deserting them. Jörg felt it wise to leave with the army, to stay with Tilly's soldiers, at least until some better chance came his way. It was rumoured that the war was already over, and the army to be demobilized so he thought he might be able to obtain a farm in the deserted lands that rampaging troops had ruined.

Tilly's army left a plundered Prague and marched west hoping to subdue the Bohemians for good, its destination the Upper Palatinate. Jörg was elated when Katarina joined the ranks of the camp followers.

After each day of marching, in spite of the harshness of camp life, Jörg found Katarina to be of much help and a good companion. She was tough and strong-minded, and while she and Jörg sometimes fought, he recognized in her good breeding and a refined spirit. She was Lutheran, which sometimes created danger for them in a camp of the army of the Catholic League, but she was intelligent and disciplined enough to avoid trouble. Although raised a Catholic, Jörg had no strong religious feelings and Katarina was slowly converting him to her spiritual ways. He was surprised to find he did not mind.

Whatever it was the Duke and the General had in mind for the military campaign, the people of the countryside suffered terribly. Soldiers looted villages, drove the people away and devastated the country. They took all they could carry, then burned towns and killed the citizens, even babes at their mother's breasts. The people wanted to surrender, but instead were forced to flee for their lives, leaving behind all the goods and supplies they needed for survival. Some had to abandon their wives and children. People hid in haystacks and barns, but the soldiers burned them. Crops were dug up and burned. Animals were slaughtered for food or left to starve.

Maidens were abducted and violated. Aristocratic women were forced to serve a soldier's needs, then to give him money. Husbands were killed in front of their wives and children, who the soldiers then abused or sold to other soldiers for their pleasure.

The peasants blamed their misery on the leaders and conspired to kill them, even at the cost of their own lives, because of the penury and hardship of supporting soldiers. Nobles fled to escape the peasants' wrath.

At Pilsen, the army took possession of whomever and whatever it encountered on the streets and lanes. Twenty-seven large fires burned in one night. People ran from their beds, and if caught, were thrown into the flames. Before the army left for the Oberphälz, the cities and the countryside lay in ruins. The people had run away, leaving nature and the animals to take back what man had despoiled.

At night, Jörg and Katarina found shelter in a makeshift tent at the edge of the camp, but it was getting colder and Jörg decided they needed a more substantial home. He could use a horse and cart, or a team and wagon. This would allow them to better carry their few goods, and, with a cover, provide a warm sleeping place. Without sufficient money, there seemed two means to get a horse and vehicle, to claim one as booty after a battle, or to join the looting parties. When he had considered looting in the past, he thought of his father, and how hard he had worked to gain just a few possessions over his lifetime. Jörg could not look a peasant in the eye while stealing from him so he would have to wait for an opportunity to capture a cavalry horse.

In early autumn, the army stormed the town of Cham. Mansfield, the commander of the mercenary army fighting for the Protestants, surrendered to Tilly for a large sum of money and a promise not to fight for Frederick, who, after his flight from Prague, was trying to rejuvenate the Protestant cause. In the short but brutal battle before Mansfield's surrender, Jörg was able to capture a rider-less cavalry horse and lead it off into the woods without an officer noticing. He tethered the horse, and after dark went back and managed to lead the horse to camp without a challenge. He was overjoyed when he found he had not only a horse, but also a saddle, and tied to it, a musket. The gun was an older model with a wheel-lock firing mechanism, but it seemed in perfect condition, although lacking powder and balls. He took away the saddle and halter and replaced the latter with his own hemp rope halter, hoping that without its saddle its owner, if he were still alive, would not recognize the horse.

In possession of a riding horse, Jörg could now roam over the countryside to find a cart or a wagon. Close to the end of October, he found an abandoned two-wheeled cart almost completely buried in a swamp. Jörg guessed a unit of Mansfield's army left it after the soldiers had spent a considerable time trying to dislodge it. The spokes of one wheel were broken. It took Jörg and the horse two days to remove the cart from its incipient grave, and another three days to fix the wheel for transport back to camp. He arrived about midnight of the fifth day, and walked the horse and cart to camp.

Mansfield dishonoured the treaty he had made with Tilly and immediately went westward to join the English. Tilly's army was too small to challenge both Mansfield and the English, and his army spent the cold and snowy winter terrorizing the people of the countryside when they were not in camp trying to keep warm.

In the spring of 1622, Tilley's army joined a Spanish army commanded by General Gonzalez de Cordoba, and together they marched to Wimpfen on the Neckar River to meet the Protestant armies. The Battle of Wimpfen was joined on a low hill near the Neckar.

Jörg was in the fifth rank of pike men. At the first barrage of artillery, he knew it would be fierce. As the day wore on, there was no relief from the choking smoke, the din of the cannon from both in front and behind, and dead and dying troopers underfoot. The enemy cavalry tore up the battlefield and it became a sea of mud and blood. Jörg felt a retching sickness but he had nothing in his stomach, nothing to vomit. He was starving and sick at the same time.

The rank kept in close formation during the early minutes of the onslaught from the enemy cavalry, but as the pike men in the ranks in front fell, one after another, the formation weakened. Sergeant Schiller was shouting, "Hold the line for the Duke." Suddenly a great blast boomed over the general chaos, and when Jörg looked up a white cloud engulfed the field. All was quiet. Behind, he heard a gasp, and then loud and clear, magnified by the invisibility, the words, "*Mon Dieu, the Virgin Mary—Victory, Victory is ours.*" The regiment surged forward and slowly the enemy was re-engaged. Jörg's rank was now man to man with the enemy soldiers who were only recognizable by their blue hat feathers. Soon it became necessary to engage anyone in front, friend or foe. He was growing very weary, his arms aching and his legs numb from the weight of his breastplate and heavy leather jerkin.

He forced himself to stay afoot, which seemed safer than falling under the crush of bodies surging forward from behind. While the excitement buoyed his energy at first, the strain had gone on too long, and he just wanted to lie down in the mud and sleep. Suddenly a large white horse came out of the smoke and reared directly in front of him, and at the same instant, he was knocked backward onto the rank behind. He involuntarily rolled himself into a ball, but found it odd that his right arm did not work. Then the pain came, a gut-churning pain, a mind-numbing pain. He swooned in a swirl of colour. He saw himself floating like a bird, feet first, heading toward a black cliff, and as he got closer the cliff receded. He was lifted higher and higher. For what seemed an eternity all was silent, then he heard screaming. Screaming released the shock, and, as he became conscious of his body again, the pain seared through his shoulder and he began to realize that he was not dead. A mass of blood was forming over his chest, and he could taste and smell his life force as it seeped into the mud of Württemberg. Suddenly calm, he bunched up his undershirt with his left hand and pushed with his ebbing strength to lodge the wad under his breastplate and into his shoulder. He tried to get to his feet and collapsed. It was only then that he became conscious of the pain in his leg. The pike men of *Anna Magdelena* swept over and around him, then, suddenly he was alone.

As he lay in the cold mud, his thoughts turned to Katarina. They had been together, it seemed, a lifetime. Her dark luminous eyes haunted him now; eyes that revealed her humour and tenderness, but also her strength and determination. He found her wilful at times, and they quarrelled. But at night her soft body took all the anger from him. A wave of regret came over him that he was not able to fulfill her most passionate wish; that they marry. He was not against marriage, but she insisted he must be Lutheran. He resisted, not so much because they were of different faiths, but because a wife was expected to take on the religion of her husband, and he could not bring himself to surrender his patronage. Now it did not matter. If God saved him, he vowed to please Katarina always. If only he could be with her again. He tried to crawl to the camp but after a few minutes there was only blackness.

Katarina searched among the dead and dying on the battlefield while the battle was still raging at the base of the hill where the enemy army was pinned. After long minutes of despair, she began to doubt that she had received a call from Jörg when the battle was about three hours old. Perhaps she was overwrought and he was not hurt. Her search led her closer and closer to the gunfire. Then she saw him, crushed into the wet earth, and her heart stopped. He looked dead. On closer examination, she saw blood oozing from his shoulder and silently rejoiced that he was still alive. She took him by both legs and dragged him into the wood at the edge of the battlefield, and after making him comfortable went back to the camp for the cart. She half-carried and half-dragged him until she managed to load him onto the cart, and walking, she led the horse back to their camp. The raw, red hole in Jörg's shoulder she cleaned with turpentine. She boiled her fine undergarments to clean his wound, and tore her petticoat into strips with which she bandaged his shoulder. She prayed.

The battle had been a murderous exchange, ending in a rout for the Protestants. Tilly's troops suffered many casualties and needed rest, and the horses needed fodder, so he kept his men in camp to reorganize and repair their heavy losses. The day after the battle, the regiment commander sent the camp surgeon to the cart to look at Jörg. He bound his leg to bring the bones together and looked at his shoulder, but told Katarina she had done all he could and gave him over into her care. In spite of the care she gave, Jörg developed a fever and was in and out of consciousness for three days.

There were many wounded from the battle in the camp, and enemy mercenaries who had escaped and sneaked into the League's camp saw it a rewarding place to loot and molest women, while many of the men in camp were indisposed. For two nights, Katarina stood guard over Jörg with the musket. Occasionally she heard the muffled scream of a camp woman being ravished while her man was dying, but no one came to her aid. On the third night, two men appeared at the edge of the light made by the small fire she set to cook soup for Jörg, who was now conscious. The interlopers had removed the blue feather that was the mark of the enemy soldier, but their eyes glistening in the firelight revealed their ambition. The larger one edged toward her, offering a friendly greeting, but with lust in his eyes. He saw the gun, but hesitated only briefly, believing she would not use it. She told him in sharp language to leave. He ignored her warning and kept edging closer. Meanwhile, in the corner of her vision, she saw the smaller man begin to circle the ring made by the campfire light. She raised the loaded musket. The trooper rushed toward her with a wild, carnal shout and she shot him full in the face. With horror, she saw his face become a messy pulp of blood and bone before the blast propelled him back, sprawling into the fire and spewing soup in all directions. The other man ran off into the darkness.

That same night she hitched horse to cart and they left the battlefield. Katarina and her wounded soldier headed south.

2

HANS
The Refugee

atarina's heroic actions came to be known by the family as *The Miracle of Wimpfen*. She cared for Jörg as they made their way south along the Neckar River, managing to avoid roving soldiers until they came to the town of Marbach. There they found a secluded spot in the wood below the town wall close to the gate tower and above a bend in the river. They could look along the river to the vineyards beyond, and it was there they finally set down the cart, made a shelter for the horse, and prepared for winter. They were married by a Lutheran pastor at his house in the town. The pastor invited some of his worshippers, and from these Katarina made a few friends that winter.

Jörg began to adjust to his new condition. The bone in his leg had knitted quite well and he only had a slight limp. The sword that had pierced his right shoulder caused major damage and left him little use of his right arm, although he had some use of his hand. He began to develop more strength in his left arm and hand. He practiced using the musket from his left side with his right hand tied to his chest. After several weeks he could handle the musket quite well. At first Katarina had to coax him to her bed because he was embarrassed by his ineptitude. Soon his strength returned, making him feel more of a man, and he was thankful that she was happy. By the spring of 1623, Katarina was heavy with child. Both were weary from their travels, especially Katarina, who was anxious to be settled in a home. She told Jörg she did not want the child born on the battlefield, so he decided to leave the war behind and go back to his home in Carinthia. They headed south once more.

They sold the horse and cart in Ulm. Jörg was able to work for their passage to Ragensburg on a bateau with a cargo of woven cloth from the looms of Württemberg that would be made into trooper's uniforms for the Catholic League. After some days, the couple was able to get passage to Salzburg, Jörg to pay for Katarina's passage by helping to work the boat. After resting in Salzburg a day with the Ursuline sisters and Victor, they bought an old horse for Katarina's comfort and walked over the mountains.

Coming out of the final pass that separated the war from his old world, the scene below brought tears to his eyes. The brown hills and green valleys seemed in sharper relief than Jörg remembered. He believed the peaks had, like a shield, protected the valley from the war that was raging to the north. He was heading home. Katarina, who had grown up in a town, had mixed emotions at the prospect of entering a new and strange alpine world.

As they proceeded out of the hills, he could see that his homeland had not escaped the ravages of war. The villages were mostly empty; churches were burned to the ground, churchyards desecrated and coffins dragged to the roadside. As he saw more and more destruction he realized the war had not spared his homeland after all. It was a very different place. Mingled with anxiety for his country and his family was the disappointment that Katarina would not know of his early life.

When they came close to the house where he had been born and where his parents lived, he was aware something was wrong. The place seemed very quiet. Then he noticed there were no birds singing. There had always been birds; his dog had chased them. Turning a familiar bend in the path that hid the house from the road, Jörg and Katarina faced the empty eyes of his home. The old weather-beaten house looked weary, and with a start he realized it was abandoned. It became clear after a few moments that no one had lived there for some time. Someone had chopped out the name above the door, leaving a permanent scar. A carved wooden devil mask with cowbells draped over it was nailed to the door, the same mask he had used to chase away the evil spirits of winter. A shaft of fear pierced his heart, along with remorse for the fate of his parents. Katarina, sensing his fear, kept repeating, "They may have moved elsewhere."

It was late in the day, with the valley already in shadow from the retreating light so there was nothing to do but stay overnight. Jörg knew of a way into the house that he had used many times as a child. They walked to the back of the house and stopped before a door. He released the lock, which was a hidden wooden bar that could be grasped from the outside through a hole in the door. Leaving Katarina at the entrance to the cellar, he stepped into the dark interior of the musty and damp room but even in the darkness he knew the precise position of the trapdoor to the room above. He pulled his body through the opening and scrambled into the house.

Walking to the front door, he noticed in the dim light from the moon that there were no furnishings. He thought briefly that Katarina may be correct; that his parents had moved somewhere, perhaps to live with his sister. He walked around the house, then brought Katarina inside and tried to make her comfortable.

Jörg found some hay in the barn and fed Katarina's horse, then he took the blankets and pouch of food they carried on the horse's haunches into the house. He gathered some firewood and, after building a fire, he and Katarina sat on the floor and ate a meagre meal. Wrapping themselves in the blankets they had brought they both spent a restless night, Katarina due to the discomfort of her pregnancy, Jörg wrestling with nightmares brought on by the tragedy he imagined for his parents and his guilt at having left them.

The next morning, a man appeared on the pathway and looked toward the house. He had seen smoke from the chimney. Jörg told him who he was and questioned him. The man said, "Your mother died about a year ago. A blessed thing for her too! They are banishing all Evangels they can find. Confessors of Christ's most holy word, their wives and babes are forced to leave their homes, sometimes before sunset on the very day. Men of God and teachers are tortured most cruelly and their holy books burned. Churchyards and resting grounds for the dead are most barbarously pulled down and made level with the ground." The man's face was red with indignation during this outburst.

Jörg knew of the situation that was making the man so angry, but he never thought tragedy would come into his parent's home. Shaking with emotion, he enquired about the fate of his father. The man explained, "Shortly after your mother passed away, Gurt came with several soldiers and took your father away with all his possessions. They told Kaspar it was land belonging to the Emperor and no longer his to farm. They have sent away from the valley many of the landed, and their tenants have to follow or find their own way somewhere else." Jörg knew of Gurt, a nasty neighbour, who had lusted after his family's livelihood since he had come home from the war with one leg.

"Where is my father now?"

"I think he is living with your sister in Spital. You know, Gurt does not want anyone to live here; he wants the land because he thinks there is red iron rock in the hill at the back of the farm. He has been digging there since Kaspar was taken away."

"Then I must find Gurt and shoot him down like a dog."

"Should you not seek out your sister and your father?" interjected Katarina.

He was quick to listen to her; she was getting close to her time. So, after taking a last look at his childhood home, Jörg and Katarina set out again, this time on the road to Spital.

By the time they reached Millstätt in the late afternoon, Katarina was feeling pain with every step of the old horse. They stopped at the Abbey where the three remaining monks fussed over Katarina and took care of the horse's needs. The next day, they made their way beside the lake, which was covered in mist. It was a distressingly slow pace they set, but when the sun appeared, the nomadic couple were cheered a little, and by late afternoon they trudged through the town gate into the main square of Spital am Drau. They found the Post Haus, which faced on the square, and enquired after accommodation. Frau Khlesl, the innkeeper, seeing Katarina's advanced condition asked, with some concern, "For how long?" Her *Hausfrau's* mind urged her to send them away, but her woman's heart whispered otherwise. On being assured that they wished to stay only until they located Jörg's sister the next day, she summoned her boy to care for the horse. Then she said to Katarina, "I have a fresh bed you might find comfortable. Come." That night, just after the town clock struck midnight, Katarina's waters broke. Frau Khlesl was summoned, and annoyed that her straw tick was ruined, roused her boy to find the local mid-wife. Katarina's pains were heavy and frequent when the mid-wife in her nightclothes arrived at Frau Khlesl's *Gasthaus* and with brusque authority sent Jörg from the bedchamber occupied by Katarina. Noise from the street informed him that the business of the town was well underway when he heard a wailing from the bedchamber, and soon after, Frau Khlesl came hustling from the room. With some agitation, she told him that Katarina had surrendered a healthy baby boy. After he was summoned to her bedside by the mid-wife, Katarina said she would call the boy Johannes Georg. Jörg was pleased with mother and son.

The next day, since the baby seemed to be in fine health, he went to the *Rathaus* where the town records were kept and was able to find out the location of his sister Eva's house, which was on the road along the river they had taken the previous day. Hoping that Katarina and the baby would be taken off her hands soon, Frau Khlesl dispatched her boy to the sister's farm to inform Eva of the events of the previous day. Later the same day, Jörg mounted Katarina's horse and set out to find his sister's farm.

He found his father hoeing weeds from the small vegetable garden in front of the house. Kaspar pressed his hand, but showed little emotion; there was no pleasure in his eyes at seeing Jörg again after his three-year absence. His father had aged greatly, mentally broken from his hard life as an alpine farmer and the terrors of war and religious intrigues. He told Jörg of his mother's death a year ago, and of his removal from the farm. Kaspar was not bitter, accepting his fate calmly. He lived in dangerous times; to be alive at his age was all he could expect.

"What happened to Erasmus? He was running the farm when I left."

"Erasmus? Two months after you left the soldiers came and took Erasmus away. They put him in the dungeon at Graz. He died there." Tears came to his father's eyes; Erasmus was his favourite. His father continued, "Gurt stole the farm. He wants the red rock from the cliff."

These last words seemed to utterly defeat Kaspar, and he quickly turned and walked toward the house. Jörg noticed how small and bent was his father.

His sister Eva came from the washhouse, wiping her hands on an apron and flushed from her efforts. Jörg was startled by the change in his sister. Her girth had expanded and she looked much older than he expected; it was only three years since he had left, but she, like his father, had gone through terrible times. She greeted him with a hug but showed no real pleasure at seeing him. Or so he thought. The reunion was dampened by her fear that Jörg and his wife expected to live with her and Amos. Amos would disapprove.

She said, "Amos is not at home. He and the boys have taken the animals to the high country pasture for the summer. They are due back on the second Sabbath."

"Is my boy old enough to be shepherding?"

"Your Leonardt is five come Michaelmas. He is a grown boy who loves Amos.

He and my boys go everywhere with Amos."

Shortly after the reunion with his father and sister, Jörg caught the horse and headed back to Spital. He was despondent. Eva seemed not to have forgiven him for leaving. And he was disappointed not to have seen his son. He feared Leonardt was lost to him, God's punishment for the sin of abandoning a son. Aside from the problems with his family, he lived in fear of the authorities, which were exiling anyone who spoke out for Church reform, as Katarina was wont to do. He could see no good future.

The experiences of war made him unfit for farm life, but he had no other trade. He had acquired some knowledge of weaving and tailoring from Katarina, and with her help they might survive by catering to the citizens of Spital. His sister had told him that there was a need for men with skills with so many young peasants killed in the war. "The guilds are not strong here," she had said. As he approached Spital he thought fondly of Katarina and her infant son and he began to hope there might be a future for them after all. He was only twenty-four years old, still young and energetic.

Jörg and Katarina leased a small house. They worked in the weaving and cloth trade and after five years Jörg was able to join the weavers' guild. Over the years they prospered within their humble class. Katarina had another son, Matthias. The family attended the Evangelical Lutheran church nearby, which somehow escaped destruction, and became a stable part of that small but active community. Although Jörg never managed to exhibit the enthusiasm most of his pious neighbours did, he was at peace. His salvation came with work and he spent most of his days working. It was his silent demonstration of love for his Maker.

His peace was shattered one gloomy morning a year later. Amos came to his door leading an old brown horse. He had a large gash across his brow, and was clearly exhausted. Jörg could see by his manner and the bloody wound that he was the bearer of bad news. He came to the pantry where Katarina was scrubbing pots with ash and sat at the table before he said a word. Johannes Georg was helping his mother and little Matthias was crawling about underfoot. Leonardt was off playing in the woods with some boys his age.

Katarina left Johannes Georg to the scrubbing and put a kettle on the fire. When Katarina came to sit at the table with Jörg, Amos spoke, first in a mere mumble, but as he gathered his courage he became more coherent.

"They came last night and took your father. Accused him of sedition against the Emperor and dragged him from his bed. With his age he was suffering from pleurisy and was in pain. He was confused, asking who was torturing him. I tried to stop them, and the one in charge flattened me with his blade. Anna woke, screaming. One of the soldiers went to her and treated her roughly, but due to her young age did not molest her."

Jörg, anxious to hear of his father asked, "What did they do to Kaspar?"

"They took him from the house to the big oak tree along the road. A torch was lit and the soldiers stood as if on parade and the officer read from a piece of paper the charge of sedition. Then they put a rope around your father's neck and hanged him on the tree. They rode off, leaving him in the tree for all to see."

Jörg was beyond anger. He slumped in his chair and covered his grief with his hands. Katarina wondered about Anna and the other children. Amos spoke quickly, "They are safe. Anna is still frightened but the oldest is looking out for her."

Katarina was suddenly aware that Johannes Georg was still in the room. She went to him and embraced his small, shaking shoulders. "Your grandfather has gone to heaven. You must be brave."

But Johannes Georg did not feel brave. He wanted to cry but he was old enough to know that crying was not proper. He loved his grandfather and the many times they had walked together into the hills behind his house. His grandfather knew the names of all the trees and the birds that made their nests in the branches. He taught Johannes Georg how to milk the cows in the high pastures and to haul the milk cart down the crooked path to the barn. He helped his grandfather sharpen the scythe that the farmhands used to cut the hay for the cows and the two horses that were kept in the barn. He could not believe his grandfather would no longer be his companion. Uncle Amos must be wrong.

That afternoon Leonardt, Johannes Georg, and Mathias sat in the back of the cart as their parents drove to Kasper's farm to give their grandfather a Christian burial. When they arrived, Johannes Georg looked for his grandfather hanging from the tree, but he was not there. Amos and two neighbours had cut him down and he was now lying in a box in the house beside the hearth. Aunt Eva said that it was, "A good place for your grandfather, since in his late years he was always complaining about being cold in winter."

Toward evening a man in a black coat and large slouch hat came to the house and Johannes Georg's grandfather was put into the ground under a shade tree at the edge of the woods. Aunt Eva said it was his favourite spot to sit in the summertime.

Amos made a wooden cross and drove it into the soft earth over Kaspar's grave.

In the weeks following, the children from the church told stories about dead bodies of people the Emperor did not like being dug up and burned, after which the coffins would sit beside the roads until relatives got enough courage to take them away. Johannes Georg had nightmares in which his grandfather hung from a tree and as he looked his grandfather fell into a hole. Some men with spades came and dug his grandfather from the ground and roasted him on a hot fire. His grandfather opened his mouth wide but no sound came. Johannes Georg woke trying to scream.

Whenever Johannes Georg visited his aunt and uncle he went to his grandfather's grave to see if he was still there. One day the grave was empty. He looked for his grandfather beside the road but he was not there. His mother spoke to him, "Your grandfather has gone to heaven." But Johannes Georg wondered.

Leonhardt went off to the war in his sixteenth year. Katarina was distressed but did not object; it was the destiny of mothers that their sons go off to war. Jörg was numb to the violence of the times and took the news as if this was a natural part of being a man. He could not blame Leonardt for following in his father's footsteps when he was a young man, and he simply said to him, "God bless you, my boy, and may He bring you home safely to us!" Then he went back to his work.

For many weeks after Leonardt left home, Katarina waited for some word as to his whereabouts, but no word came to her. She would not believe he was gone forever, and she spent many weary nights alternatively weeping for his soul and praying for his safety. Eventually she accepted that he was lost to her.

One day a trooper from the Duke's army stood in Katarina's doorway. He told her that he knew Leonardt in Bavaria and that, sadly, he had died from gunshot to his stomach. He told Katarina it was not painful, but she recalled her experiences on the battlefield and was not fooled. She had seen men die in terrible agony, deeply sunk in the mud and grime of the earth. When Katarina told Jörg the news, he said nothing. After a moment of strained silence between the two of them, Jörg went back to his weaving.

Jörg held his grief inside, but Leonardt's death aged Katarina. She became listless and withdrew into her own grief. For many months she shed tears at the most unusual times. Johannes Georg was witness to her tears and silent grief, but was unable to change his mother's moods. Often they wept together.

Johannes Georg was twelve when the family heard of Leonardt's death. He was almost an adult, but still had the emotions of a child. It was to Johannes Georg, because of his young age, that the news of his brother's death was most painful. Leonardt had seemed to be so much bigger and smarter. He kept Johannes Georg out of trouble. When his father told him of Leonardt's death he went to his cave above the river. In truth it was a crevice in the rocks that he and some of the young boys of the village had covered with tree branches and the undergrowth of the forest. Here the young boys imagined they protected the village from the Roman Legions coming up the river to kill them and steal the women. It was in this pretend fortress, high above the river, that Johannes Georg mourned for his older brother. Sobbing and shaking as if with a fever, he whispered to his dead brother that he would see him again in heaven. Now he was a man and had to act like a man. He climbed down from the mountain crevice to the river's edge and spat into the water to consummate his resolve.

Katarina could see that Johannes Georg was unhappy, and she sensed he wanted to leave home. She could not discourage him, because, in truth she was not really happy living in the mountains. She found winter in the mountains particularly harsh. And the valley was becoming very inhospitable for those who did not profess the Jesuit way, even those who owned no land, and she could see no future here for her sons. She dreamed of her childhood of privilege, and the tragedies that had befallen her after leaving Graz. Calling Johannes Georg to her side one evening when she sat spinning the yarn that Jörg used for his loom, she told her son of her earlier life: roaming in the grain fields and apple orchards with her father when she was a child; of the evenings of music, when her mother's friends had come to their house, wearing large hats and flowing petticoats; of her first husband Benedict, who died of the pest; and the birth of Johannes Georg's little step-sister Anna, taken by God at an age before she discovered life. She told of her mother dying in agony from the pest: of her father, beheaded and burned in the family hearth; of the world of beauty created by God, and the ugly brutality of war created by man. Johannes Georg listened with the impatience of youth, thinking her stories were the ramblings of old age. It was much later that her words to him as a youth sustained his resolve in times of tragedy.

K atarina died from the shaking disease when Johannes Georg was eighteen. He had been endowed with the outbound spirit of his mother, and with her gone his future in the brown hills and green valleys of Carinthia seemed not only dangerous but also constricting. But he was the oldest surviving son with a great sense of duty to the family, so when his father asked him to learn the weaver's trade he had to bury his ambition and do his wishes.

He was now well known in the town, where the people called him Hans, son of Jörg the weaver. Johannes Georg was known outside the family as Hans because, as he was growing up in the society of the village children, little Matthias, who was his constant companion, could not say his full name and reduced his effort to the shorter Hans. So Hans became his public name and stuck with him into adulthood.

In time, Hans thought of his old ambition to leave the town where he was born and seek a future beyond the hills and valleys of his forefathers. His own father was well established now and he could survive without him. Matthias was Jörg's apprentice and seemed to thrive in the work and culture of the cloth trade and was destined, Hans was certain, to follow in his father's footsteps. But Hans, like his father before him, wished to see some of the outside world. Katarina had often talked about her world beyond the mountains, and, partly to honour her unspoken wishes for him to search out his mother's heritage, he fantasized about leaving home. While he wished to escape the confinement of the mountains, he could not yet bring himself to make the break with his past, and that of generations of his family.

But the decision was taken from him. Shortly after Katarina's death, a regiment of the Imperial army marched into Spital am Drau with all its colours flying. The troops were assigned billets with the residents of the town and the surrounding area. The people dared not object for fear of banishment in exile, which had become common, even for the lowly tenant farmers and merchants. Jörg had to house two soldiers for several days while the regiment was organizing to march north. Rumours were circulating in the church community that the regimental officers had ordered the soldiers to take with them all the young men who professed Protestantism. They were to use force if necessary. Hans told his father of a plan by the local men to hide from the soldiers, and he wished his blessing to join them. Jörg said not a word, but went to the shelf above the hearth and took down his musket, his most prized possession. He handed the gun with its wheel key to Hans and said only, "Take care of it." Holding back tears, Hans hugged his father, to the latter's embarrassment, and quickly prepared to leave. He and Jörg both sensed that it might be the last time they would see each other. Suddenly, about to leave, his whole life crowded in on him. He had trouble breathing, certain this was a final parting. Cradling his father's gun in the crook of his arm he went through the door with a heavy heart and misty eyes.

Hans joined a group of men from his father's church and hid out in the woods. He and a friend, Tomas, climbed to the cave above the river determined to shoot any soldier that found them. When four troopers appeared on the rocks below, Hans' gun would not fire; he had forgotten to wind the wheel. In the ensuing struggle, the troopers overwhelmed his friends and took Hans' gun. The soldiers captured several more "recruits" scattered about in the woods. When they left the area the next day, Hans and Tomas were with them, bound in chains.

The "recruits" were marched under close guard beside wagons with straw that were to be their beds for the night. The next day they were formed into units of five men, each unit guarded by a trooper carrying a musket; Hans' unit by a rough giant called Kurt who carried one of the new flintlock guns, and looked mean enough to use it with pleasure. In their common adversity, the men from Spital, some of whom were strangers to Hans, became united against their enemies, which were not so much the soldiers with whom they lived in some harmony, but the Jesuits who were persecuting them. Although a prisoner, Hans found his days not unpleasant. Wandering north towards the war he found companionship with his fellows and soon he had little intention of returning to his family and church. He thought of his mother and her desire to have him see the world beyond the mountains. And he had secretly wished something would relieve him of duty to his father. Now he was on the road to a world yet unknown.

But the road ahead had two paths, north or west. He could go north with the regiment. The companionship suited him, but he could see that the army life of constant scrounging, heavy drinking, and brawling, was not pleasant. It gave security, but also great danger. His father did not like war, both from his own experience and from the loss of Leonardt, and would be very upset if his second son died in battle. And Hans himself had no taste for the adventure of war.

The second path of the road was toward the west. His mother had talked fondly of the winter she and Jörg spent on the slope of the river below the town of Marbach. That region was a refuge for those who adhered to the reformed church and was, he had heard, a safe haven for people of his faith. His brother was buried somewhere in Bavaria. And he had been told that his ancient grandfather Jacobs had come, "From óver the mountains to the north and west." All the urgings of his spirit told him to go west.

There was little discipline in the regiment; the troopers lived off the spoils of the area they were travelling through on any given day. They bullied residents for beds, they stole food and sometimes molested the daughters of the towns and villages through which they were marching. Hans had to fit into this pattern of behaviour; he would not survive otherwise. He stayed with the soldiers as the regiment moved north along the Lieser River and over the mountain pass of the Katschberg into the village of Hallein. Here the regiment made camp to wait for other "recruits" from the east that were to join it before they proceeded to the Danube. The regiment was now well into Salzburg Bishopric where non-Jesuits were welcome by order of the new Bishop. He decided to risk leaving the regiment and attempt to get into Bavaria.

On a moonless night, he took wine that he had stolen and managed to get the guard of the arms wagon drunk enough so that he slept. He retrieved his musket, stole some food from a village home, and hid out in the woods on the slopes of the Dürrnberg above Hallein. During the night he listened for noises of pursuit, but he heard nothing. After a cold and wet night, Hans decided he was safely away, so he clambered upward until he found a trail he thought would take him to a pass that would lead into Bavaria. Not far along the path he came to a large clearing in which he found the entrance to a salt mine. This was a surprise, which forced him to think of his immediate circumstances. Still out of sight of anyone that might be nearby he sat on a rock and ate some of his stolen provisions. He thought he might earn money in the mine to buy a horse so he made the decision to be a salt miner until he had sufficient money to move on.

A man in a roughly-built shack, somewhat surprised to find a body willing and able to go into the mine without being forced by the Bishop's decree, took his name, gave him two sacks, and sent him into the mine. Hans knew nothing of the routine but he waited in the semi-darkness of the upper gallery until a small group of miners appeared. He watched them as they sat on their sacks and slid down the wooden rails to the next gallery below. Beside the rails of the ramp there was a rope strung on posts in such a way as to allow a miner to slow his progress. Hans sat on his sacks, and following the actions of the miners, slid down the steep ramp at a terrifying speed, burning his right hand in an attempt to slow his plunge into what seemed like hell below. Reaching the bottom, he saw the glint of water in the dim light provided by firebrands placed every few metres in alcoves cut into the rock. The air here was smoky from the torches, making it difficult to breathe. He wanted to get back outside to fresh air, to run up the steps located beside the sliding ramp and into sunlight. He felt like he was buried alive. He looked at the miners which were getting far ahead, and, forcing himself to follow, trailed them as they walked around a pond of what he learned later was brine collected from the crevices in the mountain and piped through tunnels to the outside.

Hans was deep under the mountain. He could barely see the roof of the gallery, and in the blackness he imagined the mountain was crushing him like he used to squash frogs into the mud with rocks. He wanted to take in great gulps of air and sit down. But the air was so smoky he choked in the attempt. He forced himself to go forward, hoping the smoke might not be as thick below.

After three more steep tunnels and brine ponds, the miners reached the gallery that was being mined. Here they had to dig into the rock-hard salt that escaped the erosion of the water. The miners then filled their sacks and carried them to the brine ponds. At the end of the day, each man would be given a few coins as payment, depending on the number of sacks delivered. In the open air the work would be tiresome. Here in the dark and smoke-filled air it was work for slaves. In truth, many of the miners were shackled prisoners sent to the mines by the Bishop's court where they were watched and herded by a guard. In one way they were favoured because they were provided with a bed and some food. All others had to scrounge, much as he had experienced in the regiment. If a miner lasted long enough he would eventually settle himself down with some family or at a local guesthouse, using a portion of his meagre payment. But for Hans, still fearful of soldiers sent out to take him back to the regiment, this underground place seemed safe enough if you could avoid a fight. So he stayed, going down into the mine each day, trudging from the pit to the brine pools with two sacks on his back, then back to the pit to swing the pick at the salt seam, dig enough of the rock-hard salt to load the sacks again. It was backbreaking work.

He managed to find a room in the house of an old widow woman and in time he was accepted into the miner's community. It was a rough community, in which the miners slaved in the pits during the day, fought among themselves over money and women, and spent their evenings in the beer gardens of Hallein, mostly getting drunk and carousing with the resident harlots.

Eventually Hans tired of the miner's life and he began to think that it was safe to move on. He was told there were tunnels on the Bavarian side of the Dürrnberg at Berchtesgaden where salt trains were loaded to be sent to destinations within Bavaria. But he discovered from the miners that the Bishop of Salzburg would not allow Hallein salt to be sent to Bavaria, so he made a plan to go to Salzburg where he hoped he could find a way to get to Berchtesgaden and overland to the Lower Palatinate. So one morning before the sun was over the peaks, he picked up his small bundle of possessions, hid the money he had saved in his boots and walked down the mountain into Salzburg town. Here he was able to find shelter and food with the brothers of St. Peter's Abbey in exchange for a few pennies.

He began the search for transportation to Ulm, where, he had been told people were taking in refugees from the war. He was anxious to leave Salzburg and to get settled somewhere in safe territory before the winter rains. At the docks he saw a small group surrounding a man who was shouting in a coarse manner. As Hans reached the group, the man stopped talking to the assembly and began a quiet conversation with a large man who sported a great mane of yellow hair. Hans asked a man what was happening. "He is looking for guards on a salt train to the west." There were several rough-looking fellows milling about, waiting for the man to make his choice and Hans had to wait before he was able to talk to the man. Finally, it was his turn. He told the man that he would protect his cargo on the journey to Ulm. The man peered at him with his sharp, calculating eyes and examined his dagger for an edge. "Let me see your musket." Showing his father's gun, the man asked with a grunt, "Do you know how to work it?" Hans told him his father had brought it home from the war and that he was very good at working the machine. The man nodded his head and said, "I am Otto. We leave at daybreak from this place." He called out to a large blond-haired man, who came forward, fingering the hilt of his long heavy sword. Otto told them that a cart would leave at the break of day. The big blond man looked quizzically at Hans, as if he did not believe such a small man would be able to protect the wagon, but said through a very large moustache, "I am called Alvar." Hans told his story, and Alvar volunteered that he was a former fighter with King Gustavus. He had gotten lost and was anxious to join up with his regiment, which he said was moving into the Palatinate. More likely drunk than lost, thought Hans, but he said nothing. They broke apart with mutual suspicion, but agreed to be at the meeting place on the pier the next morning, from which they would travel west.

Hans spent the night in an old, rickety lean-to shed attached to the cliff at the edge of the town. It was meant as a place to feed animals on their journey from the river to the countryside, but was not occupied. Finding bits of hay scattered about, Hans gathered it up and made an adequate, if uncomfortable, bed. The hay was wet with dew when he woke. He was very hungry, but he knew he needed to be at the pier before daybreak. He gathered up his small bundle and headed for the river. In the centre of town, merchants were beginning to set up their kiosks for the day's trade. The smell of fresh loaves was irresistible. He could not chance stealing, so he spent a tiny part of his estate and purchased two loaves and a sausage. Armed with this sustenance, he hurried to the river and found Alvar amongst the bustle of fishermen heading out for their daily catch. They spied Otto walking along the road beside the river leading a horse. Otto met his two neophyte guards with a grunt that said, "Come with me."

The trio walked to the edge of Salzburg with the horse in tow. When they were out of sight of the town they left the road and walked into the woods. At first it was a struggle since there seemed to be no track, and the horse, which was not young and also stubborn, was more of a hindrance than otherwise. After some time threshing about in the woods they came upon a well-trodden pathway. Otto informed them, "We are now in Bavaria," at which point he mounted the horse and rode ahead. He waited in the trees beside the pathway until his guards caught up to him. Otto's behaviour was his way of spying highwaymen ahead. The detour through the woods was to avoid the toll station on the main road, and was part of a pattern for the whole journey that was to follow.

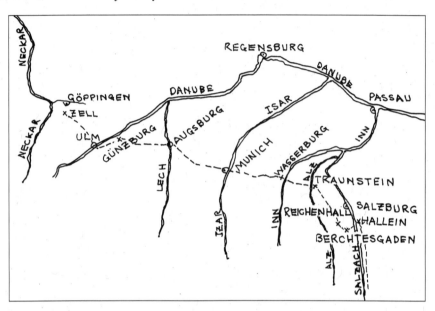

It was late in the afternoon when they came upon the salt train of six wagons strung in a line and attached to each other. The train was hidden in a clump of trees, just off the approach road to Berchtesgaden. A small house sat in a clearing with a wisp of smoke rising from the chimney. Leaving Hans and Alvar with the wagons, Otto rode off toward the house. He returned an hour later with a team of four oxen and three other men of different ages, whom were Otto's sons. They nodded to acknowledge the presence of the newcomers, and without saying a word proceeded to hitch the oxen to the six wagons. Since his help was superfluous, Hans took the opportunity to examine the train he was commissioned to protect. Five of the wagons were piled high with sacks of salt and covered with a linen cloth impregnated with hot beeswax. This served as protection for the precious cargo of salt from the rain and snow they would encounter on the mountain detours. A small cart was attached to the train with wooden boards, forming a manger-like container stuffed with fodder for the animals. The hay was also covered with waxed linen and tied to the cart with twine.

On the sixth and foremost wagon had been built a wooden shed-like structure with a small chimney poking through its roof. Peeking around a heavy blanket covering the opening, Hans could see in the dim interior four sleeping platforms and a very small fire pit. Clearly this was the living quarters for Otto's family. He wondered where he and Alvar were to spend their nights.

It was the middle of October when the little band of six men, four oxen and one horse began their journey across Bavaria. Otto talked of the difficulties that might befall them; highwaymen, toll collectors, Swedish troops, and difficult terrain with many rivers to ford. He went on, "Being this late in the year, the pest may not be as vicious as it was in the hot months of the summer, but the sexton is still the busiest man in München so we will avoid the towns except where we can sell our salt." He also had an unspoken reason for keeping away from towns, which was to keep his sons out of trouble at the beer taverns along the road. While he had their attention he laid out the rules. Hans was told to walk before the train and Alvar to follow behind, Otto would scout ahead on the horse, and his sons would drive and care for the oxen. Their first camp was to be near Traunstein at the fording of the river Alz.

At Reichenhall, Otto bribed the toll collector in lieu of a much larger toll. Reichenhall was very protective of its own mining works and imposed punitive tolls for salt coming into the town. But most merchant suppliers would bypass the town to avoid the large official toll so the toll collector worked his philosophy as, "a bit for me, a bit for the *Bürgermeister*, or nothing for either."

A fork in the road before Traunstein allowed the salt train to bypass that place and by mid-afternoon it reached the crossing of the Alz. The water was low and the crossing well marked, making the fording quite easy with only one mishap; a wagon wheel dropped off an edge stone, twisting the cart at a dangerous tilt, but the salt load stayed in place. They stopped for the night at a spot on the river's bank that was used regularly by Otto and other merchants. The oxen were fed, belled and hobbled for the night. Hans retired to the edge of the camp for a small meal of sausage and cheese, washed down with a few drafts from his wineskin. Otto and his boys built a small fire. Ernst, the middle one of Otto's boys, brought out an accordion, and after some warming up, the camp joined him in singing the old mountain songs of shepherds. Hans had no singing voice but he hesitantly joined the singing group, careful not to intrude on Ernst's melodious and emotional renditions of the songs. After the fire died, Otto instructed Hans and Alvar to stand watch through the night. He gave them blankets made from empty salt sacks stitched together by Frau Otto. The blankets were made of a double layer of sacks so they could either use them as a covering or stuff them with hay or straw to make a bed. It was agreed that Alvar would be on watch until the moon reached its zenith. Hans took his bedding and settled himself, sleeping in the cart with his salt sack blanket spread on the fodder and the waxed covering as a blanket. He slept soundly until he was called to stand watch.

The next day on the road to Wasserburg, Otto came riding back from his forward scouting position and instructed Freidreich, the youngest of his boys and the team driver, to get the train off the road and into the woods. A troop of Imperial pike men was marching toward them and Otto did not want to have an encounter with the soldiers. Fortunately, just ahead they found a path leading away from the road. They had hardly reached the trees when the soldiers came around a bend. The troopers were walking in pairs, in a somewhat disorganized column. There was much revelry among the men, some of it clearly nurtured by wine even though it was early in the day. The soldiers were so preoccupied with their own business that no one saw the wagons or the team of oxen, and soon they were marching down the road and into the distance. After this incident, the salt train proceeded along the mostly deserted road without further trouble.

At the Inn River, below Wasserburg, Otto stopped. Leaving the wagons in charge of his sons, he rode down the river's bank to find a buyer for his cargo. He was gone two hours before he rode back with bad news. He was able to sell only one wagonload to a man who would re-sell it downriver. He and Ernst uncoupled one of the wagons and left the camp to deliver the salt.

Otto had many reservations about going into the town, but he had no choice if he was to sell his salt. So when Ernst and Otto returned they broke camp, crossed over the river, paid the toll and entered the town of Wasserburg with the remaining wagons. This was much to the pleasure of Otto's sons, who looked forward to some revelry after their long and dusty journey.

Wasserburg was a typical medieval town built on a sharp bow of the Inn River, which protected the town on three sides. It was almost an island with a very narrow neck of land connecting the town to its hinterland. The town afforded an enemy almost no access except from the river itself or by means of the bridge they had just crossed.

Once over the bridge, carts and wagons from Traunstein and elsewhere parked their wares along the road at the river's edge where the boats that transported the salt bags downriver were moored. On the day that Otto's salt train arrived, there were only two boats, but many wagons. Consequently the price for salt was low, and Otto was able to sell only one wagon at a price he found acceptable. After delivering the required sacks to one of the boats, Otto was anxious to leave the town. He wanted to avoid the perils of the crowds and get on his way to München where he was sure he could get a better price for his cargo, and while there to pick up a load of linen bolts to deliver back to Berchtesgaden. His older sons objected to this plan; they begged tiredness and the need for some entertainment. Otto promised to release them to their own pleasures in München. But they argued with their father and eventually Otto gave in to their entreaties and told his crew they would stay overnight.

That night in Wasserburg would change Hans' life. With Alvar promising to guard the wagons, Hans was allowed to go into the town with Otto's sons. After securing the wagons against the elements and feeding the oxen, Hans and Otto's two oldest boys set out for town. After many days on the dusty road evading bandits, and hungry for human company, the men were exuberant at the prospects they imagined would be theirs. They headed for the nearest *Biergarten*, a place called Switzer Haus, situated close to the river's bank. It was very crowded, and even so early in the night the noise of beer steins pounding tabletops and wild singing could be heard, with the strains of the revellers floating for some distance on the night air.

Hans and the others found a place at a crowded table and were almost immediately served by a young girl showing her copious bosom behind the bib of a snow-white apron. It was not long before the men from the salt train became as boisterous as the rest. Hans' place socially was not normally with Otto's sons but tonight they were comrades, and under the influence of the drink they became soul mates. The beer flowed freely, they sang, told lewd stories and the young server rubbing against their bodies in the crush brought them to a high state of excitement. After all the days and nights living in the rough with only men as companions Hans longed for intimacy with a woman. Just then, like a dream fulfilled, he felt a tugging of his shirt. Turning from his drink, he saw a light-haired woman motioning towards the entrance. She grabbed his hand and pulled him upright. With a silly grin he waved to his drinking companions and let the woman take him away. With a mixture of caution and pleasure he followed her out into the darkness.

It was now pitch black. She led him down a path dimly lit by lanterns hung from trees. He had a stein full of beer in one hand and the woman's hand in the other. In the flickering light from the lanterns he could see that she was not unattractive, but much older than he was. She asked for money. He opened his purse and gave her what she wanted. He would not normally choose her as a companion, but these were not usual times. She did smell nice. Even with his acute loneliness from the weeks without female company he was not deceived. He knew who she was and what she was about. But his desires got the best of his common sense.

She led him to a bower formed by overhanging boughs. There was a dimmed lantern hanging from one of the boughs and in its flickering light he saw the object of her intent; a love mat spread on a bed of dry leaves. She pulled him toward her and as she did so he saw fear in her eyes. Even though his senses were dulled by wine he felt danger. They lay on the mat and when Hans was in a most compromising position the attack came. Two men charged out of the trees, one of the men brandished a heavy piece of wood. Hans was suddenly very sober. Waiting for the blow to come he gathered strength, and as the club descended he rolled off the woman and at the same time sought the knife hidden in his boot. The man had swung the club with such force that it hit the soft ground with a thud between Hans and the woman. The club wielder stumbled over the woman and Hans rose with a bound from his prone position and caught the bandit square in the stomach. He made a loud grunt as the knife went in and then unaccountably began to curse. The second bandit, the one given the job of pilfering the unconscious victim, hesitated. Hans aimed a blow with his foot straight into the man's crotch. He connected, and sent the thief, doubled-up and groaning, running crabwise into the trees. The wounded man lay sprawled on the mat that was meant for a more romantic purpose. The woman was gone.

Suddenly alone with the wounded man, fear overtook Hans and he began to shake. In a few moments, standing in the darkness with his assailant bleeding at his feet, he got back his reason. He would drag the groaning man to the river and let him drift downstream, perhaps never to be found. It seemed a monstrous thing, to deliberately kill the man. Perhaps if he left the groaning man as he was on the mat, either his woman or his partner would come back and rescue him. Since they were engaged in clandestine and illegal business it was not likely they would inform the authorities. In the end he turned the man over, tore a strip off his shirt and used it to stanch the wound. Then he walked out of the bower and ran to the place they had left the wagons.

He had a few words with Alvar who told him the boys had not yet returned and in his opinion would not be back until daybreak. Hans took over guard duties from Alvar, determined to shoot anyone who came near the wagons.

Otto's boys returned during the small hours of morning, still singing and full of good cheer. Hans breathed not a word of his ordeal, implying he had had a good time with the light-haired woman. They smiled at his secret. Hans told no one the truth, but for a long time afterward expected someone would come looking for him for what he had done.

By directing their journey along the road and through the woods on little-known trails with which Otto was familiar, the three remaining wagons of Berchtesgaden salt reached the capital town of Bavaria in two days' time. Otto made camp on the road that led to the eastern gate of the town. Pestilence was rampant in the country towns and the *Bürgermeister* of München had decreed that all trading was to be done by citizen merchants, who must venture outside the gates for supplies. Thus, the road leading to the gates was a thriving commercial centre. Country people came with their carts loaded with produce and other goods, and set up their businesses along the road. Much competition developed to get as close to the gate as possible, so there was much jostling and arguing among the dealers; sometimes a knife was drawn and bloodshed would ensue. At night the camp came alive with open fires that revealed the singing, dancing, drunkenness, and debauchery that made for a lively, if dangerous, place. Some hardy folk had established permanent shops, and there were makeshift taverns clustered around the gates. It was a breeding place for all the sins and ills of mankind. Especially the pest.

Otto had no paper to enter the town so the train was drawn up as close to the gate as possible. Once the oxen had been watered and tethered on a small patch of grass, a fire built and a meal taken, Otto's crew settled down for the night. During the night, Otto's fear of bandits became a reality. It happened about three hours after midnight on Hans' watch. The grey overcast cloud that had prevailed during the day continued after sunset, obscuring the recent starry brilliance of the heavens. It was very dark. Hans sat propped against a wagon wheel beside the fire, which had burned down to a few coals. Having had little trouble so far, Hans was off his guard and was desperately trying to stay awake when he heard a sharp noise. It seemed to come from the vicinity of the third wagon. He peered into the darkness. From the glow of a nearby fire he thought he saw shadowy figures. There were three of them, trying to undo the canopy tied over the salt bags. He ran toward the bandits, setting the wheel on his musket as he ran.

He was terrified, not so much by the thieves, but of the anger that would be brought down on his head by Otto for any loss of salt. He shouted out, but the bandits showed no signs of backing off. Hans hesitated in his headlong dash, suddenly fearful that they might have muskets or pistols. He waited for a shot. When it did not come he ran toward the shadowy figures, having set in motion what could not be reversed. He was still too far away to be sure musket fire would drive them off. He shouted loudly, hoping to scare them off, but as he approached the bandits they stood their ground. Still frightened, but now free of the panic that had gripped him earlier, he advanced slowly, and when he was sure a musket ball would reach the target, he dropped to his knees, aimed at one of the shadows, and fired.

The noise from the musket echoed throughout the camp and a great pall of smoke obscured his vision. Moving sideways and crouching behind a bush, he fumbled with the gun, hoping to reload, but in the darkness he could not. When the smoke cleared he could no longer see the bandits. They had run away.

Lights began to appear and men jumped from their beds, some cursing for being awakened from their sleep. Some showed interest, but most were indifferent to Hans' concern since driving off bandits was routine. Otto came into the group, talked quietly to some of the owners, and they soon faded away, back to their beds. Otto was pleased with Hans and assured him the bandits would not be back that night. He said, "They always try to steal from the newcomers on the first night to test their defences. Those three will not be back tonight, but others might come out of the woods. Along here the trees hide many thieves that will steal the very shirt off your back if they can. So be on your guard for anything." Hans returned to his post until Alvar relieved him.

Otto was out early the next day hawking his Berchtesgaden salt. But selling one sack at a time meant it would take several days to unload his wagons. His crew settled in for some days of relative leisure. Hans and Alvar took turns guarding the treasure at night, but bandits did not bother them again.

It was in this anthill of human smells and animal waste that Hans met Gertrudus. On the third day encamped, about mid-day, a merchant from the town was seen getting supplies put into a small closed cart drawn by a lively brown horse. By the words on the side of the cart, the merchant was one Ernst Gruber—

Fleischwarren. The spirited horse was being driven by the most beautiful girl Hans had ever seen, who showed a spirit in handling the horse that was equal to that of the animal. When the horse and cart pulled up in front of Otto's wagons, Hans could see in more detail this lovely creature handling the reins. She had long black hair covered by a red bonnet with a red string tied at her throat. Her eyes were black as coal and were set in an alabaster face. She was sitting on a seat attached to the cart, wrapped in a red cape hiding all but a vague outline of her curves. Hans carried a sack of salt to the butcher's cart and in passing this delightful creature was rewarded with a smile. Nearly choking on the words, he said, "*Guten tag.*" This black-eyed beauty said nothing and in deference to her father's presence crafted a disdainful gaze in Hans' direction. But, with the feminine guile that fathers do not see, there was an invitation in her look. Her father, the butcher, settled payment with Otto, climbed aboard the cart and she was gone, leaving Hans transfixed. For several moments he peered in the direction of the departed vision. Her smell lingered in the air where the cart had rested.

Until this moment there had been no particular direction to his wanderings, but suddenly, with this girl's brief presence, he saw clearly what he had become; a wastrel. He had had very little experience with women, mostly playing at love in the woods with two or three of the young girls he knew from the church. He had never lain with a good woman, and in his present state he could not take up with a decent woman. That night he did not sleep. His brain was alive with thoughts of the girl he had encountered in the afternoon. For the first time since he left home he was ashamed of his condition. He was dirty and always hungry. Katarina would say he was living in filth. He noticed that his straw stank even more than he did, and for the first time he realized that he was physically uncomfortable. He imagined bugs crawling on his body.

He squirmed and twisted in the night, trying to get rid of the face of the girl who had infected his peace. He finally drifted off to sleep and dreamed he was a knight with a long feather tucked into his bonnet and riding swift as the wind on a prancing horse as white as new snow on the mountains of his home. She drifted below him, covered in a film of silk, her black hair streaming behind her like a storm cloud. He drew his sword and with a delicate thrust of its point flicked away the gossamer web that hid her nakedness.

He awakened, the pleasure of his dream only a momentary relief from his misery, and he lay through the rest of the darkness in mental and physical agony. He had to leave Otto, but he was sure he would send one of his boys to find him and bring him back, no doubt with force if he resisted, since he had broken their contract. So he had to get far away, quickly. He decided to circle the town walls and try to enter from the west gate, where he hoped he could find a way to enter the town. If he could somehow get inside the town walls, which were heavily guarded to keep strangers out, he was sure he would be beyond Otto's grasp. He was already a runaway from the army recruiter, and maybe a murderer. Breaking his promise to

Otto was just another crime he would have to live with.

Before the break of the new day, he got up from his resting place and prepared to leave Otto and his salt wagons. He retrieved his musket from under the straw, his purse from its hiding place tied above the axle of the cart, retrieved his powder horn and wineskin, stuffed the rest of his belongings in a new shoulder pouch he obtained at the Wasserburg fording, and quietly walked away from the camp. It was getting light in the east and turning his back to it he plunged into the darkness of the woods hoping to encounter the river, which lay to the west. Soon he came upon the river some distance below the dark mass that was the northern wall of München. He followed the river downstream until he came upon a small cove. Here he built a fire, stripped off his filthy garments, and plunged into the freezing cold stream. He applied a bar of lye to his private parts and after splashing water over his whole body he left the water. The fire helped to dry his skin. It was then that he noticed red welts on his legs, probably caused by the cold water. He had a heavy winter coat he had stolen from a drunken man at the Wasserburg fording, but it was very dirty and he was reluctant to place it over his newly cleaned body. He also carried an outer cape that was not too dirty, and he draped this around his shoulders to ward off some of the cold early morning air. He gathered up his garments, and back at the river's edge, washed them thoroughly and hung them around the fire on branches that he had arranged beforehand.

He sat on a stone and ate some bread and cheese washed down with a draught from his wineskin. After his garments dried he set off down the river's bank to find a boatman who would sell him passage across. At the junction of a path from the east he found evidence of a river crossing and a boat proceeding from the opposite shore towards him, and by and by he was ferried to the distant side for a small payment.

His aim was to get inside the walls. But first he must find a cache for his gun. He walked into the thick woods that bordered the river until he found a secluded outcrop of rock in a dense grove of trees. Prying loose a large flat rock, he made a hole large enough to accommodate the gun. He smeared the firing mechanism with pig grease he carried in a pouch, hoping it would protect the gun from rust. Hans carefully wrapped his father's musket in the dirty winter coat, the weather now being warm and a heavy coat was of little use. He wedged the bundle in the hole and covered the opening with the flat rock. He kept the knife on his person, hidden in his boot. After fixing the location of his cache from a short distance away, Hans struck out for the western gate of the town of München.

When he reached the road, he could see that the gatehouse was in the steeple tower of a church. As he approached the arched opening in the tower he encountered a number of artisans and merchants as well as returning townsmen on the road leading to the gate. Looking over the crowded entrance he saw a man leading a horse that pulled a large wagon loaded with a cargo that required a covering. Hoping he could crouch beside the wagon and penetrate the walls without being seen by the guard at the gatehouse, he quickened his pace. He was surprised to be challenged by a second guard who stepped out of an alcove opposite the guard-house. As the guard pushed him back with his musket, Hans noted that the alcove was a porch with a door behind, leading into the church itself; likely the Sexton's entrance. This discovery gave him a new idea. He retreated and walked along the church wall, which was part of the town wall. At the corner where the church met the town wall there was a clump of bushes. Partially hidden by the bushes, he spied stone steps descending to a heavy door. At the bottom of the steps was a small covered porch to protect local peasants and pilgrims while they waited to gain entrance and give their confessions.

Descending the steps, he banged loudly on the door. At first there was no response, but after Hans banged on the door several more times a small panel in the door opened and a face appeared in the opening. Hans said, "Father, I have sinned." The face at the window muttered, "I ar'nt the Fath'r," but a scraping noise came through the door. It swung open and a very old man stood in the opening. Hans entered a dark room. By the light from a flickering candle held by the old man he could see he was in a small chapel. The old man closed the heavy door and dropped an equally heavy wooden bar across the opening. He lit a torch on the wall, directed Hans to a confessional and went off through a small door to get the "Fath'r." Hans immediately left the confessional and followed the footsteps of the old man through a low archway just visible by the light of the chapel torch. After ascending a few steps he encountered a trap door that he could not move, even by putting his shoulders against the heavy panel. This must be the verger's entrance to the chapel. Thinking that the priest must have a separate entrance to the con-fessional, he quickly retreated to the chapel, unbarred the door to the outside and left it wide open. Then he ran back to the trap door and curled himself in the dark corner hidden by the steps, hoping he could not be seen by a casual inspection of the passageway. Hiding there he heard the priest mutter, "What is it my son?" After hearing this query repeated with no reply, Hans could hear muffled sounds of the man of cloth opening his confessional. Then he heard the heavy door to the outside world banged shut and the scraping of the bar being dropped. The chapel torch was extinguished, leaving only the moving light from the candle the priest carried. The passageway was briefly illuminated by the priest's candle as he heard him retreating to the church, muttering to himself.

It was pitch dark. Hans could see nothing. But now he had an indistinct im-pression of the relation of the underground chapel to the church nave. He touched the wall of his hiding place and by feeling with his fingers he crawled from the trap door into the chapel. Again following the damp wall, he located the booth that comprised the confessional. Praying to God for forgiveness, he opened the door to the priest's booth, and on the wall he felt a heavy curtain that appeared to cover the door to a passageway. Entering this space behind the curtain, he tripped over steps, which led him to another door. Remarkably, this had been left unlocked by the retreating priest, who neglected to secure it in his anger at the old man. As he had expected, Hans now found himself in the church nave. Briefly kneeling at a pew he prayed formally for his soul. "Please God, forgive me for the desecration I have done today." Then, abandoning his plan to exit through the Sexton's tower door, he simply walked out of the church into the town of München.

It was almost noon. The sun hanging over the twin steeples of the Fruenkirke in a brilliantly clear azure heaven provided welcome warmth as he walked, almost skipped, along the Marienplatz where the hawkers were hard at work selling their wares. His body was clean and his thoughts were light. He felt joy as he bought a loaf and a wedge of cheese from a dusty man sitting on a stool under a gaily-painted awning that protected his goods from the sun. Hans sat to eat his meal on a small barrel that he found next to the wall of the giant Cathedral. Suddenly, as the hands of the church clock reached their zenith, a thunderous sound from the church bell towers enveloped the square. Looking around at the shouting merchants, the ladies buying and haggling over provisions for the day, the bright sunlight making sharp shadows of movement, and the booming noise from the Fruenkirke bells, he felt peace. But soon daggers of worry quieted his euphoria. He had to find shelter from the police, but above all he must find the one with the black eyes and skin like snow.

During the rest of the day Hans explored the town, and gradually became aware that he felt like a caged animal. There was no longer a link between the activity of the town and the quietness of the forest; it was not possible to wander between these two realities. He could no longer find shelter under a tree in an open field, or in a pile of hay, beside a rock, or even in a stable. After wandering for hours he spied a decrepit, weather-beaten inn, which he thought his meagre purse could support.

The innkeeper was an attractive middle-aged woman who appeared to have escaped the ravages of multiple childbirths. She was small and slim with sharp blue eyes in a square face and hair the colour of clover honey. She had an air of suspicion when she examined Hans, and he recognized that she was not to be trifled with, either by her lodgers or by the rough fellows who were lounging in her *Biergarten*. She seemed satisfied with Hans, and they negotiated a place for him to sleep. For his meal she would prepare whatever food he supplied. They agreed on a price and she led him up a crooked, steep passage barely wide enough for him to squeeze along. A handrail of hemp strung through iron rings fixed in one wall was all that prevented him from a fall on the worn steps. His landlady preceded him through a low door at the very top of the passage. He was in a small room. Sunlight streaming through a window in the roof revealed a narrow bed along one wall and a table with a washbowl and pail opposite the door. A single chair with a towel draped on it completed the furnishings of this roughly made sleeping room at the peak of the house.

On the second day of searching, Hans found the shop of Ernst Gruber–*Fleischwarren*. Herr Gruber sold fresh and preserved meat. It was a small shop on a narrow street behind the Fruenkirke. The façade was colourful and neat, sure evidence of women's care. There was an outbuilding that Hans assumed was a stable. He went into the shop with two older women, hoping he could get a glimpse of the black-haired girl. The man behind the counter he recognized as Herr Gruber, the man in the meat wagon who came to buy Otto's salt. Another young man was cutting swine chops, possibly Herr Gruber's son. He waited for the women to haggle over the price of their cuts but could see no sign of the girl. When the two women left the shop, Hans bought a small sausage.

Thereafter he went back to the shop each day to observe the proprietors and buy small amounts of meat. On his second visit to the shop the girl was still nowhere to be seen. Over several days of visits, he managed to catch the occasional glimpse of her, but more often made his purchase from Frau Gruber, a bosomy, attractive woman called Christina. The times he saw the girl in the shop she seemed oblivious to their meeting at the salt wagon on the road to the east gate. By listening to the talk amongst the family members, Hans concluded that she was indeed Christina's daughter and that her name was Gertrudus.

He lurked about the premises on the days of each visit to the shop and soon came to know the way of the business. Herr Gruber and the boy Johannes travelled out to the farms where the animals were slaughtered and brought fresh meat to the shop. Some of it would go on sale that day and perhaps the next day, but much of the meat was pickled for another butcher or for future sale in the shop. The pickling was done in the stable building where the family kept the horse, a cow and some ducks and geese. He often saw Gertrudus come and go, and came to the conclusion that she helped with the meat pickling process. Frau Gruber ran the shop while Ernst and Johannes prepared the meat for sale. It appeared as if Gertrudus was expected to help whenever she was needed.

One day, while Hans was dawdling over his sausage purchase, an old woman came into the shop and from the sad words she exchanged with Frau Gruber Hans understood that the Gruber family had lost an older son in the war, and this was making the work of the shop very difficult. "Of course," the old woman observed, "the war has destroyed many families and there are no young men left to do the work that needs to be done." This was met with a nod from Frau Gruber. The next day Hans was his most charming self with Frau Gruber, subtly suggesting that if the family needed hired help he would be willing to work for food and shelter. He explained that he knew the weaving trade, and that butchering was new to him, but he was sure he could be of help with some instruction. She looked askance at Hans and said, "Oh! Herr Gruber would never agree to that." So he said nothing more, paid for a sausage, and left the shop. Her appraising eyes saw him out the door.

Two days later, while he was selecting his purchase, Frau Gruber hustled from the shop and returned in a few moments with Herr Gruber, who, looking him over asked, "You want work?" Hans responded with a simple, "Yes," and negotiations began. Herr Gruber was very cautious, not knowing if he could trust Hans. After questions about his parents and his reasons for being in München, Gruber asked if he could pickle meat. Hans said that he had learned the weaving trade from his father; that he had never worked with a butcher, but he was anxious to do whatever work Herr Gruber wished if he could have shelter and food. This seemed to be the answer the butcher wanted and, after a moment's hesitation he said. "Come." He led Hans to an outbuilding, comprised of a washhouse next to the shop and through a short passage, stalls for the animals at the rear. Herr Gruber pointed to a parchment tacked to the wall beside the entry door. He said, "Read," and left. Hans peered at the paper on the wall, but his learning had not prepared him for understanding the directions printed there. Most of the words floating before Hans' eyes were unknown to him.

When Hans was six, Katarina sent him to a school run by Pastor Heidler, who held classes in the basement of his Lutheran Church. Pastor Heidler made sure his pupils learned sums, the stories of the Evangelicals and some history, but he had only the Holy book as a resource for reading instruction, making it difficult to prepare children for their adult world.

Anxious to please the Grubers, Hans struggled with the words on the parchment and was able to understand that he was to cut each carcass into pieces and wash the meat. He could see that the meat was to be salted and put into barrels. It appeared that many other mysterious ingredients were to be added, and while he was trying to compare their names on the parchment with labels on open-faced bins that hung across the wall over the table where the meat lay, Herr Gruber came into the room. The butcher, sympathetic to Hans' difficulty, showed him how to clean and cut the meat, the proper proportions of salt, saltpeter, bay leaves, rosemary, and coriander to add, and how to rub the spices into the meat. Hans looked on as the butcher took the spiced meat, placed it in layers in a barrel and pounded each layer with a mallet to pack it tightly. When the barrel was full, he hammered home the lid and took it to another room for storage.

Herr Gruber then took Hans to the loft above the animal stalls, which was accessible by a crude ladder. This, he was told, was to be his shelter at night. "You will be given food and water by Frau Gruber or Gertrudus when the animals are fed. Now," instructed Herr Gruber, "you must work." He was shown the location of the tools and material needed and thus he began to pickle meat for shipment. He had seen nothing of Johannes or Gertrudus. The object of his desire seemed oblivious to his love, but perhaps in time she would see some merit in his presence.

Later that morning, Johannes appeared and pointed out mistakes he had made. They worked mostly in silence, packing and storing barrels of pickled beef. With his food and shelter needs met, if not what he would wish, Hans began to plan for the future. The rains would soon come and he hoped he could live with the Grubers over the winter.

Frau Gruber had found her lost son, and she hustled about and made a comfortable loft for Hans. She fixed a bed and used planks stretched across two meat barrels to produce a crude table. A milking stool was sacrificed for his comfort. Given a bucket for washing, he had all the comforts one could ask for.

Shortly after he became settled in his new quarters, he fell ill. It started with a pain in his head. In the dead of night he awoke soaking wet with sweat that ran down his cheek like a river. Where he lay was a pool of water. Getting out of bed, he felt dizzy and could hardly stand. He was able to get to the waste bucket before he vomited. He spent a most miserable night retching as if his bowels were being turned inside out, alternately sweating and shivering. By morning the fever had made him delirious; hallucinating, he felt armies of insects ravaging his body and tearing him to shreds as he lay in a dung heap.

His delirium made him a child again. He was hiding in the woods when the men came. In the dancing yellow light from the flames engulfing the church he saw shadowy figures digging into the ground. The ghostly figures were moving frantically to pull large square objects out of the bosom of the cold earth, a coldness that he could feel through his feet, causing him to shiver even though he was sweating from the heat of the burning church. Shrouded figures were being pulled from boxes lying scattered on the ground where they had been dragged by the shadowy figures, which he could now recognize as soldiers. The shrouded cadavers were yanked from the boxes and thrown into the fire. One was his grandfather, screaming in agony as the flames consumed his frail body. Hans was sick all over the ground. He tried to run but something held him tied to the horror until the fire was spent and the soldiers had finished their grisly night's work. He cried for his missing teacher, Herr Heidler, who had been taken away, and others strung up into trees along the road leading out of the village.

When Frau Gruber came to find him, fearing that he had run away, she saw him curled in a ball with his legs drawn up, rolling and thrashing in the hay at one end of the loft. His eyes were yellow and sunken in his head. His protruding tongue was swollen to fill his mouth and was coated with thick white foam with bright red edges. His breathing was shallow and rapid. He appeared mad. She cursed under her breath, and whispered into the foul smelling air, "God bless us," and backed down the ladder. Her survival instinct told her to leave him, hoping the poison would break through without her care, but her motherly instinct urged her to help him in his sickness, even with the sure conviction that he would die.

She retreated to her kitchen and set to simmering a broth of bay leaves and vinegar. Her head under a linen cloth, she proceeded to take deep draughts of the fumes to protect her from the disease. She then located her family. Herr Gruber and Johannes told her to leave the boy to his fate, God protect his soul. He will surely die. "We must not allow word of the pestilence to spread, or the business will be ruined." Frau Gruber buried her mother's love in the wisdom of her men, and resolved to follow their wishes and wait for God's judgement.

God's judgement was kind. Hans lived. On the third day of his madness the fiery red carbuncle on the inside of his right leg burst, spewing yellow pus and a stream of scarlet blood into the hay on which he lay. His fever broke, leaving him very thirsty, but he was not strong enough to rise from his foul-smelling bed. After several hours, he could crawl to the bucket of washing water that sat on the end of his table of planks. God had spared him once again. His loins had been purified

H ans spent that winter with the Gruber family. After his illness he was of no use to Herr Gruber, but Frau Gruber, with skittish help from Gertrudus, nursed him back to health. When he was well again he learned the butcher trade, but had no success in wooing the hand of Gertrudus. Brought up a Jesuit, she feared attachment to a dispossessed Lutheran drifter and ignored him most of the time. Then, one day while he was stirring the brine, he caught her looking at him with a strange stare. About a week later Hans found her pitching hay to the horse, making soothing sounds to keep the horse quiet while she was in the stall. He found a hayfork in a corner and proceeded to help her. This brought a flush to her face, and as soon as the job was finished she left, "…to help Christina."

As the winter wore on, their encounters became frequent; she seemed to be everywhere Hans was at work. In the times together he found her to be a free spirit tied to the conventions of her upbringing. She wished for adventure, but whenever he tried to touch her or speak in intimate ways she shied away, always with an excuse to be somewhere else. Slowly, Hans became aware that Frau Gruber was watching her daughter with a very suspicious eye. The lady had no intentions of letting her youngster fly the nest until she decreed it. Still, Hans and Gertrudus were drawn to each other's company when the work of the butcher shop demanded it, but fear of her mother's anger kept Gertrudus from accepting her admirer's advances.

The earth grew warm and steam rose from the small garden plot in front of the butcher shop where snowdrops were in bloom. The air was soft and the breezes balmy. It was at this time of freedom from the rains of winter and the promise of new things that the butcher told Hans he had to leave his household. Since he and Gertrudus were now very close, Hans had expected his dismissal because of her mother's fierce resistance to their friendship. So, although it was spring, the time of year a young man's heart yearns for love, it seemed there was no love possible and it was time to move on.

It was Herr Gruber who asked him to leave, but it was Frau Gruber who fussed over him as he was preparing to depart her company. She had loved him like a son, but for her it was a choice between the future of her daughter and a travelling boy from the south who would do her daughter no good. She liked Hans, but when all was done he was not one of them. She was both sad at losing him and angry that his stay had turned threatening to her daughter and herself. She was close to tears as she made a slight bow and bid him, "A good and safe journey whither thou bound"–and with a note of hypocrisy–"come to our shop when you are again in München." She embraced him.

Hans had come to think of the Grubers as his family and was disappointed that neither Johannes nor Gertrudus were there to see him leave. The thought of leaving Gertrudus, of being forced to leave without any resolution of his love for her, wrenched his heart. He wished he could at least kiss her farewell like a sister. He tried to blame Frau Gruber for her fierce resistance to allowing them to be close, but he could not. She had been like a mother to him; but also to her daughter, which was his loss. He bid the Grubers a thankful farewell, expressing his appreciation for all they had done for him during the winter and his sickness. Still hopeful that Gertrudus would appear, he lingered over the meat, but it finally came time to go out the door. With a slight wave he left their presence.

He immediately retired to the stable loft to collect his possessions, mainly his knife and the purse he had saved during the winter. When he poked his head through the trapdoor that was the entry to the loft, he was startled to see a strange boy sitting on the bed. His muscles tightened to attack, sure he had startled a bandit. But the boy just sat there with a parcel on his lap. As his eyes adjusted to the gloom he noticed that the boy had a face of unusually fine features. He was surprised, startled, confused but somehow pleased; all emotions mingling as he stood dumbfounded in front of her. The figure on the bed spoke, "I am going with you!" After a long silence she continued, "If you will take me," suddenly fearful that her scheme would not please him. Wanting desperately to take her with him he blurted, "Do you realize the wrath you will bring down upon us if we do this; your parents mostly, but also the church, your friends and relatives, and the disgrace you would bring onto the whole family. They would hunt me down and put my head on the end of a pike to be paraded all around the neighbourhood." She began to shake, and broke into tears. He said, in an attempt to quieten her sobs, "I want to take you. I have wanted to be with you since I met you that day so long ago when you appeared in front of Otto's salt wagon like an angel come down from heaven. But you have shown no attraction to me." She blubbered, "I wanted to, but Ma was so angry with me she would have killed me if we were caught. But my heart has ached for you all winter, and I am going with you."

Like a dam bursting, Hans lost his senses and hungrily embraced her, and she returned his ardour with the wild spirit he had seen in her that first day. The die was cast. He knew he would take her with him whatever the consequences. They were destined to live or die in an adventure both knew would likely end in tragedy. Between arduous embraces and copious tears they made a plan. She would hide her clothes in his loft room and in two days' time would meet him dressed as a man at the rock cairn beside the road that marked a distance of one league from the western gate of the town. She would be there at noon two days hence. She trusted him, she said, to keep the rendezvous, and he swore he would do so.

So that very morning he walked through the streets of München with a light heart and a song on his lips. Like a well-bred horse anxious for the race he danced through the town gate and left a lifetime behind. He had a bulging purse; a beautiful woman soon to be at his side, and the day was full of joy.

Clearing the town, his first thought was to retrieve the musket. The woods had changed with the season and he had lost some of his woodman's skills so it took him some time to find the rock where he had hidden the gun. The coat he had sacrificed was mouldy and mice had eaten through the fabric to make nests. It was ruined, but surprisingly the gun, although showing some rust, appeared serviceable and his powder was dry.

Taking the gun in his hands brought sudden sadness. The gun had killed men, and in his mother's hands ended the life of a soldier intent on debauchery. It was the only material link to his parents that he had left. He sat down on the rock that had, for the winter, protected his past, and wept.

He was waiting in the woods near the rock cairn well before noon the day he was to meet Gertrudus. What she planned to do was so drastic that Hans had come to believe that she would finally cling to her parents and abandon the scheme to meet him. He secretly wondered if he would be disappointed, because he was aware of the difficulties presented by the responsibility for a dependent partner. But just before noon he spied a young man walking along the road, and as the figure came closer, recognized it to be Gertrudus. At the sight of her he lost all his doubts and ran down the road to take up a position beside her. They did not embrace, fearful that she was being followed, so they walked along together to a spot where the trees came down to the road. Hans looked about, and seeing no one, took her hand and led her into the woods where they embraced, with hot tears of relief and love in Gertrudus' eyes.

So it came to pass that Hans and the butcher's daughter walked boldly away from her parents and the town that had nurtured her and given him great happiness and a new start in life. Hans was anxious to get away, fearing his enemies would find him and put a rope around his neck. He was sure also that Herr Gruber would send someone after Gertrudus.

They travelled west. Hans' experiences with the army and in the salt mines taught him to pilfer food safely, even in a countryside that had already been ravaged by soldiers and disease. In the towns he found comfortable inns, which pleased Gertrudus.

Having a woman by his side and in his bed at night changed Hans. He was now responsible for someone and this gave him maturity.

They had reached the Donau near the village of Günzburg when Gertrudus became ill. Hans made a contract for a sleeping chamber at an inn on the river. He did not mention that Gertrudus was sick. Even the most Christian of souls was terrified of the pest, and any suspicion would have brought refusal for a bed from the innkeeper.

Gertrudus died in grotesque agony on the sixth day. Hans suffered through her last days with equal parts agony and anger. No doctor would come to her chamber. The *Hausfrau*, a good Christian in the event, left water and food outside the door of their chamber. But her survival instincts forced her to have a guard posted at the door. Hans was able to get into the streets around the inn late at night by crawling out a small window over a very steep tiled roof and down a drainpipe to a large bush below. Avoiding the night watchman he looked for someone who might be of help, but no one would come to his aid. People would not even let Hans get close to them. Finally he found a hag who sold him a small bag of white powder at an obscene cost, claiming it would cure the sick. He was grateful to this wreck of a woman, but like all else the white powder had no effect on the disease.

In the early days of the disease, when the carbuncles under her arms were not large, she urged him to leave her, frightened for his life as well as hers. But Hans tried to convince her that having had the disease he would not get it again. He sat with her. He cleaned up after her; put wet cloths on her brow to quell the raging fever that was destroying her body. By the fourth day Gertrudus was mad. She did not know him and tried to fight him off.

She died screaming in agony. In death Hans could not look at her. She had gone from a sweet beauty to a horror in six days. Hans was relieved for both of them.

He passed a message to the innkeeper to send for a sexton. The sexton came and took Gertrudus away to be thrown into a lime pit, the common resting place for so many in those horror-filled years when the plague destroyed the good citizens of the towns of Germany.

When the maids came with a barrel of lime to clean the chamber Hans was told to go. Since he was destitute of purse after caring for Gertrudus he had no choice but to go on the road again. He was twenty-three, but his youthful wandering was not finished. He left on a cloudy, drizzly morning to continue his drift westward.

3

GEORG
The Nomad

Hans agonized over Gertrudus' death for weeks, but mourning was a luxury only for nobles. A journeyman had to find food or starve. When he left Günzburg he traveled to Ulm, and was able to feed himself for a while as an itinerant meat processor, but he could not get guild membership. He stayed in Ulm for the winter as a refugee from the religious war, and as soon as the air became warmer he crossed the river into the Duchy of Württemberg. He walked into the hamlet of Zell unter Aichelberg destitute, weary, and in rags. He had not had food in three days and very little sleep. Just at twilight he found the church where he hoped to find a meal. A very large woman, both in length and breadth, sat him in a chair and brought bread and soup. When he finished the meal, the woman took him by the arm, marched him to a basement room under the sacristy, and bid him sleep. There were about a dozen men in the dungeon-like room in various stages of eating, relaxing, and sleeping. None of the men greeted him; to them he was just another poor refugee from the war. He found a spot against the damp wall and slept.

When he woke it was day. Most of the men had gone. He wandered to the church kitchen and found sausages and hot soup. He was preparing the leave when the fat woman came into the kitchen. She asked him about his prospects and intentions, and told that he had a butcher's trade she brightened. "A butcher! You could be of help in the town. If you wish to settle here you can call this your home until you find work and lodgings." Little did she know, he thought. But weary of life on the road, he had found someone who cared, so he accepted the offer.

So it was that Johannes Georg Weger, known as Hans, came to Zell unter Aichelberg. He let it be known in the village that his name was Georg Waeger, hoping to confuse those he had harmed while in Bavaria if they were looking for him.

He prospered in a humble fashion and was soon able to marry Gretha, a young widow of the church community whose husband, a farm hand, had drowned at nearby Göppingen. Gretha was twenty-two, a farmer's daughter who had seen tragedy very like Hans' loss of Gertrudus, and this common past brought them together. Hans, now known as Georg, married Gretha in the spring of the year the war ended. Gretha had seven children that survived. Leonardt, the youngest, was born in the autumn of 1665.

L eonardt, known as son of Georg of Spital am Drau survived the usual childhood diseases of the time and grew to manhood in his father's household in Zell. He began adult life helping his father and three older brothers in the butcher trade, but when he was sixteen he fell out with his father. Being the youngest of the boys he was forced to do all the dirty tasks associated with killing the animals and cleaning up afterward. Fearfully he confronted his father, saying he did not want to live as a butcher. After several weeks of arguing, his father gave his permission to leave the family fold and find his own way.

He set out on his own and after several months of rough living, feeling the results of hardship, he accepted the offer of an apprenticeship to a local master tailor. Two years later, at age nineteen, he met Anna Catherina from the neighbouring village of Neidlingen. Frau Schaufelein had contracted with his master to sew a gown for her daughter and Leonardt was asked to deliver it. At the Schaufelein house he met Anna and was struck with her light and airy personality. She was three years older than Leonardt, a robust woman of twenty-two. He courted her and they were married. It was whispered about by the ladies of the village, that Anna had inherited property and was a good catch for Leonardt, who had few prospects beyond his apprenticeship. But Anna was a strong woman who was determined that Leonardt would not fail her. So Leonardt made his way as a respectable citizen of the village and as an itinerant tailor. Anna birthed four surviving children while she and Leonardt lived in Zell unter Aichelberg. Georg, their fifth child, was born in the year 1696.

It was Georg Waeger, son of Leonardt and the great grandson of Jörg Weger from Schrott #7 above the village of Radenthein, who took his family to America. But before his epic journey many years intervene.

When Georg was eight, Duke Eberhardt Ludwig von Württemberg began the construction of a large castle on the Neckar River, creating employment for men from the countryside. The castle and environs was the centre of the cloth trades and also produced fine hock wines. Leonardt, young Georg's father, believed he could prosper there, and took Anna and his family to the town of Poppenweiler just across the river from the castle keep. Anna bought a house with her share of the inheritance from her father in Neidlingen. Leonardt and Anna lived in Poppenweiler for the rest of their lives.

Georg's early childhood was spent in Zell, but he remembered little of that place. He came to know that his father worked at sewing cloth together into military uniforms, apparel for the better off, and many other items of household use. From a young age he knew his mother was not happy. She found any excuse to visit relatives at her former home of Neidlingen. As he grew older he came to realize that her home seemed to have no real meaning for her. But she was a dutiful wife to his father, producing many children, brothers and sisters, for which Georg was thankful, since he had to rely entirely on his older siblings to show him the ways of the world. When her childbearing days were over Anna Catherina became quite out of sorts and was reduced to a cranky old woman, angry at the world.

S oon after being brought to Poppenweiler, Georg had an experience that changed his life. The English and Dutch favoured a Bavarian Prince as successor to the Spanish throne over one from France. War was once again the result of conflicting ambitions. The Dutch and English formed an alliance and sent an army commanded by the English Duke of Marlborough against the French army.

One day, word spread in the village of Poppenweiler that Marlborough's Army of the Grand Alliance had crossed the river at Mundelsheim where it was camped. The people of Poppenweiler were excited on hearing that the English Duke's army was camped downstream, and appeared likely to march along the river toward their village. After two generations of religious strife and the horrors of the French armies, there was finally a possibility of liberation, but the elders, having been disappointed so many times, were not moved to hope for freedom by an English Duke. They had suffered through a Swedish occupation that was supposed to liberate them from the tyranny of the Empire and the French, but the Swedish soldiers were as bad as any bad lot could be. Except for the elders, most villagers had seen too much of war with no improvement to their lives, and were hopeful that finally some peace would come to the area once the French armies had been banished.

The children were excited beyond themselves at the prospect of witnessing a huge army with the clanging of armaments, many thousands of horses, the colour of the regimental standards flying proudly in the sunlight, soldiers in their colourful uniforms, the noise, the smells, and men speaking in different languages. There was news of the mounting excitement in the towns and villages on the route of the march, with many stories of contact with the soldiers, romance for some, brutality for others, but all as grist for the rumours that had begun to spread over the whole district. Since part of the army was under Prince Louis of Baden there were soldiers known to the villagers of Poppenweiler, and some men from the village had gone off to Großheppach where Prince Louis was to join the Allied army.

The night before Marlborough's army was to pass through Poppenweiler, Georg could not sleep because of the tough straws that poked at his body. The suffocating, acrid smell from the straw wafted around him, trapped under the heavy, rough blanket covering him. He tried to keep his eyes tight shut, but they kept popping open as if with a will of their own. His father had told him that if the English army passed tomorrow the workers in the field could stop to watch. In his excitement, he wished the night to be over so he could go to the fields and see the army. Georg peeked at the window to see if it was daylight. There was a shaft of light but he knew it came from the moon; it was not yet morning. He lay in bed, breathing quietly in the dark so as not to wake his brother Bernhardt. In the stillness he heard his mother snoring from the floor below the loft where he and his brothers slept.

Then his father was shaking his shoulder, urging him from sleep. He leaned over the bed, brushing his long beard across Georg's face, and shook Bernhardt awake. Bernhardt was going to the fields with Georg although Anna Catherina had not wanted Bernhardt to go to the fields with the men because he was too young, but he begged his mother to let him go with Georg until finally she gave in.

Georg slid his feet out from under the blanket and let the touch of the cold floor wake him. Bernhardt crawled over the foot of the bed. By the time he had splashed cold water on his face and neck from the pitcher under the window, Georg could hear the rest of the family stirring. Sister Anna would soon prepare breakfast with her mother. Sister Greta would be out collecting the eggs from their ten hens. Jacob would be going to the fields soon, to begin the day by milking their four cows. Georg's mother seemed to spend most of her time with Christianus, who was always sick.

But this morning Georg and a sleepy Bernhardt left the house quietly to join their father and uncle Johann, who had already arrived with the cart to take them to the vineyard. It was still dark. They carried the breakfasts that had been prepared the night before so that they could be in the field before daylight.

Everyone knew the regimen established by the allied army. The agents for the army were sent out ahead of time to arrange food and other necessities for the troops, but they were not able to negotiate for the supplies without divulging some information. From them it was learned that the troops would break camp at three in the morning and march in ranks until about nine, longer if need be, to reach a satisfactory campsite. The soldiers rested every five days. Presumably Mundelsheim was a rest day, and they would be marching out that day. Georg's father had told him that the soldiers should be near Poppenweiler before nine that morning, and they needed to get to the field before daylight.

Georg had never gone to the field this early, but the road was so familiar he could identify every landmark, even in the dark. But even with its familiarity, he was frightened. He fancied he was going to Satan's vineyard; a story told of the Evil One disguised as a troubadour, meeting a pious old man in a northern village. The old man is thirsty and asks Satan for a drink. The Devil tells him of a wine in the south that exceeds any he has tasted, and finally convinces the old man to trade his soul for this exceptional wine that is grown in Satan's own vineyard, which indeed produces exceptional wine. The old man drinks of the sweet wine with the flowery bouquet and christens it *Liebfrauenmilch.* The Devil is furious that his wine is called "The Milk of our Blessed Lady," but the Holy Virgin is so pleased with the name she cancels the bargain made between the old man and Satan. Every day since, the Devil continues to search the vineyards for another foolish old man.

Georg was terrified that the Devil, disguised as a troubadour, would visit the wine garden this morning, looking for a foolish man.

The little band of wine-dressers went north from the village on the Neckarblick road for a short distance, and then turned left toward the river. The river valley was darker than the surrounding countryside, since the moon that kept Georg awake the night before had already set. The field they were working was in the centre of the vineyard just where the river starts its second turn as it winds its way north. As they retrieved tools from the cart and located their clogs from under a bush where they normally kept them, the sky to the east was getting lighter, showing the hard outline of the ridge above them. Georg could hear others arriving, and in a few minutes the field was dotted with workers. The owner's agent appeared and proceeded to assign each person a role in preparing the vineyard for another season of growth during which the juicy white grapes would be turned into a Riesling hock, although not of the exceptional quality sought by the old man and provided by Satan for a high price. By and large the men were assigned the jobs related to the production of the crop, while the few women and many young boys were assigned jobs related to the serving of the men to make the burdensome work as comfortable as possible. Bernhardt wanted to be with Georg, but the older brother told their father that he did not want his little brother following him all day. To avoid two sulking boys, Bernhardt was made to stay with his father.

Georg carried water for one of the crews assigned to hoeing the rows between the vines, which were just showing new leaves. Water came from a small brook dropping into a pool of clear, cold water about midway between the crest of the escarpment and the river. Georg carried two buckets hung from a wooden yoke into which pockets had been carved for the shape of his shoulders. Unfortunately, he had grown since last year, making the pockets too small and painful, and he tired quite early. He daydreamed about the water nymph that lived in the pool of Staufenberg and the handsome knight that immediately fell in love with her as he drank from the pool. Georg supposed he was the knight, in black armour with a great plume of feathers swaying from his helmet as he fought with his steel sword in far-off lands, overpowering his enemies amidst the thunder of the cannon. He stooped and grabbed a stick from the ground and swung it overhead and thrust down, a sword demolishing his enemy as his great-grandfather Jörg had done at the battle of Wimpfen. A sharp pain shot through his right shoulder, and he cried out. Georg looked around and saw no one. He trudged down the hill to fill his water buckets.

It was on his third trip to the pool that he heard a noise down by the river. Around the bend there appeared a little band of horsemen. At their head rode what appeared to be a knight on a magnificent white horse. He was dressed in a long red coat, that even at this distance, Georg could tell, since he lived in a house of tailors, was of the very finest wool. Trimmed in gold with large cloth-covered buttons, the red coat was surmounted by a gold coloured sash circling the throat of a very handsome man. His blond wig was crowned with a black tricorn hat trimmed with gold braid. A long sword with a decorated hilt protruded from under the red coat until the end of its scabbard reached the horse's knees. There was a runner with the leader, walking beside the horse, followed by several other horsemen, some in red coats, some in brown. Then, closely following the small group of horsemen, were what he guessed to be English regiments of men in red coats with their muskets at their shoulders and their bayonets bristling in the rising sun, which had now cleared the ridge. One of the English soldiers carried a giant white standard with a red cross. As more and more of the army came into sight, noise filled the valley; sounds of squeaking leather, of horses' hooves, of harnesses clanking, and the talk, laughter, and singing of the marching soldiers.

Georg was pulled in by the majesty and power of the scene. He hid the water buckets in a thicket. Without concern for the consequences if he lost them, he ran down the hill to the road's edge just where the long line of horses and footmen were turning away from him at a bend in the road. He stood still, in awe. His heart was pounding from fear and the exertion of running. When the troopers spied him, a few lowered their bayonets, pretending to run him through. He stood on the roadside for more than an hour as the vast army passed with all its colourful standards flying. The infantry and cavalry were followed by wagons carrying cannons. He tried to count the cannons but the numbers were greater than his learning allowed. Next came the carriages of the officers with their field household retinue. Then came the camp followers: children, women, and some old men. Some were in wagons, some on horseback, but most were walking.

When the tramping of the troopers and rumbling of the wagons died, Georg saw himself as part of the marching men, a soldier on a white horse with a long sharp sword going into battle against the hated French. He was about to run through a Frenchman when suddenly his father came out of the bushes with a fierce look and a long switch; he must have seen him on the road from the vineyard above. He was waving the switch and yelling that the workers wanted water and Georg was wasting time. Georg ran up the hill. Energized by his daydreams of glory, his father could not catch him. When he retrieved the buckets and got back to the workers all seemed as usual, except for the occasional argument about details of the army's passing. When his father arrived puffing and saw all at peace he said nothing. The glorious colours of the standards, the noise of the wagons, the fineness of the uniforms, the smell of horse dung, the clatter of hoofs, the camaraderie of the men, the thrusting of bayonets, Georg talked about the rest of his life. Even into his adult years he felt an odd familiarity with this unusual experience.

It came the time in his young years when he was expected to begin to assume adult ways. Georg's father had tried to find him a position in his guild, but it was closed to new members at the time. One day in late autumn, returning from Marbach with bolts of linen cloth piled high in the cart, Leonardt, concerned about the work ahead in making shirts and pantaloons from the bolts of cloth, talked of Georg's future. He had expected that his son would follow him in his trade, and assumed Georg would want this. But there would be no opportunity for Georg to advance in the trade without guild membership. He tried to explain his concern for the future.

"For many years the French have tried to subdue the people of the Palatinate and make them papists. French armies destroyed castles and burned peasant's homes sending them out into the countryside to shift for themselves in winter's cold and snow. The refugees from this destruction had to go to wherever they could find food and a pillow on which to lay their heads at night. Some were taken in by the English Queen and sent to America in her ships."

When Leonard stopped speaking, Georg looked up at his father and saw that he was staring at the river with an odd look in his eyes, lost in his own thoughts. After a few moments he continued the story of the homeless Palatines.

"Many of the peasants and poor farmers wandered about the countryside until they found refuge, or perished from hunger. They caused a great tumult. The small children that survived the French atrocities were well looked after by the women, but some of the men were bad, robbing our houses, stealing our food and even molesting our young girls. Young boys were running in the streets looking for anything of worth and causing all sorts of trouble. There were so many of them that the guilds made a rule that only boys originally from the village could be apprenticed, but many outsiders lied and they stopped taking in any new members. Also, the guilds were losing power to the large trading leagues. So, to protect their members they shut the doors."

Georg was not disappointed with the loss of an apprenticeship; he was not sure he wanted to be a tailor and follow in the footsteps of his father and grandfather. He wanted to be a soldier like his great-grandfather.

Leonardt's hope to place Georg in a trade brightened the next spring. The previous winter had been the worst in living memory. Rivers froze for two months. Fruit trees and wine gardens were killed by the cold. Cows in open fields froze to death, newborn babies died from diseases brought on by the cold weather. Many people perished. It was an unbearable winter, especially for refugees from the recent war. Many made the journey to Rotterdam.

The English Queen rescued the poor peasants and displaced farmers and gave them passage to London in her ships. Thousands were set up in refugee camps at Blackheath. But soon Londoners got so tired of feeding and housing the destitute peasants that they sent agents to the Rhineland to stop the flow, with little success. Word soon spread in the village that many of the people who left had reached America, the new biblical land of milk and honey. It was a blessing in disguise for those young people who were left, since it opened new work opportunities.

With some determination and persistence to secure a non-military future for his son, Leonardt found an opening for an apprentice in the local guild of Weavers. So young Georg was apprenticed to a Herr Brimbauer, a prominent master weaver of the district. Although Georg could live with his parents and enjoy his mother's meals, he now had the responsibilities of a man and was expected to bring money home. Herr Brimbauer's shop was only a short distance away so he could easily walk to his work. Thus, walking through the village morning and evening with other tradesmen, avoiding the danger that lurked just off the streets and pathways, he began to mature. Now he could wander in the fields and wine gardens that he loved and also take part in the social life of the young people of the village.

Herr Brimbauer had two other apprentices. Johannes had been with the master for three years and was looking forward to being made a journeyman. He was a small boy, his most distinctive feature his bright red hair that seemed always to stick straight from his head like flaming spikes of fire. He tried to make up for his short stature by lording his seniority over the newer boys. He could work a loom and this gave him the cockiness to make life miserable for the younger boys with his many demands. Johannes was quite adept at keeping the master frustrated by slyly resisting harder work than the guild expected of a senior apprentice.

Fritz was a year older than Georg. Unlike Johannes, he was overly keen to please. He was a meek, drooling boy who instantly attracted disdain. It seemed clear to Georg that Fritz would do poorly in the world.

Georg tried to do his assigned tasks with energy and thoroughness without being subservient. As a beginning apprentice his tasks were to keep the spools full of warp threads and the quills full of weft threads. Herr Brimbauer made the calculations for the amount of threads needed for each design being worked upon, and Georg was to get the threads in position so the master could proceed with his work on the loom at any time. He hung the skeins of yarn, loaded the warp board with the required amount of thread, and ran the linen yarn to empty spools, making it ready to be threaded through the heddles and the dents of the reef board. He was not yet trusted with this latter task. His other main task was to fill the quills in the shuttles. When he had been with the master for a few weeks he was occasionally sent out with the cart to pick up bales of spun linen yarn. As the trust grew between Herr Brimbauer and his apprentice Georg was allowed to take the finished cloth to be sewn into garments. Sometimes this required him to stay overnight in a nearby village, an experience he thoroughly enjoyed. It was at these times he wished his apprenticeship to be over so that he could travel from village to village like a wandering troubadour.

Georg was growing in his trade. He worked for Herr Brimbauer for long periods, but sometimes he went about the countryside and found his own work. His brother Jacob was a tailor living in Bietigheim and Georg supplied him with cloth to make military uniforms. It was while he was staying at Jacob's house that he met Maria Catherina. Maria was not a pretty woman, except for her eyes, which were very dark with red and orange highlights that seemed to smolder like burning coals. Her face was square, with a strong jaw, and this was placed on a very thin body giving the impression that her head was large. Maria's beauty was her passion for life. She was energetic and intelligent, showing interest in all with which she came in contact. She was tempestuous and also a temptress. Emotionally, she went easily from laughter to brooding anger. She teased Georg relentlessly when they were together. He asked Herr Ernst for her hand, and since Georg had prospects as a journeyman weaver he gave his blessing.

Georg and Maria Catherina Ernst were married in Bietigheim near the end of August 1717. They took up residence over her father's butcher shop.

Two years passed. Georg had settled into his adult life and for a year was pleased with Maria Catherina, but when no child came Georg became anxious for an heir. They tried desperately to make a child in the big iron bed but without success. Georg fought with Maria and she became very despondent, blaming herself for being a failure as a wife. She spent many nights weeping. Eventually she began to refuse Georg, making matters worse. They quarrelled, long and often. After one quarrel he shouted, "Come see the Magistrate and we will end this." After six years he was free. Maria's father took her back but Georg was left seeking a new home. Jacob and Catherina agreed to take him in temporarily. But they were not happy to see him.

Jacob urged him to go to America. One evening he challenged Georg, probably at the urging of Catherina, who had been complaining about the cost of flour.

"Many men are planning to go to America where there is land and an abundance of everything. Why don't you go? It would be better than your situation here."

Georg was angry that his older brother tried to control his future so he responded, somewhat sarcastically,

"Why don't you go?"

"You know I can't go. Catherina would never consider leaving Bietigheim. We are settled here and I have a good trade. I know your situation with Maria was poor, but you have to get her out of your mind. You cannot wallow in regrets. You have had time to get over her and find someone else."

Georg did not want to talk with Jacob about his marriage to Maria, so after a long silence while his anger dulled, he spoke.

"I wonder what life is like in America. Do you know anyone who went there?"

"Well, I have seen a letter from America, sent home by cousin Johann Jacob to his uncle inquiring about an inheritance from his grandfather. In the letter he wrote that he was living under the New York government on the Hoosick road, three hours from a town called Albany. He now has a large farm after paying tithes of rye and corn for ten years. He wrote in his letter that he grows corn and owns black cattle, with horses, sheep, swine, and plenty of wood. It seems cousin Johann

Jacob has prospered since leaving Germany with his father. If Catherina would leave her village I might go. You have no one to tie you down since Maria has gone back to her father. And you're still young."

Georg and his brother Jacob talked about going to America over drink at Jacob's table many evenings, but it became clear to Georg that Jacob was too settled to seriously agree to leave Bietigheim. He suspected that Catherina and Jacob were promoting America because they were anxious to have him leave their home. Georg did not let it bother him, but chose to believe they had his best interests at heart. Besides, he had the impression that everyone in America was a farmer, and he did not want to be a farmer, neither in Germany nor in America.

Then, by a stroke of good luck Georg was given a contract to work with the master weaver at Schmellenhof, near Wüstenrot, a place in the hills close to the ancient Celtic town of Schwäbisch-Hall. The journey would take him into the heavily wooded region of the Schwäbischer Wald where he would likely encounter bandits, since some of the roads were mere pathways through densely treed forests where highwaymen could rob without detection. His only protection from bandits was a wicked dagger that he had removed from a dead soldier whom he had stumbled across, hidden in the bushes at an isolated spot on the river's bank. The dagger had been rusty, so Georg took it home and brought it back to life so that it glistened in the sunlight when removed from its scabbard, but it had never tasted blood by his hand. Although he had practised using the dagger, Georg would not really know how to use it as a weapon if his life was threatened. He desperately wished for a pistol, fired by flint. He hoped that his assignment at Schmellenhof would

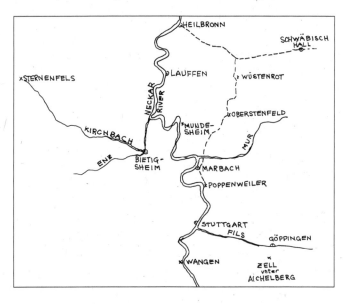

allow him to buy a pistol of the latest make.

Thus he set out one sunny spring morning with joy in his heart and the anticipation of a changed life. After the hiatus with Maria Catherina, he now felt some enthusiasm to settle into a more regular life with his own property, and he hoped for some sons in the future to help him as he aged. Before this day he had not felt a need, or desire, to accumulate wealth, his sole possessions being a lazy brown horse and harness, a small cart, his loom, a knife and some clothes. It was just as well he owned little, since travellers tried to avoid carrying valuables on their person because of the number of bandits roaming the countryside.

From the cart he steered the horse out across the open fields to the town of Marbach, cutting off a large bend in the river. From here he took the road that branched to the northeast and by late afternoon he was in the forest. He camped in a clearing of trees overnight, hoping to start well before dawn of the next day, and perhaps reach his destination before the bandits came out of hiding places and began their dangerous occupation.

His plan almost worked, but about noon he was walking the lazy horse when he spotted a wagon sitting in the centre of the road. Four people stood clustered around the wagon, presumably having been relieved of their valuables, and hoping to get on their way soon. The bandits were ransacking the wagon for anything of value. The robbers being otherwise occupied, Georg came up as close as he could without being seen, and then, jumping into the cart, he whipped the startled horse into its full speed and swept around the group standing on the road. The victims of the bandits seemed as startled as was his horse. He heard the thump of a pistol, but the ball missed him and went whistling through the trees. He whipped the horse cruelly, frigid with terror, expecting that the next ball would find his back. None came. When he was sure the bandits did not follow, he decided that they had no horses, and he let the frothing horse slow to a walk. He had escaped this time, but the incident made him proceed very cautiously for the rest of the journey.

Having encountered no more bandits he was at the gates to the manor house of Schmellenhof by late afternoon. A guard told him to step down and give his business. Georg produced the letter he had received listing the conditions of his commission. The guard peered at the document for a few seconds, pretending he could read the letter, and seeing the manorial crest gave a grunt and pointed to a path leading to the main building of the manor. Slapping the horse into motion with the reins, Georg could soon see a modest manor house built of stone with a steeply pitched slate roof, the gable end truncated and carrying the same slope as the main roof. The house was smaller than he had imagined, but it looked comfortable. There were several outbuildings whose functions Georg could not fathom, except for a large barn, which would normally house stables and lofts.

This property was the residence of Adam Bahye, a merchant who had gained his initial wealth from the salt springs at Hall, but had found new opportunities in the textile trade. Herr Bahye was a respected man in the community, but he was not of noble birth, which made his ambition to become a public overlord out of his reach. This did not overly frustrate him, since he was a practical man. He would realize his destiny through wealth, not family.

Georg reported his arrival to a sickly looking man at a small desk at the front of the manor house. The man summoned a young boy who took him to one of the sheds he had seen from the road where there were straw ticks with thin coverings on several sleeping platforms. He saw evidence of four occupants in the shed, and boxes of personal belongings at the foot of the occupied platforms. There was no one about at this hour except the boy, who told him that the workers were in the fields. He put his box and small items that he had taken from his cart on the bed he had been given. The boy told him there was a stall for his horse in the barn. He could also store his cart and loom in the barn. "You will have no use for the loom at Schmellenhof, we have a shed full of looms. You will have to find a heavy cover to protect yours from dampness."

On the way to the barn Georg took some time to examine the arrangements. Beside the sleeping area there was a kitchen with a planked table for the preparation of food. On one wall of the kitchen was a door into a pantry. Beyond the kitchen a short passageway led to another large room with a very large table made from heavy planks and about a dozen chairs in disarray. This was where the field men ate their meals and entertained themselves with drink and bawdy songs of military life and female conquests.

The next morning at dawn the ringing of a bell woke him from a dreamless sleep and, after meeting his new work-mates at breakfast, he prepared himself mentally for his first day at Schmellenhof. A brutish-looking man his mates called "*der böse Boss*" told him to go to the barn where he would be employed on the brake. Having no idea what a brake was, he objected to "*der böse Boss*" that he was not a farmer and that he thought he would work with Herr Schellenburger, the master weaver. The man became red in the face and told him roughly that there were enough loom men on the farm and what he needed was a brakeman. Georg kept his tongue and went to the barn where he found three men operating different contraptions. One of the men, with a kind face, left his machine and offered to give the neophyte an explanation of the process of making linen yarn from the flax stems as they came from the fields. "The rotted and dried stems, when they arrive here, are first broken to remove most of the wood from the fibres. That is your job." He showed Georg a long and narrow wooden frame with heavy slats running lengthwise set into the frame. There were slots between the slats. A long handle with ridges that fit into the slots was fastened at one end to the frame. Georg was to place a handful of stems across the slats and push the handle so as to crush the bundle of stems and thereby separate out the long, silky fibres from the wooden core of the stems. The wood waste would fall through the slots and be collected below. "Now try a bundle and see how it goes." The man helped him through the process of breaking a few bundles of stems. Then he showed him the other tasks to achieve a final braid-like skein of silky fibres that would be sent to the women in town for spinning into yarn.

It was at Schmellenhof that Georg became a flax farmer and a maker of fine linen cloth. He worked with the men from the village as they sowed the flax seed. When the plants were ready to be harvested he pulled the flax from the ground when the bottom leaves were yellow. Then he had to stand in the putrid ponds of water where the flax was left to rot in order to help loosen the fibres from the woody core. When the plants were rotten he had to pitch the retted flax into wagons where it was taken to a pasture to dry in the sun. He also helped bundle it for processing when dried. He operated the brake, combed the fibres, separated the short tow fibres from the long line fibres that were then bundled into hand sized bunches and sent to the village to be made into yarn.

He learned to hate the fieldwork, especially the pulling, which was a very dirty task. Pulling gave him cuts on his hands and was always done in a rush to get the ripe plants out of the ground and dried in the sun before the rains came. It was exhausting work and he was grateful when it became time to process the fibres. Although painful for his arms and shoulders, he found the rhythm of working the brake gave him peace of mind, as it was almost like working the loom. It gave him great satisfaction to watch the waste boon separate from the long silky fibres that became the linen yarn that was then made into cloth. Working the brake made him forget the trauma of being married to Maria.

Some days, after the fibres had been processed, he was asked to take the bundles of fibres the hackling crew called "bridesmaid's braids" to the women and girls in the village who would spin them into yarn. After finishing this task he could linger in the tavern, have a stein of beer, and socialize with the tavern girls. But socializing was as far as it went since he was always fearful he would not get the horse back to the farm before "*der bose Boss*" started looking for him.

Eventually, he was asked to work on one of the five looms housed in a stone building with many windows. Master Schellenburger was a harsh taskmaster but Georg felt at home on the loom and occasionally thought of his future while he listened to its song. But at night in the warm darkness of his bed he dreamed of Maria. He ached for a good woman to share his bed. It was the missing fact of his life.

In late October, when the harvesting was done, Adam Bahye, as he did every year, gave a feast for his workers in celebration of *Reformationstag*, a public holiday for Protestants in that part of the country. Large tables were set up on the lawn of the manor house and covered over with heavy linen cloth in the event of rain. The household women laid out a feast of many meats, potatoes, cheese, cakes, and pies. Barrels of beer with spigots attached were set on trestles. There was *Apfelsaft* for the ladies and *Schnapps* for the more serious-minded of the men. The ladies were dressed in their very best raiment, the girls flirting with the young men of the village who had been hired to help with the harvest.

One of the women serving plates of food and flagons of beer was Sarah, the second daughter of the manor, whom Georg had seen at the stables on the days that she decided to go riding. She was unmarried and already tending to some fullness of figure. He guessed she was about his age. With her round face and straight nose she could be thought of as pretty except for her rather thin lips. Georg had seen her at the stables, but she was above him socially and he made no effort to engage her in conversation, fearful of her father's wrath.

As she passed out plates of food, Georg was struck by her long fingers, which seemed somehow to be at odds with her ample figure. The plain frock she was wearing was stretched tightly across her hips, and as she walked among the tables the passion he had had for Maria came back to him. When she turned her hazel eyes toward his, he saw in them evidence of a resolute nature; they were eyes that did not smile easily. But he put thoughts of conquest aside; Sarah Bahye was above him in status and he could not even be seen to be interested in her. He tried to ignore Sarah and joined in the merriment caused by great quantities of the bittersweet Schmellenhof beer.

One day soon after *Reformationstag* he had a chance encounter with Sarah when she came to the barn dressed to go riding. He helped harness her horse and as she was about to mount she casually asked, "Would you be kind enough to come with me?" Startled and too intrigued to make up an excuse he quickly saddled up his old horse and they rode off together, a lady of the manor in her fine clothes on a spirited mount and he, a lowly journeyman, dusty and grimy from hackling flax all day, sitting atop his lazy old horse. Certainly a disparate pair.

She galloped off toward the woods leaving Georg loping far behind. But at the edge of the trees she stopped and waited. They walked the horses side by side through the trees. He was quiet until she asked about his life and whether he was happy working on the farm. At first he avoided any discussion about his marriage, but she seemed genuinely interested, so after some false starts he told her of his marriage with Maria; a loving union turned bad because of their frustrations in trying to have a child. With this intimacy he became more comfortable with her, but could not fathom why she was interested in his life. They walked on into the woods in comfortable silence until Georg was moved to tell her the story of his encounter with the bandits on his journey through the woods between Marbach and Wüstenrot. She expressed delight with the story. When the chill of the evening settled around them it was time to turn back. Saying so, she raced her horse through the trees until he could no longer see her and he only caught up back at the stable as she was finished grooming the horse. The episode left Georg very puzzled, but he realized that if she asked for an outing again he would be unaccountably happy.

It did happen again. And again. The outings in the woods became a pleasant interlude for Georg. Since he was on the loom much of the time, the meetings were rare, but when they did happen he enjoyed her company. He even bought a riding horse at great expense from a man in the village. Georg thought he and Sarah were meeting secretly, but his work mates, on learning of the new horse, chastised him for reaching beyond his station. The rude jokes from the men living in his shed began to bother Georg because, somewhat to his embarrassment, he insisted he had no romantic intentions. She was of the manor house and he was just doing her wishes. Amid the rumours Sarah avoided him. He felt disappointment at her sudden aloofness, but then one day he found a note tucked in the reed of his loom. She wrote that her father knew of their liaisons and refused to let her go riding. She wrote that her father, "in great anger" forbade her to associate with Georg.

Georg expected he would be released, but to his surprise he was not asked to leave. He had no way of knowing that Sarah's mother did not disapprove of her daughter's romantic behaviour. She worried that Sarah's prospects were diminishing and her daughter would remain a maid the rest of her life. She knew it was selfish of her but she looked forward to seeing a granddaughter from Sarah. Georg would not have been her first choice for Sarah but she seemed to be happy with him. So she conspired against her husband and argued that he should keep the new man. She told Adam, "Your health is going and you need his help in the fields." Hence, Georg was not let go, but Adam vowed to keep a sharper lookout for any errant behaviour towards his daughter.

For his part Georg was determined to put Sarah out of his thoughts. The noisy loom had always been his solace when life became difficult so he turned to his weaving with renewed passion. Herr Schellenburger's weavers were making table coverings for the grand houses of the region and beyond. Preoccupied with his work, Georg was startled one morning to find another note, almost hidden in the reed. She would wait in the ruin of an old tower at the edge of the woods they had often visited on horseback. She would be at this place at two of the clock in the afternoon on the Sabbath next. It was signed *Marie Sarahye Bahye of Schmellenhof.*

He read the note with sadness. He could not meet her or he would be in deep trouble with her father. But as the Sabbath approached he began to lose his resolve, and finally gave in to desire.

As the appointed time for their liaison came and went Georg became increasingly despondent. He was thinking of leaving the old tower when he spotted her loping across the fields. Since she had finally decided to defy her father she flew across the fields with abandon. Georg stood watching her progress, at once thrilled and frightened. When she came to Georg, all breathless and sweaty, he was startled by her passion.

The tower ruin became their rendezvous. Whenever Sarah could escape her father's protective eye they met during many soft summer evenings in a leafy bower of spreading birch trees while overhead came the hopeful song of the brown thrush. Their budding romance blossomed and became love. Soon Georg, losing all inhibitions about the differences in their social standing, was anxious to consummate their union but Sarah, still frightened of her father and jealous of her chastity put him off. Finally Georg, on a languorous sultry Sabbath afternoon said to her, "I wish to talk to your father." The thought of including her father into their love for one another still frightened her. She jumped from his embrace and said, "No! No!

You shan't do that!" But after a few moments of retreat into her own thoughts she relaxed and sat down on one of the stones of the ruined tower. After more silence she finally said, "No, I will tell mother and see if she can help persuade father to give his blessing." Georg was satisfied with her plan.

It took more than two weeks for Sarah to carry out her plan and to approach her father for his blessing. Her mother was already secretly celebrating Sarah's impending marriage. Adam was furious. He suspected Georg's motives. He threatened to disinherit Sarah, thinking that would deter Georg. He tried to send Georg away, but Sarah and her mother would not have it. He threatened religious damnation for her disobedience. But in time Sarah's mother, who understood Sarah's resoluteness more clearly than her father, convinced him to agree to the marriage. Adam finally gave in but would not agree to Sarah's inheritance. She fought with her father, saying it was against the laws of man and God to cast adrift his own flesh and blood, but he held firm. With this cloud hovering over their heads, Sarah and Georg were married in the Lutheran Evangelical Church of the Reformation at Wüstenrot in the middle of November 1724. Georg moved his personal belongings into the manor house at Schmellenhof at the insistence of Sarah's mother. A year later, a little girl, Maria Margaretha, was born. Grandmother was overjoyed. Adam became more agreeable toward Sarah and his son-in-law, but he would not budge on removing the dark cloud hanging over the family.

For two years Sarah fought with her father over her inheritance, to no avail. He told her that Johannes would inherit the estate to keep it intact. And, to keep her privileged position in the family, Sarah's older sister, Anna, sided with her father. Then one cold day in October Adam got a chill as a result of wading to his waist in one of his retting ponds. His lungs filled with liquid and by the fourth day he could barely breathe. That night God took him as one of His own. Sarah was devastated, partly from guilt due to her stubbornness about her inheritance. Her mother tried to explain that it was in fact Adam's stubbornness that caused the trouble between them.

Surprisingly few people came to give last respects, considering Adam's attempt to obtain a high status in the community. But the funeral helped Sarah come to terms with her guilt and grief. Three days later, her mother informed Sarah that she and Johannes had agreed to give Sarah her rightful inheritance of 155 florins. Sarah was also given all her clothes and a few pieces of her mother's furniture as well as a Bible and prayer book.

In the same year that Adam died, Georg received word that his mother had passed away one day after the celebration of St. Nicholas' Day in December. Two days later, after a heavy fall of snow, he saddled up his riding horse, and, armed with a new pistol he had purchased that summer in Wüstenrot, he set out to travel to his old home in Poppenweiler. The snow made the road difficult but there were no highwaymen operating in the depth of winter so he reached his father's house in three days without incident. Anna had already been put into the ground. From his father Georg enquired about his mother's wishes for the distribution of her estate, to be told that she wished it to be given equally to her surviving children when his father died, but that she had wished that Georg would inherit the house when his father had no more use for living there. After visiting with Jacob and Bernhardt he rode through the deep snow back to Sarah.

Shortly after his mother's death, Georg and Sarah made plans to leave Schmellenhof. She and Georg left her family home to live in Poppenweiler when the snow was gone in the spring.

Sarah purchased a small house with a garden, located in the churchyard of the Poppenweiler Evangelical Lutheran Church. With help from his brothers, Jacob and Leonardt, Georg was able to resume his former life. During the next four years of their marriage Georg and Sarah had two more children, Gottfried and Jörg Jacob. Gottfried died at three months. Sixteen days after the birth of Jörg Jacob, Sarah was taken by God. She left Georg with infant Jörg Jacob and Maria Margaretha, now five years old.

Sarah's older sister Anna came from her home in Marbach for the funeral. Afterwards she angrily accused Georg of abusing Sarah. It was true that he and Sarah had not always gotten along. Their wedded life had been stormy, worsened by the circumstances of the period, but occasionally struck with love and passion. She had nagged him about the time he spent at his loom and about their poor position in the community. When times were good they made passionate love. Although furious with Georg, Anna loved her sister and undertook to get a wet nurse for the baby, and to care for infant Jörg Jacob and his sister Maria Margaretha until Georg, whom she did not trust with their care, married again.

Jörg Jacob joined Sarah only a few months later. Georg grieved over his infant son's death more than he imagined possible. For a month the tragedy of his life with Sarah overwhelmed him. In his grieving he grew closer to his daughter Maria Margaretha and undertook to care for her. She made his life seem worthwhile again.

When Georg examined Sarah's effects he discovered she had left her estate to their sons Martin Gottfried and Jörg Jacob, and daughter Maria Margaretha, with Georg Waeger to be their guardian and trustee. With the papers giving the distribution of her estate, he found copies of letters written by her brother Johannes to relatives in America. The letters, after greetings and news of family matters, were mostly about the sickness of the older folk and the heavy taxation exacted to support soldiers marching up and down Germany, even though it was a time of peace. One letter that Johannes had written to a cousin of Sarah's in America worried about the Turks, who were threatening Christendom, and read, "…*if a bitter war breaks out there will be hard burdens and all kinds of new and heavy exactions. We would be oppressed and brought to poverty, and the people of Wüstenrot and Schmellenhof ask urgently about America.*"

On reading the letters, Georg resolved to approach his brother Leonardt about going to America. He knew nothing of America, but letters from people who had gone there were full of the wonderful abundance of the land. He had nothing in Germany, except the right to live in Sarah's house until Maria came of age. But when Georg approached his younger brother, Leonardt gruffly told him he had no interest in leaving Germany, unless the war situation flared up again. Georg was undeterred by this refusal, since he had felt the same way two years ago. He did not put his ambition aside.

Ambition or no, Georg did not go to America. Not then. That winter his father died from a chill he had caught while hunting boar in the snow. Georg inherited his father's house as Anna wished. As he had no use for another house, which was inferior to Sarah's, he let it to his younger brother Bernhardt and his wife Barbara, who at the time was living with Barbara's family. Since Leonardt got the vineyards as his estate, Georg was still the poor brother. He had houses but no land. Without land he was a citizen in name only.

Shortly after Sarah's death he met Margaretha Egermayer from Wangen, daughter of a vinedresser. Margaretha was a young widow with a lively spirit. She was also fatally attractive to men. At age seventeen she had run off with an officer of the Imperial army in defiance of her father, who himself had come down in the world from being an infantry officer with the Duke of Savoy. He knew that no good could come of Margaretha's wilfulness in marrying a soldier. Margaretha's love for Gerhardt was deep and passionate but soon he began to spend more and more time apart from her. It turned out that Gerhardt was more interested in his army mates than in Margaretha. Then one day Gerhardt did not come home. The official solicitation she received was that he was killed in battle, but she found later that that he was run through with a brother officer's sword in a duel fought over a male lover. Margaretha, alienated from her father, took solace with her grandmother, who had always been her support in times of stress. Her grandmother spoke to her, "Gerhardt was a weak man! With your beauty there will be other men, good men." So when Georg was introduced by her father she was no longer grieving for Gerhardt; and fearful that her childbearing years were shortening, she accepted his advances. Her father was acquainted with Georg and his brother Leonardt, and on his word she agreed to marry Georg. It seemed like destiny; two unhappy people finding each other.

On a spring day in June 1731 Georg Waeger and Margaretha Egermayer were married. He brought his new wife to Poppenweiler. Georg's life took a new turn when a son was born to Margaretha at the tail end of winter in the year of 1732.

E berhardt Waeger was born into very modest circumstances. Above the Neckar River, above the vineyards, on a small promontory protecting the flat plains of farmer's fields to the east stood a large church of the Reformation. In the shadow of the church was a small house under a large tree, bare of its leaves but sprouting a few buds in the renewal of its cycle of life. The small house, a cottage really, was made of faggots woven together in a mixture of clay and lime, held against the autumn storms and snows of winter by weather-beaten hewn boards. The steep roof of straw thatch covered the inhabitants from the elements. A door in the north side of the cottage led, by a worn path, to a shed that served the functions of a washhouse. The cottage itself had two rooms, one to house a loom, which was used to manufacture the linen cloth that was the sustenance of the family. A small curtained window, adorned with a sprig of some neglected flower plant, caught the morning sun. Adjacent to the window was a rough door that led to a footpath running the length of the church and beyond, and which connected the cottage to similar dwellings in the village of Poppenweiler.

On the day Georg and Margaretha's boy was born, there was muffled activity within the cottage under the budding tree. The boy's young mother was happy. It was her first child and he appeared healthy. The father, after one look at the child, returned to his loom and continued with his weaving. Margaretha was his third wife and the boy his fourth child, with only Sarah's Maria Margaretha surviving, Gottfried and Jacob being taken by God soon after birth. Margaretha's boy was healthy, but Georg had learned during his hard life to depend on fate. Some things must be left to God, and it did not do to hope.

Eberhardt Waeger was born in the afternoon of a bright, crisp day, attended to by Margaretha's mother, Anna Egermayer, who had lived with Georg and Margaretha since Margaretha's father had died half a year before. Twelve days later the baby boy was christened on a wet, cloudy day in the adjoining church. Since the boy appeared healthy, Margaretha had delayed the christening so that her sister Dorothea and Georg's family could attend. Georg took no part in the arrangements, hiding his apprehensions about the child's survival in a weaving project that the Duke's people had commissioned. Margaretha wanted a proper christening, so a letter was dispatched via the boat captain to her sister in Wangen, and Maria Margaretha was sent out with notes to Barbara and Bernhardt Waeger and Leonardt and Catherina Waeger, announcing the baptism of Johann Eberhardt Waeger by the Reverend Mattaeus Blumgardt on the 22nd of March, 1732. Leonardt and Catherina were asked to be sponsors of the boy. Margaretha wanted her friend and neighbour, Anna Kolbien, with her husband to be special godparents to the child. On the sixth day Margaretha received a note from her sister stating that she was not able to attend because of the cost.

So on the appointed day and hour, the little band of sponsors gathered in front of the small house, all to walk a few steps to the Lutheran Evangelical Church of Poppenweiler. Margaretha carried with her a copy of the Nurnberg Handbook, a family treasure, which contained the baptism ceremony, and a worn Bible in which she recorded the thoughts and events of her life. They were welcomed at the church door by Pastor Blumgardt, who directed them in their respective roles during the baptismal service.

"*In Holy Baptism thy gracious heavenly Father liberates us from sin and death. We...*" Georg had heard all this before, but words like "liberate from death" were meaningless to him. Those words did not liberate his sons Gottfried and Jacob from death. He prayed this time the pastor would get it right. As the pastor droned on about "fallen humanity," the "resurrection of Jesus Christ," and how baptism makes us reborn as "children of God," Georg's mind began to wander to the work in which he had been engaged that morning. He was distracted by the intricate weave and lively pattern of Anna Kolbien's shawl. As he was admiring the skill in the weave of the shawl, she moved, perhaps seeing Georg's eyes on her, and the shawl dropped away, displaying a glimpse of forbidden flesh. His mind was jerked from indecent thoughts back to the business at hand by a hard look from Margaretha and to the words of Pastor Blumgardt, "*...body of Christ. As we live with Him we grow in faith, love, and obedience to the will of God.*"

Then after the promises to bring him to God's House, teach him the Lord's Prayer, the Creed, and the Ten Commandments, the pastor poured water on the babe and intoned, "*I baptize thee Johannes Eberhart Waeger in the name of the Father, and of the Son, and of the Holy Ghost. Amen.*"

With these words, Georg began to have hope for the child, even a moment of pride. His mother appeared in good health twelve days after the birth, and the boy was ruddy and looked healthy. Georg's hope was based on the boy's legacy; a line of sturdy mountain men who had come from a homeland in Carinthia, and who had survived many hardships in a dangerous land.

After the few moments of hope held in his heart for the new babe, Georg returned to his loom in order to ward off thoughts of once more being betrayed by God. The loom was a hiding place from the fears that beset his soul, and over the years his loom had become the solid oak tree that kept him from being blown away by the tempest. He worked the treadles and watched for the rise and fall of the harnesses to free them from the inertia that seemed to invade them from the time of the last use. He checked the warp and examined the bobbins of the shuttles for the fine linen thread that he was using for the present work. The finished cloth would be sewn into a suit for some soldier of the Duke so that he could die in the mud in the style of a hero.

He was ready to begin the day's work. As the shuttle flashed to and fro between the warp threads by the flick of practiced wrists, and as the treadles moved under his feet, the noise from the harness frames and the thwack of the reed beating the weft into place, he soon began to hear the song of the loom. He played the song like an organist in a great cathedral. This was peace. Over the years he never tired of making the loom sing its song. With the birth of a healthy boy he could hear the loom sing the song of his people, and a paean to the legacy he would pass down to his son.

A year after Eberhardt Waeger was born war broke out again, this time between the Bourbon Kings of Spain and France, and the Austrian Hapsburgs. Georg was required to house a soldier at his own expense at a time when he could barely feed his own family. To help pay the stipend, Margaretha began to spin worsted, but it was not permissible to sell her yarn privately, only to large merchants that paid too little money. The weaver's guild was a tightly controlling entity. And the municipal guilds were being threatened by rural ones even as large merchant companies were threatening both. She was criticized by un-married women, once even leading to violence, who believed it was their privilege to do the spinning since they were not allowed to survive otherwise except by begging, or on poor relief. In addition to their poverty, Margaretha appeared much attracted to the soldier. Georg feared she might run off with him.

Because of the expansion of the guilds into the countryside it was harder and harder for Georg to get a contract. With the added burden of taxes to support troopers, especially officers, it was becoming difficult to buy the food they needed to stay alive. He was taken off to the gaol for a few days until Leonardt came to pay his tax. About six months after this Sarah's legacy ended for Georg when Maria Margaretha died at age nine. It was in this, the bottom of his life, that he again thought of going to America.

Georg recalled the letters extolling the virtues of abundant land in America. One dreary October day in the year Eberhardt was four, in the late afternoon when Margaretha seemed content at her wheel he spoke to her, "I am thinking of going to America. Leonardt has changed his thoughts and is thinking of going now that little Christina has gone to heaven, and he thinks we would have a future there." At first Margaretha paid no heed to Georg since she had heard many of his unfulfilled wishes, but when mention of Leonardt being willing to go her ears perked up and she thought to herself, "perhaps Leonardt will finally convince him to do it." She was torn between her natural thirst for adventure and the tradition and expectations of her family in Wagen. She wondered whether her son would have a good life in America.

For now, culture and her family won over her restlessness for a new life. But she knew that if Georg decided to go, the same tradition said that she had to obey his wishes. She said to Georg with some frustration, both at her own reluctance to change her life and his lack of ambition, "We do have a future here if you would go looking for it. Frau Stoufer says there is work in Sternenfels." He saw that she was upset and said nothing. Perhaps the situation in Württemberg would improve in the next year.

In his travels around Württemberg, Georg had learned there was work in Sternenfels where *Stubensand,* an abrasive for cleaning pots and pans, was being produced. But he considered it ditch-digging and he did not want to be reduced to digging sand out of the side of a cliff. His grandfather Hans had dug salt out of the mountains and ended up a pauper. He himself had spent many years to learn the weaving trade, and was a member of the guild. He was above digging ditches. But like Margaretha, frustrated with his life, he was also frightened of breaking away. So he took his family to Sternenfels, even though he still had Sarah's house in Poppenweiler, which he let to a young family of his guild. Georg became a citizen of Sternenfels and dug sand but their situation did not improve.

After two months of grubbing sand in the sandpits of Sternenfels he learned to hate the work. He was strong enough, but the effort was too much like pulling flax and standing in the retting ponds of Schmellenhof. Then, little Christoph was taken by God in the darkness of night after only nine months of earthly life. For Margaretha it seemed like the end of her life: Elizabetha and Gottlieb and now Christoph, all gone. She lost her youthful vibrancy and became sulky and moody, and angry with Georg for Christoph's death. She cried at night, and denied him his rights as her lawful husband. He talked of going to America but Margaretha wanted to return to Poppenweiler, where his prospects were no better than at Sternenfels. So it was during this hiatus in their natural wedded life that Georg spent many rainy afternoons and evenings that winter at the Heinricherhaus across the town square from the small house he had let from Herr Braun.

So it came to be that one stormy evening five years after Eberhardt was born Georg slammed the house door against Margaretha's cruel words and headed for the Herr Heinrich's tavern. The rain was coming down in torrents, sizzling on the cobblestones and engulfing the feet of anyone foolish enough or desperate enough to be out of doors so late in the evening. On the farthest corner of the square the lights of the Heinricherhaus flickered through the sheets of rain, a beacon that drew Georg toward its entrance. Inside, shadows hid all but the centre of the room, with a few flickering candles showing the outlines of dark furniture and sawdust on the floor. The sawdust was stained red with blood and wine that the young men of the village occasionally spattered on the floor while settling arguments over women.

Georg found he was the only patron of Heinrich Hesse's inn. He sat on a bench in a corner opposite the entrance at a small table, bare except for a candle. Georg had been a frequent patron for the past year so without having to ask, Heinrich delivered a bowl of ale. Being the only patron he was studied by Herr Hesse, who believed knowledge of his patrons was his business.

Georg, now forty-two years old, had not aged well. He was altogether unexceptional in appearance, with the ruddiness of skin, rough dress, and shapeless hat that identified him to the innkeeper as a labourer, poor in body and poor in spirit. The light from the candle on the table disclosed an inner sadness and torment, a man suffering in solitary anguish. Heinrich had seen many such men. He had come to know that Georg was not violent with drink so he paid him little attention.

Just then a more interesting man appeared at the inn doorway. A large man wearing a woollen hat and a brown cape crouched as he came through the door, pushed into the room by the slanting rain, which covered the floor around the entrance. Quickly shutting the door, he chose a seat at a table close to where Georg was drinking. Georg looked up from his drink, but knowing nothing of the man he only grunted a greeting. Herr Hesse enquired after the newcomer's wishes. The latter asked for beer and sausage, which were quickly delivered to his table.

Georg picked up a paper and read slowly and painfully by the light of the candle. He carefully laid the paper, a letter, on the table. He was silent for a few minutes, and then he shuffled in his seat and looked into the face of the man at the next table. "Are you a soldier?" Startled, the other man said, "No!" Scarcely waiting for an answer, Georg mumbled, "When I was a child I dreamed of being a soldier, but when I was old enough it was a time of peace and I wed Maria instead. Now it is war again, but I am too old to lie all night in the mud. But it is not only soldiers who suffer in war."

Angrily, he grabbed the letter from the table and waved it in the air. "Now we have suffered through another war against Louis. Johannes, in this letter he wrote to Sarah's cousin in America, speaks of the hardships he has had to endure. He has written that Wüstenrot has for half a year quartered a company of Imperial soldiers, together with seventeen officers. Every one of the soldiers must have money every week, and beer or brandy, and cash money for the officer's provisions and lodging. The parish paid over ninety-six taxes or duties. Nine thousand gulden it cost the parish for the provision of the officers alone, together with the bandsmen and lodging money, not counting the provisioning for ordinary soldiers."

The innkeeper had heard this story many times from many patrons and had learned to close his ears, ever conscious of a visit from the authorities.

"Nine thousand gulden! Imagine! I cannot feed my woman and child, yet a fortune for war! I have to dig the sand to scratch out an existence." Tired, Georg put the letter on the table and continued his solitary anguish in silence.

After a few moments Georg looked at the man in the brown cape and spoke with defiance in his voice, "Have you a child?"

"Yes, I have a daughter who I have not seen in some years," said the man.

"I buried my sixth child." Georg felt more grim than sad.

"I am very sad to hear of this. How was he called?"

"His name was Christoph. His age was nine months. He had my resemblance."

The stranger in the brown cape said nothing. After a short silence, Georg continued, "We had little Maria up at the Schmellenhof. She was a sweet thing with curly hair and blue eyes. Her eyes were so blue! Bluer than heaven even. Her eyes now make heaven even bluer since she was taken from me when only nine. Did your daughter have blue eyes?"

Without waiting for an answer he rushed on, "Christoph was a beautiful child. They put him in a wooden box and lowered him into the ground under a tree close to the church." Looking at the stranger, he added, "May God rest his soul!"

Having no plans for the evening, and not wanting to face the rain, the stranger asked, "Is this your home?"

For a few moments Georg said nothing; then, "I am from Poppenweiler. I am the son of Leonardt the tailor, who lived there since my birth and died there some years past. I learned to make beautiful, strong uniforms from my father, but all the soldiers we see going through here get their uniforms somewhere else now. I am now a ditch digger of brown sand. I was a linen weaver, making fine cloth for the Duke but that is gone. Have you sat at a loom all day, picking? Under and over, under and over, under and over, under and over. My brother Leonardt is a wine farmer. Hoeing, seeding, picking, crushing. All is the same. When I was a boy I dreamed of fighting French soldiers, but we fight now to stay alive. Once, long ago, I saw the English army on its way to glorious victories at Hochstadt and Landau. How I wish I had run away with the army, to grow up in the army. But my father was a tailor. I am a weaver. I wed Maria, then Sarah who died, and now I have Margaretha."

He drew some coins from inside his shirt. Waving a fist in the air he called for more ale. His face in the light of the candle told Heinrich of strong emotions sweeping over the huddled figure. Sadness became a dark cloud of anger, then desperation and fear.

When Heinrich came up to him Georg grabbed his arm, insisting that he hear his story. But the innkeeper took the coins from the table and pulled away. Fortified with a swallow of new ale, undeterred by the innkeeper's indifference, Georg was bound to tell his troubles to the stranger in the brown cape.

"Beautiful, young Margaretha. She came up from Wangen and took me after my failures, and lusty Margaretha has given me a healthy son. She gave me Elizabetha and Gottlieb too, but they died. Then Christoph. I have one child left to me, Maragretha's Eberhardt, may God be praised. I hope he is not a sand digger, nor a weaver making uniforms for soldiers going off to do battle with the bastard French. The bastard, Popish French. But are they worse than the Duke and his tax, which grind us into the ground so he can live in his castle with all those people and their fine linen goods? And the food they waste. A man was through here the other day, it was right in this room, who told of food being thrown to the dogs because it was not tasty. We have freezing winters with poor crops and no wood, and our own German bastards that live on the hill throw our food to the dogs.

"We are all kept poor. We must outfit the troops from head to foot with new equipment inside and out. And they are scoundrels, every one of them, stealing, getting drunk and molesting the young girls, even women with babies; they don't care who they attack. So much cost that it keeps us all in poverty."

With this outburst Georg's reason broke through the haze of drink. He looked around the near-empty room as if to be assured once more that there were no soldiers or "German bastards." He peered intently at the stranger, appeared to be satisfied that he was not an agent of the Duke, and continued his harangue.

"When I was a child my grandfather told me stories of horror when we were naughty and said he would lock us in the mouse tower at Bingen if we did not behave.

"You know the story of Bishop Hatto?

The stranger said, "No, I am not from these parts."

"One year the rains were so heavy the crops rotted in the fields and the people were starving. Bishop Hatto's barn was full of grain. To keep the starving poor from rioting, Bishop Hatto opened his barn door and said to them, 'You shall have food for the winter.' When all the village people were in the barn, Bishop Hatto bolted the door and set the barn alight.

"They jailed me once, the Duke's men. Said I stole money from him. They said it was his tax money, and due him. I am a good man, but now I feel like I'm locked in the barn, waiting for Bishop Hatto to light his fiery brand. They put me in the filthy dungeon of the town hall until Leonardt paid them."

Georg slumped in his chair, very tired. After a long silence, he looked up at the stranger and recited the rest of the story of the mouse tower as told to him by his grandfather.

"Bishop Hatto was pleased and had a merry supper. That night he slept like a child. The next day the rats came; thousands of rats, eating everything. Stricken with terror, Bishop Hatto hastened to his tower on the Rhine and barred all the windows and doors. But the avenging army of rats crossed the river and poured in upon the Bishop. He was counting his beads when the rats devoured him, gnawing his flesh from every limb. They stripped his bones until they were white."

After this story of Bishop Hatto's judgment day, he straightened his back and glared at the stranger, his spirit revived. Georg said, "I think it was when Leonardt paid money to cover my tax debt that he finally thought about going to America. Have you heard about America? They have everything there. They have so much wood they burn it in the fields. Burn it in the fields mind you! We had no wood to burn last winter to keep little Christoph warm."

After a short silence to control his emotions he said, "Poor little Christoph, he might still be with us if we were in America."

Again he slumped over the table. All was quiet in the room except for the beating of the rain as it slanted onto the windows, tearing at the thin shelter, trying to get at the people inside. Suddenly Georg rose from his slumped position, and in a paroxysm of rage shouted to the room, "I am going to America! I am taking Margaretha, and we are going to America. Margaretha will become young again. Eberhardt will do well there."

Heinrich the innkeeper listened to Georg's shout, and was startled by the finality of the words. It was as if the man had been contemplating this for some time, and now at this precise time, the irrevocable decision was made. But of course he was full of ale, and Heinrich knew the next day could take a different turning. He had seen it before. The same man would have the same sad story the next day.

4

MARGARETHA
Cutting Roots

When Georg came home from the Heinricherhaus at Sternenfels in a drunken state proclaiming that he had decided to take her to America, Margaretha located a long letter hidden between the sheaves of her Bible, where she kept her letters. She had received the letter from her cousin Frieda the same year Eberhardt was born. Frieda and Pieter had gone to America some years back and seemed to be well settled there. After Georg had gone to his bed Margaretha once again read the letter in front of the fire.

> *Dearest Cousin Margaretha; with good wishes for all good things and with greetings from your Cousin, and Pieter and little Johann and our dear daughter Ottilia. We wish you peace, happiness, health and blessed life back in our beloved Germany.*
>
> *Our dear God has granted us fortune. We arrived at the American port in this place, the colony of New York, in September of the year 1731 after a journey of four months, sixteen days from leaving our dear Wangen. We are now settled in the region styled Kirkehoek in the said colony. We have eighteen hectares of good land and two hectares of trees. We now have four cows and three horses as well as some chickens and geese. We keep some sheep, as there is a mill near our farm where we can buy blankets and cloth for clothes. Pieter has built a nice log house of two rooms with a washhouse adjacent. Timber is very plentiful here. We have surplus wheat to sell and grass for the cows to eat and a vegetable garden for our food. We have healthy water with our meals instead of wine, as grapes are not grown here and wine from outside is very expensive. God has been good to us with a church we call the German church, to which all the religious people go on the Sabbath. There are Reformed, Calvinists and Lutherans. We meet at different times of course. Our community has been granted a plot of land of two hectares near us, and the men are planning a Lutheran church of stone.*

Margaretha was pleased for Frieda. She had been a plain, shy girl when young and as she grew into her childbearing years without prospect, her father became desperate to see her married. So when the young scholar Pieter showed up at his doorstep with apparently honourable intentions, Frieda's father made an offer to provide Pieter and Frieda with sufficient funds to emigrate Germany and settle in America. From her letter it seemed Frieda was pleased with her lot in the New World. Margaretha wiped a tear from her eye, not for Frieda, but for herself. She read on,

> Dear cousin we did not always please God. Our journey was full of fear, misfortune and expense. Pieter bought us passage to Koblentz with Herr Schneider, where we boarded a sailing ship, which was to deliver our family and belongings to Rotterdam. At Koblenz, we were required to stop overnight at inns for food and lodging at great expense, and to buy food for the journey to Rotterdam. The journey from Stuttgart to Rotterdam required three weeks and two days.
>
> On arriving in Rotterdam, Pieter contacted our agents Kaan and Horst, and agreed on a ship to America. The ship had two masts and was named Arnthore which I was told means Eagle of Thor. It was a merchantman type ship that seemed smaller than the others, but the agents told us it would take us to America in fewer days.

Margaretha had never been north of Wüstenrot where Georg had worked. Even then she was very young when her father took her to Hall to visit Uncle Freiderich Egermayer who had made money in the salt trade. She had never seen the Rhine. She felt a surge of anticipation at the thought of travelling on the mythical River and tasting the spirit of the legends that her mother had read to her when she was a very small girl. As she grew older she often dreamt of beautiful and strong Siegfried and wished to be Queen Brunhilde. She suddenly felt very warm, and lowered her eyes to Frieda's letter.

> Our ship, commanded by Captain Keiler was to sail in six days. Our agreement was that we would provide provisions for ourselves, which would be stored aboard ship to be distributed by the ship's surgeon while at sea. The supplies required a barrel of good and dry and durable provisions. We were told to buy extra supplies for the journey to the seacoast. We then set out to provide ourselves with grains, peas, beans and potatoes.
>
> We were delayed under anchor with poor winds for six days before we reached the open sea. Our extra food supply that had caused great expense in Rotterdam was mostly gone.
>
> We went on the open sea with a strong wind from the side so that the ship rolled angrily. Sickness came among the passengers. Pieter and I held out quite a while until we too had to vomit. In spite of the rolling back and forth we stayed on the foredeck with no thought of eating until it became

very cold.

The next day the wind grew stronger and many people became sick again. We felt not too well but by evening we could eat a little. When morning arrived, we could see land no longer.

With dawn the next day came the wind again from the side. By evening it had become a violent storm, and in the night it became so frightful that it was impossible to sleep. The wind drove the ship so to the side that we had to put ropes across our bed to keep from being thrown to the floor. The waves struck the ship with such fury that streams of water rushed down between decks. For two days we dared not to think of cooking, nor had we any appetite. It was frightful during the nights. Some cried out when water rushed down into the deck; others cursed and blamed the good Lord for their misery; others screamed when the waters came against them in their bed. One man went mad. Children cried from cold and fear.

Margaretha felt sick. She rose from her chair and went out into the night. The air was fresh; it cooled her fevered brain and settled her sick stomach. A million stars twinkled in the arc of heaven. Did the same stars shine over the heads of Frieda and Pieter this very night? America was halfway around the world and perhaps Frieda and Pieter saw different stars. Only God who made heaven and lived there would know. Her mind clear and heart at peace she returned to the chair to finish reading Frieda's letter.

After three days the wind subsided somewhat. At once came a good strong wind. Mountains of water broke against the ship and rolled over the decks. The Captain had planned to stop at the Azores, but because of the favourable wind we continued south to close to Madeira where we had to turn sideways, and the next day found our course to America. With calms, one very violent wind where the ship's crew had to pull in all sails, rain and very pleasant weather we slowly advanced toward our new home.

You can imagine the rejoicing when we could see the coastline of America, being almost a quarter of a year on the ship. We arrived safely in New York where Pieter made arrangements for a bateau and we journeyed on the river Hudson to our present home.

Dear cousin, our new circumstances allow us to forget the horrors of the journey to this place. Our home is humble, but we have all the necessities that a loving God would wish upon us. Above all our pleasures are that there are no wars, we never see a soldier. We are not required to keep soldiers, nor do we support Dukes in their military adventures and castle building, nor do we support Duchesses in their fine dress and parties, as in our dear still beloved Germany.

Pieter and I and Johann and Ottilia wish you and yours dear cousin

*all the blessings of God in body and soul here in this temporal life and there
in the everlasting eternity.*
Your loyally devoted cousin,
Frieda Egermayer

Margaretha put the letter back in her Bible where it had rested so many years, not wishing it to be read by Georg. She began to tremble even though the fire was still warm. Then she left the chair and retired, but sleep did not come. She was at once terrified, angry, and exhilarated at the thought of going to America. To leave her known world of friends and relatives frightened her, although most of the time she was angry with one or the other. But, they were familiar and familiarity was a comfort to her. And she feared she would need intimates in the next few months because there had been no blood in her flow for several weeks. As she lay awake staring into the dark she tried to remember how many times she had suffered childbirth with only Eberhardt to show for her conjugal duty. Her first Elizabetha, from Gerhardt's seed, was taken by God after only eight days because of Gerhardt's sin of perversion. Georg's Elizabetha died from gout after giving her hope for a daughter that would grow to be a queen. Her future queen lived three months. Gottlieb, a brother for Eberhardt, went to heaven at one year. He was her most beautiful child, was Gottlieb, with bright blue eyes and curls the colour of honey. Then Christoph; poor little Christoph. He was taken from her in nine months. She had to put his tiny body in a grave far from Gottlieb and his sisters. It gave her hope that they will play together in heaven.

Of Georg's seed, Eberhardt was all that was left. This child in her belly would be her sixth. She was still young and strong and another birthing was not a great burden, but she was frightened to birth a child on a sailing ship to America with only strangers to ogle and help in its delivery. She had told Georg nothing of her condition, nor of her fears. When Georg was taken to prison for debt, Margaretha was disgraced and kept to herself. She had encouraged him to work in Sternenfels to avoid being reminded by her friends of the scandal, angry that a wife had to suffer for her husband's transgressions. *Does God find my husband sinful* she had written in her bible, *does he not care for the welfare of his family?* Perhaps by leaving Württemberg they could find a better life. With this hope she turned to the wall and slept.

Before leaving Germany, the family had to return to Poppenweiler for Georg's renunciation. Back in their former home, Margaretha was moved to relate the contents of Frieda's letter, particularly the section about the terrifying sea voyage. He knew no more than she of the conditions they were about to face if they went to America, but he said to her, "Don't listen to Frieda. She was always jealous of your beauty. Pieter has done well over there, and Frieda, in her jealousy, does not want you to come and spoil her happiness. She does not tell the truth in her letter. Put it out of your mind."

Frustrated and hurt by his lecture and the rejection of her fears, she went to visit her sister-in-law Catharina.

Catharina was her only confidant. When they talked, it seemed as if all the people of the village were planning to go to America, a far-off place where things were said to be much better than in Württemberg. But no one seemed to know very much about America, except from the letters that told stories of its grandeur and new opportunities. Last year had been a harsh winter in Württemberg, with grapes freezing on the vines and cows dying in the field from cold and the scarcity of feed hay. All winter there were guarded conversations between Georg and Leonardt about how bad it had become. Catharina knew that Georg was trying to persuade Leonardt to go with him, but she was calmer about the prospect than was Margaretha. When Pastor Blumgardt had made the final arrangements to shepherd a group from Poppenweiler to go to British America in July, Georg and Leonardt had decided to go with the group. Margaretha made a fuss, angry at not being told of Georg's action.

Margaretha was sad for her son Eberhardt. He was just becoming wise to people and God's creation away from her petticoats and it would be very hard for him to leave his newfound world. He would not see another summer with its warm moist days. The bare trees along the river would have turned green, giving a new splash of colour against the rolling brown hills and wild flowers dotting the emerging green and yellow meadows. New vines would be planted, the fields would bloom, and then harvested. Margaretha would make the preserves that her boy liked.

She knew the most memorable event of the year for Eberhardt was the wine harvest, when the boys of the village helped in the pressing of the juicy grapes from the vines and took part in other jobs when the clear amber fluid was processed and put into bottles. During the summer, the vines were loaded with green grapes, bursting with life and a haven for birds, insects, and small animals. In full bloom, the vineyard provided a refuge from the demands of his father. Gone would be her son's refuge in the vineyards, or would he be able to hide in the hay pile in the field below the house. The hiding place from his father was a secret to all except mother and son.

So that winter when Margaretha sat with Eberhardt and told him in halting words that father was taking them to live in America he tried to hold back the tears, but they came anyway. He was angry with his father and sobbed that he wished to live with aunt Catharina and Paulus. When Margaretha told him that aunt Catharina and Paulus were going to America too, he stopped blubbering. "Is Agatha going?" Margaretha was more than a little intrigued by this question about a little girl he and his cousins played with the previous summer. Wanting to cheer him up, but not wanting to lie she said, "I do not know if Agatha is going but many people of the village are leaving with Pastor Blumgardt. Perhaps Agatha's parents are with them."

Most everyone was talking and making plans to leave the village, and gradually anger and frustration turned to excitement, mixed with fear of the voyage on the unknown sea. No one in the village had even seen the sea. Letters from America told horror stories of its cruelty and as the time drew close, Margaretha became very quiet. The joy of the last summer was gone from Eberhardt too.

Georg and Leonardt had many duties to attend to. It was no easy matter to leave Württemberg in those days. First it was necessary to sell those things that could not be taken on the voyage to those who did not leave, the poor and indigent. And to distribute treasured possessions to relatives, in the hope that someday they might be seen again. Then one had to clear all debts and contract obligations to the satisfaction of the Magistrate.

Leonardt had already sold his holdings. The vineyards, meadows, and herb gardens at Hochdorf, Erdmannhausen, and Marbach had been sold easily to neighbours. Sometimes in anger and frustration with her husband, Margaretha taunted him with the fact that Leonardt and Catharina had valuable lands and he did not. But with the sale of Leonardt's lands, they seemed as poor as she and Georg. With so many people leaving Poppenweiler prices for houses were low and with the sale of Sarah's old house and kitchen garden next to the church wall, as well as meadows that now belonged to Georg, they were worth very little. Leonardt's house in Rellingsgaße and his acreages were worth twice as much, allowing he and Catharina to go to America with a large estate.

Margaretha would not ever forget the day they cut all roots with the past. It was on a wet day in February, 1738, with piles of snow on the ground, that Leonardt and Georg went to the Sessions Court and stated that they and their families had the intention of emigrating to strange lands, and being free of all debts and obligations, renounced citizenship and their willingness to forego all claims to the benefits, rights, and privileges of citizenship on their and their children's behalf, for life. Margaretha was surprised that Barbara, Catharina's sister, was listed as emigrating with Leonardt's family.

When Georg signed his petition on behalf of herself and Eberhardt, Margaretha cried openly.

I t was the day of leaving. The families Kolben and Fritzen, whose boys Eberhardt had played with, came out of their houses to wish them luck, and expressed hope that God would be in their presence during the voyage. Margaretha was moved by this gesture since she had not been intimate with the two neighbour women. For the first time ever in the years they had been living side-by-side she hugged each of the women. Her anger had subsided over the months and she looked to the future with a mixture of excitement and fear as they made their way down the rough path and onto the road of timber that led to the river's edge. Eberhardt was trying to be brave but like his mother had difficulty keeping back the tears. Georg was grim. He had spent the morning in silence, making several trips to the riverside with their few treasured possessions after selling most of the furniture. The final end of life in Poppenweiler came when Georg carried the metal parts of his loom from the small house to join the pile of goods that belonged to the Johann Georg Waeger family.

Besides Leonardt's, there were several other families from the village. By mid-morning all had deposited their belongings in little humps, some larger than others. Pastor Blumgardt, all in black, was going from group to group asking questions and giving directions. Ev-

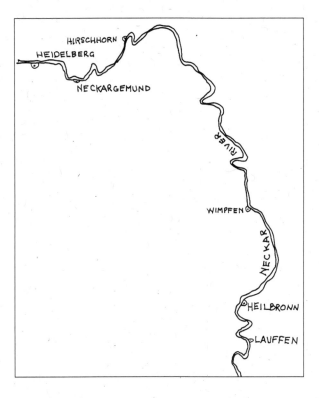

ery few minutes he would take off his floppy black hat and wipe his bald-head with a red bandanna. Soon the boat arrived with three crewmen to take the emigrants down river. The men of the village who had come to bid farewell to their friends loaded the piles of belongings in the boat, covering each pile with a blanket to keep it dry. Then the women were ushered aboard, along with the children. Barbara was looking after Paulus and Elenora and keeping an eye on Eberhardt as well. Elenora was crying, distraught about something she had to leave behind. Paulus, the oldest of the cousins, wanted to help his father but was silenced by his aunt.

All was loaded about noon and the boat crew pushed the vessel away from the small jetty, and the sweep manoeuvred the boat into mid-stream. The huddled band, refugees from hunger and politics, took a last longing look at the village they were leaving. The actual site of Margaretha's house was not visible from the river, but the church of St. Georg, stuck its spire into the noon sky giving her a last look at the home she was leaving forever. As the boat entered the curve in the river the vineyards began to obstruct the view of the church and its surrounding village, and soon nothing could be seen of the homes the people of Poppenweiler were leaving, some after many generations of joy and hardship. No one spoke, each absorbed by private sadness.

Margaretha had mixed emotions. She was fearful, but her heart was full. She had not yet reached thirty years with little experience beyond her father's and her husband's worlds. When young she had been tied to the life of her soldier father, who had not always been of such a low station. He fought with the Grand Alliance against France and afterward settled in Württemberg. She grew up in a military camp where she had been given some learning of German history and language, purchased by her father, with higher hopes for his daughter than a soldier's wife. She was a beauty with a lively spirit, and the same swarthiness as her father, which had come from ancestors that originated in the south. When she was a little girl her black hair, hazel eyes and dark skin set her aside from the northern girls who were of the ruling class, and because of her difference she spent a lonely childhood. Nevertheless, the forced solitude gave her a sense of self and an unruly streak in her personality, and as she got older, she found she could use her beauty to get what she wanted. She was continually in conflict with her father's wishes and she defied him, which was scandalous to the people of Wangen. Her mother said it was because they were alike that they fought, and she did not take sides, loving Margaretha but keenly aware that she could not publicly defy her husband.

In the arguments with her father, her grandmother Egermayer came to Margaretha's defense. She was fond of saying Margaretha was like Elizabeth Stuart, the English princess who became the Queen of Bohemia; known as the Winter Queen, since her husband the King was deposed and exiled after one short year. Her Grandmamma told Margaretha stories of Elizabeth.

For Margaretha, Elizabeth was an example of perfect womanhood; she was attractive, gay, vibrant, and ambitious, a trait not admired in women at the time. Before she was sixteen she had been wooed by both the King of Spain and King Gustavus Aldolphus. The Prince of Wales, her brother, wanted her to marry Frederick, the young Elector Palatine, to bring the religious reformers of England and Germany together. Elizabeth's mother-in-law, Queen Juliana, tried to turn her into a simple German hausfrau, but she would have none of it. She preferred men's ways. There was a story that while she and Frederick were touring London, before their wedding, she grabbed the match from a gunner and fired off one of the big guns of the Tower. She was a daring huntswoman and keen equestrian. She was brought up to go first into dinner, as befitted a Queen. She was never bored, she had enough brilliance of her own to keep the world shining around her, and she made no demands, except for a kingdom or so, and unlimited money to squander.

Elizabeth Stuart bore thirteen children; all were splendid specimens of beauty, vigour and intelligence. She turned the German state upside down, made a man out of the shy, retiring, sad-eyed Frederick and girded him for the great challenge that was the horror of the Thirty Years' War. When offered the Kingdom of Bohemia, he vacillated, and took to his bed with the anxiety of responsibility. She coaxed and teased him into ambition, and asked why he had married a king's daughter since he dreaded being a king. She entered Prague well advanced in her fourth pregnancy in five years, at the head of eighteen coaches of her possessions.

Margaretha had named her baby girl Elizabetha, but she died. Perhaps Elizabetha would have been a queen had she lived. Perhaps the child in her belly would be another Elizabetha, Queen of America.

Margaretha dared to hope she was setting out for a queenly life in America. Sometimes in the dead of the night, after Georg had exhausted himself, she lay in a half sleep dreaming of sweeping down a grand staircase in a lacy gown with all eyes of the men below on her, pleased to see the anger and the jealous fright of their women. She had had the same dream with Gerhardt, but his dreams were of seduction, war, and perversity. When Gerhardt was killed in a duel, fought over a brother officer, she was both mortified and very angry with her father who had arranged a sick marriage with Gerhardt because he was military. She never forgave her father and had thought her life was over, so when Georg approached her father and asked permission to see her, she consented. Being older and a widower he seemed to exude the stability of life that she longed for after Gerhardt. And life was very hard for a widow, especially one that was alienated from her father.

While Margaretha was daydreaming, the captain of the bateau had steered them to a place where the river flowed serenely, winding its way through the landscape of pasture, forest, and vineyards. Rounding a bend in the river, sitting on a high promontory was a town that shone in the sunlight like a golden paradise. It was Marbach, where a toll was to be paid. As the bateau approached the town Georg was telling Eberhardt the story of his great-grandfather and pointing out the exact position by the river gate where he and his great-grandmother had camped during the winter of 1721. Georg was familiar with the town and had walked over the very ground he believed his great-grandparents occupied so long ago. It was important that his son should know his story.

The familiar countryside opened up to Georg like a ripe flower. So much of his life was tied to the towns along this river. Beitigheim was up the Enz a short distance on the left. It was here that his brother Jacob lived and where he and Maria were wed. It was a beautiful town but one of sad memories for him. Poor Maria. As the boat passed the mouth of the Enz, Georg was suddenly anxious about Maria's fate, and wondered if she was still alive. The last time he spoke to Jacob, she was still living with her father. He and Maria had a happy year or two, but her barrenness defeated him and after six years, he had had no heir. She was the first to go to the magistrate, but in the end, it was she who was found guilty. Because she was barren her father took her back, and for a while, Georg felt free, but he never got over the hurt.

The party spent the first night on the river at Mundelsheim, where Marlborough forged his Grand Alliance of Protestant Princes. The boat crew manoeuvred the bateau to a small jetty where there stood a small inn at the end of a road up the hill from the landing place. The captain was paid a fee to secure belongings, after which the emigrants walked to the inn and settled there for the night. The children were tucked into straw beds in the barn that was attached to the inn. Some time in the night it rained.

They were on the river early the next morning. The rain had stopped but the day was dark and foreboding. The boat crew manoeuvred around the bends in the river as it meandered through the low hills until they reached the town of Lauffen. The boat was steered ashore at Lauffen where a toll was collected. Taking overnight necessities only, the little band of travellers climbed the steep banks of the river past the church and the fortress to arrive at the Lauffenhaus, a guesthouse beside the road that wound through the centre of the village. Some of the bateau's number, worried about the expense, decided to camp in an open field at the edge of the few houses in that part of the village. Margaretha persuaded Georg to open his purse for a comfortable night in a proper bed at the inn. For Margaretha this decision proved to be an error, a mistake from which she suffered afterward.

The public room of the Lauffenhaus was a large space with the hearth at one end and a long table at the other end where the owner served beer and food to his patrons. A cookhouse where vegetables were prepared was at the rear. When Georg and Margaretha entered the room after putting Eberhardt to bed, meat was roasting on a spit in the fire pit. Curious eyes examined the newcomers. Now it must be said that Margaretha was a very attractive woman with her dark wavy hair, wide-set hazel eyes set in a narrow face with a straight nose, prominent cheekbones, a strong chin, and a full, sensuous mouth. She was somewhat taller than the average woman, and when she moved, healthy men imagined a fulsome body under her frock. Men and women both noticed her, but for different reasons. She had to be wary of unwelcome advances, which sometimes not only annoyed her but made Georg angry. At such times he called her a gypsy.

They joined the Ritter's, a couple from the bateau. During the meal, served by the surly owner, Margaretha noticed a man, heavy with drink, ogling her every move. His attentions made her feel very uncomfortable. She was frightened that Georg might notice, but soon the man rose from his seat, said something to the men at the table eliciting great laughter, and weaving across the room, left the inn. She finished the meal in silent contemplation while the men discussed plans for the next day.

After seeing that her son was safely asleep in bed with Paulus, Margaretha decided to walk in the village to make up for the long day of sitting in the cramped bateau. Outside, the sun showed to her only a thin orange crescent peeping over the hills across the river, and within minutes it had disappeared and darkness was creeping over the village. She walked along the road observing the few scattered houses that flanked it. After a few minutes she was feeling tired from her walk and she turned back toward the Lauffenhaus. It was now quite dark.

Suddenly, from behind a low wall made of stone, a man, in a surprisingly quick move considering his drunken condition, lurched toward the road. She immediately knew his intent. Frantically she looked for help but no one was about. Margaretha gathered her skirts to run but she had taken no more than a few steps when the man grabbed her billowing frock and dragged her down. He pulled her to her feet and dragged her, struggling hard, behind the wall. He pushed her to the ground and began to paw at her underclothes. She fought his hands, at the same time dug her heels into the soft earth, and pushed her body away from his. He lay on her, trying to subdue her writhing movements. She fleetingly feared for her unborn child but still she fought him with tooth and nail. She thought she would faint, as much from his body smell and his breath as from her efforts at fighting him. She kept struggling, ignoring the thought that he would choke her if she did not comply with his lust. He pulled the frock over her head. His odours no longer sickened her but now she could not breathe. He was choking her with both hands around her throat, leaving her arms free, and she beat on his head with her fists. At the same time, weak and breathless, she kept struggling and pushing backwards with her heels.

Almost exhausted, she made a final push, and in what she thought was her last struggle before having to submit, she felt a hard object under her left shoulder: a stone that had fallen from the wall. She clutched at the stone and with a final effort, for she was suffocating, she swung it in a powerful arc and heard a dull thud as it hit its mark. She hit the man repeatedly in a mad frenzy until he no longer moved. Extracting herself from the weight of his unconscious body, she ran onto the road and made toward the guesthouse, smoothing her clothes as she ran. It was only when she was at the door, quite breathless, that she calmed down, and had the suddenly frightening thought that she had killed the man.

Georg was sleeping soundly, apparently unworried about her. Furious at his lack of concern for her safety, she undressed and neatly folded her clothes. She sat in a chair next to the window for almost an hour. When she crawled into bed beside her sleeping husband she had lost her anger towards him and was, for once, thankful for the warmth of his body next to hers.

The next day was a horror for Margaretha. All day she expected to see a boat following theirs, full of friends of the drunken man whom she thought she might have killed. She was limp with worry when the boat reached Wimpfen, a place embedded in the folklore of Georg's family. She had heard many times the story of Georg's great-grandfather Jörg's battle wounds and Katarina's courage in rescuing him from the battlefield. Georg had tried to make Eberhardt understand the importance of this event that had taken place a century before. So as soon as they came ashore and set up camp in the early afternoon Georg took him, along with Paulus, to see the site of the battle. After more than a hundred years, there was no evidence of the battle, just a pasture for cows. Margaretha, tired from her day of anxiety, rested under a large hickory tree. She had told no one of her terror beside the stone wall, and as she sat in the shade, she prayed to God that the man was not dead.

The following day the hills became higher and the river became wider. The bateau with its passengers reached Hirschhorn late in the day. The town was high up over the river with the monastery and castle higher still, brooding above the town. From the river, it seemed it would be a tiring climb to reach an inn for the night, but the boatmen put into the beach on the opposite side of the river from the town, at a landing where there was a small inn. Again, as at Mundelsheim, the men and boys slept in a small barn. Pastor Blumgardt made sure the children were prepared for God before letting them sleep.

In the morning, the sun glistened off the spires of the churches of Hirschhorn, the whole town bathed in a soft glow, the houses of the townspeople pushed up against the castle fortifications and monastery, as if God would protect them if they were close to His house. Preparing to leave, a noisy argument broke out between Paulus and two other boys about who should sit in the bow of the boat. A slap to Paulus' ear by his aunt appeared to settle the matter, although he pouted until noon. By this time, the bateau had turned into the river mouth at Neckar Gemund, the captain explaining that the crew had to obtain provisions. The boat was beached near a covered bridge linking a small part of the town on one bank to the larger part on the opposite bank. The captain and crew disappeared and left the families, telling the passengers that they would not be gone more than one hour. Some sat on the boat while others went to the beach, and it being midday, prepared a hasty meal.

After two hours had passed it was clear that something had happened to the boat's crew. Four hours later, the captain returned alone, heavy with drink. He informed his passengers that they would stop here for the night. Georg, Leonardt, and Herr Gephardt were by now very angry, and were sure the crew was drunk. They talked of going into the town and dragging the members of the crew back to the bateau by the hair of their heads, but their more sensible wives convinced them to calm down. So, in the end, they acquiesced to the captain's suggestion that they spend the night on the beach. The women concurred quickly, knowing that if the men tried any overt force on the errant crew there would likely be a brawl, and the rest of the journey and the remaining days would be very unpleasant. Pastor Blumgardt objected strongly, invoking God's wrath on the captain and crew, but eventually sided with the women and accepted God's will as a punishment for the drunken crew. Leaving the captain with their belongings, which he promised to secure, the families, with much grumbling, prepared to walk into the town and find an inn for the night. With the church steeple guiding them, a small inn was spotted close to the rear of the largest church. Here they settled for the rest of the day, and after an evening meal slept in very pleasant circumstances, with the women and girls in one chamber and the men and boys in a separate chamber. Although the expense was greater than Georg liked, the night was quite satisfactory, and pleased Margaretha, who had been quite glum after the incident with the drunken crew.

All resentment faded the next day. A beautiful sight greeted the boat passengers as it turned round a bend in the river. Heidelberg was nestled between the river and the mountain with its great castle standing above the town, its turrets shining in the bright sunshine. The crew, seemingly unmoved by the beauty and history of the place, lowered the stayed mast so the craft could clear the covered bridge that linked the fortifications of the right side of the river to the town of Heidelberg. The captain's destination was not the main gate but a river port further along. As the boat cleared the bridge Margaretha could see, in all its beauty and impressions of imperial power, the castle and its adjoining gardens situated on the mountain above the town. She marvelled at the splendour of the place and could truly imagine life as the Winter Queen, bending the court and the Elector Palatine to her wishes. Georg saw the castle through less romantic eyes. For him it stood for exploitation and tyranny, reasons he had to leave his country to start a new life in an unknown, far-away land. At Heidelberg the passengers were to leave the boat, its captain and crew, and to arrange for another, larger boat for the first part of the journey on the Rhine as far as to Koblenz where they would change to a sailing vessel. Some Palatines would be joining the group of Württembergers at Heidelberg.

After three days at Heidelberg, Margaretha was ready to move on since Georg and Leonardt complained about the expense for her and Christina's comfort. Herr Eckardt from Esslingen had arranged for a larger boat with a mast and two sails, which he said was a suitable vessel for the currents of the Rhine. The boat had covered accommodation in the rear for women and children, and at the front for the captain and his crew, but the men had to make do as best they could. Everyone was pleased to be underway again, so early in the next morning, the baggage and enough food until Koblenz were loaded by his crew of three, on the orders of Captain Schwinger. The boat moved out into the river well before noon.

The boat entered the Rhine at Manheim and from there to Mainz the river flowed peacefully through a district of vineyards that came right to the river's edge. While Georg was paying the toll at Mainz, Margaretha told Eberhardt that it was here that Herr Johannes Gutenberg had lived, and it was here that Herr Gutenberg had made her bible.

After passing Rüdesheim, the river narrowed as it plunged between the Hunsrück and the Taunus mountains. The river turned and headed north and soon could be seen the white water that Herr Eckardt called the Binger Loch. Margaretha said it looked as if the water was boiling as it jumped and twisted its way through the notch.

At Bingen, Herr Eckardt, who, of all the passengers, seemed to know the river best, said that everything may have to be unloaded and the passengers walk to the other side of the reef on the tow path that river boat captains used to haul their boats upstream with horses. Making light of the danger of the rapids, Captain Schwinger laughed at Herr Eckardt and said he and his crew had gone through the notch many times downstream without capsizing. This did not allay Margaretha's fears. For her, the dark cliffs keeping the sunlight from the river made the wild, untamed rapids ahead look life threatening. She was frightened that the white water would throw the boat and all in it onto the rocks.

More passengers came aboard at Bingen until Margaretha thought the boat could take no more, but the captain kept taking on people so that the boat became crowded and uncomfortable. It was a heavy boat that left Bingen.

While the captain and crew were fighting the current to keep the boat from being pushed on to the rocks, the children oblivious to the dangers of the rapids, were excited by the sight of the Mäuseturm. Margaretha told the story of Bishop Hatto hiding in his mouse tower to the children. One little girl burst into tears when she heard that Bishop Hatto was eaten by rats for his sin of locking the villagers in his barn and then setting fire to it.

They entered a truly nasty section of the notch where the boat rolled from side to side threatening to throw its passengers into the foaming stream. Twisting and leaping forward, the craft was kept under control by the captain. True to his word, he managed to steer the boat, through the notch and past the Mäuseturm, which stood on the very end of an island in the middle of the river. Safely past the maelstrom, the river widened and far in the distance could be seen the Pfälzgrafenstein Castle emerging straight from the waters. Ruined castles rose up on the hills on the left bank; castles destroyed in the religious wars of a century earlier and by the armies of Louis of France when Margaretha was still a young girl.

Captain Schwinger steered the boat into Bacharach with its *weingartens* pushing right up the hill to the Strahleck castle above. He prepared to leave his boat, announcing that he would return early the next morning to continue down river. This caused great alarm since no one had planned for this. The captain was adamant, saying that he lived here and he had not been home to his wife and family for fourteen days. "There are inns here and my crew will stay on the boat to guard your belongings." There was much fury expressed by Herr Eckhardt and two other men, but eventually everyone calmed down and it was agreed that Herr Schneider would stay on the boat overnight to guard the guards. Magaretha told Georg that she would be willing to sleep on the boat since it was a clear warm night, so while Leonardt and his family went off in search of an inn, Georg made comfortable sleeping spaces for Margaretha and Eberhardt. As the moon rose over the river Margaretha marvelled at the heavenly dome of the starry sky, turning it into a silver ribbon that beckoned the little family into the future. Soon, with the gentle movement of the boat from the current, all fell into a comfortable sleep.

As promised, the captain came to the boat early the next morning. The passengers who had gone ashore showed up with the anger of the night before gone, hoping to get the journey over with. With hunger satisfied the journey was continued. At the *Pfälz* castle a chain was drawn to the surface to hinder their progress and a toll was collected, the money supporting the burgers of Kaub. There was grumbling about the expense of the toll, but humour restored everyone when it was noticed that an outhouse was attached to the rear of the castle. The edifice truly looked like a stone ship striving against the current.

As the boat approached the Lorelei rock, a discussion broke out as to whether the Lorelei was a water nymph who sang songs to draw mariners onto the rocks or a beautiful maiden from Bacharach who jumped into the roiling stream just as the ship of her loved one was being wrecked on the rocks. The argument had no winner. Passing the rock safely with deft manoeuvring by the captain, Koblenz was reached with no further incidents.

It was necessary to hire a scow at Koblenz because the promised sailing vessel was not there, and after two days of waiting Pastor Blumgardt arranged with a Captain Hager for passage to Rotterdam. To Margaretha it looked like a very uncomfortable vessel. The accommodation was a large covered area at the centre of the boat wherein the passengers had to make do with whatever they could arrange for themselves. A rude fire pit with a few pots and pans and other utensils were available for meals. There were sheltered areas at the bow and stern for protection of the sweeps and quarters for the captain and crew. Margaretha was sure a child would fall over the side at night and be lost. She was not happy with the arrangement, but it seemed the only possible means to complete the journey.

During the time at Koblenz, Georg purchased food for the rest of the journey. It was necessary to put up at an inn with much grumbling at the expense from Georg and the rest of the men. The first night at Koblenz it rained hard and Margaretha was pleased that she had a dry bed after the rough nature of sleeping on a boat. On the third day, again threatening rain, they left Koblenz. Captain Hager was a difficult man, with a surly demeanour, and a patch on his right eye that made him appear all the more ferocious. Cousin Elenora thought he was a bandit and was fearful of being robbed and put ashore on the riverbank to be eaten by wolves. Paulus, behind the captain's back, pulled his cap down over his eye and pretended he was a soldier, brandishing his arm up and down as if skewering a Frenchman. Margaretha said Herr Hager was probably dishonest, and was not pleased to put the children's safety in his hands, nor indeed all their possessions, but there was no choice, they must get on with the journey.

They were with Captain Hager for a week and three days on the Rhine, stopping for tolls and to purchase fruit. The adults enjoyed the landscape and told stories to the children, stories of the legendary heroes and heroines who lived along the river in ancient times. Margaretha knew most of the legends of the river and enjoyed telling the stories to Eberhardt and his cousins and the other children who sat at her knees and listened with awe. One story she told was of Siegfried the Count of Andernoch, whose castle passed shortly on the left bank after leaving Koblenz.

> *Siegfried was a Christian who, being pious and a warrior, joined the Crusaders and went off from his wife, the beautiful Genofeva for a long period of time. When he returned, Golo spoke to him of the unfaithfulness of his wife while he was absent. The slander of Golo made Siegfried very angry and he banished Genofeva from his sight. Genofeva fled to the forest of Laach, where she gave birth to a baby boy. So, for many years Genofeva and her son lived in the wild forest with its robbers and wolves and other beasts. One day Siegfried went hunting in the remotest part of the forest, and lo and behold, he came upon the very place where Genofeva and his son had been living all these years. It was the son whom he had never seen. Siegfried, being pious, knew it was a miracle that his wife and child had survived in the wild all those years. Seeing the evidence in the child that Genofeva had not been unfaithful, he bore her and his son to his castle.*
>
> *There was joy in Andernoch. The palace rang with revelry, the city blazed with light, and on a pike atop the Roman gate could be seen the traitor Golo's head.*

Thus, the rest of the lazy voyage on the river passed with story and song. Many of the passengers had not been on this river of legend and they marvelled at the richness of the towns and the beauty of the castles on the hills, many now in ruins. Although there was much rain, making everyone uncomfortable, the time passed pleasantly. Near Godesberg the rain cleared, and at sunset the Drachenfels ruins was like a golden shrine pushing upward to heaven itself, an image that Margaretha talked about the rest of her life. This monument always brought her back to her roots in a beloved Germany.

Half way up the craggy rock was a dark cavern called the Dragon's Cave where the fire-breathing monster, half-beast, half-reptile, lay in wait for sacrifices of maidens to be brought from the surrounding towns. "My grandmother used to threaten me when I was bad by telling me she would send me off to be fed by the dragon of Drachenfels unless I behaved." The rock held no romance for Georg, as it seemed to do for Margaretha.

A whole day it took at the frontier and then they were in the flat lands of the Low Countries. With the news that the end of the river voyage was close, the men began to organize their families and possessions, and everyone began to put their personal belongings together for embarkation. While not expressed aloud, everyone was glad to see the end of Captain Hager, who had not been a cooperative master but kept to himself, making his presence felt only when one of his crew needed disciplining. Margareha's fear aside, he had proved honest enough and carried out his contract dutifully, if with no pleasure.

One morning after breakfast Captain Hager announced that Rotterdam would be within sight before noon. Margaretha was relieved at the near completion of the journey from Koblenz in a very uncomfortable boat with its irascible captain. About eleven o'clock, the sweep steered the scow around a slight bend in the river, and about half a league distant appeared the town of Rotterdam. The town itself was hardly visible behind the port full of ships at anchor, with its church steeples seen only through the rigging of the ships. The white sails stowed on the yards glistened in the sunlight, making a virtual forest of giant Christian crosses. Margaretha saw the sight as a gift from God, His promise of good fortune on the sea voyage ahead.

As the scow weaved through the anchored ships, everyone wondered if each ship that passed would be their ship. Approaching the main wharf, Margaretha recalled her cousin Frieda's letter from America. She had memorized every word and had passed the letter to Georg before leaving Poppenweiler, hoping that the contents would help him get through the problems of negotiating for a ship and provisions for the ocean voyage. She knew Georg had shown the letter to Leonardt and she prayed the two brothers were well prepared to negotiate a passage with favourable conditions.

To the Württembergers, the landing place was chaotic, small boats going to and fro, hawkers selling their wares and everybody shouting. Various inns, close to the port of Rotterdam, had boys at the wharf enticing passengers on incoming boats to hire them to carry belongings to their inn. The two Waeger families hired a neatly dressed, yellow haired youth of about thirteen. Georg and Leonardt loaded their possessions on the boy's cart and they followed it along a cobbled street to a small building, which sported a weather-beaten sign naming their temporary home as *Geervliet Huis.*

This pleasant inn was home for a week, during which Georg and Leonardt set out each morning to arrange passage to America. On the last day of the week, the brothers returned to the inn and announced that they had obtained passage to sail in three days. During the ensuing excitement the men took their wives aside and gave them the bad news; the families would not be together for the voyage. To get passage to New York within a reasonable time it was not possible to accommodate them all on one ship. The *Anne* and the *Amsterdam* were to put to sea early in the new week, but it was only possible to provide for one family on each ship. The next sailing from Rotterdam to New York was in three weeks, so the men had made the decision to go earlier because of the expense. Georg and his family would go in the *Anne*, a British ship, while Leonardt and Catherina and aunt Barbara and the cousins would go in the *Amsterdam*, a former Dutch East Indian man-of-war. Pastor Blumgardt would go with those assigned to the *Anne.* "We leave in three days."

Margaretha spent the time before they sailed in a state of anxiety. Until now, she imagined she could always turn back, but the finality of cutting her roots for good was now upon her. She tried to keep herself occupied with the trivia of re-arranging their belongings and spending as much time as she could pretending to laugh with her sister-in-law, who seemed to accept the arrangement as inevitable, and to see the joy in each day. Margaretha also took long walks along the river, keeping to the barge path for horses hoping to avoid being attacked, her memory of the terror in Lauffen still haunting. Walking through the trees disturbing all the small creatures in her path freshened her mind and calmed her heart, but at night the old fears of leaving her homeland for an unknown future came back to her.

For Eberhardt, the journey on the river took away all his childhood terrors. He was in a new world of excitement and anticipation and when he saw the big black ship with sticks that looked like God's crosses and which seemed to soar to heaven that was to take him to America, he could hardly wait to explore its mysteries.

At mid-afternoon on the day before the scheduled departure Georg and Margaretha said their teary goodbyes to relatives, and after a prayer seeking God's blessing and protection, they parted at the wharf, perhaps never to meet again. The ferryboat was making its way out into the harbour towards *Anne*, while Margaretha was still mourning for Christina, Barbara, and the children as if they were gone from her life forever. Her son was excited, shouting with joy and jumping up and down between her knees, threatening to expose her underclothes.

She looked up at the slowly approaching ship bobbing slightly in the surge created by the river current meeting the incoming tide. From the small ferryboat, the ship looked large; larger than anything she had seen on water. In truth the *Anne* was a smallish three-masted barque owned by Ogelvie and Brown of Portsmouth, a cargo vessel adapted for passengers due to the increasing trade in refugees going to America. It had brought a cargo of skins, cotton, and tobacco from Mexico and New York to England. It was returning to New York with a cargo of German refugees. It was a small ship for the Atlantic crossing, as its passengers would discover in the coming weeks. The *Anne* was just over 100 feet in length and 180 tons burthen. She was built in Portsmouth in 1720 and had her original copper bottom. Her rating for seaworthiness was "good." Although large in Margaretha's eyes she was much smaller than the *Amsterdam*, which was at this very moment receiving the other half of the family. Perhaps after all it was fitting that Leonardt, with his wealth, would choose the larger ship.

The furled sails of the *Anne* nestled on the yards glistened white in the sunlight. The ship was bonded to earth-bound man by the mass of ropes freshly tarred, running like black sentinels from the masts and yardarms to the ship's hull. The name *Anne*, freshly painted, was sprawled across her bow. The most arresting feature of their new home was the carving of a half-naked woman with her hair streaming along the bulwarks, and proudly showing her bosom to the sea. Margaretha was startled by this display of woman's nakedness, but she was secretly pleased. A half-wild, gaily-coloured, naked woman would transport her to America. She and *Anne* together would master the hardships of the voyage to come.

A stair-like ladder was lowered from the ship and the passengers scrambled aboard, the women with as much dignity as possible while managing their children. One little boy about four years old began to scream as if he was destined to the fire pit. His mother roughly pushed him up the ladder, obviously having faced his screaming many times. The crew carried the very young children aboard. The passenger's belongings were hauled to the ship's deck by ropes and slings manned by several sailors. Twelve families went aboard the ship, and once on board all clustered beneath the main mast waiting for everyone to assemble. A young man with blond hair and beard, dressed as an officer in the military, met each of the new arrivals. When all were assembled he addressed them, his words translated by Pastor Blumgardt: "Your quarters are amid-ship below deck with access by the hatch you see between the two sets of steps to the quarterdeck. The quarterdeck belongs to the captain of the vessel and you are not to go there under any circumstances, unless invited by the captain. The captain's cabin is below the quarterdeck. That area of the ship is sometimes known as the aftercastle. If you now turn toward the bow of the vessel you see the fo'castle. This is the sailors' quarters and under no circumstances are you to enter. You are standing in the waist, which is available for your use for taking air and exercise, except during bad weather when you will not be allowed above decks. Now if you follow me below I will show you your quarters."

The little group's belongings had already been piled at the bottom of the companionway steps on the floor of a large room with a long eating table. At the aft end of the salon sat a giant stove, now cold. At the opposite end of the room, past the table and through a door, were sleeping quarters, consisting of two lines of cubicles along each side of the ship. Margaretha was surprised to see that some of the cubicles were occupied, having been taken by families that had previously boarded. The blond man said a few words to Pastor Blumgardt who in turn announced that he was responsible for assigning the cubicles. He asked the group to stay in the salon and to keep with them only those belongings needed on the voyage, as the rest would be stored below. The adults were to line up in front of him.

Each family was directed to a space with two narrow sleeping platforms one above the other. Margaretha said, "It is very small." As Georg stored the necessities for the voyage under the lower platform, Margaretha surveyed their new home. In the small space there was a wooden frame with a removable basin for washing, a pail for waste, a very small table and a foldable chair with a canvas seat. Straw littered the floor. A heavy, dark curtain hanging from the deck beams was all the privacy they were apparently entitled to. Margaretha's immediate concern was for her son. The sleeping platforms were very narrow, hardly wide enough for adults let alone children. The only possibility was that Eberhardt squeeze in with her on the lower platform, which was slightly wider than the one over. She must talk with other mothers to see what sleeping accommodations they were planning to make for their children. Since it was late in the day, the family retired to the salon to have the meal of bread, boiled eggs and sausage brought with them from the inn. Cook had prepared a kettle of tea. No one knew that first night the filth, sickness, fear, and outright terror they would need to endure before leaving the ship.

5

THE SAVAGE SEA

On the 29th of June, at six o'clock in the morning, riding an ebb tide and favourable river current, the three-masted barque *Anne* sailed out of Rotterdam for America. The silence of the early morning was shattered by the boatswain's call, "All...ll hands on deck... ahoy there... sharply, men!" Almost instantly the sailors scurried about, the mates shouting strange commands from the fo'castle and the after deck. The second mate, Mr. Johnston, called for the rowers from his port watch. On the fo'castle deck, the first mate stood over ten sailors loosely grasping the anchor rode while four men braced the windlass. The pinnace rowers in place, the anchor was slowly hoved-to the bows with much grunting and chanting. "Heave-ho... heave-ho... heave-a-ho-yo!" The pinnace rowers, under the supervision of the second mate, towed the *Anne* past the cluster of ships at anchor, and when clear of the ships towed it out into the river. The pinnace was hauled aboard to the chanting of the sailors as the ropes hummed and the mate shouted, "Heave... heave... ho... heave!" At the same time, sailors scrambled aloft to loose the sails. Captain Mills stood beside the helm and quietly gave the orders to Mr. Johnson, who, through his clasped hands, shouted the order to the men on the yards. "Set topgallants!" In unison, the sails were loosed and the men on the deck braced the yards to catch the early morning breeze. The wind from the southeast raised small wavelets that shimmered in the light of the rising sun that was just appearing over the sand dunes. The few trees that the burghers nurtured to keep the dunes from washing away in the violent storms that ravaged the coast in winter looked like shadowy skeletons at the start of the new day. The waves appeared to be laughing at such a small vessel manned by fragile men heading out into the cruel sea.

Slowly the ship began to move in the water. The sailors aloft crawled along the foot-rope of the topgallant yards, down the shrouds and along the topsail yards to make ready to loose the topsails. "Set the topsl's!" By the time the yards were braced and the sheets belayed, the *Anne* had the bone in her teeth and was making substantial way. The captain looked over his shoulder at the rain clouds moving in and apparently decided the south-easterly wind would hold until they reached the open sea. He ordered the staysails set.

"If this wind holds we should be at sea by early afternoon." The captain seemed pleased as he spoke to Mr. Roberts, the first mate.

"Aye, sir."

"Hold to mid-channel, Mr. Roberts."

"Aye, sir." Mr. Roberts voiced his opinion that they would be extremely fortunate to cover the seven leagues to the Hook on a fair wind without a tow or lay-over.

The captain was pleased to have Mr. Roberts aboard. The mate was a sailor from Bristol, England who had left the Royal Navy in 1728 when his ship was decommissioned. The Navy assigned him to a post in London because Britain was in a period of peace on the high seas, but he was unhappy at a desk; he wanted to remain at sea. The British trade with America was very active, so Mr. Roberts left the Navy and joined Ogelvie and Brown. He was berthed with Captain Mills, a twenty-year veteran of the Company. The mate's Navy training was a complement to the captain's more relaxed approach to discipline, which had occasionally gotten him in trouble. This was their third trip together, and Captain Mills had found the mate to be dependable and able to discipline the crew without generating trouble. As the captain turned to leave the ship in the mate's hands, he said, "By the by I notice some of our passengers crowding around the bottom of the companionway steps. If they wish to come topside I would permit them. Do you think you could make them understand?"

"Aye, sir. Cook was with Marlborough and can speak German. I will send him to them."

On second thought, believing he might have less trouble with the passengers if he spoke to them himself, the captain said, "No, I will see them myself. Assemble all the family heads, the pastor and the cook at eight bells, and I will address them." With these orders he went to his cabin.

The mate went to the after-castle, and shortly he reappeared with a short, fat, ruddy-faced man dressed in dirty pantaloons and a bright red jerkin that matched the colour of his face. He carried a smile on his lips as if it was permanently etched there. He filled the companionway opening and stood blinking for a moment to adjust his eyes to the gloom below. He spoke in very bad German to the small group of people standing there, informing them of the captain's orders. Margaretha was one of those at the companionway steps to get fresh air, and when she heard cook's words she went to find Georg and her son.

At noon, the Germans gathered in the waist awaiting the captain's appearance, anxious because few knew the reason for the meeting. They stood respectfully, quietly waiting, as was their habit. Soon the captain appeared at the breast rail of the quarter-deck with the cook and first mate. He threw his right arm forward in a gesture meant to demand attention and began to speak slowly to allow the cook and Pastor Blumgardt to find the words in German. Cook relayed as best he could when the captain paused and the pastor helped to make sure that

117

everyone understood. The words of Captain Mills were:

"Gentlemen, in a short while we will be at sea. It will be a long voyage with much hardship. Your wives and children will find it extremely difficult, as the life here is very different from what they have experienced. Some of you may not survive, so what I say must be taken very seriously for your own safety, that of your loved ones, and indeed the survival of us all. You must be aware of the rules under which we sail and keep your people from jeopardizing not only his own well-being but that of us all. The captain will not tolerate bad behaviour.

"Below us are stored bales of cloth for the American market. At Plymouth we will take on more cargo, but you will not be allowed ashore and you must not hinder the work of the crew while we are berthed there. This is mainly a cargo vessel, but the owners, recognizing your plight, have contracted with the government of England to take you to British America. Thus, we have in the past few weeks, converted the mariner's quarters to make it more acceptable to families in transit. While your accommodation may not meet your expectations, we are a small ship, and you must be aware of the circumstances of adding twelve families to such a vessel. You have the freedom of the salon, the starboard aft quarter of the fo'castle deck, the main deck, and the heads. Under no circumstances, unless invited, are you to be found on the quarterdeck. You must go below in a storm, and in no way hinder the work of the ship's company. I am sorry that at such times we must close the hatches, which you will find very uncomfortable, but it must be done for the safety of us all. Lamp oil is not to be used during sleeping hours. You are responsible for your own victuals. The provisions you have brought aboard are stored in the room behind the fire hearth at the port side of the bow on your deck, and are available at the discretion of the captain. You can also purchase provisions from the ship's stores if available. The galley will be available to the women after the crew has been served, but when the weather is poor, there will be no fire.

"There are French and Spanish privateers on the sea and we may need to defend the ship. For such purpose we carry six guns, a quarter of the complement the ship was originally designed for, but when the *Anne* was sold to the present owners and converted for merchant use, most gun positions were lost. In the circumstances of an attempted boarding by privateers you and your families must go below and under no circumstances leave that part of the ship. Mr. Johnson is your advocate and any communication you may wish with the captain will be delivered to him.

"Now, for the ship's log, I must confirm your actual presence on board my ship. Mr. Johnson will go among you and check off your name, the names of your family members, as well as your estate, against the ship's manifest."

The captain then turned to Mr. Young, the cook, and asked if his message was understood. Receiving the reply, "Aye, sir," the captain went to his cabin.

Some of the women and children watched the scene from the fo'castle deck. The breeze carried the words of the captain and those of the cook to them. Margaretha could understand most of the message, and she listened as Mr. Johnson called out the names of the passengers, many names that were familiar to her. The business being ended, the men drifted apart and began to return to their families. Many of them gathered around the companionway and Pastor Blumgardt suggested a prayer of thanksgiving. He expressed his favourable impression of the captain and thanked God for deliverance into his hands. Then he asked God for a safe journey and the Lord's protection, "In the name of Jesus Christ, our saviour." When the prayers were finished most of the passengers remained on deck.

As the Dutch shoreline drifted past on both sides Margaretha was surprised that the ship had not yet left the river. Georg explained that the sea was still some distance ahead. The clouds grew thicker and the sky looked like rain so people began to leave the deck. Georg was quiet as he led his family below to begin to face the coming ordeal.

The wind increased and the rain began. That evening, Captain Mills made an entry in the ship's log for the first day at sea:

29 June, 1738 - 4 o'clock p.m. - Weighed anchor, Rotterdam 6 o'clock a.m. on ebb tide and following current. Cloudy. Wind SE at F3-4. Course WNW at 4 kts. All passengers accounted for. Cleared Hook at half three o'clock p.m. Course WSW 5kts. Wind backing and freshening. Mercury falling. - 8 o'clock, p.m. ESE wind rising, est. Half gale, F6-7. Heavy rain. Reduced sail starboard watch. Set topsails, reefed fore course, fore topmast stays'l and spanker for o'night.

Margaretha woke from a dream in which a young prince with a feather in his cap carried her to his castle high up on the Heidelberg. She felt guilty dreaming of a handsome prince. Since the captain's discourse at noon Georg had said little. During the whole period of their marriage, Georg had spoken about going to British America. But now, facing the very reality of death for all of them, fear had taken hold of him. Georg was afraid, and she had learned that his fear brought anger. Over the years she had controlled his anger by providing relief through his loins. She hated it and thought God punished her for making babies without love. But it made life bearable. Only Eberhardt was made in love. She dearly wished for another love child, a little girl; perhaps God would let her live. Perhaps in British America her wish would come true.

She felt a violent movement of her sleeping platform. The boards beneath her were heaving and rolling. She thought the blackness of the cubicle would smother her; each breath served to magnify the fury of the motion. Then she was aware of the smell of fresh vomit, piled onto the smells of tar, mildew, ancient excrement and the sickness of those before; smells that seemed to permeate the very wood around them. The ship's owners had placed straw on the planks of the sleeping stalls and had supplied buckets for excrement, but the vomit from several of the stalls was making her feel sick. She tried to shut out the thought of having to lie sick in the mess.

She strained to hear Georg breathing, but the noise from the workings of the wooden ship made her give up. He must be sleeping, she thought, oblivious to the chaos engulfing them. To affirm that she was safe in this black, undulating hole she felt for the side of the ship and discovered it was wet. She was wide-awake, her mind racing. It flew to the wet wall. Was the ship sinking? She whispered a prayer, "Please, God, keep us safe." She couldn't face the thought of a watery grave in this cold, desolate, Godless place. If they were sinking she wanted to be with her family. She determined to wake her husband and raised her body to go to him. Suddenly she was floating free above the sleeping platform and in the next instant came crashing down on her belly. The nausea that had been gathering in her gut now spewed forth into the black void. Mortified, she settled back in her sleeping place and lay there, waves of terror surging through her, until the change of the watch when the hatch opened and she could hear the crew carrying on as normal. This gave her peace and she got a few moments of sleep before the day's activity began.

The German women rose at daybreak, even though their quarters were in deep blackness, obeying some internal timepiece rather than the presence of daylight. Lanterns were lit and the women applied themselves to cleaning up the mess from the night just past. Frau Götz was of the organizing kind and she spoke to Margaretha about a plan for the duration of the voyage. The ship was still pitching and rolling, but by the light from lanterns the two women decided that the soiled straw on the floor had to be removed. Also, there was the problem of the slops. At this point in their planning, Frau Ernst and Frau Schatzel joined them. Frau Ernst brought the news that the Reinhardts were already weak from sickness and were causing a mess in their sleeping place. She suggested the captain be approached to make him aware that they intended to keep the place clean. The group voiced their concern to Pastor Blumgardt, who was already cleaning the straw from his stall. Frau Götz voiced her concerns very forcefully, "Our quarters smell worse than a pig-sty. Unless we get some fresh straw we will all be sick unto death before this crossing is made." Pastor Blumgardt suggested a delegation go to the captain. The decision was made that he and Margaretha should approach the captain. She covered her head with a clean bonnet and with Herr Blumgardt set out to find Mr. Thomson.

30 June, 1738, 8 o'clock a.m. - Wind veering. SSW at F 5-6. Sea running high. Harden sails at 4 bells, larboard w. Mr. Roberts reports leak in fo'castle trunk, and stopped up. Shook out reef in forecourse. Set jib and staysail. Course W to Riv. Thames. Mr. Thompson advised delegation of passengers wish to see the captain re. cleanliness. - 8 bells, starboard w. - Met with preacher and a Frau _____. Gave permission to keep quarters clean, but when straw is gone, it is gone. Refused permission to wash their deck. Said necessary to keep cargo dry below deck.

1 July, 1738, 8 o'clock a.m. – Wind veered o'night to NW, at 15 knts. Sky clearing with heavy seas. Course SSW to Strait of Dover with wind on starboard quarter. Plan to make Strait at ebb tide. All sails set and pulling.

Many of the German families were on the fo'castle deck to observe the white cliffs of England. The ship was trouncing along like a rocking horse driven by a steady breeze from over the quarter. The clouds were breaking up above the spars, and ahead lay blue sky. It was enough to make them forget the shambles of the last two nights below. As the day wore on, the Germans began to figure out ways they could help each other. Some people were quite sick and needed fresh air. The Reinhardts seemed no better; they lay abed all day and no amount of coaxing would get them on deck. Everyone was aware of the need to look after the small children, who in their exuberance sometimes went too close to the rail and had to be admonished and kept close to their mother's skirts.

Daily household chores were carried out without fuss. Pastor Blumgardt held a short religious service just before noon, and this too became part of the daily routine of the voyage in fair weather. During the day, the south coast of England was clearly visible, and much of the social discourse of the group involved speculation about the small communities they passed. Once the captain appeared on the forecastle deck and enquired about their state, and although some did not comprehend his words, they were grateful for his obvious concern.

That evening, after the others had gone below, Georg and his son lingered at the rail under a bright moon in a clear sky. Beyond the sea, the lights of England twinkled in the darkness. For the first time since leaving Württemberg Georg told his son that he had good feelings about going to America. Eberhardt did not know what to make of his father's words.

The next day at about two o'clock in the afternoon the crew of the *Anne* brought the ship to anchor in the busy port of Plymouth, England. She lay at anchor for ten days, first to take on provisions and cargo, and then to wait for favourable tide and wind conditions. The Germans were not allowed to go ashore, which, in spite of their grumbling, brought them together as a group and gave them substantial time to become accustomed to life on a small ship. During the time at anchor, they developed a cooking rota and allocated the chores that needed to be done each day. Margaretha found that she had skills of organization that had never been required of her, and the task of scheduling made her as happy and content as possible under the circumstances. She also was elected as a go-between the Germans and the captain. Eberhardt had found a young friend,

Heinrich, and the two of them were always together somewhere, roaming about the ship away from her care, if not concern, so her boy caused her very little trouble.

Margaretha was exhilarated. She found a coil of ropes on the port side of the foredeck where she could sit in the mornings and watch the scene on the wharf below. The traders haggling with the ship's agents over the sums to ship their goods, the seamen trudging back and forth on the gangplank with the goods, and the men in dandy coats and hats who were undoubtedly the owners. There were children running in and out of the mob below to get a few coins in whatever way they could. Occasionally a fight broke out and a policeman would suddenly appear as if from nowhere and drag the miscreants off by the scruffs of their necks.

While Margaretha was enjoying her days in port, Georg was having the opposite reaction. Since he had told Eberhardt of his pleasure about going to America, he had been quiet and lethargic. He was absent from the fo'castle deck during religious services, and afterwards Margaretha would find him in some remote corner of the vessel. He ate little, and more telling than all these unusual actions for him was the fact that he did not bother her at night. For the first time in their marriage, she did not have to indulge his passion in bed. But some nights she thought of the way it was before Eberhardt.

Those days in Plymouth were sunny and hot. About noon each day a breeze would spring up from the west and blow over the hot land mass. In late afternoon, the wind would disappear. Sometimes about midnight the wind came up and blew towards the sea. Curious about this, Margaretha asked a crew member about the wind changing direction between day and night and the sailor informed her that the winds were called sea breezes in the daytime and land breezes at night, that they were local winds and not a reason to go to sea. "The winds in the strait may be completely at odds with what you see here in port." So they rested at anchor until everyone was anxious to continue the voyage, even Margaretha, who had tired of the inactivity.

One day, in the early morning hours, a different kind of wind began to rattle the rigging and the ship began to shudder in the gusts. At daybreak, shouting came from the quarter deck. "All hands for away!" "Make haste, ye hardies!" "All hands to sails!" "Mr. Thomson, see your men to the windlass and heave-to the anchor." "Set topsails." Then shortly, "Back foretops'l!" "Bo'su'n, see to those larboard braces." "Break out the anchor!" "Set jib and staysail!" The ship began to move through the water, then the thunk of the anchor being lashed to the cathead could be felt, and the *Anne* was finally under sail, bound for America.

12 July, 1738, 8 o'clock ante meridian. Weighted anchor half four a.m. Wind ESE F6. Cloudy. Course SSW to Ponta del Gada. Full rig flying. Noon measure on Mr. Charles new sextant device gives lat. 49 degrees plus 50 min. est. longitude 4 degrees plus one half degree. Lizard Head 15m. to starboard. 8 o'clock p.m. Wind backed to ENE and freshening. Rain.

Clewed up royals and forecourse 4 bells. Mr. Thomson reports one of pas-
sengers missing. Name of Hans Gerber, bachelor, about 34 years. Preacher
said he was unhappy; suspect he left ship just before sailing from Plymouth.
No further action to be taken.

13 July, 1738, 8 o'clock a.m. Wind NNE F6. Rain. Noon. lat. 49 degrees
N. est. long. 6 degrees W. 8 o'clock p.m. Wind F7 Cloudy. Course SSW.

14 July, 1738, 8 o'clock a.m. Calm. Mercury falling one inch per hour.
Furled tps'ls at 9 am and brought tps'l yards down.

The Württembergers were on the fo'castle deck, just beginning their noon prayers, when the storm struck. Some had wanted to cancel the service when they saw the sky to the west; an indigo slash mottled with crimson hovering above the horizon. The whole ship seemed to vibrate with a low moan from wind in the rigging. The pastor began the service with a prayer for deliverance. He announced to the gathering that Herr Gerber was gone from their midst, having abandoned the voyage at Plymouth, and a prayer was said for his eternal peace. "*I will Arise and go to my Father, and will say unto Him, Father, I have sinned against Heaven and before Thee, and am no more Worthy to be called thy Son. Dearly beloved brethren, the scripture moveth us in Sundry places to acknowledge and Confess our manifold sins and Wickedness: and that we...*" A gust over the port side caught the petticoats of the women and lifted them high in the air so that white undergarments were visible. Some men lost their hats before they could secure them.

Margaretha, grasping her petticoats with one hand and Eberhardt's arm with the other, wondered aloud where Georg had gone. She had ceased to expect his presence at the daily religious gatherings, but suddenly she was concerned for his safety. Her concern was torn from her by a second tug of wind in her petticoats, followed almost immediately with a blast that wrenched her bonnet to the back of her head and tore through the rigging of the ship with a loud roar, twisting the yards and loose canvas. A limp sail exploded with a bang like a cannon shot. Mr. Roberts was shouting from the foot of the main mast, "You! Go below... quickly now! Hurry... all below!" He was waving his arm to the Germans who had quickly begun to disperse and were rushing to the companionway. The men of the watch were running to various parts of the deck to make certain the hatches were closed. By the time the group of worshippers reached the stairs, they could barely keep to their feet against the shrieking wind. A sailor was shouting and waving his arms, urging them to hurry before he closed the hatch. Reaching the familiar blackness of the salon, the hatch immediately banged shut behind the last straggler. Before any further action was possible, the deck planks disappeared from beneath their feet, pitching them across the rough pine to crash into the wall of the ship.

Margaretha clutched Eberhardt's clothes and when they stopped mother and son lay huddled in a ball wedged between two timbers of the ship's hull. Margaretha held Eberhardt tightly, afraid of losing him. He was shaking with shock and fear, but had not yet begun to cry. Somewhere close to Margaretha's elbow someone was screaming, an adult voice. She was sure they were dying and began to pray and ask forgiveness for her sins and for God's redemption in her death. She prayed for the soul of her son. Where was her husband? She did not want to die alone.

Her panic gradually abated and she became aware of the noises about the ship. She was alive. The distant roar of the wind, the vibration of the ship that seemed as if might shake itself apart, and the moaning and shouting of people in confusion and pain would be awful in daylight; in the blackness of the bowels of the ship it was terrifying. A child, close by, was piercing the dank air with its screams. Between the screams of the child, shouting and cursing men's voices were coming from some distant corner of the salon. The sailors on deck were running and shouting to control the ship.

After what seemed several minutes the ship was moving slowly in the water. As it moved it began to right itself. A lantern was lit. The scene in the salon was of utter chaos. In the circle of light from the lantern stood Frau Schatzel, who had had the presence of mind to grasp the vertical wooden struts supporting the deck. Frau Schatzel was clinging to the post with the fear of death in her eyes while most of the passengers and a few sailors were sprawled in a tangle of arms and legs between the deck and the hull of the ship. A small child, wedged under a pile of bodies, was screaming. As the ship righted, the people on top of the pile were able to crawl on their hands and knees, then to gain upright positions and begin to relieve the weight on those below. Someone found a coil of rope and spread it between the posts in the salon, making it easier to clamber upright. However, about a dozen people did not get up, including Frau Duchardt and old Frau Müller.

Just when the ship appeared to be upright, it rolled in the other direction, although now with the life-line and light from the lantern most managed to keep to their feet. In the dim light from the swaying lantern, Margaretha scrambled for the life-line, pulling Eberhardt by the neck of his shirt, all she could find of him in the darkness. After a few minutes of being thrown to and fro, the rolling subsided a little and the sound of the water on the hull told them the ship was gathering speed.

When Georg appeared, Margaretha was angry with him for deserting her. He was silent at the time, but afterwards told the story of his near death experience. It was a confession of sorts.

"When the squall hit the ship I was in the main starboard chains, watching the storm roll across the angry, black sky. There was not much wind, but even a man living on the land all his life knew heavy weather was on its way. I admit I was fearful for my life."

Georg's life had been guided by understanding the vagaries of the elements, but the weather he had known had not been life threatening. On this alien world of the sea, his fear stemmed from not knowing what to expect. He did not have Margaretha's faith to help conquer his fear. For several days he had been assessing his situation to try and understand how he should respond to the new circumstances in which he and his family found themselves. Margaretha seemed almost to enjoy the hardship and filth and seemed to find power in this, while he felt unable to rise above the degradation. It was shame that had made him seek solitude in the chains, his melancholy relieved by the buffeting of the wind and the erratic movements of the ship.

"I felt the first gust and heard the mate shouting at those on deck to go below, which convinced me that my life was in danger. I grasped the lanyards and was scrambling for the rat-lines to climb back on the fo'castle deck when the ship seemed to roll on top of me. I saw the green water of the sea rushing toward me but was helpless to do anything but hold tightly to the lanyards. I curled my arms about the bundle of ropes, wedging them into the crooks of my elbows. When I felt one of my feet slip off the chain plate I thought I was going to be carried away, but I curled my leg around the sheave and braced for the shock that I knew was coming. The cold green water rolled over me and then I was being dragged through the water with such a force that I was sure I could not hang on. I buried my face in the rope, hoping this would somehow keep the water from my nose and mouth. I was under the rushing water for what seemed an eternity."

When he felt he could no longer hold his breath, the sea gave him up. He climbed into the waist of the ship and hung on for dear life. It was only when the companionway to the fo'castle was opened that was he able to get out of the storm and find his way to the salon, only to be greeted by more chaos. At the end of this discourse, Margaretha so was moved by his trauma that she kissed her husband on the cheek.

K nowing her family was safe and unhurt, Margaretha staggered along the salon deck to see what she could do for Frau Duchardt and Frau Müller. Frau Duchardt had befriended her when Georg was in prison and she was particularly concerned about her condition now. There were two other women trying to stem bleeding from her mouth and ears. The bedclothes were soaked with great amounts of blood and Frau Duchardt's skin was ghostly white. Despite the women's attempts at stemming the flow of blood, Frau Duchardt died that night. Old Frau Müller never recovered from shock and died the next day. One man, one woman and four children injured that morning survived.

The storm raged for three days, three days of misery below decks. The hatches were not nailed closed, but Mr. Johnson told the Germans they were not to go on deck or they risked being washed overboard. The ship rolled from side to side and pitched so wildly that it was not possible to move about without using the life-line the sailors had rigged. Water came in through seams in the hull and dripped through the decking until the bedding became wet. The German women worked tirelessly to keep their cooped quarters clean and reasonably dry. Even with their efforts the smell of mould joined those of urine, vomit and feces. Sickness among the children was a never-ending problem for the mothers. As Margaretha said, "We are only a few days from Plymouth and already sickness and death have visited us. God help us all!" During the storm Frau Asche delivered a baby girl. Fortunately, one of the women had done midwifery, and Margaretha, who helped her, said of her, "She saved two lives this day."

It was early on the third day of the storm that the captain summoned Margaretha to his cabin to report on the condition of the Germans. For the first time she took Eberhardt with her. The storm had abated a little, but the seas were still heavy. The water was crashing over the bow and sloshing across the deck of the waist, making it difficult to keep from being swept into the gutters. Margaretha found a lanyard, strung by the crew for their safety, and, tugging the hand of her son, pulled him to the after part of the ship. Windblown and feeling unwomanly she staggered into the gloom of the officer's quarters with wet feet. Making her way around the officer's dining table, past the cabins of the surgeon, cook and second mate, she and Eberhardt entered the captain's cabin. Captain Mills sat at the side of a long, intricately carved table framed by the light from the windows behind. He was dressed in an old naval uniform. Eberhardt's eyes went to a long cutlass mounted over a cabinet at the end of the table. The captain greeted Margaretha with a slight bow, but did rise from his chair. He pointed to a chair on the opposite side of the table and asked her how the Germans were making out. Margaretha had practiced a few words of the captain's language in preparation. She told him it was difficult to keep their area clean and dry, and about the sickness caused by the filth below deck. When she tried to report on the deaths he raised a hand and said, "I know. I am sorry. They will be buried at sea as soon as we have a fine day." Margaretha had no more to say and prepared to leave his presence.

While Captain Mills and Margaretha talked, Eberhardt wandered about the cabin under the close eye of the captain. Captain Mills, sensing the boy was intelligent with a curious mind, and to please his attractive mother, said to the boy, "Would you like to learn the way of a ship?" The boy did not know how to answer, so he looked to Margaretha, who nodded. "When my duty allows I will summon him and we will do some work with the sextant and the ship's log. He will like that, I think. In the meantime, tell Mr. Johnson that he will allow the boy to see the ship when it is convenient for him. But, he is not to ask. Is that clear?" Again Margaretha nodded. He stood, signalling the end of the meeting, and then to Margaretha he said, "Madam, I will try to get you some assistance to make the rest of the voyage more comfortable, but we have not made much progress to date." He walked to the windows and pointed to a line on the horizon slightly darker than the sea. "That is the coast of England. The storm has driven us back." When they left, Margaretha was weeping silently.

16 July, 1738, 8 a.m. On 14 July, 1738 at noon, the ship was struck by a line squall from the west with unusual force, the first blast struck her broadside and she broached to. The fo'ard and the main courses both split, making the ship almost powerless as the spanker was furled. The jib and staysails pulled the ship out of the broach and we were righted. Shook out the spanker for balance. Almost continuous squalls drove the ship back towards Plymouth. This morning we were able to see land, bearing ENE. A conference with Mr. Roberts and Mr. Thompson ensued in which we came to agree that the landfall was Lizard Head, a point not possible to mistake in fair weather, but we are hindered by mist and flying sea. Wind is veering to the north and the ship is in no immediate danger from the lee shore. If wind backs, we must run to the Bay of Biscay. Sea still running very high and waves sweeping deck. One sailor lost, Danial Bronston, from the topsail y'darm. We tried to find him for several hours with no success. May God rest his soul! A funeral will be held when fine weather next blesses our little company. The Germans suffered greatly and many are injured and sick. Two of their elders died from injury and fright. We must thank God the ship is safe, and we see no permanent damage. Mr. Johnson brought German boy for lesson. Taught him meaning of some terms from the logs. Anne is now skipping along to the SSW under a F6 NE fair wind.

It was a time of mourning below deck. After the storm, the ship's surgeon came to the stalls to remove the bodies of Frau Duchardt and Frau Müller. The Germans refused to give them up. Pastor Blumgardt, intervening, insisted that the bodies of the women had to be properly respected, mourned over, and prepared for their final rest in the dark, satanic waters. The surgeon retreated while the dead were washed with some of their precious drinking water and dressed in their finest clothes, for which they would have no more use. Pastor Blumgardt then said a prayer over the women and the congregation sang prayers for the souls of their dead sisters. Afterward, the sail-maker covered the bodies with worn out sailcloth and the men helped to remove them to a resting place in the hold until burial could take place. The Germans gathered in the salon where the women served tea and biscuits.

At last, as if rid of a heavy weight, the lady *Anne*, pushing a roll of white water, took off toward the Azores in a gusty breeze as if she had been given a new life. The singing of the wind through the rigging accompanied the shouting of sailors, and the sight of acres of bulging white sail above brought on a feeling of euphoria for both the crew and the Germans. The women cleaned up the mess below while the sailors on watch repaired sails, wrapped and served rigging and scrubbed the deck until it was bone white. The remaining healthy Germans, seasickness now mostly a horror of the past, came out into the waist and found places to sit in friendly clusters. The men smoked their pipes and the women talked among themselves while knitting, crocheting or sewing their family's garments. The ship with its white wings tapering to the heavens made a sparkling sight as she pitched into and out of the white-capped waves that rolled beneath her bow. The bosomy woman of solid oak that guided her course seemed happy.

Occasionally a white-topped rogue wave splashed across the waist and filled the lee scupper with green water, causing great excitement among the women as they danced away from the foaming water to keep their skirts dry. Porpoises began to congregate and frolic in the bow wave for an amazed and delighted audience. There were flying fish, many of which landed on the deck and were stranded there, which gave lie to the story that they could truly fly. The cook collected these each day and produced fresh fish for the crew's kit. As promised, the captain had instructed Mr. Johnson to allow Eberhardt privileges, and it was during this period of fine weather that he began instruction on the ways of a sailor's life and his ship.

This lazy life continued until about noon on the third day after the storm when the order was given by the captain to "wear" ship, and with much running about, shouting and singing, the ship turned across the wind. The sailors, singing in unison, "Heave... heave... heave," on the starboard braces while the rest of the larboard watch freed their lines from the belaying pins at the foot of the main mast. *Anne* was now into the Portuguese trades and racing south and west at eight knots.

On the 20th day of July, the captain and crew of the English barque *Anne* and all the Germans who were able gathered in the ship's waist for the funeral of Danial Bronston and the two German women, Frau Barbara Duchardt and Frau Anna Müller. The bodies had been tied tightly with hemp twine to protect them from the wind and to give some dignity to the dead, even though the canvas coffin did little to preserve the remains from roving sharks. The captain came down from his quarterdeck and said a prayer in his language. Pastor Blumgardt then said a prayer in German. *"Forasmuch as it hath pleased the Almighty God in His great mercy to receive unto Himself the souls of our dear sisters here departed: we therefore commit their bodies to the deep, looking for the resurrection of the body when the sea shall give up her dead, and the life of the world to come, through our Lord Jesus Christ. I heard a voice from heaven, saying unto me from henceforth, 'Blessed are the dead which die in the Lord: Even so saith the spirit, for they rest from their labours.' Amen."*

After the prayer, Mr. Johnson tipped the gurneys, committing Frau Duchardt and Frau Müller to God's grace in the hereafter. Since the ship's carpenter had only had time to make one extra gurney, the sailor, Mr. Bronston, was jackknifed off the port bulwark by four of his shipmates and was catapulted by the curve of the ship's hull into his final resting place with a small splash that remained with the motionless ship for a few moments. The wavelets from the splash soon dissipated and became part of the vast ocean that swallowed the soul of Mr. Bronston. The Germans sang *We Hail Thee Now*, while the sailors, not knowing the words but knowing this might be their fate someday, stood with respect in their places.

17 July, 12 noon. Gale winds from NNE. Clear weather. Latitude, 46 degrees, 24 minutes. Est. Longitude, 9 degrees, 24 minutes W.

18 July, 12 noon. Winds veer to SE at force 6. Cloudy and rain. Tack to SW by W.

19 July, 8 a.m. As yesterday. 12 noon. Wind backed to NW at 4 about 10 a.m. Clear sky. Backed to S at 11 a.m. Latitude, 45 degrees, 10 minutes. DR distance noon to noon 118 n.miles. Est. Longitude, 10 degrees, 40 minutes

20 July, 12 noon. Calm. Sunny. Funeral for Mr. Danial Bronston and two German women at change of watch. All hands attended. Captain said English prayers. Mr. Blumgardt gave Lutheran prayers.

29 July, 1738, 8:00 a.m. Sunshine and fair winds from the NE at force 5. Continue SSW by S to Azores, and Ponto Delgada for potatoes and port. Also 6 casks of water for crossing. Cook wants more meat, but not sure Owners would authorize expenditure. Also fresh vegetables. At noon Latitude 40 degrees 21 minutes, DR distance noon to noon 130 n.miles. Est. Longitude 25 degrees 32 minutes. Mr. Young gave German boy instruction on use of lines, braces and sheets.

A smudge on the southern horizon brought the sleepy lookout on the topmast trestletrees to his feet with a shout of, "Land, ho!" All but the off-duty watch gathered forward to see the hump of land emerging from the sea on the starboard bow. It was the island of Pico, recognized instantly by the seasoned sailors from its distinctive peak banded by streaks of wispy cloud shining in the early morning sun. Captain Mills stood at his usual station on the starboard quarterdeck, looking anything but pleased. This was not his intended destination. He was perhaps a whole minute and one half, some thirty leagues west of where he was supposed to be. He decided to go into de Horta on the island of Faial, just west of Pico, where he would re-provision the ship and take on fresh water.

With land teasingly close, the fair wind failed. At midday a calm stopped the ship, to be replaced by a slight breeze from the islands of the Azores. Thickening clouds appeared high overhead and by evening the breeze had freshened from dead ahead, threatening to push the ship back to where it had been. At the change of the evening watch, Captain Mills gave the order to heave-to. The *Anne* lay-to for two days, with everyone on board becoming irritable with land so close, yet not attainable. On the morning of the third day, a breeze from the northwest pushed the ship into the bay of Faial, where the port master came aboard and piloted the ship to an anchorage.

At three o'clock in the afternoon of August 3rd they dropped anchor in twenty fathoms of water, about one half mile from the town. The port master came aboard to collect the port fee, and after determining there was no disease on the ship, he clambered into his launch and was rowed back to port.

The ship being cleared, the on-duty starboard watch was given permission to go ashore at eight bells. Its work of bringing provisions aboard would begin the next morning. Mr. Johnson went ashore with the boat to wait on the Governor and enquire about the ceremony of saluting. On his return, he announced greetings of welcome by the Governor, but no return of guns was in order.

Several of the Germans lined the rail of the fo'castle deck, the part of the ship closest to the town, and talked among themselves about what they could make out of the nature of the place. The Portuguese town of de Horta sat at the top of the bay, flanked by two castles, one on each of the headlands. A continuous wall of stone from the castles to the town gave the residents security except from cannon balls.

Behind the seawall stood several religious structures, the Jesuit College, five monasteries and eight churches. The whitewashed residences were plain in their appearance and looked quite inhospitable with the window shutters closed.

Several ships lay off the town; an English brig, a Portuguese barque, an American sloop from the Amazon, and others that no one could identify. Two Portuguese whaling ships were very evident by the odour that wafted over the surface of the anchorage as their crews moved the cargo of whale oil to agents in the town. As the sun set over the western headland, outlining the dark crenelated castle walls in a delicate pink, the scene seemed serene and beautiful after a month on the rolling, pitching, wet and stinking ship at sea.

The *Anne* lay at anchor in the Bay of Faial for ten days while she took on water, wine, flour, corn, and potatoes. While in port, the ship's crew dined on fresh beef, fresh vegetables, and fresh fruit from the Island of Pico. The able-bodied male passengers, but no one else, were allowed to go ashore to supplement their provisions. There was no wind and it was very humid, causing great discomfort to the passengers left on the ship.

14 *August 1738, 8:00 a.m. Depart Faial Bay 7:20 a.m. Falling tide. Winds NE 11Knts, Bar. rising. High clouds, clearing. Est. Faial Lat. 38 deg. 31 min. S. Long. 28 deg. 48 min. W. Course SW 270 deg. Had Mr. Young and master Eberhardt working the log for DR.*

Well-provisioned and with a rising breeze from the northeast, the *Anne* set sail on a falling tide. Clearing the cape at the westernmost point of the island, Captain Mills set the ship on a course to the southwest to find the southeast trade winds that would drive them to America. With the trades, he hoped to lay Bermuda and continue north to New York on the Gulf Stream. His main concern was running into a hurricane off the coast of America.

When *Anne* left the island of Horta the German women had thoroughly scrubbed the salon and cleaned the sleeping quarters, but, in spite of their efforts, it was the weather that would dictate the state of the ship below decks and above. One storm and all their work would be for nought.

After leaving the Azores, the weather was fine and the passengers spent the days on deck, mostly on the fo'castle deck. The *Anne*, fully rigged to catch any breath of air, slowly made her way south and west. After ten days, the wind dropped completely, leaving the ship sitting on a flat sea. Some of the crew took to the pinnace and tried their hand at fishing. They caught a giant sea turtle that the cook prepared, resulting in a riotous supper with loud laughter and rum-induced singing drifting up through the fo'castle companionway. During the night, the captain could feel a surging of the ship and knew she would soon be in the southeast trade winds.

The next morning at dawn, the wind began to blow out of the southeast and increased during the day. The *Anne* flew toward the setting sun with all but the stunsails set. After two months at sea, the Württembergers quietly gave thanks to God in their innocent belief that the worst hardships were behind them.

For a week, the fair weather drove the ship west. Even the old and infirm were on deck to enjoy the warm sunshine. The sea, which the Germans had seen in all its rage, was now providing the ship's passengers sights and sounds they had not experienced so far on the voyage. The children laughed at the storm petrels dancing on the waves. The passengers lined the bulwarks and watched tuna chasing herring, which flew out of the water to escape only to be caught in the air by shearwaters. The porpoises were now so familiar to the passengers the children had given some of them names. Flying fish landed on the fo'castle deck by the bucketful, which the sailors, who had light duties in fair weather, let the children collect. One day a pod of whales heading north crossed the bow of the ship.

Margaretha and Frau Götz, with whom she had formed a sisterly bond, sat at the catheads at night and watched the silvery backs of the porpoises and the phosphorescence that played in the the bow waves as the *Anne* ploughed through the water. They counted stars, and became friends with the bosomy maiden who pointed toward their future. They called her *die Wasser Nymphe*.

The lazy days at sea were short-lived. After ten days of fair weather, the glass was falling. High, wispy clouds floated overhead, harbingers of foul weather. The next day the barometer had fallen six points and thick dark cloud covered the whole sky to the horizon, denying the mate his daily sun shot. A squall was developing off the port beam. The barometer was now falling one point every hour. The wind was backing to the south. All hands were called out to reduce sail. The sailors furled all square sails, flying only a jib, a main lower staysail, and the mizzen spanker.

That night the storm came down in all its fury on the fragile *Anne* and raged all through the night. The ship bucked storm winds and monstrous seas. Waves washed over the ship, clearing everything that the heavy weight of water could loosen. Sailors had strung lifelines fore and aft, but only the helmsman and men of his watch who were needed to control the ship ventured on deck. When the fore mast staysail was torn to ribbons, leaving the ship unbalanced, the captain ordered the starboard watch to bring the *Anne* into the gale and heave-to. The ship wallowed in the troughs lying a-hull, and waited out the tail end of the storm.

The storm's fury lasted four days; four days of force ten winds, mountainous seas, and deluges of rain.

Hatches were nailed shut during the storm. Everyone below huddled in cabins and prayed; sure their fate was a watery grave. All hope of hot food was dashed by the cook, although he managed to make tea using the flame from a lamp. Because of the pitching and rolling of the ship the passengers were hardly able to get to the salon without being thrown against a post. Three men were badly hurt trying to get food for their families.

Pounded by wave after wave, the main deck seams began to leak with the twisting of the hull, even though the port watch had recently caulked them. So, all along the lower deck, water began to drip into sleeping quarters, making it almost impossible to keep dry. Added to the misery was the smell. The slops were not able to be sent above regularly, except during an occasional lull when the bo'sun lowered a wooden barrel to collect the excrement that had accumulated, sometimes for as long as two days. Sickness became part of everyday life. Old Herr Schmidt, a Palatine, found his gums swelling and his teeth coming loose. It was the first evidence of scurvy on the voyage. Georg went for the surgeon, who gave Herr Schmidt a navy concoction, but it seemed to have no effect. Little Anna Hertz, four, caught a fever and died before the storm was over.

Margaretha was tormented by fear for her unborn child. She had told no one yet of her condition, but she was afraid her secret would become evident if they did not reach America soon. She was restless, beginning to accept the life of the sea, and she wanted to get out on deck and breathe fresh air again. Driven by necessity and pride, Georg went about helping wherever he was useful. When the storm finally abated, the wet, battered, sick, hungry, and filthy Württembergers emerged from their prison, to be greeted by a cloudy sky and moderate winds. The ship was still moving violently beneath their feet, but they could stand and move about. They congregated on the fo'castle deck and said prayers, led by a dishevelled Pastor Blumgardt.

The *Anne* encountered two more storms before land was sighted, but none as harsh as the one that, the captain told them later, almost sunk her. Dead people were dropped into the water almost every day.

On the long voyage Margaretha had become aware of different degrees of blackness in her living quarters on the salon deck. During the daylight hours on a fair day when the companionway hatches were open, it was possible to distinguish the activities of her fellow passengers, but during a storm when all hatches were belayed-to, no light penetrated the dank gloom of the corner where she rested. Gerog had purchased candles in Rotterdam but they were of such poor quality that they lasted barely an hour and were used only at mealtime. Sometimes the galley stove gave off a glow, which provided some light and made the space actually comfortable. On a dark, stormy night the blackness was complete, but after so many days in such close quarters she could sense the mood of the ship and her fellow passengers.

One morning, just as the blackness of was giving way to the first light of day, a shout came filtering through the heavy planking of the deck. Margaretha was not able to hear the words, but she knew instantly that land was sighted. All the previous day the Germans had talked about nothing else. People were stirring and whispering, the excitement of the women and children was sweeping the deck at the prospect that this miserable voyage was to soon end. Many, who in private cursed the very day they left Germany, felt relief that the ordeal may soon be finished. Even those who appeared to enjoy the voyage in spite of the hardships, wished to end it. Many were on deck, not having been able to sleep. The crew, confined on a small ship with their smelly comrades, was excited at the prospect of going ashore to taste the delights of civilization after almost two months at sea. The shout from the trestletrees changed the ship's company from a mood of anticipation to one of action, marking the beginning of the end of the voyage.

Margaretha gently shook Eberhardt awake, and dragged him, still half asleep, to the fo'castle companionway to join those who were already on deck. A slight breeze was blowing from the starboard quarter, with the ship carrying full sail before it. She was heeled slightly, requiring Margaretha to plant her feet solidly on the sloping deck. For a brief instant she saw the beauty of God's creation, the last vestiges of the moon throwing the full white sails into relief. The movement of the ship through the water made a sound like the waterfall near her home where she used to steal away from her parents and stand naked under its cooling spray. In leaving behind the storms in which the little barque had plunged, rolled, and twisted like some savage beast, joy possessed Margaretha. They had made it! After the sickness, death, hunger, filth, and terror of the journey, she could finally allow herself to believe it was over and she could dream of a new life in a new world. She lifted her constraining petticoats and strode to the high side of the deck with long, deliberate steps, pulling her boy after her.

She was able to find Georg, who was standing at the forward starboard rought-ree rail peering toward a faint light that was just visible on the horizon. As her eyes adjusted to the image, someone said, in English, "It looks like a ship burning." This set off a murmur amongst the crew, and suddenly an argument was in progress about whether it was ship burning or a lighthouse. But soon, the men had to turn away as they had duties to attend to. This left room at the rail and Margaretha looked around Georg's shoulder at their new homeland. As daylight moved toward the ship and its people, a faint grey line appeared off to starboard that looked different than the waters of the sea. Margaretha was startled to find land beside them, as she had expected it to appear over the bow of the ship. Then she remembered leaving Rotterdam and watching the security of the land drift beside them for two days before the vast ocean, with all its terrors, confronted the little ship and its precious cargo. Perhaps New York was like Rotterdam, some distance up a river. It was then she realized the voyage was not over, and she lost some of her initial enthusiasm.

As the sun rose over the taff rail, the light breeze disappeared. All morning, the ship appeared to sit motionless on the surface of the sea with landfall no closer than it had been at daybreak. Margaretha's spirit was soaring as she prepared the family's belonging for leaving the ship, yet her enthusiasm dulled as the ship seemed to sit still with America getting no closer. She told Eberhardt to be patient for a few more hours, but her words were lost on him; unlike the adults he was sad to see the end of the voyage. He had learned some of the ways of a ship and wanted to be a sailor when he was old enough and strong enough to survive the rough life.

The ship was slowly approaching the new world on the current of the flood tide. About noon, the tide began to reverse and to avoid being pushed back the captain ordered out the long boats. With the mates shouting and cursing, the strong oarsmen of the *Anne* towed the ship forward, and using the advantage of small local breezes the barque was worked along the southern coast of Long Island.

At sunrise the next day, an opening in the coastline appeared to indicate a broad river valley. A small breeze was blowing from the northeast and the ship's crew set to work to harden the sails to the wind so that the barque could sail into the estuary. At about eight o'clock, a tip of green was observed jutting into the river, which the first mate declared to be the British Colony of New York. As they rounded the point to port, the first signs of civilization in this new world were an old windmill and a fort. The ship dropped its anchor in the waters off the small settlement of New York at noon on October 12th, 1738.

After the sails were furled, the ropes coiled and belayed, all passengers were allowed to go on deck to see their new home. Some were sick, some were lame, most were stiff from the long confinement in such a small space. A child had died during the night, a little girl who would never see the new world, never feel joy, never marry a frontiersman, nor have children that would create a new civilization. Her father stayed below with her, cursing the circumstances that brought him to this tragedy. All the others, with the exception of old Frau Trescher, went on deck and clustered around the bow rail to see, hear, and smell their new home.

Word spread that the *Anne* was sitting off Fort George, the fortifications protecting New York from the Dutch and the French. The Germans were told they would be confined on the *Anne* until the quarantine officers and the Governor's officers gave the captain permission to lower boats and take the passengers ashore. "It might be some time before the paperwork is completed for those who are healthy, and possibly even days for the sick and dying." Margaretha was very disappointed at this news. Her twin emotions of anxiety and anticipation frustrated her new-found sense of adventure. Nevertheless, she steeled herself to accept the inevitable, because the Germans were in no position to influence events. Her interest turned to the other ships sitting at anchor. One of them looked like the *Amsterdam* but she could not be sure. Georg thought it was the *Amsterdam,* and they asked a prayer to God that Leonardt and his family were safe and had survived the voyage without death visiting them.

She asked Mr. Johnson permission to approach the captain. He returned shortly with a positive answer and escorted her to Captain Mills' cabin. He was siting at the table with some papers, and when she entered he looked up with a friendly greeting. "What is it Frau Waeger?" She made a slight bow in deference to his station and said, "Captain, I hesitate to intrude into your busy life with a small request, but I am very anxious to let my sister back in Germany know that my family has arrived safely in America under your guidance and skill." The captain stood up and directed Margaretha to a chair at the end of the table. "Thank you for those kind words." He waited for her to speak.

"I have written a letter to my sister and I would be pleased if you could post it when you arrive back in Rotterdam."

"Well, I have been instructed to ship lumber to Liverpool on my return voyage. If it would help, I would be pleased to post your letter in Liverpool. It should arrive safely in Germany."

Having troubled the captain with her homely task she could not now refuse his offer, so she pulled the letter from the sleeve of her blouse and laid it on the table. "I thank you for your kind offer and trust in God that the letter from Liverpool will reach my sister in due course." Looking down at the table to avoid his eyes she said, "Also, thank you for your kindnesses to my son during the passage."

At these words, Captain Mills, somewhat flustered said, "It has been a pleasure to know you and the boy. Your boy is well instructed by Mr. Young and could almost ship out as a midshipman!" When she looked him full in the face to show her gratitude he said, "I wish you the best of good luck and happiness in America." It was Margaretha's turn to be flustered when he extended his hand in the English style to grasp hers. She allowed him to touch her hand, and with a slight bow prepared to leave his presence. He escorted her to the door and opening it said, "Goodbye, Frau Waeger. I will do my best to deliver your letter." She was blushing as she joined the other passengers to disembark, but in the general excitement of going ashore, no one noticed.

Shortly, a boat appeared alongside the *Anne* with two men in uniform and one man dressed like a gentleman carrying a black bag. The three men climbed aboard via the rope ladder that had been dropped from iron hooks clutching the topgallant rail and now lay dangling alongside the hull of the ship. The men were British colonial officers and a doctor. Margaretha observed the men in the red, white, and gold uniforms and seeing the look on Georg's face knew that the sight of a man in a uniform similar to these along a dusty road long ago was the reason the three of them were standing here on the deck of a British ship preparing to begin a new life in a British colony.

After a discussion between Captain Mills and the colonial officers, the captain sent orders for Pastor Blumgardt to join them in the Grand Salon. After what seemed an interminable wait, the preacher came and told the men to join their families and their belongings. Each family member was to be examined. The Götz family was first. When cleared for landing they were directed to take a position near the rope ladder for disembarkation. The families were examined one by one and instructed to wait with the family Götz. As the group became smaller, the Ernst family was detained and sent below. At this development, Margaretha's fears of being left on the ship heightened, and she was in a fever pitch of worry as the last but one of the group went to be examined. Then her family was examined. The doctor asked many questions in German and physically examined Georg and Eberhardt, but did not touch Margaretha, except to look into her mouth. Then, they were free to go ashore.

When all were gathered, a sailor that the ship's company called Blackbeard opened the rail, and the Germans were sent down the rope ladder and into a waiting boat, women and children first. When the boat was loaded except for the officers and the doctor, who remained to do their duty with other passengers, the rowers took over and the boat turned toward the fortification sprawled along the point of land. Smoke was spiralling from many chimneys and the sight of this prompted Margaretha to say she looked forward to again having her own hearth with her family enjoying the comforts of home, however crude it might be. She praised God for deliverance from the brutality of the past months.

It was late autumn when a tattered whaling schooner sailed into Nantucket with survivors from a three-masted barque that one of them, a bearded seaman, told his rescuers had, "run into the Devil's own gale." The story quickly spread on the docks of Nantucket that the barque *Anne*, carrying lumber bound for Liverpool, had gone aground off Horse Island, and the fierceness of the storm, "broke her up." Most of the crew went down with the ship except for some half dozen men who were still alive. They were rescued by a long boat from the trader *Greit Halverstolm* and brought to the infirmary. Two of the sailors died there, but the mate and two others survived to sail again.

In June of the following year a man from the Hudson River schooner *Wind-song* stepped ashore at Kip's Landing and enquired after the settlement called the Witaberger Lands. Getting a satisfactory answer he hired a riding horse from Heideger's Stables and left town. That afternoon the same man was heard to enquire after the residence of Mrs. Waeger, one called Margaretha.

Margaretha was spinning linen yarn when the man came to her door. At first she thought him a stranger, but on looking into his face, he seemed in some way familiar. He introduced himself. "I am Mr. Johnson, the former first mate of the *Anne*. I believe you sailed in the *Anne* to America from Rotterdam."

"Ah! Mr. Johnson. I see it is you. What brings you to my door?"

Her thoughts flashed back with fondness for the help Mr. Johnson had given her during that terrible voyage, and she was about to invite him into her home when caution made her hesitate until she learned the reason he was standing at her door.

He held out to her a letter wrapped in waxed linen cloth and said, "Your ship, the *Anne* foundered on the rocks off Horse Island in a storm. Capt'n Mill's chest was crushed when the mains'l yardarm broke loose. He died while the ship sank beneath him. But before the end came he passed this letter to me and said, 'Mr. Johnson, I am gone. But I have fond memories of a Mrs. Waeger, a woman with a small son who was one of our German passengers on my last voyage to New York. Her name is Margaretha. If you survive I would wish that you deliver this letter to her so that she might know that it was not possible for me to accomplish my undertaking to her.' He was very agitated and anxious that you receive the letter."

Margaretha hardly recognized the letter she had written to her sister, it seemed so long ago. The letter was smudged with the marks of dirty fingers, water stained, and yellowed with one corner torn away. The sight of the battered missive brought tears to her eyes. Through her tears she observed that Mr. Johnson was embarrassed, and, wiping her eyes with her apron, she invited him into her house for supper.

He graciously declined saying, "I must catch the evening schooner back to New York Port. I am now Master of the frigate *Amanda* that is anchored there, and I must return before the day following the morrow when we sail to New Liverpool on the coast of Nova Scotia, where there is trouble from American pirates. But I have not yet fulfilled my promise to my dead capt'n until I have seen your son." Holding out a thin canvas covered book he said, "Capt'n Mills was fond of your boy and told me he spent many hours pouring over the ship's log with him. As the *Anne* was sinking Capt'n Mills said to me, 'The Owners will believe this to have gone down with the ship. I would like her boy to have it.' He gave me the log. He seemed to have Devine assurance that I would survive to carry out his wishes."

Margaretha took the book and said, "Eberhardt is in the woods hunting with his father, but I will give him the book which he surely will keep safe. I am extremely grateful for your captain's treatment of my son during the voyage; and for these gifts, which I will treasure the rest of my days."

"Today I have fulfilled a promise to my dead Capt'n, which I must admit has been a burden on my mind for several months. Good day to you madam."

Disappointed, but grateful to this man whom she hardly knew, Margaretha bid him good day. As he turned, about to leave, she whispered, "I will pray to God for your safe journey, and for the soul of Captain Mills." Then he was gone, leaving her with an empty heart.

Before retiring she re-read the words she had written to her sister about her safe arrival in America. Then she lodged the letter between the sheaves of her bible, and placed the ship's logbook beside it.

BOOK TWO

THE PIONEER

"For men being all the workmanship of one omnipotent and infinitely wise Maker- being all equal and independent, no one ought to harm another in his life, health, liberty, or possessions." — John Locke, An Essay Concerning The True Original, Extent, And End Of Civil Government.

PROLOGUE

I n *The Pathfinders*, using Margaretha Waeger's old Bible and faded letters, I brought members of the Waeger family from the hills and valleys of Carinthia to the mouth of the Hudson River in America. Then I encountered a conundrum. The last entry in Margaretha's Bible read: *Johann Eberhardt Waeger m. Magdalena Kerver, 1760, Emigh's at Backway, Dutchess Cty.* The entry told little of Eberhardt's life.

Eberhardt had been anxious to have his story told and I had promised it to him, but the story had to come to an end with the last page of Magaretha's Bible, or I would need to begin the hard work of putting flesh on his bones in some other way. During the nights I spent with him in his cabin so long ago, he told fragments of his personal journey to Ganneious, but they were only verbal scraps, and in retrospect not very coherent. So in my frustration I spent many months following his footsteps in America. My sorties to the State of New York to try and pick up a thread of the story gave me some context to his life in America, but did little to discover the man himself and his personal story.

As I was ruminating on my quandary I again heard from my ancient grandfather. It was many months later while I was in Kingston vising a childhood friend that I heard his voice calling me to his side. My friend Harvey and I had much in common, having grown up in the same village and it was while Harvey told of his ancestor, one of the Palatines that settled in Ireland before coming to America, that I heard in his monologue the voice of Eberhardt. When it seemed no longer impolite to escape from the verbal clutches of my friend, I went to Eberhardt's cabin in the wilderness of Ganneious.

I stood on the road leading to the log cabin hoping to see someone, but there was no life about. There was no smoke from the chimney and all looked cold and abandoned. The roof of the animal's shed had collapsed. The iron kettle used to scald hogs and make soap was tipped on its side and held water from recent rains. It was a place of ruin and I wondered if my intuition had deceived me.

The door was unlatched when I walked into the room that was still familiar to me after those feverish nights waiting out the storm several months ago. Adding to the sense of abandonment was the lack of a fire, for though it was still summer the day was chilly. Wondering whether or not to leave, I heard a voice, faint and reedy, coming from behind a blanket strung across the corner of the room. "Is it you, my grandson?"

I found the old man, sick and lying in a pile of confused blankets on a small bed. He had grown a large beard, which emphasized the whiteness of his face. His hair was matted and greasy and I suspected lice were growing in the long tresses flowing over his dirty pillow. It was clear that Hanna was not looking after her sick father.

As I stood before his bed, he roused himself on an elbow and his dull blue eyes suddenly shone with a spark of energy. He was gruff. He came quickly to the point of his call to me in these, his last days. "Have you made my *ototeman*?"

When I read aloud the words I had written to my ancient grandfather he was silent for a time. Then he snorted, "My daughter Hanna is now married to her man. My second wife, Elizabeth, has gone to heaven. I am alone with thoughts of my death. As I lay on my straw facing eternity I recall the old Indian's words: *That a man is a mere shadow of himself without a story, a rock on which to cling in the tumultuous stream of history.* You tell of Margaretha and Georg, but not of me. Old *Deyohyogo* said I should know my *ototeman*, but you have said the story of others."

"But grandfather" I objected, "Your story carries all that comes before you. Remember what *Deyohyogo* said, *A drop of water carries the story of the stream.* I used Margaretha's Bible and her letters to piece together the lives of your ancestors, and now I want to hear your story." He did not seem surprised that I had mentioned Margaretha's Bible.

Pushing aside his blankets, he sat up. "I was very young when we set sail on the ocean, but in the months at sea I lost my childhood. The sea was a coming of age; as if my childhood was snatched from the ship's deck by a huge wave and drowned in its dark waters. In port, the *Anne* was a thing of beauty, but once upon the deep ocean she showed her true character. She was a living monster in the fierce storms, threatening every second to drive herself and all her doomed innocents into the bottomless depths to be devoured by the creatures that lived in those black waters. My years have dimmed much of the terror of the Yankee war, but the horrors of the ocean voyage remain always.

"It was the dead and dying. Some nights the horrors and stench of the ship are still with me and I wake up in a cold sweat. In my nightmares, I vainly try to climb out of the waste pit behind our house in the old country, and for many years after the voyage I had nights dreaming of the ooze that kept trying to suck my head under its foul surface. The endless rolling, pitching, squeaking, and banging of the ship, the vomit and screams of the injured and dying people were horrors, but worse was the sickening smell of the dead before the crew could come and take the bodies away. Afterward, the women were left to clean the mess from the beds, the final resting place of the dying: an obscene and tragic ending for innocent farm people who were highly superstitious, and fearful of a watery grave.

"It was the dead children, some of my own age, who seemed to stink the most after two days lying in their own waste. There was much wailing of the women when a sailor would finally come to carry off a dead child and wrap it in a shroud of worn-out sail cloth hoping to see the corpse, full of disease, dumped into the sea without further ceremony. There was always a struggle from the Germans to delay the burial until they could gather together to properly send the soul to God before the small body was thrown overboard to be torn apart by sharks. Those beasts seemed always to be following the ship waiting for human flesh and a small morsel would be quickly gone in a grisly feeding frenzy. My nightmares continued until mid-life, when a pile of bloody bodies, dead and dying in the mud of some battlefield or other, replaced the waste pit."

I interjected, "Was it all blackness for you? Margaretha's story of the voyage was not so grim."

"In the first days at sea, I made friends with three other young boys called Matthias, Heinz, and Johannes, and before many days passed we had found a hideaway in the forepeak with the coiled ropes and the folded sails. We recited the legends that had been passed down by our kinfolk, and we made fun of the odd characters with the funny language that kept the ship moving across the sea. The captain was quite taken with mother and she was often invited to his cabin to report on the welfare of the Germans. The German woman began to gossip that Margaretha was altogether too friendly with the captain for her own good. For correctness, shae always took me with her and it was because of those visits that I was seen by the crew as a favourite of the captain. Word got around, and as a result, the sailors treated me kindly. I was allowed the run of the ship, and on good days during the voyage they taught me the ways of a square rigged ship of that time. On hot sunny days when there was little wind, I carried water to the sailors and two of them I came to know as Davie and Snub, became quite friendly with me and allowed me to help with light tasks. They told me many sea tales that were hardly-believable."

"Margaretha seemed to almost enjoy the voyage while your father seemed moody."

"At first Margaretha was very frightened when she could not find me, but father was more concerned with other things. Mother was brave during the daylight hours if her family was safely under her care, but during the long nights I often heard her weeping. Some mornings she complained of being sick, and, turning me over to Georg, kept to her bed, praying to God. In spite of his ministrations, father could not make her rise, even on days when the sea was calm and the sun shone brightly. It was on those sunny days, after a short prayer by the captain that the dead were thrown overboard wrapped in old sailcloth, and became food for the big fish that always followed our ship.

"While Margaretha appeared to enjoy the voyage at times, father seemed angry and frustrated. He was moody, and sometimes he struck out at mother, not knowing she had his child growing in her belly. After the death of Sarah he had always been kind to mother, and I never knew him to strike her at any other time. On fine days he disappeared and secreted himself in some part of the ship, coming below for meals only, and during days of foul weather."

Suddenly the old man was on his feet, full of energy. He drew two blankets over his filthy nightwear, and on spindly legs shuffled toward the hearth. He mumbled over his shoulder in what appeared to be frustration, "You ask too many questions. Come build a fire and I will tell you my story in my own words."

Thus, I sat with him through the season of colour and beyond the falling of the leaves. As he told his story, I wrote every word he said in a notebook. When he finished his story, he again took to his bed, assured that his story was recorded and hopeful that he would no longer be a shadow in the annals of history.

6

EBERHARDT'S RHINELAND

It was not until we were settled on the Witaberger Lands near Ryn Beck that I learned of my mother's terror in leaving the old country. She had made the journey sure she was carrying a child. On the journey down the Neckar River she was assaulted by a drunken man at Lauffen, and feared that she might lose her child. Afterwards she thought she had killed the man and had kept the matter secret until the day she told me. By the time we arrived at Rotterdam she was resigned to whatever the future would bring, but the voyage across the cruel sea was a trial for her.

In her new world she took pleasure in taking me to her sanctuary in the woods to tell me stories; and sometimes she carried baby Johann Leonard on her hip. In spite of her fears he had survived the ship's journey safely. Although I was only a boy I remember the stories, and the joy she seemed to get from recalling the legends from her childhood. Now, after more than three score years of my own rough life it is time to tell my own story.

My childhood in the old country is now a distant memory. When mother told me that father was taking us to America I was angry, but soon anger at father went away and I believe I grew beyond my years during the next months. After the breast of mother my first awareness was of my sister Maria. She was about seven years old at the time and considered old enough to look out for me when mother was helping in the vineyards at harvest time. Maria was both my first love and my first tormentor. As I grew she fed me, but afterward teased me and grabbed my playthings and ran away from me setting me into a great howling, until she relented her jealous pique and gave them back. Her brothers Martin Gottfried and Jörg Jacob had died before I was born so I remained her sole sibling on which to perpetuate girlish guile. She strutted about and showed me to her cousins as if she was my mother.

But then Maria, my first love and comforter, was taken to serve God just before her tenth year. Although Maria was from another woman, mother cried for days after putting my sister in the ground. Despite some joy, ours was a sad house at that time. Mother told me I had had a little sister Elizabetha Dorothea who died when a mere babe before I was born. A baby brother Gottfried died the same year as Maria. Father had work at first but then we had to move to another village so he could dig sand. Christoph was born when I was four or five years old, and for a time there was some joy, but he also died. Margaretha wept over her lost children and visited Christoph's grave each Sabbath day.

But she was not always sad. Sometimes I heard her singing when I helped her put up preserves for the winter.

When Christoph died father was plunged into gloom, and spent his days tramping up and down the riverbank muttering to himself. He spent his nights drinking with rowdies in the Heinricherhaus.

My most vivid memory of that sad house was the day the magistrate came with some soldiers to take father to the dungeon because of his depts. Mother was silent as they took him away, frightened I now believe, more for my welfare than for her own. She sent me off to my aunt and uncle in Poppenweiler to be with my cousins. Paulus was a year older than me, Elenora a year younger but she seemed older and took Maria's place in bossing me about. After a month Uncle Leonardt paid father's debts, and Margaretha and Georg came home to our village. Father was by now determined to go to the new world across the seas, and he and Uncle Leonardt made plans to leave Germany the following spring.

The last summer we lived in Poppenweiler I touched life beyond the skirts of Margaretha. Two other cousins, Agatha and Bernhardt lived close to Paulus and Elenora, and we cousins spent most waking hours together roaming the country-side, sometimes with other children from the village. We played rope jumping in which the girls were bullied into holding the ends of the rope while we boys jumped around like clowns. The girls turned hopscotch into a dance. Many hours were spent playing hide and seek in the cornfields outside the village. We hid in chestnut trees and dropped nuts on old people's heads. I knew my mother would say this behaviour was childish and cowardly so I kept it secret, but during that summer I began to see the world outside our house as an exciting place.

I got involved in other pranks that I am not proud of now in my old age. Herr Fuchs was a rich merchant who owned a large apple estate near the village. When the big juicy apples were bright red, he invited his tenants and their families to harvest the apples in return for a small portion of their pick to keep for preserving. On the appointed day in the late summer all his tenants gathered for a day of apple picking. Old man Fuchs provided schnapps and beer, but in limited quantities to ensure his pickers did not get too much to drink and find a place to sleep in the bushes. All the children of the village who were not from tenant families would gather in the woods, and when the harvesting was in full progress dart in and out of the pickers and gather as many apples as they could cram into their shirts before being chased away. Besides stealing the apples it seemed fun at the time to have the pickers chase us into the woods in hopes of taking a miscreant to the magis-trate, but we were too nimble to be caught. One old man chased us far into the woods, and then collapsed. I was terrified that he had died, but after a few minutes he rose up and went back to the orchard. Parents of the really poor people turned their backs to such behaviour from their children, since, although they were pious

Christians and stealing was seen to break God's commandment, they saw minor pilfering as a right reward for the way they were denied everything beyond mere survival. Many of the village families had relatives who had taken up arms against the nobility at various times in the past.

A highlight of that last summer was the harvesting of the grapes and pressing them into wine. The children of the village helped this production in small ways, but the adults did not take their contributions too seriously, so most of the time the children ran in and out among the vines and eating their fill of the juicy grapes until irate mothers caught them. That summer Paulus found a cave down by the river, which in truth was only a small cavity under an overhanging rock cliff, but to him it was a great fortress. The girl cousins were sent out to gather sticks to place in front of the cave to keep it from being viewed from the road. We ate stolen apples and grapes, and stored corn that we stole from the cornfields near the cave. We could not stomach raw corn, so most of it became rotten, and when it began to stink, we made the girls throw it in the river.

It was in this cave hideaway that summer that I became aware that boys and girls were different. Father said they were like fire and water, but he did not say which was fire and which was water. The behaviour of Elenora and Agatha I found very strange: secretive, giggly, and saucy. When I was alone with Agatha she bossed me about without shame, and I did her bidding without any thought of being bullied. It was a sweet and sour time of my childhood.

For me, the journey down the Neckar and the Rhine was a great adventure. I played on the boats, and sometimes fought with Paulus and Elenora, and we made fun in secret of the odd captains and their crews that took us down the rivers. My tragedy in the rapids of the Saint Lawrence River much later in life still bring back to me the childhood fright of the Bingen Notch. The fears that came to me on the rivers of Germany in the blackness of night were driven away each day by Margaretha's stories of the Rhine and Neckar legends.

The savagery of the sea tore apart my childhood imaginings so completely that the ocean passage still comes to me in vivid colours. The years have dimmed much of the terror of the American war, but the horrors of the ocean voyage will remain with me the rest of my days, few as they will surely be.

It was through mother that the voyage of the *Anne* was a learning experience for me. As the voyage progressed she was often called to the captain's cabin to report on the situation with the Germans. Most of the time she took me with her. It was because of the captain's favourable opinion of Margaretha that he treated me like a son and allowed my freedom to run about the ship, except in stormy weather. During our meetings with the captain, Margaretha and I began to learn the strange language that we would need in America. He allowed me access to the ship's log and some of his books as a way of teaching me his language and the way of a ship.

It was the very end of summer when the *Anne* docked in New York harbour. During the voyage the adult Germans often gathered around the table in the ship's salon after a meal and discussed their future plans for living in America if they survived the ship's crossing. Some had relatives in the Dutch community of Ryn Beck who had written letters stating that much wood could be had and no taxes were to be paid. It was voiced about the ship that German Palatine refugees had settled in Ryn Beck in former times, and to most of *Anne's* passengers it appeared to be a satisfactory place to make a farm since large landowners were leasing land to settlers for payment in kind. So after much wrangling among the men a pact was made to proceed to that place.

After landing at New York, examined for disease, and cleared for embarkation from the ship, a red-coated soldier took us through gates into the place he called Fort George where English officers examined us once more. Margaretha clutched the Bible in which she kept the letter from cousin Frieda Egermayer close to her bosom for fear the English officer would take it from her. The letter was her only link to family in the new world. She asked if Ryn Beck was far distant from Kirkehoeck, where she had kin, but got a blank look in return; the officer knew not the location of either Ryn Beck or Kirkehoeck. After a pause, she asked of the man if the Dutch war ship *Amsterdam* had arrived. She was told, "It came yesterday."

The officers seemed satisfied that we were not enemies, had no contagious disease, and released us after warning that we had to leave the fort right away. Enquiring of transport to the region of the Palatines, an officer told father to go to the wharf adjacent to the entrance to the fort and seek out a sloop, which he could hire to take his family up the river. Margaretha was fearful for Leonardt's family, worried they had perished from disease or been eaten by sharks, so before seeking transport she insisted father find the whereabouts of the passengers from the *Amsterdam*.

Her fears were for naught. Uncle Leonardt and Paulus met us as we emerged from the fort, and after tearful and thankful greetings, Uncle Leonardt told of their crossing. His family had had more comforts in the bigger ship, but they too suffered from many storms, sickness and death. Safely ashore, they had spent the night at an inn on a street called Broad, and their belongings were still at that place. Father and I stood guard of our possessions while Magaretha went off with Uncle Leonardt and Paulus to the inn. They soon returned with Aunt Catharina and Aunt Barbara, accompanied by a man leading a horse pulling a cart, which carried the goods and chattels of the family. Cousin Elenora was skipping along after the cart until she saw me and ran ahead to shyly stand before father and me. The owner of the cart unceremoniously dumped its contents on the road leading from the fort to the town, was given some coins by Uncle Leonardt, and left without saying a word.

By early afternoon the English officers had processed all the passengers from the *Anne* and word was passed to re-assemble in the square at the entrance to the fort. The adults gathered around Pastor Blumgardt with bowed heads while he led a celebration of thanksgiving for their deliverance and a memorial prayer for those who had perished at sea. After a prayer for our future safety and health, we all sang *Christus, Der Ist Mein Leben*. No one then knew how difficult it would be to conquer the new land.

New York in those days was a small place and consisted mainly of Fort George and a few buildings. Across the square from the fort was a small structure with a hip roof that Pastor Blumgardt said was a church, and he praised God that the place was not entirely of heathens. Mother asked Georg and me to accompany her to look inside the church but we were pulled along towards the port with the others, who were anxious to be moving out of the city where they were not comfortable. The port of New York was dirty and noisy, a very alien place to us. I saw a man chained to a post like a dog. His skin was black. Men in tall hats and white skin stepped from the crowd that surrounded the black man. Each white man felt his muscles and opened his mouth to peer at his teeth. The scene brought memories of the day I went to the countryside with my grandfather, his intention to buy a horse. Grandfather felt the horse's muscles and looked into its mouth before he paid money. At the port of New York white men were buying black men like my grandfather bought his horse. If a buyer thought the man sound, he held up fingers to say how much he would pay. The owner, standing beside the post with a whip in his hand, nodded when the deal was made. The man with the whip then undid the chain, and the other man led the black man away. I asked mother if black men in America were horses. She said, "Shush! It is nothing to us."

Right after I saw this happen a man brought a black woman to the post in the midst of shouting and jeering. She was naked except for a flimsy cloth covering the middle part of her glistening body. She was young and looked healthy and the bidding was furious, so she did not have a long time to suffer humiliation before her new owner took her away. There were more black men and women being herded off the boats and urged forward by men with whips.

What I saw in America those first few hours were a fort, a church, and the slave market.

P roceeding to the wharf as advised, Herr Eschert showed a letter to the *Anne*'s shipping agent. The letter was from his great uncle, and informed Herr Eschert to contact a Mr. H. Beekman of Ryn Beck in the province of New York. The agent told him that Ryn Beck was about one hundred miles up the river. "A sloop is berthed over yonder at Coenties slip that will take you and your party up-river tomorrow." When Herr Eschert brought this news to the group, the women objected, refusing to get on another ship, insisting they would walk first. A delegation of the men went to the agent with Pastor Blumgardt as an interpreter and asked the agent if there was another way of getting to Ryn Beck. The man pointed to the dusty street and said, "Well, if you strike out in that direction you will meet the Boston post-road which will take you to the river, but from there it is just a track that is wet and very muddy this time of year. There are hardly any bridges and the countryside is very rough and swampy from here to Fishkill. You might get there by horse, but a freight wagon would be impossible. You will not get to Ryn Beck before winter on that road" and, he added somewhat amused, "even if you are not all killed by savages." The agent pointed to the Coenties slip and said, "The *Maria* sitting right there at the wharf could take you and your chattels to Ryn Beck in two or three days if the winds are with the sloop." When the pastor translated this message someone asked about savages and he said to them, "The people here call the Indians savages and believe they are wild people who live in the woods." On hearing this, the women agreed to go on the river by boat. After a discussion, during which some of the more suspicious members of the group thought the agent might be in the employ of the sloop's captain and may not be telling the whole truth, there really did not seem to be any choice in the matter. Mother said to me, "It's the name of your sister; that is a good omen." The men enquired about the sailing and were informed that the boat was leaving on the rising tide tomorrow. The man said we could board the *Maria* right away and find shelter for the night. The fare seemed unreasonably high, but after several minutes of haggling a suitable fare was negotiated.

Leaving the women, children and the old men to guard their goods, the able-bodied men went off to find some of the necessities for life in the wilderness before suitable houses could be built, since they were told there were very few supplies where they were going. It was about two hours before Georg, Uncle Leonardt and Herr Götz returned with small tents and some cooking utensils, implements that they had not brought with them. Aunt Catharina and mother were not too pleased with the choices their husbands made in the pots and pans they had acquired, but declared themselves able to do their work, if not as they were accustomed.

The other families were making similar arrangements and by late afternoon we were ready to begin the last stage of the journey to an unknown place. Most were full of good nature, but also apprehensive about the future.

Late in the afternoon, we boarded the sloop *Maria* to sail to the northern wilderness. The accommodation in the stern of the sloop was a covered section over the deck where some of the women and children could squeeze closely together and get some rest, if not actually sleep. Getting the children settled, the women prepared a cold meal and after a singsong and some prayers the night was spent in some comfort. At dawn, two couples and a man, who, because of the captain's deference was thought to be a man of some importance, came on board the sloop and were shown to quarters in the cabin. This small group of people seemed to know each other since they were talking and laughing as they settled in their quarters. They pointedly ignored the tired and ragged Germans huddled in the stern. About one hour later, Captain Jones, seeing no further business, and it being a rising tide, ordered his two-man crew to cast off the lines, and the sloop sailed out into a bay at the mouth of a large river.

The instruction I had taken from Captain Mills of the *Anne* allowed me to follow the river voyage with some interest and excitement, which pleased mother. The wind was light and straight in the face but as the *Maria* rounded the promontory where the fort was located and turned into the river the wind was favourable, it being a rising sea breeze. The morning sun and the pleasant motion of the boat pitching gently into the current gave all on board a sense of wellbeing that lasted all day. As evening approached, the wind died, so Captain Jones and his crew put into shore and dropped anchor to maintain their day's progress against the current. Some time during the night, as dawn approached, the wind rose against our progress, but in spite of the ill nature of the weather, the *Maria* weighed anchor shortly after daylight and headed out into the current toward the opposite shore. All that day the crew criss-crossed the river against both the wind and current. Undeterred by the perverse direction of the wind, the captain, looking at the overcast sky said, "Tomorrow we will catch a following breeze, mark my word." Sure enough, during the night the wind died and rose with daylight, this time favourable to the sloop's progress. The third night after a rainy and windy day the *Maria* was berthed alongside the wharf at the mouth of the Fishkill. We were able to leave the ship and camp on the riverbank, as the captain intended to spend the night there, "to deliver the post."

That evening as we camped at the mouth of the Fishkill an old man, walking on the road that was close by, spied our fire and came limping into camp. He looked around at the assembled company and began to berate us in loud words, waving his walking stick so wildly that some of the mothers feared he was bent on hurting the children. At first, it was difficult to understand what it was about us that made him so furious. But after a prolonged display of anger we began to piece together fragments of his harangue and the subject of his outburst became clear. He had heard our voices as he traveled on the road and thought we were New Netherlanders. Through the pastor's translation it came out that his father had been killed in the English war with the Dutch in 1673 and he was furious that "you people" had the nerve to come to "my country." "There is already too many of you here already." The pastor explained to him that they were not Dutch, "Not Netherlanders; Württembergers!" Not understanding, but somewhat mollified, the man became quiet and with his next words wondered if we had anything, "to whet my whistle." On being told we had no alcohol, he limped out of camp sputtering and mumbling to himself about "you people" crowding the countryside. He disappeared from the light of the fire still waving his stick, dramatically poking its point to the heavens in time to his words.

At dawn, Captain Jones and his crew came shuffling along the path and began to prepare the sloop for the onward journey. They showed all the signs of spending a night drinking. Margaretha, furious with the captain and ignoring my presence said to father, "He's just another drunken one like he who left us overnight at Neckar Gmund; likely carousing with women who earn their keep by pleasing men." I asked her what she meant. She seemed surprised that I had heard and put me off, saying, "Pshaw! You don't need to know."

The new day promised to be sunny, and soon the gloom lifted and the crew turned to, making it out into the river where *Maria* caught a rising breeze. In bright sunshine with the sloop blown up the river by a following wind, there was a spirit of anticipation throughout the boat. The captain, now over the effects of the night before, stood on the bow of the *Maria* singing some sailor's ditty and between verses shouted, "Look at 'er go! She shur 'nough got the bone in 'er teeth now. We'll be in Ryn Beck in no time a' tall at this rate!" The Germans, used to being tied to the land, had little sensitivity to the joy expressed by the sea-going captain and were more taken with the country bordering the river; struck by the similarity of the country to the one they had left many weeks ago. There were clearings with signs of habitation that were like some of the wild places along the river in the old country. Occasionally there was a fine house with open fields, which at this time of the year were brown, but being farmers the men could visualize the green that would come in the spring when new life began to sprout. The trees along the banks of the river were a blaze of yellow, orange, and red colours. It was the dark and foreboding forest of pine and fir trees pressing in on the river at places that brought fear of wild savages lurking in the shadows.

I n the afternoon on the fourth day since disembarking the ship *Anne* we came into a landing that we learned from the captain was called Vanderburgh Cove, two miles from the town of Ryn Beck. There were passengers waiting at the landing who were bound for Albany, and to take advantage of the continuing up-river breeze the captain was anxious to unload our chattels and get underway as soon as he could. Left on the river's bank with our possessions, we gathered together on the wharf to plan what to do. The "important" passengers were now perceived to be residents and they quickly disappeared up the road that led from the landing place, and we were left alone in some wonderment as to what to do next. I attached myself to father, whom, with Uncle Leonardt and Herr Götz walked up to a tavern that was close beside the road. Enquiring after Mr. Henry Beekman Jr., we were directed to a point along the road where we would find his house. The informant was sure he was not at home, "but someone at the house would surely hear your story and give further directions." Returning with this information, the tired Germans walked up the hill to the house of Mr. Henry Beekman Jr. to enquire as to where they should proceed.

Henry Beekman Jr. was indeed not at home but a man with a waxed moustache covering most of the bottom part of his face introduced himself by the name of Rutsen, a nephew of "Colonel Henry." Mr. Rutsen looked at the tired, raggedy group standing meekly before him and, excusing himself left the room. He returned shortly and informed us that Colonel Beekman would be home tomorrow, and that in the meantime we could take our comfort in the stables for the night where a milkmaid would provide blankets. A boy appeared quietly in our midst, at which point Mr. Rutsen said, "As the day is drawing to a close, I expect you are hungry. Jim here will take you to the kitchens where the cook will be pleased to supply you with sustenance until you are able to see Colonel Beekman on the morrow." We followed Jim to the kitchen, where a meal of venison, bread, and cheese was provided. We ate heartily, if silently, not wishing to disturb the household, and on finishing the meal Jim led us to the stables where we were pleased to be able to rest with some space about us, unlike the crowded condition of the ships and the sloop that brought us to this place. The next day would tell of our future.

The sun was well up when Jim appeared the next morning and motioned for the heads of the families to follow him to where Colonel Beekman would receive them. I tagged along with father. Leaving the women and most of the children along with the chattels in the barn where we had slept the night before, the men followed Jim to a smaller room at the rear of the main house where we found a man sitting behind a large, dark desk. As we entered, he stood and came to the front of the desk. He was a tall, spare man with a strong chin and a prominent nose, altogether a handsome man. He looked fit, as befits a man used to the saddle on the back of a spirited horse.

On the desk was a large map, unrolled and fixed flat with two stones, homely items against the dark richness of the wood. The colonel asked if Herr Eschert was a member of our group. When Herr Eschert stepped forward, the colonel said to the assembled group, translated by Pastor Blumgardt, "I had a correspondence from Herr Eschert some twelve months past informing me that he knew of a number of families who wished to migrate to this country. He wrote that since a number of Palatines had settled at this place a generation ago, some of whom are relatives of Mr. Eschert, and having obtained my name from said relative, he wondered if I would be pleased to consider additional settlers on my land, which you will see outlined on this map." The map, the colonel explained, was a drawing of the patent awarded to the colonel by his father, as well as additions he had later purchased for himself. Colonel Henry explained that he had drawn off in the southeast corner of these lands a section that he had intended for our people and which it pleased him to call the Witaberger Lands.

"That section has been surveyed into leases, and once delivered to the lands you will draw lots for the leases. Each lease has a quit-rent of two shillings per annum in proper currency and eight bushes of grain in kind, or its equivalent, at my discretion as to equivalent kind."

Colonel Henry looked us over to see if there was any dissent and after a moment he continued, "If this is understood I will arrange pack mules to transport your estates to these lands, and I myself will ride ahead to direct you thither."

Herr Eschert had enquired about reasonable land rents from his nephew who had lived here some years and he satisfied the rest of the men that the rent was fair and equitable. Georg asked if their lands were near to Kirkehoek as his wife had a cousin living there. Colonel Henry answered it was, "some four miles." To pre-empt the next enquiry, being experienced in these matters, the colonel said, "The lands are high and fertile, some three miles from Ryn Beck where all necessary supplies are available. With clearing and habitation the lands will make excellent and secure homes. You may trade as you wish so far as the quit-rent is received for the total amount of two shillings and eight bushels for each lease until such time as you can purchase your lot. If you wish to sell to anyone other than someone currently living on the Patent you must have my approval. My permission is needed for lands set aside for schools and churches."

The Württembergers knew they really had no choice as to the arrangements so they readily acquiesced and began to break apart, preparing to leave. The colonel showed them out of his office and went to round up some mules and a herder to load the possessions of his new tenants. By noon a short train of mules led by the colonel on a black-and-white stallion, followed by a line of bedraggled and dusty new settlers, left the Heermanse, which the Beekman Manor was called in those days, and proceeded up the hill to end their long trek to a new home in the wilderness.

The road led northeast alongside Landman's Kill where we observed through the trees two mills at the water's edge. The road brought us to the settlement at Ryn Beck, a town of several houses and shops. A tavern, with a sign bearing the rough-hewn word *Traphagen* sat at the crossroads that separated the settlement into

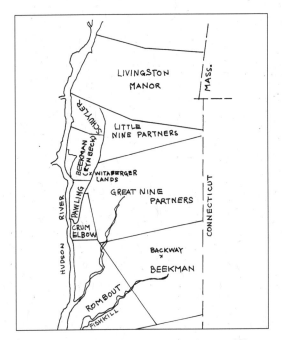

four parts. The colonel did not stop but hurried the mule driver through the town before any of the thirsty men could be tempted to visit the tavern. After a short distance, another road bore off to the southeast, and the procession led by the colonel turned onto this road. It was rocky and rough, but dry, and after proceeding for about three miles we came to a stop at a natural clearing surrounded by dense forest. While waiting for stragglers, the settlers looked around, kicking at the soil. Someone asked the colonel about water. He pointed to the east and said, "There is a good-sized creek that runs through the lands, beyond those trees, about four hundred paces yonder." Pastor Blumgardt had already picked the clearing in which they were standing for the site for his church. By and by the mules were unburdened and the colonel and his muleskinner were gone and we were left to our fate.

Shortly after a prayer of thanksgiving, the ringing of the axes that had been purchased in New York could be heard in the woods as the men cut firewood. The women collected the cooking utensils since the time for the evening meal was fast approaching. When the woodcutters returned to the clearing they built fires and began to assemble the few tents that we had brought. After prayers and hymn singing we ate a communal meal sitting on stones around a large fire in the clearing that was already being called "Our Church." Afterwards everyone, according to his or her circumstances retired for the night.

The next morning when the sun was barely up, the head of families proceeded to draw lots from the rough drawing of the plots left with them by Colonel Beekman. Uncle Leonardt drew a lot just adjacent to the church clearing. Father drew lot number nine, which was near the creek. When all lots had been drawn there were some that were not allocated, and some trading took place. Uncle Leonardt and Herr Götz ended up with adjacent lots. Margaretha was satisfied with lot nine, as she liked being close to the creek, so Georg kept his drawn lot. Once this process gave each family a site for a cabin, the axes came out again and the building of shelters for the coming winter began.

Uncle Leonardt and Georg decided to build one large house for the two families so as to save time and effort until permanent houses could be built. So they set to work cutting trees and stripping them of bark. The trees were cut into lengths and one end of each log was squared off and then piled for future use. The next task was to dig a square hole, ten paces to a side and as deep as a man. The earth was packed tight until such time as sawed lumber for a floor could be had. The logs were planted, palisade style, around the perimeter of the hole, and bark used to seal the outside against dampness and the collapse of the earth.

The construction of her home underway, Margaretha called for me and we walked to the crest of the nearby hill. Afterward, she told Catharina of the pleasure she found in the woods on the first day in our new home. Her words were written down by my aunt and became part of the family lore:

The morning sun revealed to the west a vast plain of red, yellow, orange, and green plumage forming a canopy over the silent forest, as if to create nature's cathedral for the dumb creatures that lived beneath its great arches. Eagles and hawks searching for the first meal of the day swung and looped in the rising air currents that were pushed heavenward by the warming earth. The wily chipmunk scrambled from bush to bush searching for food, all the while keeping a watchful eye for the shadow of death above. The twittering junco followed the chipmunk, hoping it would leave a mor-

sel behind. A deer with her faun minced with delicate steps into a clearing, disturbing a hidden partridge that took to the air with a thundering explosion of sound, only then to expose its hiding place under a huckleberry bush. The thump, thump of the partridge hung in the air for some moments.

In the woods that first morning Margaretha was quiet in the midst of the sights and sounds of the forest. She took me by the hand and pulled me close. She said, blinking back tears, "Eberhardt, this is life abundant. You and I are part of the woods as is the faun and its mother that we see yonder through the trees. A new life is growing in my belly as it did with the mother deer, giving life to her faun." I was not old enough to understand her words at that time and I said nothing. After several minutes while she listened to the sounds of the woods we walked to our new home to the ringing of axes and the sweet smell of wood smoke that was curling upwards into the still air of the new day.

When we returned the other children were gone, having been sent off to find river stones in the creek to add to those that had been dug out of the ground. As they staggered back, they dumped the rocks on the pile that was growing beside the large hole in the ground. A discussion took place as to the best location for the hearth and its chimney, and finding that the prevailing wind was from the west, Georg and Uncle Leonardt after much talk decided that the chimney should be placed on the east side of the dwelling so the smoke would blow away from the house.

The walls of the house were fashioned with a view to the south and on each side of the door opening was a small widow opening. Logs were split and put in place to form a roof structure and strips of bark from the basswood tree were wedged between the roof beams. A partition was constructed of small logs running the length of the enclosure, stopping some two paces from what would become the entrance to the house. By the first of November, the house was ready for occupancy, except for a timber floor and a door. In the meantime, the windows and door openings were closed with heavy blankets. The signs of winter were all around; the leaves had fallen, leaving spindly ghosts of trees in the moonlight, the air was cold and in the mornings the dew was very heavy. The birds had gone south, and some of the animals were already in hibernation. Some families had not yet finished their shelter so father and Uncle Leonardt went off to help others, leaving Margaretha to make a comfortable home. By the middle of November, the new settlers in the woods of North America waited for heavy frost and the first snow.

That first winter we lived in the same house as Uncle Leonardt, Aunt Catharina, and Aunt Barbara, the two families separated by a partition with a door that was kept closed with a rough blanket. Father made me a bed in one corner from some rough boards that he and Uncle Leonardt had got in trade from the sawmill at the river. The families shared meals cooked on the hearth, and lived together except for sleeping. Cousin Elenora took over from Agatha in bossing me about. But she and Paulus were my constant companions, and even though Paulus was the eldest of the tree cousins, Margaretha said to me, "You must see they keep away from bears and wolves." I did not always obey mother's wishes but we children survived many wanderings in the woods without a major mishap, except that Elenora told stories, and mother became more watchful of our safety. She set down rules that we were to follow.

By the time the house was fit to live in Margaretha was very heavy with child. Just before Christmas, she took to her bed, confined from my curiosity by a curtain of blankets that Georg nailed to the rafters of the roof. Besides Catharina and Barbara, Frau Götz came often to visit my mother and care for her needs. Mother gave orders to the women not to let me see her. By Christmas day, Margaretha's time was getting close, so Catharina sat with her while Aunt Barbara took Paulus, Elenora, and me to the Christmas service that Pastor Blumgardt conducted in a tent that he had consecrated. Afterwards father and Uncle Leonardt joined us for a meal spread on tables set up following the service. The new community of Lutherans enjoyed the meal of venison and duck, along with corn, squash, and beans that had been bartered from the Indians in exchange for homespun blankets that the women had made during the cool nights of autumn. Everyone brought a loaf, and in defiance of convention some brought strong drink, which helped the assembled group reach a state of merriment that the pastor turned his back upon, comfortable that after all it was a celebration of the birth of Christ.

About a week later, I knew that soon I would have the baby sister that Margaretha wanted. Catharina and Barbara sat with mother night and day and Frau Götz came often. Then one night I was awakened by loud moans and stifled screams from Margaretha's bed. The noises of great pain seemed to last half the night, but in truth it was about two hours later that a baby's screaming cry filled the cabin with noise. I got from my bed in time to see Georg and Pastor Blumgardt summoned by Barbara from where they had been keeping a blazing fire. At the time I did not dream that mother could have died from all the pain she endured; she was so strong and such a powerful presence in my mind it was not conceivable to me that she could leave me. So I went back to my bed and went to sleep.

Margaretha's wishes for baby girl turned out to be a brother for me. A few days later Pastor Blumgardt christened him Johann Leonard in his small log church built during the winter by the settlers of the Witaberger Lands. Afterwards Georg, with a determined expression, took to the woods with his gun, "to kill squirrels," he said.

Margaretha recovered quickly, being up and about by the middle of January. By spring, she had regained her liveliness, and we began to walk in the woods, even before the snow had completely melted.

The men and boys of the Witaberger Lands had spent much of that winter clearing the forest for planting in the spring, and hunting deer. The creek froze solid but Paulus and I cut holes in the ice and caught fish. Father had brought his loom reed and shuttles from the old country, and during that first winter when the weather was bad he constructed the wooden frame for a loom.

The forest was teeming with game, and we ate well, but I missed my mother's preserves, which were not available that winter. Mother collected ash from the burnings and made lye soap, but she missed her delicacies from back home, so when the weather made clearing and burning impossible, a trek to the village was organized to buy flour, bacon, and salt. An old widower who had lived in the village for a long time took a shine to Margaretha and gave her his dead wife's spinning wheel. "I lost Marta last year and in heaven she has no use for a wheel, and you will have more use for this than an old man like me." When she protested he said, "Faith, I have no one else. You might as well get some use from it. I hear Georg was a weaver in the old country and this might help you survive in this wilderness."

Uncle Leonardt bought a team of oxen, two cows and a pair of breeding pigs, some chickens, and a red rooster to make sure of a continuing supply of chickens. I begged father for a dog, and one day he came home from the village with a beagle puppy, who was my faithful companion for nine years. I called him Dog, to show that I knew the new words of the village, and made a place for him under my bed.

The spring after that first winter, when the snows were gone, the streams free of ice and the ground around us steaming in the hot sun, Georg cut trees and built a house for Margaretha on lot number nine. It was built of logs with notched ends to join the corners. It had four windows and a large stone hearth. Mother was so pleased to "live on the ground instead of a cellar." Lot nine was smaller than the average because of the creek, but our family being small, father said it would fill our needs. Once the cabin was declared liveable by my mother, we cleared away most of the roots from the clearing with the help of Uncle Leonardt's oxen, and began ploughing the rich, black earth for planting. Father planted corn on about half the cleared area, the rest with barley and flax. Mother made a garden down by the creek beside a grove of willow trees in which she planted potatoes, beets, and tomatoes. An Indian woman, with whom she had become friends, gave her seeds for squash and beans.

Margaretha developed a love for the woods of America that one would not have thought likely from her fondness for things queenly. She told me once that if she could not be queen of the court she could be queen of the woods. It was that spring that she began to take me into the woods where she had found her throne, a large granite rock at the edge of the trees surrounding a sunlit clearing. Sitting on her throne with her petticoats spread over the rock she could truly be a queen about to address her subjects. It was that summer; at age seven that I began to learn the way of a good life. Margaretha became my source of knowledge for all the wonders of the world and all its tragedies. She not only pointed my empty mind to where I belonged in my family, but using many stories from her Bible pointed me to the possibility of a rewarding future life of the spirit. Her teachings were as strange and confusing to me as were Pastor Blumgardt's, but she was much more gentle and loving in bringing the stories into our surroundings in the woods, which was full of its own kind of life. That summer I came to love Margaretha in the woods in a way that I could not love her in the kitchen. She put me in touch with the spiritual world as well as providing the comforts of a good mother.

It was that summer too that I became aware of the woodland people that lived on the fringes of the European settlements that many in our group called savages, and accused them of killing white settlers. One day Paulus, Elenora, and I were fishing the waters of the creek without catching any fish. In an attempt to find the trout, we had wandered far from the settlement. Sitting beside a pool that seemed as empty of fish as the rest I looked up from my fish pole, and across the creek stood a man that I instantly recognized as an Indian from his dress and jet-black hair. Terrified, I whispered to my cousins and we started up and prepared to run. But realizing that the creek separated us from the savage there seemed no great danger so I looked again at the man. He smiled, and then pointed to a shady backwater downstream. Then as suddenly as he had appeared, he was gone. Ashamed to go home with no fish I urged my cousins that we try the pool downstream. Paulus was of a like mind, but Elenora wanted to run. Being afraid of getting lost on her own, and having the protection of her brother if she stayed, she agreed to stay, and we found our way through the bushes to the place indicated. Throwing our hooks into the water we caught several trout and went home triumphant.

Several days passed, and then one day the Indian who had frightened my cousins and me while fishing appeared in our settlement with a young boy about my age. He left the boy standing by the door of our cabin and as silently as he came, he disappeared. The boy was very scared, and Margaretha, seeing how thin and scrawny he was, coaxed the boy to take some of the stew that was meant for our supper. He took the bowl of stew in his hands and looking about ran away taking the food with him. Later we found the bowl at the root of a tree. This happened several times that summer.

The Indians thereabouts were not warlike, and little by little a few of the newcomers to the land and the original inhabitants came together in mutual understanding. Over time and proximity our family came to know the boy and his father. The boy's name was Nupi and the father was called Hahanu, which we learned meant, "He laughs." Margaretha became very friendly with the boy, and had no worries of letting little Johann Leonard be in his company. Father and Hahanu went hunting together, and sometimes Nupi and I went with them. It was thus that I learned some of the ways of the Indian and the nature of the woods.

I could not say we prospered greatly, but our family survived those first years in America. The second year, Georg planted more flax than barley, and mother and he began to sell bedclothes and a few items of women's underwear to the wealthy households along the river. This allowed my mother to trade her wares for some of the things she desired to make the household more comfortable. The small clearing around the cabin that Georg had cut produced the necessities.

When not doing chores I roamed the woods with my cousins and other boys of the settlement, including Nupi. We snuck into the village, wandered the creeks and ranged up and down the river. We lived in our imaginings of life on the river, with the sloops and their captains plying their trades and enjoying the delights of the taverns that were springing up and attracting those women who helped supply the captains' delights. Indeed, not only the delights of the river boat captains. We were all sons of tenant farmers and when a boy saw a prominent landowner staggering away from Traphagen's tavern it was a story to be taken home with the satisfaction of knowing the rich and powerful were not so grand after all.

There was a large house at the very edge of the village that we were not to go near; it was sufficient bait to hook the insatiable curiosity of young boys. The house had a large garden surrounded by a wall made of stone, and it became the aim of every boy to climb the wall and peer into the garden without being caught. It happened there was a large oak tree beside the road that ran behind the garden that overlooked the rear of the house. In summer when the tree was in full leaf the boys took turns climbing into its leafy bower to observe the young ladies gambolling about and sunning themselves when not entertaining men from the mills.

When I was nine my life moved from a love of the American woods and its creatures to the harsh reality of the society into which my parents had placed me. Mother was again heavy with child, and in the spring of '41 she had her baby girl at last. She knew she would never be the Queen of America so she put all her hopes in a new generation that would carry her likeness. She wanted to call her daughter Elizabeth after her heroine, the Queen of Bohemia, but having had her first daughter go to heaven after only three months of life, her superstitions of poor luck with Elizabetha caused her to call her daughter after herself, hoping the babe would live to a ripe old age.

While mother was overjoyed with her new baby girl, Georg was not so pleased. He had wanted another son. I think he sensed that I would not be at his side during his declining years, and Johann Leonard was now just two and of unknown quality. Greta, as he called the new baby, was another mouth to feed in lean times.

It was a bad year for us, with mother's garden drying up that summer for lack of rain. She was frightened we would all starve and blamed father for our troubles. After a hard winter, the worst in people's memories, with livestock dying from the cold and the prospect of the ground being too wet for spring planting, Georg went down to New York to find an opportunity to help feed and clothe us. Jobs were scarce with economic troubles and the cost of the Spanish war dampening the demand for Georg's weaving skills. The sawmills and woollen mills were not taking on new men, forcing Georg to go farther afield to find something to support us. His quest took him south to New York town.

Margaretha took baby Greta, Johann Leonard and me to the Vanderburgh Landing to see father off. The ice had mostly retreated from the creeks, the air was fresh and still from the release of the weight of winter. While I stood, wondering why father was leaving us, he took his pack, slung it over one shoulder, and climbed into the waiting riverboat. Margaretha waved until the boat was out of sight around the headland.

One morning, some four months after father had left us, mother and I were in her garden working the earth to plant potatoes when I looked up from my job and saw father walking down the road. Margaretha saw him at almost the same instant and we dropped our hoes and ran to meet him. I was full of excitement and asked many questions, but he said very little except it was good to be home. He said something to Margaretha out of my hearing that seemed to please her. She said, "Come, you need a bath and some clean clothes."

I was of an age when I was beginning to be curious about the outside world. For weeks I pestered father to tell me about New York, but he said very little about his time there that held my interest. Sometimes at night I heard Georg and Margaretha arguing with stifled voices, as if they did not want me to hear the words. It was about that time that my friends told stories that they had heard from their fathers of the burning of New York by Negro slaves. One day that summer Thaddeus and I were fishing in the creek where I had first seen Nupi's father. Thaddeus' father often journeyed to New York as a justice of the law and when in his cups at Traphagen's he told stories about the men and women who came before him. These stories were oft-times repeated when there were guests, sometimes in the hearing of Thaddeus.

So that summer's day at my favourite fishing spot I asked Thaddeus if it was true that some Negro slaves had risen up and tried to burn down New York. Thaddeus said nothing at first, hesitant, I think, to tell tales against his father, but after while he said, "Father said there were white men too; an alehouse keeper called Hughson was hung by the neck. A priest was hung too. A whole bunch of Negroes were burnt at the stake."

"Why did they try to burn down New York?"

Thaddeus was getting into the story. "They did not burn down the city. Fires were set so they could rob the burning houses. The robbers helped the owners of the burning houses take out things before being consumed by flames. They took the stolen property to Hughson's tavern. A fallen woman hid some of the stolen goods in her room at Hughson's."

"Did Hughson sell the stuff?"

"The police found some in the fallen woman's room. Father said most of the stuff from the burning houses disappeared, not to be found."

"Did the police find the robbers?"

"The people were in a panic, fearful for their lives and property. The police rounded up many slaves, some from a Spanish ship, and put them on trial. It lasted all summer. Father told Herr Pottenburgh that thirteen Negroes were burned at the stake and sixteen hanged. Besides Hughson and a priest, two other white men were hanged. A great number of the suspects were banished from America."

Just then Thaddeus had a bite. The fish took the hook and while Thaddeus was heaving on his bending pole to land it, it jumped in a curving arc, throwing rainbow-coloured drops of water as it plunged again into the stream. It was a big trout and in our excitement we forgot about the burning of New York.

We caught five nice-sized trout between us that afternoon.

Walking home with Thaddeus, I again thought about the burning of New York. Father had been there at the time of the fires but he had said nothing about the story Thaddeus had told. I wondered why, but being a small boy whose father could do no wrong I turned to more childish concerns.

As I was growing up, neither my father nor Margaretha revealed what had happened to Georg while he was sojourning in New York. It was only much later, when I was preparing to go to New York for the first time, that I asked my father's advice. His only comment was, "Stay away from Hughson's alehouse by the North River. Hughson was hanged in '41 so it may not be there now, but it was trouble then and maybe still is." It was my first inkling that he knew of the robberies and the hangings, and his secrecy forced me to believe my father was more than a little involved. But I did not ask, "Why stay away from Hughson's?" because I did not want to know the answer. The true story of my father's time in New York in '41 went to the grave with him.

During those years in Ryn Beck my life was as full as any young boy could wish for. That may be the reason I was not aware of trouble brewing in our cabin. Only gradually did I become aware of mother's complaints about my father spending so much time in Traphagen's alehouse. Then one day she told me we would be going away, leaving Uncle Leonardt and Paulus to look after our few acres.

It was some years later that I understood what my immature brain did not see. Uncle Leonardt was building a grand house, and mother would say to father, "While we are still living in the same old log cabin." Always father's retort to this was, "Leonardt has two women to please him, while I have none." And at this, mother would break into tears and run to her spinning wheel, sobbing that Catharina was "all worn out" and weeping for hours on end while busy at her spinning machine. Father's response was to leave the house with his gun and return only after I had gone to sleep. Now I realize this trouble had been hurting my parents, and I guess they believed that if they got away from Georg's brother Leonardt, who was younger and stronger and more ambitious, they might come together again. So, at mother's urgings, my father talked to Leonardt, and one day in the spring of 1742 father and my uncle went off to see Mr. Beekman. It was agreed at this meeting that Leonardt would take over father's lease. Father purchased a new lease from Mr. Beekman for land near Poughquag, some two score miles to the south and further from the river.

So in the early summer of that year we boarded the boat at the Vanderburgh Landing with much weeping and long good-byes, and with all the possessions of our small family we headed down the river to a new home. We unloaded at the landing at the mouth of the Fishkill, and took a scow up that stream until we could go no farther. From there we trekked to our small plot of land on the slope of a hill called Vette Bergh that the locals knew as "Fat Hill."

I was ten at the time, too young then to really know our state of affairs; I did understand that father was gone from our cabin much of the time working either at the Elseworth Mill or cutting trees to build roads in the area. Mother planted her garden among the tree stumps behind the cabin, and soon the pattern of life was much the same as at Ryn Beck. Mother seemed happier, and my father seemed more anxious to please her. Greta appeared to be healthy. Johann Leonard was growing into a healthy boy and Margaretha soon was with child again.

Niclass was born when I was eleven years old. He seemed very small to me, almost as small as Dog's newly born puppies. Dog was a girl dog and by the time Niclass was born she had had three litters of puppies which father took off in a bag weighted with a stone and threw in the creek. Each time I was very angry with him, but each time mother explained to me that it was necessary. "We cannot keep all those puppies, they would eat us out of house and home."

Mother was anxious for Niclass since she had had disappointments before, but after the first year she talked about how he was thriving in the wilderness, not being subject to as many diseases as in the old country. Now I had two brothers, but they were so much younger than me that they could not do the things I wanted, so I found other boys with which to explore the countryside. Life continued for me much as before, but I missed being near the river.

The day I was thirteen Margaretha said to me, "Eberhardt, your father has found some land in the Clove Valley, not far from here, and he is taking us there." Father had told Margaretha that Henry Beekman described the lease as a good place for an enterprising farmer and his family. "It consists of cleared acres with a pasture, an existing cabin and shed. The soil is fertile and will make a nice little farm."

I remember that day clearly because it was my birthday and I was angry because no one seemed to notice. I was angry too at having to leave still another home, and wishing that father would finally find his place.

Early one morning we loaded all our possessions in the wagon, with father's loom and Margaretha's spinning machine on the very top of our few chattels. The path was muddy from the spring rains and sometimes we all had to get out and push. After an hour or so, both father and I walked behind the wagon to push while mother handled the two oxen straining to pull the wagon through the mud. By the time we reached our new home everyone was worn out except the babies, who were restless and irritable. But the next day arrived in bright sunshine and I ran outside to see my new surroundings. Our cabin was located in a valley surrounded by high hills and deep woods. Mother was pleased with her new home, but expressed the wish that she did not move again.

Since those days of my childhood I have come to realize that Margaretha's serenity in the face of hardship was due to her faith. She was very passionate about the worship of her God, and her God's creation in Nature. There was no church close to our new home, but Niclass Emigh, a man formerly from Amsterdam who had done well in America, opened his large stone house for services on the Sabbath. It was not long until my mother found a community of like-minded souls and began to attend services at Emigh's meetinghouse. With another child on the way she also set up a sort of shrine in one corner of the cabin for her Bible and prayer book.

We obtained ten sheep, as woollen blankets were necessary for warmth in winter. Mother planted a large garden. For many weeks during the wool-harvesting season, father worked at the fulling mill in Poughquag, cleaning and de-greasing the raw wool for spinning into yarn.

Anna Maria was born in '45 and was baptized during services at Niclass Emigh's stone house at Backway. With the birth of Anna Maria, Margaretha became a different person than I had grown up with. She became moody and tearful and given to sudden fits of anger, directed mostly at father but sometimes at me. We no longer went to the woods, and she no longer taught me the ways of her people in the old country, spending most of her days in the house, except for Sunday's meetings at The Klove. She was at the end of her childbearing years. Anna Maria was her second surviving daughter, making her fiercely protective, and with Johann Leonard, Greta and Niclass, ages six, four and two, Anna Maria took the major part of mother's interest, and she turned away from me, saying, "You are old enough to look after yourself." At thirteen I was deemed old enough to work as a man and it fell to me to help work the farm, as by now Georg was in his middle years and not as strong as before. And, he had little interest in the farm. I was approaching manhood and would soon be expected to take over from him, something I did not want to do. Mother had long ago planted the seed of curiosity in my head and I wished to venture from the valley and find a life and land of my own.

Father's plot of land, besides the wool from the sheep and the small acreage of flax for linen, produced enough corn, pumpkin and beans, to feed our family but little else. Meat had to come from the woods. But the woods were the hunting grounds of the few Wappinger Indians that had survived European diseases and disastrous wars with the Dutch. While the settlers believed treaties gave the land to them or to Henry Beekman, the savages thought differently; they had not given up the woods, their traditional hunting grounds. The last winter had been a harsh one, with spring arriving very late for planting, followed by a hot summer with little rain. The regular old timers in Pawling's Tavern in Poughquag said they had never seen a winter with so much snow. The mournful howls of starving wolves could be heard every night. Prey not taken by the wolf packs died from starvation. Game became scarce, and the summer hunting season was a scramble to shoot or trap anything on four legs.

Our family also faced a winter of hunger, so father drew me aside and announced that we had to spend the fall season hunting. But, he said, "The Indians are also faced with a bitter winter so there will be clashes in the woods. We must be very careful, or we will get an arrow in the back." Forced from his town life in the old country, my father had become a keen and skilful huntsman. I spent many days in the woods with him and when about nine was allowed to carry a gun, an old flintlock from the French wars. I had become quite good with the old gun, even brought down a cougar that was crouched in a tree ready to pounce on father's back. After that, I was allowed to go out with the gun on my own, although Margaretha objected, frightened that carrying a gun would make me a target for an Indian warrior, even though warriors were not usual in that neck of the woods. In spite of mother's worry, father and I usually provided all the meat and fish necessary to feed our family, year round.

But when the water for the whole year came down in the form of snow, followed by a dry summer, it was difficult to find enough game to fill the larder for the winter that was fast approaching. It was about the first of November, in the late afternoon after a day of hunting with only a single rabbit to our credit, when my father stopped me at the edge of a place of thick trees and whispered, "I think there is a squaw bear downwind in that hollow yonder. Do you smell her?" I had to admit I smelled nothing but the musky tang of a broken puffball at my feet. Father quietly outlined his plan. "You go round the thicket and try to get behind her, upwind from where I think she is feeding. When she smells you she will start to move my way. I will walk directly into the thicket and hopefully get a shot while she is moving away from you. Make some noise, but not too much as she may charge, especially if she has cubs."

So I carried out our plan as father had instructed me. I cannot say I wasn't frightened. I crept through the thick bushes and fallen trees not knowing whether the sow was getting ready to charge or whether she was moving toward my father. I deliberately stepped on a few dry twigs, hoping that the bear was moving with me. I got a glimpse of her through some thick leaves, and was heartened to know that at least the bear was real. She quickly disappeared, giving me no time to aim and fire. Then I heard a noise off to the right that sounded like "ptsst," and another "ptsst" on my left. At almost the same time, I heard the crash of a gun, closer than I expected.

Not sure the bear was truly down, I crept through the undergrowth. Parting the large leaves of a dense bush I saw it lying in a clearing, apparently dead. Two

Indians crouched over the carcass. They already had their knives out in preparation for skinning the beast, when, with a crashing of dead twigs, father came running out of the trees. When he saw the Indians he stopped dead in his tracks, but after a few seconds he walked to his kill to claim it. Acutely frightened but unwilling to let father face the Indians by himself I walked toward the tense scene. As I approached the carcass of the bear, I could see that it had been hit by three tufted arrows. One had gone completely through its neck and blood was spurting from the wound, forming a small arc before it spilled on the ground, taking with it the life of the bear.

The larger of the two Indians had straddled the bear's neck and was slicing off its ears. Father was trying to stop the Indian, but his partner stepped between them and grunted, "My bear." Father pointed to the gunshot wound just behind the ear and shouted, "I killed it. See, a ball right into the brain." He tried to push the large Indian with the knife away from the carcass. The second one made a threatening move with his knife and I knew then that I must do something. I shouted as loud as I could in father's direction, "Paw, the Indians fired first. I heard two arrows before your gunshot." The third arrow, which I did not hear, must have been launched at the precise time father fired his gun.

This outburst seemed to calm father, and he stepped away from the big Indian and looked to me for an explanation, which I readily gave to him.

"I heard two of the arrows as they let them fly. The third must have been let go at the same time as your gunshot. The Indians were first. Whether or not the arrow through the neck killed the bear before your gunshot no one knows but God."

The two savages were looking at me and suddenly began shouting in their own language and waving their arms, sensing they had won. Indeed, I firmly believed it was their kill and said to father, "Let them have the bear. It was likely their kill and we won't starve without its meat, but they might."

Father was not sympathetic to their plight. We both knew losing the bear meant he had to kill at least one of our wool-bearing sheep for meat if another bear or moose could not be had before the deep snows set in. Nonetheless he realized this battle was lost. He prepared to leave the Indians with their "ill-gotten prize" and shouldering his musket turned to leave. Just then the smaller of the two savages took a hatchet from his belt and plunged it into a nearby log and uttered words that seemed to be friendly. The larger of the two, holding bloody ears aloft, had not lost his angry scowl. Nervously ignoring him, but being curious about their origin because the clothes and totems said they were not local Wappinger, I said to the smaller of the two, "What village?" He quickly answered, "*Tankileke*." Pointing to his partner, "*Mahiingan*." With these words he looked furtively into the woods, suddenly aware that they were hunting in another tribe's territory. The big Indian was trying to haul the dead bear into the trees and frantically waving his free arm in a motion that clearly said "Help me get this thing into the woods." They were anxious to avoid trouble with the local tribe, which, while normally peaceful would seek vengeance for stealing its bear.

I said to father, "Come on and let us leave this place before there is trouble with the local Wappinger!"

Father seemed to accept my advice and we left the glade and the Indians to drag their prize into the deep woods and butcher it to be divided among the members of their village. I was shaking as we walked away.

When we returned to the cabin Margaretha was angry with us for "stirring up trouble with the savages." But father assured her that nothing would come of it, and he turned out to be correct. When the Puritans had come in great numbers after the English Civil War, the Indians had become aware that they were losing their traditional lands and began to fight the Hudson River Dutch and the Puritans of New England. But the years of warfare between the natives and the newcomers were mostly over when I was a boy approaching manhood, with the local Indians reduced by guns and disease to a few peaceful souls. Faced with losing their lands and their culture, those who were left retreated to the woods to seek out a bare existence. But the voracious appetite for farmland by European settlers was slowly eating up even the woods.

M y childhood was a time of relative peace in our region of the country, but internally I was at war with myself. I was reaching that age when, being the eldest male, I would be expected follow in father's footsteps and carry on where he left off. But I hungered for something more than a small plot of land in the wilderness, a hunger that would be satisfied, in an unexpected way, only in middle age. Meanwhile, Georg and Margaretha were in their middle years and I carried a larger and larger share of the work to support the family. Johann Leonard was old enough to be of some help, but was a dreamer and even when older did not take to the rough life of a farmer. Niclass was the lively one of my brothers, but he was still very young and not strong enough for heavy work.

But, life for me was not all work. There were summer fairs with produce and crafts displayed and evaluated. The neighbours held suppers and dances nearly every Saturday, but everyone, sober or not, was expected to be present at Niclass Emigh's stone house for Sunday service when Pastor Reinhardt thundered his message of doom for sinners. To rid us of the salvation doled out by Pastor Reinhardt, Hendrick de Lange and I escaped from the adults who stayed on for refreshments after the service. Some of the men, in defiance of their wives, kept a jug of rum in the stone well beside the meetinghouse, and pretending to be thirsty, went in twos and threes to imbibe of their secret supply of "good drinking water." Not to be outdone by the adults, Hendrick had his own supply of rum. In the crevice of a rock behind the horse's shed, Hendrick kept hidden a crock of illegal rum, and we each had hidden a corncob pipe along with flints. We carried Indian tobacco in our coats, and here behind the shed away from the worshipers, and in defiance of Pastor Reinhardt we committed the sins of drinking rum and smoking Indian tobacco.

One Sabbath, it was a hot day in June, Hendrick's cousin Magdalena found us puffing away behind the rock. I was used to seeing Magdalena at the meetinghouse, sitting with the Kerver family, but until today I had never been close to her. Standing in front of us in the harsh sunlight, with her legs spread and her feet firmly planted, she dared us to chase her away. I saw her for the first time as more that a white face framed by a bonnet on the Kerver bench in the meetinghouse, taking in every word the pastor uttered. Her saucy stance before Hendrick caused me to sit up and take note of her more closely. She had shed her bonnet, revealing long black tresses as shiny as the feathers of a crow. Her eyes, shaded by dark, heavy brows, matched the blackness of her hair. A long straight nose and full lips framing a wide mouth set in a square face that was as white as snow gave her an otherworldly appearance that in Massachusetts would cause suspicion by the Godly men of New England. That day she wore a snow-white bodice with the strings drawn as tight as possible to emphasize her burgeoning womanhood. Even at her tender age I sensed in her the spirit of a nymph. Her presence caused me to squirm in my skin, but I felt something in my loins that made me want to be near her. Even now, in my advanced years, my blood stirs remembering that first encounter with Magdalena.

She said to her cousin, "Give me a pipe Hendrick or I shall tell on you." We had put away the rum and were smoking tobacco to kill the smell of rum.

"I don't have another. If your father knew I gave you tobacco he would kill me."

"Let me puff of yours." She sat between us on the rock, forcing me to move away to avoid intimate contact. She neither looked my way nor said anything to me, ignoring my presence altogether.

So Hendrick, as fearful of her as I was, gave up his corncob. She took a few puffs and began to cough. Satisfied, having bested us and got her way, she jumped up and waved a gay goodbye while running back to join her family. Hendrick and I put away our pipes until the next Sabbath and followed her. Returning to the meetinghouse, I felt I had entered a new, adult period of my life.

In many of the social events that summer I was thrown together with Hendrick's cousin and her friends, although she mostly ignored me until late in the day of one hot afternoon. It was at a barn-raising bee that she encountered me in a most compromising situation. At the end of the day, after working to raise the frame of the barn for finishing the next day, Hendrick, Jacob Kettel, Jonas Emigh and I went down to the river, and, hidden by a grove of heavy bush, stripped away our garments and waded into the cool water for a wash. We were splashing about when, in a temporary lull in our revelling, we were startled to hear giggles coming from the bushes lining the bank of the river pond. Patches of colour through the bushes identified some young ladies spying on us. Magdalena was one of them, and she seemed to be looking directly at me with a wide, taunting smile. She seemed to be daring me to expose myself. I felt, with a great measure of embarrassment, that it was very important for me to escape from her gaze.

We were trapped. Our clothes were lying in the grass under bushes, and while the ladies did not seem to be bent on stealing our garments, we nevertheless could not retrieve them without emerging naked from the stream. It seemed odd to me afterwards that I was aroused by this girl, who, with her mocking grin, was subjecting me to the greatest torment imaginable. After a few moments when her playful eyes had me in helpless confusion, she turned away. The other two did the same and after a few minutes we felt it was safe to retrieve our clothes and join the barn-raising crew at supper where my tormentor sat with her parents and avoided my eyes during the meal. I was relieved to have avoided her scrutiny but still I wanted to be close to this beguiling creature.

At the dance on the floor of the barn that had been raised that day, the maiden ladies sat primly along one side of the floor, with the young men, those who were not outside drinking from a jug of whiskey, stood around in clusters. The young men pretended to be indifferent to the ladies, while at the same time furtively surveying the choices. There was much strutting and playful punching of each other to show off their manliness, while across the room the ladies were mentally willing a favoured gentleman to glide across the floor to seek their company. Some of the younger men were embarrassed because their mothers tried to push them into action. Magdalena was quite popular, but after several reels by the lone fiddler stomping his heavy boots on the barn boards I saw her sitting without company. Nervously, I approached her for a dance. She accepted and we found a square that was not yet complete. She looked at the floor and avoided looking straight at me. The music began and we were soon lost in the frenetic activity necessary for such a dance. When close to her in the swings and the do-si-dos I could feel the warm contours of her body and smell the scent of her hair. I wanted the dance to go on forever but it was over much too soon. Holding her warm hand I stood at her side after the music stopped, secretly hoping she would be my partner for the next dance, but after a confusing moment she said, "Thank you," with a smile and went to meet her friends along the wall. She was soon taken up by Jacob Kettell and whirled away into the crowd.

Whirling away says it all for my future court of Magdalena. She was like a butterfly, alighting to show her beauty, but flying off when I tried to catch her. It made me all the more determined to conquer this pretty will-o-the-wisp, a determination that overcame my good sense.

I asked if I might see her at the next barn-raising bee, which was being held on the following Saturday. She consented, seemingly pleased that I had asked her. So on the day appointed, just after sunup, Niclass and I hitched the younger of our two horses to the cart loaded with hay for christening the new barn and set out for the farm of the Shermerhorn brothers, Jacob and John, about four miles down the road from our place. Mother and my sister Anna would follow later in the buggy to help prepare the noon meal for the men. I expected that Magdalena would help the women prepare food, and we had agreed on a rendezvous at the dance that would follow the raising of the barn.

During the day I saw little of her, both of us busy with our separate tasks. Work on the barn finished for the day, everyone gathered to have supper on the floor of the new barn, suffused with the sweet smell of newly-cut timber. Tables were spread with vegetables and fruits from the local farm gardens, and as if by magic the women of the community brought in large cauldrons of beef stew along with bricks of cheese and loaves of bread. Jacob Shermerhorn gave thanks for the raising of his new barn, and being a shy man, said no more but called on Pastor Rhinehardt to say grace. When the workers were satisfied with adequate food for their day's work, the women joined them. I hoped that Magdalena would sit close to me but she gave me a playful glance as she sat across from Jacob Kettell, a boy I was beginning to hate. In spite of my attempts to catch her eye during supper she studiously avoided my attention and engaged in animated conversation with the men and boys close to her, with, I thought, special intimacy with Jacob Kettell.

When the supper tables had been cleared and the barn floor sprinkled with sawdust to make it easier to dance on the rough pine boards I sought out Magdalena for the first dance of the evening, an unwritten requirement for young couples who were socially intimate. Magdalena was as sweet as sugar and fell into my arms as if all she wanted was to be there.

After the first dance to slow, romantic, dreamy music, a caller mounted on a chair shouted over the excited talk on the floor, "Take your partners," announcing the beginning of several lively reels. I managed to keep Magdalena through two square dances, which brought out the sweat in both of us. She said, "I must find mother, she is all alone and will be anxious for me."

"Will you keep the last dance for me?"

She whispered demurely, "Yes," and left me on the floor in a state of euphoria.

I forced myself to dance with other girls, but always kept an eye out for Magdalena, who came back to the floor and whirled around with several young men. We had the last dance, her body pressed close to mine bringing out both suppressed love and rising emotion at the closeness of our temporary union. I marshalled enough courage to ask to drive her home, and when she said yes I was taken aback since I had only the cart, and it was to share with Niclass. So I went to Margaretha while Magdalena went to get her shawl and begged her to let me have the buggy while she and Anna could go in the cart with Niclass. With a sly smile she agreed, and so Magdalena and I continued our intimacy on the buck-board of the buggy while her mother kept a withering eye on her daughter from the seat behind.

When it seemed Magdalena might agree to be my wife I lost heart in the pursuit. My soul was restless, imbued with the sentiment of seeking to see what was on the other side of the mountain like Georg before me. I did not always see eye to eye with father, but I had to admit that when we were in the woods he was a different person than at home. He often spoke of his frustrated dreams when he set out to become a master weaver in the old country and ended up working in the mills as a day labourer, his life much as it had been in Germany. He had little interest in farming, only a few acres of the farm had been cleared while the heavily wooded back acres, against the rugged hills remained as nature intended. Much work was needed to make the back acres more than a haven for bears and wolves and neither father nor I had the desire to wrestle with the land to make it flourish as a farm as long as it was leasehold. Many leases were being sold but father could not afford the rising prices for freehold land. So his frustration grew at the same time as my desire to move on haunted me. I had been brought up to believe the oldest son was to carry on from his father, but something in my make-up was pulling me away from duty to the family. I agonized over the direction my future should take, so I put aside any thoughts of marriage even though my affection for Magdalena was powerful, and denying myself of her brought me many sleepless nights.

Meanwhile life went on. New England was constantly at war with the Indians or the French of Canada. In those days, after largely subjugating the original inhabitants of the forests, the New England settlers had a new enemy, the Papist French to the north who had allied with the Algonquin tribes. Both sides courted the warriors of the Iroquois, but a man called William Johnson seemed to bring them to the side of the English. I thought of travelling up the river to Fort Edward or Fort William Henry to seek the fame and fortune of war, but it seemed only a wild boyhood wish when I spoke the thought to my friends. We were living in an isolated, peaceful place with no real enemies except the landlords. Magdalena wondered why I wanted to put myself in the way of danger.

Except for news from the occasional English trooper or a soldier of our own militia home for a rest from battle, the colonial wars were of little interest to most people in the Clove Valley. Some of the old men talked much of the adventure of war but little of its tragedy and brutality, There was an old man, a colonel I think, living on pension in Poughquag, who traveled around the countryside on his bay horse and spoke of the adventure awaiting any boy who joined the militia.

Of my brothers, Johann Leonard showed little interest in war at that time, but Niclass was fifteen and anxious to gain the age when he could join the New York Militia. Mother was so upset with this that she sat Niclass on a hard chair in front of the fire one evening with a letter in her hand that she had received from her cousin. The letter was to her cousin from a brother who had fought with Abercrombie during his assault on Fort Ticonderoga.

"Niclass, this is a letter written by my cousin Henry who is only four years older than you. He was excited like you about going off to fight with swords and guns. Cousin Henry went up the river to a place called Fort Edward and gave his name to an English General Abercrombie who was planning to capture Fort Ticonderoga."

"Fort Ticonderoga"?

"It is a fort where the French army lives. Cousin Henry with the large English army marched on Fort Ticonderoga. The French general had had his soldiers cut down trees around the fort and sharpened the branches, so when Henry and the English soldiers tried to reach the fort they got all tangled in the fallen trees and were brutally slaughtered by French bayonets. Henry's very best friend was killed trying to get untangled from the *abatis* and a French soldier kept putting ball after ball into his body. Henry wanted to help his friend but his captain would not let him help."

Niclass seemed uninterested in the story, prompting mother to raise her voice.

"Niclass! Listen to cousin Henry's very words, 'At noon we mounted a full-scale attack, but after five hours of slaughter we came to the knowledge that the *abatis* had defeated us. Our men were being impaled on the *abatis* as they fell. The redcoats were easy targets as they tried to cut through the branches of the fallen trees. We in the green and brown of the first battalion were better off, but in spite of our smaller losses we were even then cut to pieces. My mate, Jeremiah from Fort Edward, took a ball straight into his right eye. It almost took away his head. The red blood was spurting out of his eye and his mouth, darkening the green leaves in which he was entangled. I ran in a crouch along the *abatis* and tried to rescue him, but an officer behind me shouted, 'Let him be! He's a goner. Get back to your post!' I took a last look at my friend and spent the next three hours in a state of insanity, trying to kill as many Frenchman as possible.' What happened to Henry's friend could happen to you my dear boy if you take up arms."

Niclass listened after Margaretha's angry outburst but said nothing. I think he did not believe anything he heard.

She went on, "I do not want you to go to end up like Henry's friend. Please promise you will not go to war."

Niclass mumbled one word, a half-hearted word that sounded like, "Yes."

Margaretha, discouraged, turned away with tears in her eyes.

Mother was so appalled with the prospect of her youngest son going off to war that, for my love of her, I began to abandon my desire for adventure. If she were afraid for Niclass she would be quite shaken if I, her future security, left her. Niclass talked no more of the militia, and he, like me, did not get caught up in war until mother had gone to heaven.

Meanwhile, she was pushing me to take a wife, in particular to lay court to Magdalena Kerver. Her reaction to the talk of Niclass going to war had forced me to consider her wish to keep her boys close; and besides honouring mother's wishes the prospect of marriage to Magdalena was beginning to be attractive to me without her urgings. But I was hearing tales of her keeping company with Jacob Kettell, and since she was then the only lady that I considered for a wife I suffered secretly at the loss.

During the following Yule season an incident occurred which gave me hope that I would yet gain her hand. It was a beautiful night with new snow reflecting the light of a full moon, making the scene almost as bright as day. It was the tradition, carried over from the old country, for the young people of the community to gather together on some conveyance to sing carols as they travelled on the roads connecting farmhouses. Afterwards, there was a ball and dancing at one of the larger homes. That night, about twenty young people wrapped tightly against the cold air were singing as they huddled on a Conestoga wagon drawn by two spirited horses. The road was bathed in moonlight as it meandered along the bank of the dark river, swollen and heavy with water that here and there glistened as bright as silver where the fast flowing stream struck a rock or fallen tree branch. I lost my joy at the beauty of the night as soon as I spotted Magdalena and Jacob Kettell sitting together at the rear of the wagon with their feet dangling over the side. I had been fated to be sitting beside Ursula Smith, a plain but pleasant girl that I was sure had set her bonnet for me. It was not that I disliked Ursula, just that I was obsessed with Magdalena.

After the accident, I was told it was Joe Yeomans who had grabbed the whip from its pouch and slapped the rump of one of the horses. The horse bolted, slewing the wagon partway across the road so that the rear wheel dropped over the edge of the riverbank and the wagon lurched toward the fast waters of the river. As it dropped away beneath the carollers, some six of them were thrown into the stream. Jacob and Magdalena were the first to hit the water, followed by a tangle of other screaming bodies clawing at the bank to escape the rushing current. Most managed to cling to bushes growing along the river, but in horror I spotted Magdalena being drawn downstream by the current. Without thinking, I pushed through the carollers still on the wagon, threw off my coat, and jumped into the river. The icy water pierced like a knife and for a moment I was stunned. At that point the river was not deep, only waist high, but the current was very strong and Magdalena was moving quickly away from me. Thinking back to that incident now, I realize that it was at that moment that I knew she meant more to me than my own life.

I caught her about fifty yards downstream where her feet had found bottom. She was struggling against the current to scramble ashore when I clutched her and dragged her to the river's edge. With her sodden clothes she was very heavy and being weakened by the cold water I could pull her no farther. She too was done in, but unhurt. Catching my breath, I managed to get her to her feet and together we scrambled up the bank to the road. Bedraggled, soaking wet, and shivering uncontrollably her contrary spirit came through. She sputtered, "Your hands found places that were indecent for a proper gentleman." Looking into her face with water streaming down her cheeks like tears, her lips chastising me for indecent treatment in saving her, I could not help but laugh. Mollified, she grinned in return. It was that single moment that set the tone of our young lives together.

By this time several people from the wagon had appeared and we walked back to the site of the accident. The horses had been strong enough to hold the wagon from going into the river, and by the time we reached it the team had pulled it back onto the road. Only one of the others thrown off the wagon onto the bank of the river got completely soaked; the others had held to bushes and mostly only their legs were submerged. But all were shivering with the cold and anxious to get back to the house of our host, Joshua Barent. Someone put a blanket around Magdalena and everyone piled onto the wagon and huddled down into the straw in the wagon's bed. Magdalena found my hand and squeezed it.

The horses were whipped into a run and after what seemed forever but was only about five minutes we were back at the house, our clothes steaming in front of a roaring fire. Frau Barent took Magdalena into her bedroom and gave her dry clothes, but no one paid much attention to my plight until Magdalena returned, and seeing that I was shaking, asked Frau Barent to find a dry shirt for me. This done, we sat together in front of the fire with some of the others from the wagon that were also wet and cold. I remember finding it strange that after all the excitement Johann Wannamaker was ignoring the whole affair and going on about seeing a giant blue whale being rendered for its oil over on the river at Poughkeepsie.

Our intimacy during the river accident and Magdalena's tenderness toward me immediately afterward seemed to make no change in our relationship. She was as flighty as before, driving me to frustration and despair. We often met behind Emigh's meetinghouse while the men were socializing at the well, and on those occasions she treated me as if she had affection for me. But at socials and dances she was seen more often with her cousin Hendrick and Jacob Kettell. Later, I found that wise Margaretha understood the reason for my frustration, but said nothing to me. Meanwhile, I stumbled around, trying to court my will-o-the-wisp. Eventually our wispy togetherness led to a haymow in the barn on her father's farm, which led to his ultimatum. He was against Magdalena seeing me, but now that I had supposedly "shamed" his daughter he was anxious to make matters right. The ultimatum was not necessary. We had become betrothed before the barn incident occurred.

We exchanged vows in front of God and the senior Kervers at her home. While her father blessed our union he was not in favour of our living in his house so we lived with mother and my younger siblings until father returned from Crum Elbow, where he had gone to make sail cloth for the schooners plying up and down the Hudson River. When father came home from Crum Elbow I began to look for an excuse to take Magdalena from there and try to find land of my own.

About that time Margaretha received a letter from Aunt Barbara informing her of Catharina's passing. After hearing this news, mother said to Georg, "I suppose Leonardt will now marry Barbara," and, true to her prediction, he did marry Barbara. She gave birth to a baby girl, Elisabeth, and two years later Sebastion was born, another cousin for me. In the words of the letter I found my immediate future.

The letter informed mother that Uncle Leonardt was not well and Paulus needed a hand. This message was intended only as news and was not a serious plea from Aunt Barbara for help, but I took it as an opportunity to become independent. I wrote to Uncle Leonardt and offered to move Magdalena and myself to the old homestead. Mother was very upset by my decision to leave her. She carried on for a week, wondering what she would do without her eldest son. Johann Leonard showed no interest in the farm and had been talking about the war for Canada. He had several times threatened to leave father, with whom he did not get along. He spoke about seeking out Robert Rogers and joining his rangers. I told him he was crazy, he wouldn't last overnight with such a tough group of fighting woodsmen. Niclass was also restless and unpredictable. My heart was full of guilt for leaving them, but now that I had a wife I had to please her. She had told me several times she was not happy and did not want to live with my family. Mother took me aside one evening and whispered that she suspected Magdalena's irritability was because she had a child growing in her belly.

In the end mother had to accept the reality that I was leaving the nest, and became quieter, if not less moody. Father did not seem to care whether I left or stayed; he had almost no interest in the farm and spent most of his remaining days in the woods with his musket.

I struck an agreement with Uncle Leonardt to go back to the homestead, and took as part of my legacy two road-horses from the farm. One morning in late May of the year 1760, loading the horses with our meagre possessions, consisting of cooking utensils, my flintlock and the few things we needed to survive in the wilderness, we bid our folks farewell, and Magdalena and I set off to what was father's old farm, near Ryn Beck. We encountered no hostile Indians or bandits and arrived safely in early June to take up a new life.

The year before, Uncle Leonardt and Michael Pultz had each donated one acre of land on which the community could build a permanent church. So the summer of the year we came to the old homestead I helped build a church on the Witaberger lands. Magdalena quickly fell in with the women of the parish and being a lively soul appeared to be well liked. Nevertheless, she often was homesick and missed her mother. As it happened, one of the first baptisms by Reverend Ries in the new church was a girl child, christened Margaretha, the daughter of Catherine and Eberhardt, a cousin of mine, son of Uncle Bernhardt. Cousin Eberhardt had recently come to the Witaberger lands from Crum Elbow.

It seemed like Magdalena and I had barely arrived at father's old homestead when Aunt Barbara arrived on our doorstep with bad news. "Your father is dead. He was found by some hunters with a hole in his chest from a musket ball." I guess I wasn't too surprised that he had died; life was pretty unpredictable back then, but I was taken aback by her words of the nature of his death.

"Who did it?"

"Apparently no one knows. The first thought was that he fought with some Indians over the ownership of a game animal, since there was a great amount of blood, as if Indians had killed him and slaughtered the animal near his body. Then someone remembered two strangers on horseback in Poughquag. Suspicion turned to these men, but they have disappeared and the sheriff has not been able to find them. He thinks the two strangers are figments of someone's imagination. Georg was found face down beside a log as if he may have tripped over the log and accidently shot himself. He was found lying on his musket. The Sherriff thinks it was an accident and rather than stir up the Indians, has reported to the authorities that it was a hunting accident. Your sister Anna argued with him, but to no avail."

The story sounded unbelievable. "How do you know this? Why didn't Anna write to me?"

"Someone who had passed through Poughquag met your Uncle Leonardt in Traphagen's, and on finding out he was Georg's brother relayed the story to him. I expect you will receive a letter from your mother or Anna."

I looked down at the gun I had been cleaning and felt rage rise in my chest. I felt like smashing the gun over a rock. But my anger soon left me and I stood the gun against the doorjamb.

My thoughts turned to the day father and I had had the encounter with the Indians over a bear, and wondered if the same thing had happened and his anger had got the best of him. But the talk of strangers bothered me. I wondered if they had something to do with father's mysterious adventures in New York town some years ago. But that was almost twenty years ago. It was so long ago that there could be no possible link there, but still I was uncomfortable with the thought. Probably the Sherriff was correct; it was a simple hunting accident. After all, accidents happened frequently in the pioneer settlements. For my own peace of mind and considering Magdalena's condition I too made myself believe it was an accident.

I did get a letter from Anna that told the same story. I talked to Uncle Leonardt and his advice was to accept the Sherriff's decision, "and forget how Georg died. He had almost seen his three score and ten and had fulfilled God's wish for him." We agreed that he had had a good life with Margaretha and my "thoughts should be for her." That seemed to end the incident, but to this day I wonder if Georg had caused some trouble in New York that never came out at the time. I remember things seemed to go well for us after he returned, but I had assumed it was because of his honest endeavours. But I realize now that I never knew my father. For me, he died as he had lived, as a mystery.

7

DRUMS OF WAR

One bright spring day with nature turning green and noisy geese flying north to their summer breeding grounds, a rider came to us with a letter bearing sad news. Anna, who lived with mother after Greta's marriage had written that Margaretha had passed away. At the end, she suffered greatly from pleurisy and she died late one night of pneumonia. As I stood on the doorstep of our cabin looking down the valley and seeing it beginning to bloom I thought of how she loved the woods and the small animals and birds that made it their home. She had blossomed in the wilds of our new homeland, but in the fall of her life she had withered and now she had died.

With both my parents gone, I came to feel that our presence in America had left no footprint, and if we were to prosper, I had to have my own land. Father left very little in his passing, while Uncle Leonardt owned his own land, and Paulus, and now even Sebastion, were doing well. Georg left no such legacy except for several offspring, his loom, seed, and a few sticks of furniture, including Margaretha's spinning machine. Greta was safely married. Johann Leonardt had married Christina from Ryn Beck and they had a little girl they call Gertrout. They were living with Christina's father.

With my father gone and so little to show for his life I felt the need to break out of the web of my family and create my own affairs. The following year an opportunity came my way to lease a small acreage in the precinct of Nine Partners. It was there that Lena birthed her first son to carry my life into the future. She christened him Thomas, after her father.

Several months after mother died a team and wagon came down the road and turned into our yard. It was Niclass. As I went out to greet him I saw that the wagon was piled with household chattels and a few pieces of farm equipment.

"Niclass, have you left the farm?"

"I have that! There was nothing to keep me there so I came up here and find work in a different part of the country. Anna married the Becker boy and has gone to live with him. I gave her most of the furniture, mother's spinning machine, her clothing and the bedding. I knew you wanted father's loom. It's on the wagon."

Lena came into the yard carrying Thomas. On seeing her it set my astonished mind at work and I asked quietly of Niclass, "Do you hope to live with us?"

"Only for a short time until I get work in one of the mills. That is, if Lena will have me."

When Lena came up to us I said to her, "It's Niclass! He has brought some furniture for you and some farm equipment. I have asked him to put up with us until he finds work."

I knew she was not pleased, but she put on a pleasant face and said, "You are welcome to stay with us Niclass as long as you need to." She pushed Thomas forward and said, "This is Thomas! Thomas, meet your Uncle Niclass!

Niclass, too young to love babies nevertheless took Thomas in his arms and made the polite cooing noises that mother's expect. I interrupted his embarrassment and invited him to unhitch the team and come to have the noon meal.

With Niclass living with us we could have stayed put and paid the rent or bought acreage since much of the land around us was freehold and relatively cheap. But there was as much uncertainty about freehold land as there was about leased land in those days because of the troubles and insecurity caused by talk of civil war.

Like my father before me the politics of the time intruded on my life, and like him the politics of the day did not favour lowly people like us. Trouble was brewing. The region was filling up with settlers who were heavily dependent on the landlords for their livelihood and there was growing resentment developing because many tenants felt like slaves. Many were promised deeds to their land after a given number of years of quit rent, and too often the deeds were not forthcoming. Land disputes dragged on for years while lawyers for the wealthy men who held patents from the Crown fought the settlers. Large landlords were also fighting each other in the courts for more land. The whole countryside was aflame with hatred. Farmers began to fight for what they considered the right to ownership of raw land after they had invested their own labour in clearing fields and building homes. The feeling was that the farm was properly theirs, won by sweat. A rebellious character called Pendergrast began to organize the settlers into action against the landlords and the Crown, which had awarded large tracts of land to a few men. The protesters were called "levellers," or "clubmen;" labels that came from the English Civil war.

Mr. Robert Livingston, awarded a large patent by his king, had increased his acreage, some said on the backs of settlers. A number of disgruntled farmers refused to pay their rent, and some were threatening to kill Livingston, but their weapons were mere sticks, hoes, rakes, and shovels. Livingston's son met this ragged bunch with forty armed men and caused them to withdraw.

The next day a small army of levellers gathered at Poughkeepsie, led by Pendergrast and his lieutenants. They broke open all the jails between Poughkeepsie and Albany on the east side of the river. The government alerted the 28th Regiment of militia and it was sent north to quell the riot. The militia captured Pendergrast, and he was sentenced to die for treason without benefit of clergy.

Hanging Pendergrast was not the end of the matter; in truth it was only the beginning of a terrible and tragic time for America. In Traphagen's tavern, drunken fights kept breaking out between those who supported Pendergrast and those who supported the government, which many believed was supporting the landlords. There were rumours that in Boston officials of the government were being dragged from their houses by mobs, robbed of their silver and gold, beaten and covered with hot pine pitch and feathers, and escorted out of town astraddle a sharp cedar fence rail. The patrons of Traphagen's tavern worried that this violence would come to them. The trouble being stirred up by Pendergrast seemed to be the beginning of a chaotic situation that many thought they had left behind in Germany.

One afternoon some tenant farmers met in the tavern to make decisions on how they would stand in a civil war between the farmers and the landlords if such a situation came about. Some said the fracas was another peasant's war like that of Luther's time. At this point old Martin Froese spoke up, "I will tell you of the peasant's war. If I could just have a bit of oil to loosen my tongue." Old Martin loved to tell stories, some not so truthful, but he needed a smooth tongue in the telling. The unsaid rule was that if the patrons had not heard the story before, or if it was a subject of interest and they were inclined, they would make sure old Martin got his "oil." That afternoon he told the story of the war in which the peasants rose up against their landlords in Germany.

"It was in the days of Luther, when the landholders and urban magistrates were getting rich on the backs of the peasants who were close to the soil and the very soul of Germany. For two years the towns and the countryside were ravaged, farmers and their families slaughtered and many were the hangings. It started with the popularity of Luther's preaching of equality for all men. People refused to pay tithes and were arrested by the magistrates. Some were executed. Peasants organized and wrote their demands, much as Luther had done, in the form of twelve articles. One was the elimination of serfdom, which, by God, is nothing more than what we are. Serfs! The Swabian League of nobles put out the fires of rebellion after much bloodshed and chaos in the towns and countryside of my homeland. It could happen here too. The thing is, nothing changed; the peasants gained nothing, and their lot was actually made worse because it gave the nobles an excuse to tighten their grip over their lives more than before the war."

Many of the tenant farmers were going north where it was rumoured land was available in Albany County. Cousin Johann Jacob, who married the same year my Thomas was born, took his new wife Rosina up the river and leased land off the Hoosick Road from a Steven van Rensselaer, and from the words in a letter he wrote to Uncle Leonardt, he seemed to be prospering. At this time, my landlord was asking for more rent. The same thing was happening all through the district, with landowners and their lawyers trying to squeeze every drop of blood from us, and most of the talk in the taverns those days was of raising an army to fight the landlords. Walter Haltenburger was taking names of farmers who would join him in the fight. I did not sign, believing I would become a target for the hired thugs that were intimidating the settlers. It was hopeless to get ahead, and if it weren't for Lena and the children I would have taken my flintlock and joined Pendergrast's levellers. It was time to seek a new place close to where Johann Jacob lived, but the whole country seemed to be in the hands of rascals, and I was not too hopeful that things would be different in Albany County. But in the tradition of my kin it was time to move on to seek an ordered and peaceful future. Besides the opportunities for land-hungry people, the increasing violence stirred up by mobs in New England made me think there was no future where I was then living. Mostly, I was sad to leave Anna, my sister in Poughquag, whom I nevertheless believed capable of a successful life with the Becker boy.

So it came to pass that Niclass and I made plans to take the means to survive for one year and go up-river.

Lena was very unhappy with my plan. After Thomas and Catharina were born she had lost her playful nature. She felt isolated from her kin and she wished not to take her children even farther into the wilderness, where she believed there were savages behind every tree. Although her mother was off in the hills of Backway, itself an isolated place, she expressed a need to be close to her. I explained there were no more Indians in the north than in the woods east of our farm, and with the comfortable keelboats able to bring people down from Albany in a few hours we would hardly be further away than we were at our place. After some days of reasoning, even if she could not see the sense of my plan, she reluctantly withdrew her objections.

Niclass spent several days fashioning green basswood into arch-like bows, which he fastened to the sides of the hay wagon. When these were covered with two thicknesses of linen sail cloth he had made a comfortable shelter for two-year-old Thomas and baby Catharina, and our fragile goods were safe from the burning sun and the storms that we were likely to encounter. Niclass then bent his hand to tightening and repairing loose and broken wheel spokes, greasing the hubs with tar, and replacing some wood due to rot. A soft seat and a foot platform were rigged so that Lena could drive the oxen when necessary. When hitched to a yoke of our sturdy bullocks, Niclass declared the wagon fit for the journey.

We left for unknown parts in May, after the ice had been loosened from the rivers and creeks. When we set out for Ryn Beck that morning we were two families, for Johann Leonard had decided to take his family to the new promise land with us. We were a caravan train of yoked oxen, cows, horses, and two wagons loaded down with axes, tools and tar for repairs, guns, buckets for water, barrels of feed for the animals and father's loom. A small stove for the making of bread hung from the rear of my wagon. We proceeded noisily, with the rattle of pots and pans hung from the bows of the canopy, and the jingle of the harnesses of the oxen. Lena had to keep to the sanctuary of the covered wagon, because when she tried to walk, little Thomas insisted on walking also, but he ended up mostly pulled along the road by his mother, who soon gave up the effort and kept he and his baby sister in the wagon.

As our caravan entered the town of Ryn Beck some of the men I had known, drank and fought with, having heard of our coming stood on the steps of Traphagen's, and while some cheered a hurrah others stood silently by. This friendly send-off was startling to me since I was sure no one cared a whit about my coming or going. I was at the same time deeply moved and, giving over the team to Lena, walked from the road to shake the hands of the men that wished me "Godspeed." Old Ezekiah, a local character quite far gone with drink, fell on me, his tears wetting my cheek. I was much moved by this show of affection and wondered if I had made a good decision to leave the country where I had grown up.

Having survived this unexpectedly fond farewell, we struck the post road and turned north. The road was much improved, the government having laid down paving stones since the last time I had travelled over the road to visit Margaretha's cousin in Kirkehoek. We passed the German church in that place that the Palatines established long ago, and when our entourage reached the stone church of the Lutherans we agreed that we had now left Ryn Beck forever. For some minutes after, all adults were silent, each with thoughts peculiar only to themselves. The leaving did not bother the children, being of an age where serious matters were of no consequence.

After passing the stone church the road became much inferior, being mostly a packed earth track through grass and fallen leaves. The road was wet in many places and we soon encountered some difficult patches. Berry and Buck, our bullocks, were up to the job with only now and then a touch of the whip.

At the toll station of Red Hook we were able to have a bite to eat and to rest and water the animals.

Leaving Red Hook, we drove through the afternoon until we reached the manor of Robert Livingston. I was anxious, fearing his men would refuse us entry because of the recent troubles caused by rebellious tenant farmers. Johann Leonard was acquainted with some of the men on the estate who were sympathetic to the plight of the small farmer, and he was able to speak favourably of his kin. That first night from home we spent on the manor grounds, accompanied by an itinerant troubadour who for small coin entertained the caravan occupants around an open fire. He was a man of Norwalk who called himself St. John, prompting Johann Leonard to re-name him "the Baptist." Whatever his religious calling, he could sing a lusty ballad. He took up a position just at the edge of the glow from our fire, and accompanied by the notes from a wheezy squeeze box sang a ditty he claimed he had written himself and which seemed to be appropriate to the times. I recall the words,

> "While I relate my story, Americans give ear
> Of Britain's fading glory you presently shall hear
> I'll give a true relation, attend to what I say
> Concerning the taxation of North Americay.

The cruel Lords of Britain who glory in their shame
The project they have hit on they joyfully proclaim
Is what they're striving after, our right to take away,
And rob us of our charter in North Americay."

His story went to many stanzas, and when he had finished his song he went off a few yards and settled for the night in a somewhat rickety caravan of his own. The moon was full and showed the landscape as if it were daytime. The coolness of the air told of bedtime so we prepared for our first night on the road. Following prayers, Christina, who had a sweet and tuneful voice, led a hymn of thanksgiving, after which we retired.

The next day at about noon we arrived at Claverack, where we had to pay a road toll. Just beyond the toll station there was an inn called the Lion and Thistle that looked like a pleasant place to stop, but I was a little suspicious because

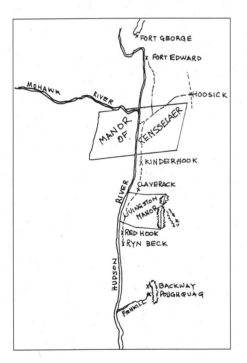

the name suggested the owner was a tory that chose to resist the republican sentiment that was sweeping the land. In those days inns and taverns were adopting names that had no association with English public houses to avoid being damaged or burned to the ground. Chancing trouble from local mobs, which was not likely during the daylight hours, we rested there, turning the animals out to pasture for a few hours on the newly sprouted lush grass. On enquiring of the road before us, the innkeeper was kind enough to give his opinion that the drying of the last few days would make the road passable. "Just yesterday we had a caravan similar to yours heading for Kinderhook, and he has not returned." But he also gave a warning. "That stretch of road between here and Mordever Kill traverses Schodack country and you may be accosted by poor Indians, bent on stealing food more than on murder. My advice is to give them what they want." After paying the man for the grass, which I could not help but believe by the amount asked included money for his advice, we set out on the road toward Rensselaerwyck and just before dusk found a small clearing close to the road where we stopped to spend the night.

The innkeeper's talk of possible hostile Indians made me think that we should post watches during the hours of darkness. Gathering Niclass and Johann Leonard to my side we decided to keep three watches of about four hours, similar to those we had on the *Anne* during the crossing when I was a boy. I agreed to take the morning watch. That night Niclass roused me from the warm bed where Lena slept peacefully. He whispered, "All is well" and headed off to his own blankets. I grabbed the loaded musket and took up my watch on a rock beside the small fire that Niclass had nurtured during his watch. I was about an hour into my watch trying to stay awake when the cold crisp air carried a mournful sound that could only be the lonely howl of wolves. They were not far from our camp since I could hear the males growling as they fought and played with each other. The thought of hungry wolves coming into the camp and killing our young ones made me shiver and break into a sweat even though it was not a warm night. As I sat on the rock my fright of these wild beasts gradually gave way to a certain admiration. It was a wild chorus in which a lone wolf began the song with a sharp bark-like howl followed by a sad and lonely wail as the pack joined in. In some profound way I felt an affinity with the pack. I thought of mother, her love of nature and her courage in facing the future with serenity. It made me feel better about what I was undertaking.

I became aware of the faint sound of drums off to the east, somewhere in the woods shy of the Connecticut River. I recognized the message of the drums as a mourning dirge for the passing of one of their number. The Indian camp was some distance from our camp and the drums signalled peace so I felt all was well. I woke Johann Leonard, told him of the drums and went to bed. Daylight came without incident although I could sense the presence of Indians all around us in the woods; they were watching our caravan, for what mischief I could only imagine.

At mid-morning as we were spread along a narrow part of the road beyond Claverack, two Indians suddenly appeared and stood at the side of the road in a grove of elm trees. They looked hungry. Fearing for our livestock and our very lives, Johann Leonard sent a ball in their direction. When the smoke cleared, they were gone. I expressed my anger with Johann Leonard, believing his action would bring their vengeance down on our heads, but he argued that our guns were our only protection against scalping. My fears were realized when only a few yards along the road a large band of warriors, dressed and painted for battle, stopped our caravan. Their number was a score of fierce looking faces behind lances adorned with eagle feathers. Each one carried a fighting axe. They looked as poorly as the two we had seen earlier, but this did not detract from their fierceness. I could see no guns among them, and seeing this Johann Leonard was prepared to drive them off with gunfire. I argued that we could possibly kill one or two, but in the end they would overwhelm us before we could have time to reload. "To protect the children we should talk with them and see what they want." I lifted my hand to them as a sign of peace.

A large, older man with three feathers in his headband, whom I took to be the chief of the tribe, stepped forward with a raised open-faced hand. He too wished to talk. He approached me with his right hand pointed in the direction of the cows and nodded his head. He wanted a cow.

I motioned him to stop and ordered our group to gather in a circle in front of the oxen. "Do we try to shoot our way out, or give up a cow?" The two women, fearful for the children, elected to give up a cow. Johann Leonard and Niclass were bound to shoot as many of the Indians as possible, believing we could escape. Being the elder and having the final say, I sided with the women, believing it was my duty to see to their safe passage. I wondered aloud whether a half-section of the hog we had slaughtered before leaving Ryn Beck would satisfy the chief. Despite loud grumbling from Niclass, who did not want to give them anything, I eventually carried the day.

Having decided the issue I carried the meat to the chief. He looked at it, and then at me with a scowl. I swear I stood in front of the chief for a full two minutes, and all that time he kept looking at the meat and then at me several times. But finally he stretched his arms and received our gift to his people. He bowed to me, making me wonder whether these men were savages after all. There were whoops from some of the chief's warriors, but it was evident that others wanted to fight. They stood sullenly while the chief carried the meat into the woods. I feared we were still in jeopardy from the belligerents, but after some tense moments they reluctantly followed the path of the chief. We proceeded on our journey, poorer perhaps, but as Christina said, "Not as poor as those hungry Indians."

The post road bent toward the Hudson River as it approached Kinderhook where the innkeeper at Claverack had told us heavy tolls would be collected. At the same time, he had revealed to us the existence of an Indian trail around the settlement, a more direct way north. "It might be passable now that the ice has gone." Johann Leonard, who went ahead on his riding horse, found the trail. It was very rough going, with swamps swarming with mosquitoes and fallen trees that had to be cut through so the wagons could be brought forward. There were no dry crossings, and some of the creeks were running almost full. Twice we had to build log bridges to ford the streams. The front wheels of Johann Leonard's wagon fell through the chinks in the logs, breaking a spoke at an especially rough crossing. Niclass damaged his leg on the logs while prying the wheel to move it forward. With much effort from both the men and the women pushing to help the oxen we finally got the wagon with its broken wheel to the far bank. There we stopped to repair our wheel, which took several hours. By this time, it was getting dark, and we had no choice but to stop at that place in the deep wilderness for the night.

We spent a very bad night, what with Niclass complaining of his leg, the mosquitos, and the dampness of the woods. For two or three hours during the early evening, the mosquitos were merciless, and it looked as if Thomas would go mad with torment. Lena covered him all over with a cloth, which seemed to help. Everyone was miserable. I took the early watch.

As the moon reached the top of its journey for the night, the mosquitos left us, and, sitting on a rock with the others safely put away for the night, my thoughts turned to wondering if I had been wrong in undertaking the journey. We were poorer than when we started with the loss of a half section of a hog, surrounded by Indians bent on thievery or worse, miserable with mosquitos and dampness, and heading into an unknown future. I thought of the stories Margaretha had told me about my kinfolk who had left the mountains to escape from persecution, and my father who left the old country to find something beyond the poverty, war and disease that had ravaged Germany in his day, only to find that nothing much had improved in his lifetime. It looked like war was coming upon us, and like my father, I wondered if I too would be disappointed with a life somewhere else. That night, with a full moon overhead and with the forest throbbing to the distant sound of the drums of those poor Indians, for the first time since being a child, I prayed.

God helped us get through the next day with more comfort, and we spent that night sheltered in a barn during a furious rainstorm.

On the fifth day we were on Rensselaerwyck lands. The road through the lands was away from the river with branches to farms along the river but most of the farms were adjacent to the road. Some of the houses we could see through the trees were very grand indeed, setting the women to talking about how good their lives would be if they could live in one of those houses. I gritted my teeth and said naught. A few hours into the Rensselaerwyck lands we came to a fork with a post and sign giving Husteed to the right hand and Schatighcoke to the left; where Johann Leonard and Christina were headed. A smaller sign pointed to Hosek on the left fork. The road on our right headed off toward the purple hills we could see to the east, while the left fork was a well-used Indian trail that had been cut wide enough for wagons. Was this the Hoosick Road? After consulting with Johann Leonard and Niclass I decided to continue straight ahead in spite of the roughness of the road. It was not long after that we came to a sizable river; our trail had brought us to a fording place. Having no experience of this river I halted our caravan to decide what to do. I was about to wade into the stream to estimate its power and depth when a rider appeared on the other side, and without stopping drove his horse into the water. Observing his progress across the river I could see that the water covered the rider's boots about mid-stream.

When he came up to our party he stopped and greeted us, "Where you headed friend?"

"To my cousin who lives on the Hoosick Road. The sign said this is the Hoosick road."

"Wrong friend, the Hoosick road is some two miles yonder. You have one more river to ford and then you are there. When you reach the Hoosick Road you will find that to your left is the Hudson and to your right hand some twenty miles distant is the Hoosick settlement. Say friend, I'm headed for Ryn Beck. How's the road."

"We have come from there some four nights ago. The road is good but we were accosted by an Indian party which took away a ham."

The rider's horse was anxious to move on so it could warm up from the stream crossing, so our new friend bid us farewell and rode off from us.

In my mind's eye I calculated that without mishap the water would cover the bed of the wagon making our bedding wet in crossing. So Johann Leonard and I re-arranged the contents of our wagons before attempting the fording. With the women and children perched high on the seat I led our team into the stream. The horses rebelled at first but once in the water they were easily led into deeper water. I managed the crossing with little trouble but as I was pulling on to the far bank I heard a scream from Johann Leonard's wagon. Looking back I could see that one wheel of his wagon had dropped over a rock, tipping the rear part of the wagon deeper into the water. As I watched, the horses with some urging from Johann Leonard pulled the wagon back to the fording surface.

Wet and tired, Johann Leonard, Niclass and I conferred and decided to push on to the next fording and cross before nightfall. This was accomplished without difficulty and we made camp on the north bank of the river for the night.

Early the next day we came to the Hoosick Road with a fork to Schaghticoke.

A parting of families took place with many tears, and then Johann Leonard took his family to the left-hand fork and Lena and I with our family proceeded east with much joy in the anticipation of meeting up with Johann Jacob who had agreed to take us in until I had land to build on. As we journeyed toward Hoosick the countryside was to my liking. The rolling hills, now covered with a fresh green mantle, gave me hope that the decision to come here was good. The soil was dark and moist from eons of seasons in which the trees gave up their nourishment to the soil that in turn nourished the foliage that brought the wild creatures to live and raise their young. I hoped that the soil would be as good to us.

The next day I spotted the church Johann Jacob had mentioned in his letter and seeking out the Pastor we were directed to Johann Jacob's farm. Soon we were with Johann Jacob. There was much celebration and prayerful thanksgiving for our safe delivery. We were put up in Johann Jacob's barn. The next morning Johann Jacob hitched a horse to his cart and took me to see a Mr. Van Den Hagedoorn who was able to secure a lease in the name of Stephan Van Rensselaer for two hundred acres of treed land not too far from Johann Jacob's farm.

We lived with Johann Jacob until I was able to cut a clearing close to the road and build a rough log cabin. I expected to obtain a deed within ten years.

In a small way we prospered during the following years. I cleared forty acres and raised milk cows and heifers, a large herd of sheep, and a few hogs. We planted corn, wheat, and rye, and had oxen to plough the fields and to haul the wagon at harvest time. I even had a team of road horses.

By the time the war broke out Lena had borne four more children. Thomas was approaching manhood and was help to me in the farm work, while Catharina and Hanna were just beginning to be of some help to Lena, mostly in looking after the little ones. The children had trouble with my name and in their mouths it became something like Everet, a name that spread throughout the district. This made me feel, finally, permanently installed as part of the settlement, although we still had no deed for the farm we considered ours by right of tithes and the work of our hands.

Although anxious about the future, Lena found joy in the beauty of the verdant landscape and the natural life that surrounded our farm. The children and the fieldwork were exhausting, but she found some time for herself. The sprouts of new life emerging from the rich soil each spring enthralled her. New generations of calves, lambs, and piglets lifted her spirits after the harsh and sometimes cruel winters. The fluffy chicks that she hatched in a corner of the stable gave her much delight. She used to say that fondling those small fragile bundles of fluff almost made up for the mess they made when they became hens. The summer brought on exhausting labour, and we were relieved when the harvest was done and the cycle of nature dictated that the earth begin a process of rest and hibernation for winter.

The Palatines had built a church some years ago and it became Lena's solace and protection from the troubles of life. Each Sabbath she took the children, dressed in their best, and set off to the Gilead Lutheran Church for worship. She enjoyed the hymns, especially Luther's own call to glory, ...*He breaks the cruel oppressor's rod, and wins salvation glorious....* The thundering morality from the pulpit made her uncomfortable, but in spite of this she usually left with a renewed spirit for the week that would follow.

Not all was peaceful in our house. Lena had periods of bitterness. She derided the fact that we did not have our own land so she could live "a decent life," which meant she wanted to dress like a Van Rensselaer woman and fill her house with goods from New York. Our lives together became quite stormy. She had the ambition to be a "somebody" that I lacked. I could not reach the grand expectations that she wished for, which could only be found, she thought, in New York or Boston. Eventually, when she was in her bitterest mood I retreated to the barn.

She did not want to give the women of the Church the satisfaction of seeing her bitterness, so she tried very hard to keep up appearances. She kept urging me to go to the Church with her and the children, hoping, I think, that this would help her become happier. I saw no need for religion except for weddings, funerals, and baptisms. However, now that I know what happened to us, I regret not making more of an effort to please her.

Looking back from my cabin in the wilds of Canada West, I wonder what led me to take up arms, since I was no longer young and had no urge to kill anyone. Perhaps it was God's will, but the future as it turned out was not an easy row to hoe.

I hoped only for peace and some orderly administration from the colonial government in Albany, but in the end, it seemed as if the country had turned against the natural order. The countryside was on fire with rumours of war. The news from Boston town was not good. We heard of battles between street mobs and the British regulars. Tories were being tarred and feathered and run out of town on a split cedar rail. Yankee traders fumed at Parliament's decree that trade must be carried out with the mother country in English ships. Smuggling became widespread. The English navy sailed into Boston harbour and blockaded the normal business of the Bay Colony. Bostonians were being asked to house and support the very soldiers that many thought of as oppressors.

Mobs were stirring up rebellion against agents of Parliament with diatribes against taxation to pay for the war that made them free from catholic New France that ambitious men claimed to be like an iron collar choking off the breath of liberty. The age-old spectre of taxes was like a wound to the body for those who, like my family, had left the old country because of the crushing burden of taxes to support armies. All of us were very vulnerable to the anti-tax rhetoric, whether or not the tax was reasonably justified, and some men, sympathetic to the cause of the rebels, were causing trouble for farmers like me who only wanted to live in peace, even if under British law.

The sound of the drums of war that we had heard in Dutchess County seemed to be leading to civil war. The rot of rebellion was spreading from Massachusetts Bay Colony, sending tentacles of violence outward like a stone thrown into a lake sends out waves. Many of my neighbours were not unduly anxious about our situation, thinking our remote location and sparse population would save us from the violence that was even now creeping up-country. But some, those who had lived in the Hoosick valley in the very early times remembered the fear and panic when French soldiers and their Indians roamed the countryside burning settlements on the way to attack Fort Massachusetts. The settlement of Hoosick Falls had been burned to the ground in '54.

The first violence in my time came in the person of Ethan Allen and his kin. At the time, the governor of New Hampshire was selling land grants that were located in territory also claimed by the colony of New York. Ethan became involved in the legal battle over the grants, and losing to New York landowners he and his brother Ira, along with cousins Seth Warner and Remember Baker, began to organize other like-minded men to chase away surveyors and uproot New York farmers they claimed were living on New Hampshire grants. Before I joined the British over one hundred farmers had been issued patents from both New York and New Hampshire, with many battles between New York officials and the Green Mountain Boys, as Ethan's followers were called.

Jim Breakenridge, a man I knew well, had a farm three miles west of Bennington under a New Hampshire grant. When the sheriff from Albany came with a posse to remove Breakenridge, claiming he was on New York land, Ethan and his followers chased them away. After that he became a hero to some, but an outlaw to others.

Jim Breakenridge's farm was only a few miles from my farm, and to me it looked like the ownership of the farms near the vaguely defined line between New Hampshire and New York provinces would be contested for years. It made me think I needed legal title to my land to be secure for my old age.

Ethan's war with New York landlords and their lawyers, with farmers in the middle, was a fight over land ownership, but the events in Boston were even more frightening than Allen. The poor farmers of Albany County were being drawn into the larger conflict, which was being voiced about as nothing less than a revolution and independence from the mother country. A Committee of Safety was established in Albany that sent agents out into the countryside forcing farmers to make a choice between joining the rebellion against the King or being branded as Tories. If named a tory, all sorts of atrocities could be carried out against you, including confiscation of your livelihood. You could be taken to the guardhouse and beaten if you did not reveal the names of other Tories that you were alleged to know. Families were torn apart by the decisions they had to make. Brother Johann Leonard in Schatighcoke was so sure the rebels would win the struggle for independence that he joined the New York militia. But the cousin we called Young Jacob, Eberhardt's son from Crum Elbow, spoke out against the chaos being caused by the rabble and was taken to Albany and put in the guardhouse.

The situation caused anger and frustration. It seemed every time I went to the Hosek Haus an argument broke out between those who wanted to fight and those who wanted peace. Lodewick Beschler was a very old man with no teeth causing him to puff when he talked, but this did not deter him from damning everything he did not understand. Grampa Luke as everyone called him had a grandson who had joined the Massachusetts militia against his wishes, which made him furious. He believed New Englanders were evil. One day during a heated argument Grampa Luke spoke up to give those around him his version of the situation in Boston.

"Yep, by gad, those Yankees aint my kind o' people but they want us to raise hell agin peace loving folk. Seems t' me they treat Tories like they use't treat witches in my day. Ye know, back in '92 I lived in Salem when a child and I saw it for meself. She was a good woman in my lights, but they could see evil in her ways and the elders condemned her. When she was leavin the gua'dhouse, I stood beside the woman they called a witch and looking into her eyes for the work of Satan I saw only fear. They took her to the public square in a solemn procession and two men marched her up the steps to the platform of the gibbet, which stood there for the hanging of criminals, blasphemers, adult'resses, and witches. This day, a man of the cloth stood beside this poor woman and in a Godly rage sentenced her soul to the eternal fires of hell."

Young Ben Schneider who was listening sang out "Halleluiah!" This caused an uproar, until someone said, "Tell your story, old man! Let Grampa Luke tell his story!"

With some hesitation, Grampa Luke continued:

"A burly man standin' there pushed a stick under her chin and forced the poor creature to look at her persecutors. For an hour, with the woman standing in the hot sun with chin uplifted by the hateful stick, the elders pleaded that she admit her transgression from the normal way of life. Then they dragged her back to the gua'dhouse. T'is Godly truth, I saw this with my own eyes when jest a child an I will rest my bones in hell before I'll sign any piece of paper the Committee puts in front o' me."

On top of the hated taxes, Parliament had enacted a law that gave the French Catholics in Canada religious freedom and decreed the unsettled lands east of the Mississippi as Indian Territory, thus cutting off western expansion and frustrating the newly created Continental Congress, which ruled that if Canada wished not to join the states in union then it must be taken. So, a month after the first shot was fired at Lexington Ethan Allen decided to attack Fort Ticonderoga for its guns, and to open up an invasion route to Montreal and Quebec. At the same time, a like-minded man named Benedict Arnold had the same idea, obtained a commission of colonel from Massachusetts and set out to raise sufficient men for the task. Ethan with his men from the Green Mountains and Arnold with his recruits overwhelmed the poorly garrisoned fort and took the guns for use by the rebels. Sure the Canadians would rise up against British "tyranny" Congress set the wheels in motion for an invasion. Ethan Allen, now a colonel of the Massachusetts militia had gone to Ticonderoga to join Major General Philip Schuyler who had been given orders to plan the invasion. Word came back to us that Ethan had gone into Canadian territory and captured Montreal. Some who knew Ethan talked of this with some pride. Then we heard that he had been captured and was being sent to an English jail. A good place for him, I thought.

An invasion was mounted that summer, led by General Richard Montgomery, a former British officer who had had a distinguished military career during the French and Indian war, and was known to those who had come up from the Ryn Beck area where he had married a Livingston woman. On garrison duty during the war, his ship had run aground off Livingston Manor, and while marooned he met Janet Livingston. After the war he took home leave to repair his health, and while in England sold his commission, left the army and became a farmer in Ireland, his home. But he returned to America to be a gentleman farmer, and after renewing his acquaintance with Janet, they were married and bought a house in Ryn Beck. When Congress decided to invade Canada he was persuaded to join the rebel cause. Given a commission of brigadier general he was chosen by Philip Schuyler to be in command of the rebel army that was to invade Canada from Fort Ticonderoga, then in rebel hands after Allen had captured the fort without a shot being fired. Montgomery, as he had done many years before for the British, captured the Richelieu River forts and then Montreal, this time for the rebels.

Meanwhile, Benedict Arnold, who was anxious to wipe a stain from his family name and gain a reputation, asked George Washington to lead a second attack on Quebec by way of the Kennebec and Chaudière rivers. He raised about twelve hundred hardy, fearless, undisciplined men, and in surely one of the great feats of the war led them up the Kennebec, through floods, over a height of land, across swamps and down the Chaudière with leaking bateaus and with winter coming on. His depleted army reached Quebec and waited for Montgomery to combine forces for an invasion of the town.

B rother Johann Leonard had gone off seeking adventure with a regiment of the New York Militia commanded by Montgomery and was sending letters of his experiences as a soldier in Montgomery's army to his wife Christina. She in turn wrote to Lena telling of Johann Leonard's exploits. Curious about the war, I pestered Lena for detail, but she told me naught except that Johann Leonard was coming home soon from the Canadian campaign. Thomas, now thirteen, also pestered her, but she was unwilling to talk about war with him. Lena resisted mentioning the war, partly because she was horrified at the rising brutality closing in on our farm, convinced that it was worse than in her beloved Clove Valley, and blamed me for bringing her to "the worst place on God's green earth." She wanted nothing from the place but her garden and her church.

Finally, frustrated with me asking about Johann Leonard, one evening she blurted, "If you are so interested in Johann Leonard and his fighting escapades why don't you go and see him? His enlistment is up near the end of January."

"You know I cannot leave this place."

"Yes, you can. Not much is needed here in winter except the milking and feeding of the animals. Thomas and the girls and I can do that. We have enough wood cut for the winter, and you don't really have to pull stumps and cut trees for the few days you would be gone. Go on! It will do you good to get this thing out of your system."

It sounded mad, travelling that distance in winter. But after spending a listless December I began to take Lena's suggestion to heart. Something was driving me to understand the cruelty that was out there, away from my homely farmer's life. Some would say I had premonitions of my future, my own brush with death in war. For a month I fed oats to Old Jude, one of my road horses, until her hide was as smooth as silk. At the end of the month she almost looked like a riding mare.

So, in early February, after a hearty breakfast of eggs, pork, and potatoes I put a blanket and makeshift saddle on Old Jude, bid goodbye to Lena and the children, and set out for the river. It seemed as though Lena was frightened to see me leave, but she had urged me to go and now could say naught to hold me.

The road was muddy, but held only a smattering of snow, except where it ran under the largest pine trees that kept the track in constant shade. I saw few travellers. It was lonely except for the odd soldier returning from the war, some in very poor shape. Just before the entrance to the Hayner farm I saw two men coming down the road, one badly wounded and supported by the other. From some distance I could tell that the wounded man had lost a leg and was struggling along the road with a makeshift stick to help support his weight. As I drew up to the men I stopped Old Jude and enquired of their purpose.

The man who supported the other asked for whiskey. Told I had none he prepared to trudge away, half-dragging his partner.

"Where did your friend get his wound?"

"This here is Jeremiah, I'm Josiah. We're brothers. Signed up with General Montgomery we did, way back. The Gen'l got killed at Quebec. Jeremiah here lost his leg. A butcher sawed it off. We're going home now."

"How far is it?"

"Jest the next farm. We're pract'ly home now. Got a ride in a cart to the farm gate jes' behind. We're almost home now. I'll never leave home agin."

I gave them a drink of water and watched them make their way down the road. The man who had lost his leg looked no more than sixteen.

About two hours after noon, just as I left the road where it turned south to Albany onto a road that would take me to the river, two men stepped out of the woods onto the track, one brandishing a musket. They wore scarfs to cover the lower parts of their faces and hats pulled low to shade their eyes. Clearly, they were bandits, bent on no good. Old Jude was not fit to outrun a musket ball, so I had no choice but to stop and let them do their worst. I mentally figured the distance to the last farmhouse I had passed if I lost Old Jude and had to walk.

I pulled up to the men, one a very tall man and one of average height. It was the tall one who seemed familiar that pointed the musket at me. He shouted, "Are you for King or Congress?"

His voice betrayed him.

"Jed Adler. What are you doing robbing a peaceful farmer?"

"Everet, is that you? Shure as damn it is you! Don't fret, your old mare is not useful to us. My friend here is Henry."

Henry said, "Let's take his musket."

"Well," drawled Jed, "it's pretty old. Not much use to us. Besides, he needs it to shoot bandits."

Here he let out a large laugh, which caused me to relax.

"Jed, when did you begin to rob travellers?"

"Well, Everet, I've always considered you my friend. I guess I can trust you not to give me away to the Committee."

"You can trust me, Jed."

"Gershom French, from over Lansingburgh way, is raising an army to fight the rebels. At one time he was fer independence, but when he found the rebels were hell-bent on violence he turned to the King. Me and Henry here have thrown our lot in with French. Right now me and Henry are relieving rebels of their assets to help the King's cause. Say, how 'bout you Everet? You should join us!"

"Jed, you know me, I'm not for King or Congress, and I don't have any assets except the clothes on my back and a bite to eat. Besides, I'm too old to be traipsing around the country, robbing people. Right now I'm going up to Schatighcoke to see my brother and sister-in-law. Do you know Johann Leonard, he came up from Dutchess County with me?"

"Can't say I do."

I did not tell Jed that Johann Leonard was with the New York Militia.

Jed turned to Henry and asked, "What say you, Henry, will we let Everet go in peace to visit his brother?" Henry grunted, whereupon Jed waved me on my way. As I left them standing in the wagon tracks Jed shouted after me, "I'll be around to see you when the snow is gone. Take care!"

The friendly parting was Jed all over. He was a good man. I had known him for a very long time and was surprised he was so caught up in those days as to rob people, perhaps innocent people. But the violent times made men do strange things.

I rode Old Jude to the Black Wolf Inn, a former stone house on the side of a hill just up from a small boat landing at the river's edge. The road north from here would take me straight to Schatighcoke tomorrow.

By the time Old Jude was fed and settled for the night it was quite dark. I found my way to the main room of the inn and seated myself at a small table near the rear of the room. Although the room was gloomy I could see a number of men, mostly locals, judging by their dress. The room was lively with arguments about which side of the coming civil war was on the side of God. There was singing from one quarter, mostly ballads about love and tragedy. There was great exuberance in the room, but no fights. The innkeeper and his son, both large rough-looking men, took care to keep the peace.

I had just settled down with a bowl of stew when two men came through the door. I could tell they were trouble. The shorter of the two wore skins and carried a musket and a knife in his belt, and he looked like he would use either at the drop of a hat. The bigger of the two loudly ordered a jug of whiskey, and after receiving it they went to a table in a corner of the room where an old man nursed a bowl of wine. Soon loud talk, more or less directed at the room's patrons, made it clear they were recruits bound for Fort Edward. From my vantage point not far away I could hear them badgering the old man, accusing him of being a tory. Suddenly, there were three men at the table hemming the two into the corner. Strong words were flung about for about a minute when the smaller of the two jumped to his feet and made a motion toward the knife in his belt. At this, about four more men jumped up from their seats, two of them very drunk. I saw a swift movement from the corner of my eye as the innkeeper's son ploughed through the crowd around the table and, with one blow, floored the man with the knife.

The other shouted, "You're all tory bastards and should be hung from the trees!" By this time the innkeeper himself arrived on the scene and simply said, "Get out! Now!" The miscreant looked at him for a few moments, but seeing the belligerence of his host, he sheepishly stooped, grasped his friend by the collar and dragged him across the floor and through the door into the wintery night. I understand they slept in the barn with the cows that night.

The incident was over quickly, but I realized I was in a nest of Tories. For some reason this made me feel safe. Perhaps, after all, these were my kind of people. It led me to wonder how I would be greeted by my brother, a potential enemy.

I woke next morning with the sun filtering through the grimy window of the room the innkeeper had let to me the night before. He had also let it to two other men. Once I had gotten used to the snores, grunts, and sour smells I had slept well after the long day and I woke up thinking of Jed and wondering where he and his band of bandits were holed up. Would any of his fellows challenge Old Jude on my journey today? I may not be so lucky to have Jed among them.

Out on the road Old Jude sensed an end to her ordeal and stepped right along, almost as frisky as a young gelding. We stopped at a house bearing a sign with the crudely written words, "Food & Hay." A black woman stood waiting on the front stoop, wiping her fingers on a colourful apron. She had very white hair and was so thin she could have hidden behind the post that held up the small awning above the door. I would not have associated her with food. When we came up to her she said, "Jake's b'hind in the barn. If yo'all want t' feed y'r horse go on back. My name's Lizzie. See me if'n yo'all want eggs and grits."

During a hearty dinner Lizzie told me she and Jake were freed slaves who had come north after hearing the talk of freedom and liberty here. But the white folks in the north were no different than at home. The couple eked out an existence on the river as long as they kept to themselves and did not "put on airs."

Old Jude and I reached Johann Leonard's place that afternoon. He was outwardly pleased to see me, but I detected anxiety in his manner; perhaps a natural wish to please an older brother whom he had not seen in a long time. It was not something I could do anything about.

Christina had borne another daughter, Anna Maria, now eleven, since last I had seen her. Johann Leonard told me later that she had lost two boys in the intervening years. He hoped soon for a son before he "kicked the bucket." And, at super time I could see that Christina was indeed carrying another child.

The girls, Anna Maria and Gertrout, treated me like their grandfather. I suppose to them their uncle looked very old compared to their father who was eleven years my junior.

The secret purpose of my journey, although I did not say this, was to learn what Johann Leonard knew about the war in Canada. After a supper of hog's hocks, hot bread, and cheese, Johann Leonard took a large jug of what I learned later was gooseberry wine from a cupboard at the end of the table. At this, Christina retired to her chair near the fire with her knitting while the girls simply disappeared from the room. It was time for men's talk.

"You know, Eberhardt, this wine reminds me of my commander; Colonel Goose we called him. He was a good man; the men liked him. He held us together in bad times at Fort St. Jean."

"You were at St. Jean. I did not know that. What was it like there?"

"It was wet and swampy. Savages were shooting their deadly arrows from behind trees in the woods. The mosquitos were terrible, their sting almost as bad as an arrow. Between the buzz of the mosquitos and the slap of an arrow in the chest of a comrade the men were getting panicky and some began to run away. Colonel Goose was able to hold our company together and laughed at the deserters. 'We need a good sheep dog to round up those cowards,' he'd say. I tell you, Eberhardt, it was easy to be a coward with the Indians whooping and hollering from the woods, working up the passion to scalp us all there and then."

Taking a long draught from his cup Johann Leonard continued, "We set about building breastworks, but by this time the guns of the fort had found us and were pounding the living daylights out of us. About this time, a resident of St. Jean, a man called Hazen, came into camp with the intelligence that the fort was well defended with reinforcements on the way. The General made the decision to withdraw to a place called Île aux Noix at the mouth of the river called Richelieu. Turned out Hazen was suspected an enemy spy, and gave wrong intelligence."

"We heard Montgomery took Montreal. Did he go round St. Jean?"

"We took St. Jean, but only on the third try. After our retreat, many of the men had come down with malaria and were in no condition to fight. But a great many men from the countryside were coming into camp, full of enthusiasm, whether for Congress or for the sheer adventure of it all."

Johann Leonard was drinking cup after cup of gooseberry wine, more than was good for him. I glanced at Christina who was looking at her husband with a pained and perplexed expression. She was anxious or angry, or both. War is not for a family man.

Filling still another cup from the half-empty jug, Johann Leonard continued, "On the second try, about nine hundred strong we marched on Fort St. Jean again and took up our old position. A stone-like silence greeted us. We sent balls into the woods at any sound, expecting a wild savage to fly from the gloom brandishing a bloody axe, intent on taking a hairy prize. Some ran to the boats, but I am proud to say that Colonel Goose kept our company from running like rats from a barn fire. When the savages started their war whoops, and it was learned that the *Royal Savage* with its brass cannon and carrying enemy reinforcements was on the way, there was much fear in our ranks. We were ordered once again to withdraw to Île aux Noix.

"It rained and it rained; a cold rain, one that penetrates your very bones. The rain kept us bogged down for several days.

"On the third attempt, St. Jean was taken, but only after fifty-five days. General Montgomery, with a refreshed army of men that had come to us from the countryside, set up three gun batteries; south of the fort a giant mortar we called the "sow," four guns across the river opposite the exposed side of the fort, and a battery of six mortars to the north west. The siege of the fort began."

Johann Leonard suddenly burst into loud laughter that brought Christina flying from her chair. She was clearly upset at me for provoking him into revealing his inner terrors. She said to her husband, "You should go to bed and get some rest." She tugged at his arm. He jerked his arm from her grasp and was about to push her away, but seeing the look in her eyes, he got up from his chair and followed her meekly to their sleeping quarters.

When Christina came back into the room she said not a word, but led me to a cubbyhole with a curtain across it that was to be my bedchamber for the night. She lit a candle hanging on the wall of the cubbyhole, the only comfort.

I thanked her for her hospitality and apologized for upsetting Johann Leonard. That seemed to soften her mood.

"Johann Leonard was changed when he came back from Canada. He is fearful of everything and everyone. I was angry with you just now, but perhaps spending some time with your brother may help him become his old self again."

"War changes men who go off to kill other men. It's an un-natural act that surely brings self-judgement, even if only from the inner workings of his mind. Johann Leonard was the sensitive one of Niclass and me; I guess I'm not surprised the war has hit him hard. Like you I do hope my visit will be of some help to him."

She said, "I do hope so!"

After an exchange of "good night," I climbed into a lumpy bed and was soon asleep.

The next morning was crisp but clear with no sign of new snow. I joined Johann Leonard to help with the morning chores. Not having boys, he had hired a young lad from the farm next door to help the milk the cows. James, the lad's name, fed the animals while the girls gathered the night's production of eggs. Johann Leonard and I walked past the pigpen onto a cleared field used as pasture in summer. With the snow glistening like a cache of diamonds spread over the hillside and blue shadows under the remaining trees along the snake rail fence, the strain of the night before seemed far away. We were brothers again. As we walked through the snow on a path made by the cows, he again began to talk to me about his war experiences, as if he was anxious that neither Niclass nor I get involved.

"General Schuyler, not knowing what to do with the ambitious Allen, sent him and a spy called John Brown to convince the Canadians to join the rebellion. Instead they schemed to mount action against Montreal, Allen from Longueuil and Brown from Laprairie. On the morning of the planned raid, Brown did not move against the village, leaving Allen exposed on the river's edge. A habitant, as the Canadian farmers are called, alerted the English general, who, with his small company of regulars, marshalled a goodly number of Canadians to march against Allen, bringing him to surrender. As you know, Ethan was a remarkable man, surely an impressive sight standing defiantly before his enemies with his fur hat and feathers. So the English put him on display and publically humiliated him before they banished him to England to be tried for "traitorous acts" against the King. General Montgomery was furious with Allen because his impulsive act brought many more Canadians against his army."

Johann Leonard seemed more like his old self than the night before. I had to admit the story he was telling was life affirming, even with all the danger. In his words I thought I could hear the joy of surviving the improbable. War it seems drives men to the peak of ecstasy and then to the depths of depression. Thus ruminating, his story broke into my thoughts,

"…on the march to Montreal we had little difficulty as Fort Chambly had surrendered to John Brown, and without incident the army reached the St. Lawrence River and occupied its south bank. This mighty river is very broad in its girth and when I saw it the first morning, glistening in the rising sun, I thought I had never observed such a magnificent work of God.

"General Carleton had abandoned Montreal and we were able to walk through the gate into the town, greeted in a friendly manner by the numerous people gathered there as the news of capitulation spread. General Montgomery addressed the assembled army and thanked us for our efforts in this great and difficult campaign. He said over one hundred men and officers were taken prisoner and said anyone molesting women would be summarily dealt with. With Montreal secure he was preparing to march on Quebec.

"The enlistment terms were up for many of his men who planned to go back to their farms for the winter, but I had signed up 'til the middle of January. Colonel Goose urged his company to go with the army to Quebec and 'finish this great effort to bring freedom to the poor souls living under a tyranny as cruel as that which our ancestors had suffered under.' His urging was impressive, but I found it not easy to choose between love of home and private honour. I recalled Colonel Goose's disgust of cowards and decided to honour my enlistment and go on to Quebec."

That evening was a repeat of the previous one. The death of Montgomery at Quebec disturbed Johann Leonard greatly. "After it was over, Colonel Goose told me that Montgomery had only undertaken the mission to keep his honour. He had come back to America to settle into the life of a farmer, met and married Janet, who was from a fiercely republican family, and entered the fray once again, probably to please her father. He longed to go home to her and only stuck it out only for his honour. His death at an early age was the greatest tragedy of the failed invasion."

Johann Leonard was again far into his cups and again Christina hustled him off to bed. She admonished me angrily and blurted, "You must not mention the war again. He is so fragile and he must find some relief besides drink. I think it best that you leave tomorrow." I took no offence at her suggestion because I knew that he needed a long rest.

The next morning after a somewhat sombre breakfast I bid goodbye to my brother and sister-in-law. The girls gave me a farewell kiss, still calling me their honourable grandfather. Johann Leonard, unlike Christina, seemed pleased with my visit and after an embarrassing embrace we exchanged mutual invitations to visit, but I expected I would never see either of them again. As I left the house Christina followed me out the door. She pressed a package into my hand. "Inside are copies of some letters cousin Elizabeth from Ryn Beck sent to me. They are letters from General Montgomery to his wife. I want you to have them to keep them away from Johann Leonard, who as you have seen, gets very upset by memories of the war."

I stood beside Old Jude for a moment not knowing what to say. It occurred to me that Johann Leonard might have treasured his letters and would be angry with me for having them. But I had to believe that Christina had his best interests at heart so I said, "Thank you for trusting me with these I will make sure to keep them safe, and return them someday when Johann Leonard gets stronger." I mounted and waved my hand to Christina. Then Old Jude and I set out on the road again, the way we had come.

It was in the late summer of '76 when a man came to my door looking for me. Lena sent him to the barn where I was sharpening a scythe. He was dressed in buckskins and outfitted with a long-barrelled rifle as well as a large knife and hatchet. Although dressed as a warrior he seemed friendly enough. He asked about the crops. After a few moments of idle conversation about the weather, he asked, "Are you for King or Congress?" I said "Neither. I am my own man." He told me his name was Benjamin Woolsely, a scout to the New York militia, and he was recruiting hale and hearty men to go join with Arnold to stop the English army from invading the colony, which was expected to move on Albany.

Having stated my position I thought it wise to appear interested, so I said I had heard much of Benedict Arnold and his defeat in Canada and wondered if he was a fit man to win a campaign against the mighty empire of the English. The scout replied,

"Having hailed from Norwich village, I knew Ben Arnold when he was a child, and a proper hellion he was, always wanted to be first to cause trouble to the authorities. The stories people told about his exploits are hardly believable by Christian folk. At fourteen he talked some local lads into stealing barrels of tar from a shipyard, and when caught dared the constable to fight. He got roundly cuffed for that trick. He used to ride the waterwheel at the millrace where we swam in the summers. There is a story that he sent a musket ball after a Frenchman who was courting his sister Hannah because he thought him a rake. The townspeople said his recklessness would lead to a short life. But, whatever happens to him in the future his march on Quebec showed him to be a leader of men.

"At Quebec he was wounded in the battle and stuck it out there for most of the winter terrorizing the English, but the ditherers in Philadelphia did not send him promised reinforcements, so in the end he had to withdraw. But, take it from me; he is a leader who gets out in front of his men. I was with him on his march to Canada and to tell you the truth I would march into hell if led by Benedict Arnold." Wavering some, and it being noon, I invited my visitor to come to the house and have dinner with us.

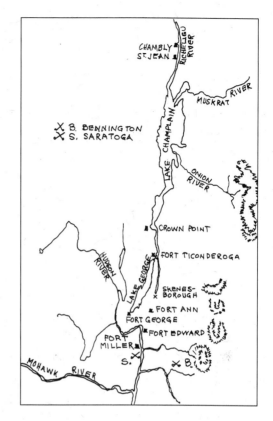

After a meal of venison and potatoes, while Lena was cleaning up, I offered my guest tobacco. It was then that the reason for his visit came out. After getting his reluctant pipe drawing, he said, "I was with Colonel Greene of the Rhode Island militia when we made the march to Quebec with Arnold."

"Oh!" I said. "Did you know Ephriam Lochwood, who lives just down the road?" He looked a bit startled and said, "Yep. We were in the same outfit."

But he would not be deterred from his mission.

"Arnold is now raising a force to try to stop the English by manning a fleet of ships he is building on Lake Champlain, and he wants anyone he can get to gain our freedom from the English King."

I protested, "I know nothing about fighting from a boat."

"That is of no concern, he will train you. You had better think about it and make up your mind before the Committee for the Detection of Conspiracies comes to your door." With that veiled threat, but still friendly enough, he picked up his hat, thanked me for my hospitality, and left.

About a week later, on a warm evening after pitching hay all day I sat with Lena on Tom's bench in front of the cabin. Thomas had worked the last winter sawing lumber for Joshua Bruhn over in Hoosick Falls and had brought home lumber to build a bench, thus our resting place on nice summer evenings was called Tom's bench.

The sun was sinking behind a profusion of flat-bottomed clouds strung across the horizon, turning the heavens to the west into a dome of soft pink. Lena said it was proof God was in heaven.

A man rode into the farmyard, his features in shadow from the last vestiges of sunlight on his back. Expecting trouble, I stood and at the same time urged Lena to go inside. She refused, so we waited. As the rider came up to us he turned to dismount giving me a look at his features.

"I swear; it is Johann Leonard. What are you doing in this neck of the woods?"

"Army orders."

"Orders?"

He said, smiling, "Are you not going to invite me to get off my horse?"

This set Lena into a flurry of confusion and she quickly went to him and said, "We are so pleased to see you Johann Leonard, no matter your mission."

On the ground he said to me, somewhat out of breath, "Yeah! Colonel Goose has asked me to recruit whomever I can for his militia regiment. He found out I had many relatives and acquaintances along the Hoosick Road and thought I could convince them the join his regiment."

Lena spoke up, "You must stay for the night. Have you eaten?"

Johann Leonard turned to speak to her. "I have been on the road since early morning, visiting farms along the way." Turning to me, he said, "I have signed up ten men today."

"Well, come in and have a bite to eat. You can sleep in the barn over the stables where Catharina and Hanna have made a bedchamber for strangers. You're not a stranger, although we do not see you often, but it's the only extra bed we have. It is really quite comfortable there."

Lena explained, "Catharina is our oldest girl, she is twelve come November. Hanna will be ten come January."

With the pleasantries said, the three of us went into the cabin so Johann Leonard could have a bite to eat.

I was silent, suspicious that my brother was at my cabin to recruit me. But I determined to keep my own counsel, even though he was close kin.

As he ate, Lena pestered him about Christina and his girls. She kept him supplied with ale, not aware that he might drink too much. I saw he was making an effort to be disciplined, the subject of family not unpleasant to his fragile nature. I avoided any talk of the war. Much to my surprise, he did not broach the subject, making me believe that I had been wrong in my suspicion of his motives. But, he was very worn out from the long day he had endured.

Midway through his meal Tom came barging through the door. After a moment of confusion he said, "Hello, Uncle Johann Leonard." I was surprised that he knew his uncle since he had last seen him when he was very little. Lena introduced him, "This is Thomas, our oldest. He has been in the back acres with his father cutting hay all day." After dutiful greetings I took Tom into our bedchamber and whispered, "I don't want you to mention the war to your uncle. He gets very upset. So watch your tongue!" We returned to the dinner table where Tom and his uncle got acquainted without mishap on Tom's part. Soon after, Johann Leonard, having eaten his fill, begged tiredness and he and I prepared to leave the cabin to get him settled in the barn loft.

On the path to the barn he asked about my crops.

"I had a good crop of corn and beans this year," I answered, "Plenty of hay, and I will have timothy and clover to sell, I think. Lena's vegetable garden produced enough potatoes, squash, and turnips for the winter. We are doing all right, but we will never get rich at this rate. And, I don't know how long it will last the way things are going." He told me, just as we were going in the barn door, that his place was much the same.

We climbed to the loft and as I showed him his sleeping quarters he said to me, "Things are bad. That is why I joined to fight for a new government of the United States. One that will replace the tyrannies of a foreign master that is trying to crush us into the dirt of the earth."

I grimaced at the word "tyrannies" and tried to put him off. "It is very late for you, Johann Leonard, and I see you are tired from your ride today. We will talk about it in the morning."

"Fine" he mumbled, perhaps sensing a negative response from me. "I will see you in the morning."

"Good night. I hope you sleep well."

With my words he climbed into the bed that Catharina had made up for him. I believe he was asleep before I left the barn.

Walking back to the cabin was very depressing. I had a mind to stay out of the coming conflict if I possibly could, and I did not want to confront my younger brother with my reluctance to catch his republican fervour.

Breakfast was pleasant; talk was domestic. Johann Leonard took from his saddlebag small gifts for my girls; a bright hair ribbon for Hanna and a shiny neck bauble for Catharina. Shyly thanking him, they soon rushed off to admire themselves. After breakfast, Johann Leonard and I retired to Tom's bench with large cups of Lena's strong rhubarb tea.

"Eberhardt, you are going to have to decide one way or the other. You cannot stay neutral. One day someone from the Committee is going to come around and ask you to sign against the King. If you do not, there will be big trouble for you. Look at Young Jacob, he's out in the woods, hiding from the Committee. If they catch him he will be thrown into the guardhouse in Albany. You're going to end up in the woods too if you try to stay neutral."

"I'm not political, I just want to live in peace. I just want all the violence to go away so I can be my own man."

"But you can't be your own man, any more than our father could in the old country. I can't imagine you can deny that all men are created equal, and with the British King ruling your life you and I will always be nothing more than serfs."

"They are great ideals; liberty and equality. But will the great words hold true? I remember stories of a boy named Jörg going up into the high pastures of the Priedrof in Carinthia to protect his father's sheep from the wolves and bears. Here, the landowners and their lawyers are like the wolves preying on Jörg's sheep. Like his sheep, we too need protection from the wolves. So I don't mind seeing a few British soldiers around."

"You are a hard man to please. We have to keep this army at our own cost and we are taxed on top of that. Without having any say in the matter."

"Will you and I, poor farmers, ever have any say? I was told the paper signed in July declares that we should have the right to life, liberty, and property so the landowners do not have to share their wealth with the King."

"No! You are wrong. That statement was changed to life, liberty, and the pursuit of happiness."

"Same thing!"

I made a move to stand up, seeing that Johann Leonard was getting upset. But he seemed to want to continue our conversation.

"But what about all these taxes they are trying to load onto us, without having any say in the matter?" he asked.

I sat down again, and after swallowing the last drops of my tea I replied, "You know we don't like taxes, nobody does. Father used to fume and curse that the Prince in the old country was sucking the people dry with taxes to build his castle on the hill. Many of our people came here to get out from under their poverty, caused by unfair taxes. It's a smart issue on which to foment a revolution. The English Parliament has handled it badly, but we will be taxed whatever piper calls the tune. Is it worth it to change one greedy piper for another?"

"Eberhardt, now you talk in riddles."

"Besides," I continued, "Fenwick Lochwood told me that Ben Franklin said in Europe that the American colonists would never agree on anything, let alone break with the mother country. I heard that the first vote on independence was a tie, and it took another try to get a bare majority in Congress."

Suddenly, Johann Leonard stood up, clearly frustrated.

"You're hopeless. I see you have made up your mind to be a tory. All I can say is, God help you!"

"Johann Leonard, it is natural for a young man like you to seek out new adventures, but I just want to live in peace with some semblance of social order, which I don't see if the rebels prevail in this conflict. Besides, I believe you are also uncomfortable with the violence."

Johann Leonard surprised me with his next remark as he made to saddle his horse, which, like him, was getting restless to begin the day's journey.

"I have been up to Canada and seen plenty of violence. Often it made me sick to my stomach. I'm not comfortable with a soldier's life, but I'm in it now. I believe we have to get the yoke of the King off our backs to have a better life. I hope I'm right, but in Canada I began to wonder whether this whole thing is different from the freedom we are promised. General Montgomery told Colonel Goose of his wish to leave the war behind and go home to his farm. But he stuck it out, he said, because of honour. His honour got him killed. Like him, with me, it is a matter of honour."

I did not mention the letters Christina had given me.

He had finished saddling his horse and was preparing to leave. I was curious about his plans.

"Where do you go from here?"

"I have a few more farms to visit and then it's home to my girls."

"Look," I said, "If you are still in the area, please plan to stay with us for the night."

"Thanks, I will see."

Lena, who had been watching with our girls, saw that Johann Leonard was about to leave and came to wish him all haste. The girls thanked him again for their gifts and Lena apologized that Thomas could not see more of his uncle, but he had to get in the hay before the rains came. "Please, please visit us again. And bring Christina and your girls next time." Then Johann Leonard mounted the horse and was off into a very uncertain future. He waved back as he turned onto the road.

I wondered what would become of him. He was not cut out to be a warrior, and too honourable to be a rebel. And too proud to admit to his fears. He had no passion for his mission, a sure condition to be brought low by a cruel world.

But in a way I thought I might be the coward, not taking a firm stand for the King.

By the spring of '77 the jaws of the vice were closing. The invasion of Canada was lost to the rebels. Arnold's campaign on Lake Champlain was lost in October, and his fleet of ships destroyed. A new English general had been appointed, and a large army of English regulars and German mercenaries from Hesse was being formed at Quebec to march on Albany with the hope of stopping the rebellion. It was a fine spring day with the sun beaming down on the black earth when I again had to think seriously of our future. I was down in the corner of the field, hoeing the weeds from between the rows of new corn, when someone made a noise in the bushes along the snake rail fence. It startled me at first, but then I saw Jed Adler waving toward the bushes. I looked out over the field and kept hoeing. I did not want to see him. He was trouble, but Jed was making such a fuss, waving both arms and pacing back and forth, that I thought it would be safer for both of us if I made my way to the side of the field. I kept hoeing, still fearful that someone was watching. When close to Jed I said, "What do you want?" He went down on one knee as if to tie his bootlace. "Everet, there's a herd of horses over near Bennington and Gershom French wants to relieve the rebels of some of them."

Stealing horses was a hanging offense. "You know I don't want to go, Jed. I'm forty-four years old with a family, and I don't want to get shot; or worse, hanged by the neck."

He said, in a voice too loud for safety in those perilous times, "But you have talked against large landowners, most who see their wealth increasing if they can rid themselves of the King; I thought you would want to get back at them." It was true, I had railed against my landlord but I had no quarrel with the Committee. It had not bothered me yet, probably because I was a tenant and had nothing the members wanted, unless I showed evidence of working for the King against them. My only quarrel with the King was his decree that forced us to house soldiers, like in the old country. But there were few soldiers in my neck of the woods.

I had a deep dislike for landowners, many whose source of wealth was the King's largesse, but I did not see how stealing horses would harm them much. Besides, it was open season on Tories, with a bounty on turning them in to the Committee. In January, two neighbours had taken in Young Jacob, where he spent five months in the stockade before he would sign the oath. I remember looking down at the young shoots of corn poking through the moist soil and cursing those who had been neighbours but who seemed to have lost their minds lately. I thought perhaps things would return to normal when the harvesting had to be done.

So I told Jed I was not going with him, and kept moving in a tight circle around the hoe, avoiding his eyes. I was betraying my friend and drinking partner of nigh onto a dozen years. Jed was the first to help me get started when Lena and I came from down river, but I was fearful; the situation was becoming serious business and someone was going to be killed. I thought it was time to lay low and keep out of trouble.

Jed was hurt by my refusal to join him. He cursed me to high heaven, calling me a coward and a liar. He carried on about how the rebels were making life miserable for everyone, but I kept to my decision and urged Jed to be quiet and leave me alone. After a minute, he could see the futility of his mission and said, "Well, Everet if you change your mind, I will be with Gershom French if you can find us." He walked into the bush and quickly disappeared. The encounter left me feeling melancholy; I truly liked Jed. Not long after this meeting, the sheriff came to my cousin's farm looking for Jed, who had escaped when one of the guards got drunk during a work stint. Until then I didn't know Jed had been locked up since he had accosted me on the road to the Black Wolf Inn.

Shortly after Jed's visit to me in the cornfield, while drinking ale at Hosek Haus Ephriam Lochwood was telling his mates in a loud voice about his exploits in Canada, a story I had heard before. I only half listened, but one thing he said made me think. Ephriam said the British Government was giving land grants in Canada to anyone who helped them in their attempt to put down the rebels. Some others were also interested and talk amongst the farmers got around to this subject. John Harper mumbled, "I heard its Mohawk country. Worse than the Appalachians and that's bad enough. Go up there and you'll lose your hair fer shure." Alonso Boomhour from over Hoosick Falls way told of an Indian who lived at his place for a while, and who had been a Huron and fought against Munro at Fort William Henry in '57. "He said Canada was full of lakes and streams with only a few settlements of white Jesuits. Don't sound too good to me, Indians and Papists, you'll lose more than your hair up there." This seemed to put an end to any hope of surviving as a farmer, especially for the Methodists around here, thought I, and left for home. But I wondered if it was true that the English were giving land in the northern wilderness to Tories.

One evening, tired and dusty from helping Hiram Coons raise a barn with some of his neighbours, I went to the Hosek Haus to whet my whistle. A large crowd had gathered from neighbouring farms and after a few drinks an argument broke out in a dark corner of the room. This sort of thing was becoming more common those days, what with war looming and the Committeemen trying to force people to support the rebellion. The argument was a good-natured one, in which men spoke their minds but were not belligerent. At a relative lull in the noise, Zack Barent stood up and addressed the room.

"Look here, men. We fight about the situation in Boston but none of us ignorant farmers really know what we are talking about. Well, we have here right in this room young Fred Geisburger who has come from his studies at King's College. The College has since closed its doors because of the rebellion, so young Fred is working for his paw. I talked with his paw who tells me that young Fred is cognizant of the true situation in Boston and New York. So why don't we buy him a drink to loosen his tongue so we all may be apprised of his wisdom. What say you?"

A short silence came over the room; the farmers startled at hearing Zack give such a long oration. Then a chorus of, "Hurrahs," and, "Yup, let's hear what young Fred has to say." Meanwhile, young Fred looked down at his hands, tightly cupped around his mug of ale and seemed less than eager to expose his thoughts to these rough men. After a prolonged chorus of, "Speak," and, "Come on, get on your feet and tell us your thoughts, tell us what you learned at that fancy school," Fred stood up, red-faced, and began to speak.

"On my journey to New York in '75 I was invited to visit an uncle and his wife in Cambridge for a few days. My lodging was on the road to Lexington. At about ten o'clock, I heard the sound of shouting from the road below drifting through my open casement. Going to the window, I saw a rider on the road waving his arms and shouting. The words were carried away by the wind so I know not what he was shouting. He raced past my lodging and up the road toward Lexington.

"It was only a few minutes later I saw a large troop of redcoats marching along the road with their white gaiters reflecting the moonlight and the rhythmic tramp of some three thousand feet turning up the dust in the road. The order and discipline, as seen in the light of an almost full moon, impressed me mightily."

There was silence in the room. Some of his audience, Fred suddenly seemed to realize, might not like his apparent admiration for the redcoats, but no one spoke, apparently giving him the courage to continue.

"When they came back down the road the next day, they were a scraggly and frightened group of men, although marching as if they had won the battle. At that moment, I realized the rhetoric being voiced all over Boston had turned to a deadly serious purpose.

"That evening my friend invited me to accompany him to Boston town, a distance of one league. Having supped, we walked on the road, sometimes dusty, sometimes wet, for the road to Boston town crossed a marshy area. The moisture from the countryside, depressing in itself, added to my apprehension of visiting this place which I had been told was not safe. Entering the narrow and irregular streets, crowded with merry citizens and revellers celebrating of the recent victory over the English at Concord, we came upon a quadrangle in front of the meetinghouse where there was a large crowd. A man of the cloth was standing on the platform of a pillory, which needless to say was not in excellent condition, and I feared that the platform might collapse beneath him, with his pious prayer of thanksgiving floating off on the wind.

"Leaving the good preacher to his fate, my friend and I were about to leave the quadrangle when we chanced upon an incident I will not soon forget. A well-dressed man of middle years was backed into a corner of the meetinghouse where the vestibule met the front wall and was being harangued and taunted by a gang of youths. Some shouted 'Tory,' some 'Traitor,' and many other obscene expressions of his parentage that do not bear repeating here. One of the youths, who seemed to be the ringleader, was threatening the helpless man with a stick and shouting, 'I know who you are, a tory and a traitor! Stealing our money, you are. We should stretch your neck on yonder gibbet and let the devil see you dance.' The man cringed into the corner which was both his sanctuary and his prison, and being a simple peaceful soul, stood in front of his tormentors with tears streaming down his cheeks and a dark stain spreading on his trouser leg. He threw his hands to the heavens and prayed silently to He whose house before which he stood. He was white as a sheet and shaking like the leaf of a poplar tree in the morning breeze. He was clearly frightened out of his very wits."

Fred stopped speaking, his face white with anger. Anxious to hear the end of the story, someone shouted, "What happened next? You can't stop now!"

Fred, mentally returning to the task at hand, continued his story.

"When it seemed the tormented man was going to collapse from fear, an older man, with a full white beard and a somewhat dirty tricorn, stepped out of the crowd and walked to a spot between the man and the youths. The old man said nothing but stood straight as an arrow with feet planted far apart. The ringleader seemed to be acquainted with the whiskered one because he hesitated and said, 'Aw, Old Elijah, this is not your business. Get out of our way.' The old man just stood where he had planted his feet and said; 'Peace is God's business and God is my business. So you young hotheads get off home with you and leave this innocent man in peace.' Still he stood, unmoving and unblinking. Someone in the crowd of youths said quietly, 'Come on, lets go from here. I hear Mr. Adams is giving a speech from the Town House balcony. Let's go and see what he says.' The leader, frustrated by Elijah's stoicism, and looking now for a way out of the situation said, 'Let us go hear what Sam has to say,' and with those words strode off with his gang of youths dutifully following.

"Sickened by this demonstration of cruelty, I had no more stomach to remain in that place and I told my friend I wished to return to my lodgings. But my friend was anxious that I hear Mr. Adams' oration, and being his guest, I could not in politeness refuse. So we walked through the streets, which were now beginning to empty for it was getting late for God-fearing people, and entered the open space at the entrance to the Town Hall. Mr. Adams had finished his oration and gone home, and the crowd that had come to listen to his familiar charge of 'the King's tyranny' was also dispersing. My friend took me to the site of the five 'murders,' as he called them. It was the place where a mob taunted a sentry on guard duty until he called to his regiment for aid, and in the ensuing melee five of the mob met an untimely end. My friend seemed proud of the event that took place there, in front of the Town Hall. The place looked very ordinary to me.

"The next morning I visited Harvard College. On seeing this simple, beautiful hall, I was struck with its serenity and the majesty of all that is civilized in world knowledge, compared with the ugliness and uncivilized behaviour of the previous evening. With this thought, I left Boston for New York, where the Sons of Liberty and their agitation for 'liberty or death' is not taken so seriously. It appeared to me that the citizens of New York were almost indifferent to the rebellion rhetoric. In thinking on this, I concluded that the relative peace there was perhaps because New York is taking in many immigrants trying to escape from the very situation existing in Boston."

I thought Fred was a little too much inclined to support the Tories, and looked around the room expecting an uproar from those who disagreed with the young scholar. But in truth, I saw no real hotheads, most of the men in the room being seasoned farmers who were imbued by experience with their own wisdom and in this instance were inclined to let Fred have his say. Young Fred, seeing no real discontent with his story, seemed encouraged to go on, perhaps even in a bolder manner.

"Now, what we know in this neck of the woods is that many of you are considered Tories and traitors if you do not believe in the rebels cause. We are left to struggle on our own against nature and our neighbour. In my opinion as a humble subject, this is what is in store for us if the rebels, now causing untold chaos all over the colonies and even into Canada and Nova Scotia, gain power."

Someone in the back of the room yelled, sarcastically, "Hey Fred, you for the King or for Congress?"

Fred, the scholar, was taken aback by the tone of the question. He was about to sit down when Zack, more sympathetic to Fred's story, said, "Fred is my guest, and I for one would like to hear if he has anything more to say. What say you all, does he continue or no?" There was a murmur of consent, and Fred, with a lot of courage, I thought, straightened his back and tried to answer the question.

Fred hesitated before going on. He was wise enough to be humble.

"It may be that I am wrong, and the commonwealth the rebels propose will endure forever, or perhaps it too will go in the manner of Cromwell's commonwealth. My professor claims that all governments tend toward corruption. Only time will tell if history can be turned upside down.

"There is a certain attractiveness in their rhetoric, in that it seems to dampen the rigidity of the class system. It may be true that with the elimination of the top of the pyramid of class, namely the English nabobs, all men, except those unfortunates who are slaves, will do better in a new system. It may elevate small landowners and merchants to a higher level. But will a new system help you, the farmers, who, after all, are the wellspring of any society? You have already seen examples of the insecurity of your land. Will you have security of your present holdings if the rebels win this war?"

Young Fred stopped speaking and abruptly sat down and hung his head as if he had committed a terrible sin. This was exactly the right thing for him to do, for although there were a few cries of, "Tory," and, "Traitor," from the floor, Fred's seeming repentance for his words quickly dampened any wide-spread antagonism, as if refuting his words would also be a sin. But, some men did leave.

Zack expressed his thanks for an "informative discourse," and the meeting returned to the usual drinking and gossip. I left.

When I was hitching the horse to the buggy for the trip home, I heard an argument erupt over behind the tavern's horse shed. A taunting crowd of men, urging them to settle their differences in the dust, surrounded some young bucks ready to fight. I went home, knowing that Fred's oration did not satisfy everyone. However, after that evening, I was inclined to side with the boy scholar.

As the horse jerked the cart along the dusty road, I could not help but contemplate the failure of my life. I was in debt for seed. Thomas seemed uninterested in farming. Lena would not let me touch her any longer. She was almost impossible to live with and nagged me to let her take the girls back to the Poughquag where her widowed mother lived. She believed they would be in less danger there than in what she thought was a war zone. I had no intention of going back, and this increased her unhappiness.

I might lose my livelihood if these rebels were not put down and some of the land problems solved, but in truth I did not see much hope for either my family or me. Perhaps I could have signed up for the rebellion, but I could see no future for us tenant farmers if the rebels were in charge. They would take my lease and deprive me of any future as a farmer, except as a farmhand. Besides, I was sure the King's army would put down the rebellion in the end. There was word of a large English army of regulars and German mercenaries gathering up in Canada with the intention of taking Albany. I had come a long way since father and Uncle Leonardt emigrated from the old country to end up with nothing. It seemed I might have to take up my gun and fight the rebels after all.

8

EBERHARDT'S WAR

Talk of revolution was in the air, and gloom hung in the air like a black cloud. Apart from the troubles caused by the Green Mountain Boys over land grants, the gathering storm as yet had little direct effect on domestic life. Some farmers believed that being isolated from the large towns along the seacoast meant they were safe from harm. But the Sons of Liberty had planted the seeds of rebellion in fertile soil, and like weeds, they were soon to entangle all peace loving folk in their fast growing tentacles, and with agents of the Albany Committee for Conspiracies roaming the countryside, some with very dubious motives, the farmers were beginning to realize they had to declare for the rebellion or suffer loss and humiliation, or even taken to the guardhouse. The failure of the rebel's invasion of Canada made me believe that the English would prevail in the end.

I was fearful that any day now that a man from the Committee would demand my allegiance or remove me from the forty acres that I had spent the last twelve years clearing and planting. Niclass, who now had a place of his own, was talking of joining the British, and young Tom was showing great interest in war talk when we were together. Young Jacob, after his stint in the guardhouse, had gone with Gershom French to harass the militia.

I no longer had any attraction to Lena, but I wished that she not be left in penury. I spoke to her about taking up the gun and fighting the rebels with the hope of getting my own land in Canada. She was clear that if it came to that she would take the children to live amongst her friends and relatives in Dutchess County. Catharina and Hanna were now old enough to look after the little ones and with me gone Lena would probably not stay on the farm although I believed she and Tom could keep up our small acreage if it was not confiscated because of my actions. As I trudged home from the Hosek Haus behind Old Jude these thoughts haunted me.

I was passing the gate leading to Ephriam Lochwood's old weather-beaten farmhouse when I had an idea. Ephriam had been with Arnold on his march to Quebec so I would consult Ephriam about land in Canada. Tying Old Jude to the fence, I walked up a small hill to Ephriam's house. He was sitting in a sagging rocking chair that squeaked and bumped as he moved to and fro, smoking his cob pipe. Smoke from the pipe curled up under his old wide-brimmed hat. In the fading light of evening, I could hardly recognize that the figure sitting there was Ephriam, but I made my greeting. Ephriam said, "Howdy. Nice evening." He was

212

a man of few words when not drinking.

I answered, "I was passing and thought I saw you sitting here."

"Want a drink?"

Begging off his offer of whiskey I sat on the front stoop and got to the point right away. "Ephriam, tell me about Canada. What is it like there? Is there free land?"

"Well, I'll tell you, all the time I was there I was scared for my life. After the battle for Quebec, we lay siege to the town until the fierce Scots with their pipes of terror drove us back to Montreal and out of the country. We suffered from the cold and the lack of food, and worn-out boots. We had to steal food, but we finally got new moccasins. It was a terrible time, I thought I would never see home again."

"Did you meet Johann Leonard? He was with Montgomery's Yorkers."

"The famine-proof veterans as Arnold's survivors were called, were from Connecticut, Massachusetts, and Pennsylvania and we looked down on the Yorkers; they were General Montgomery's men. I did not see hide nor hair of Johann Leonard."

Before Ephriam could give me a long harangue about his war adventures during the invasion of Canada, I asked, "Ephriam, what is the nature of the people and the countryside there?"

"Well, the people are open-handed. And they are full of music, more joyful than the fanatics of Massachusetts. They are ruled by priests but they don't always obey. The women will open their hand and give you the shift off their back, and are open to singing and dancing, but pushed by the priests, they have many children. They keep their maiden names after wedlock.

"In the homes are many fine things. Many have pianos. Almost every family has a fiddle, and they sing and dance the whole night through. Meals are a ritual, even in the poorer houses. There are few English, except the Governor and military officers. The Scotsmen are fierce in battle, and they dress in colourful skirts with great pride. They go into battle behind their beloved bagpipes. The noise from this fearful thing is a lonely, haunting tune, blood curdling to their enemies. The sound bounces off the hills, and when you hear this call to battle you can expect a fierce fight. A Scot is driven to fight like Satan himself."

Ephriam stopped as if finished. I talked into the silence, "The countryside, what is its nature?"

"Well, most the time I was there the ground was covered in deep snow. It was very cold and it seemed always to be snowing. There are large Popish churches everywhere; they are the centres of the farmers' lives. The farms are similar to ours, large tracts controlled by seigneurs, who were originally patrons of their King Louis; very much like our large landlords, only a different king. The farmers are called habitants and most are tenant farmers."

"Ephriam, is it true land can be had for service to King George."

"While laying siege to the town, before we were driven away by the fierce Scots, the spies we sent behind the walls came back with stories that the English, who rule the people, would give land to any American patriot who would give service to the Crown. I believe the land they were offering was in the western wilderness of the Province, it being full of Indians. I don't know if these stories of free land were true, but many believed it to be so."

I prepared to leave somewhat disheartened by Ephriam's description of where the English lands were located. Ephriam's pipe had long ago died, and as he fixed a new pipe I got up to go, saying thanks for the story. Ephriam was startled from the thoughts of war that seemed to possess him, and he stood up, again offering a drink of his whiskey. I said, "Thanks, but I need to get home before dark or Lena will kill me." After finding Old Jude and my cart in the gathering night, I drove home in deep thought.

That night, I was wrestling with a recurring nightmare in which a scaly monster stood before me with bristles along its back, and eyes covered with slime. It had webbed feet, fingers joined together by rough skin. The creature, with seaweed in its hair, and more dripping from its mouth, rushes toward me with its scaly arms outstretched to embrace me....

Just as it was about to crush me to its spiny chest I awoke with a start, my heart racing and in a cold sweat. The bedchamber was full of light. I sprang from bed, suddenly aware of fire. The window seemed ablaze with flames. I shouted to Lena, "Get Tom up! The barn is on fire!" In my nightclothes I ran to the well for a bucket of water, and only then saw that it was a haystack between the house and barn that was burning. At the same time I saw two shadows running toward the road. I swore at them in a rage, "You bastards," but then I had to attend to the fire. By this time Tom and Lena had joined me and we fought for about an hour to keep the fire from spreading to the barn. Fortunately, there was no wind that night or the whole place would have gone up in flames.

Covered with soot and sweat, and smelling like ashes the three of us went to the house where Catharina had made tea. Lena was hysterical with fear and anger and Tom was all for getting out a gun and chasing after the culprits who set the fire. With help of Catharina and Hanna, who had joined us, I got Lena to bed where she gradually calmed down. I sat with Tom watching that the fire was out until finally he went off to bed too, swearing revenge. I spent the rest of the night agonizing about who might have it in for me. My first thought was Ethan's boys trying to encourage me to leave the farm. Or perhaps it was just two kids out to create mischief; or rebels, or perhaps even Jed's friends to convince me to go to their side. Taking the musket to the bedchamber I finally slept just as the sun's rays were peeping through the window.

On a warm, sunny morning three days after the fire, Tom and I were shearing sheep when two men appeared holding the declaration of loyalty to Congress the Committee had dreamed up. The one that did the talking was a burly man, rotund, with a twisting of his mouth that produced a sneer in his expression. His demeanour was not pleasant. The second man stood aloof, mouth drooping and eyes dull, showing, I thought, some impairment in his ability to associate with ordinary men. Unlike the burly one he looked not to be dangerous except that he carried, carelessly pointing at me, a heavy musket that he seemed ready to use at a word from his leader.

The large man said, "I come to make you sign the oath of loyalty. I am also instructed to tell you that if you do not sign the oath I am to confiscate your guns and take your decision to the Committee of Safety for a ruling. The Committee could declare you a traitor, put you in the guardhouse, and confiscate all your chattels."

His belligerent words made me angry, but I held my tongue and answered calmly, "My oath is to my God and those who came before me. My father and my grandfather before him suffered lives of hardship and political upheavals from men like those on your Committee. All I want now is to work my farm in peace. God knows my loyalty is to Him only." The man then asked, "Where is your gun?" "I have no guns," I lied, having kept my two guns in the hay during the daylight hours for the last months, only bringing the musket to the house at night. The man muttered, "We will look," and he and his imbecilic partner went toward the house. This movement brought Lena with little Ephriam in her arms to the door, the other children trailing behind her skirts. They were frightened and the baby, sensing danger, was setting up a loud wail.

After the two agents ransacked the house, they left it and began searching the outbuildings, and even peered into the well. After about one hour they returned to the barn and told me that the next visit would be from the sheriff. "You can bet on it."

I blurted, "The sheriff? It's not his business!"

The surly one answered with a sneer, "Word has come to us that you have been keeping company with" he looked at a piece of paper "Jedediah Adler, an escaped horse thief. Looks to me like you are a tory horse thief." Before I could deny the accusation, they mounted up and left.

It was not much later that word of the men's visit spread to the adjacent farms; someone had seen them. Two farmers came to enquire. "They accused me of being with Jed Adler stealing horses, a bare-faced lie. Jed is a friend but I have never stolen any horses with him." I thanked them for their concern and after having tea they left wishing me well with the Committee. Lena was very upset. "I knew it would come to this. When they come back you have to sign the oath or God only knows what will be the fate of me and the children."

"But Lena," I explained, it is no longer about the oath. They are saying I stole horses. If the sheriff comes it will not be with the oath but with a warrant to arrest me for horse stealing. I must take to the woods until this blows over. When the English army comes they will drop the false charges and I will be able to come home again. In the meantime you and Tom will have to do the best you can." Lena was more often than not angry with me, but at this time of crisis she calmed down and I believed she would cope with the new circumstances.

About noon, the oldest son of Adam Schmelling rode into the yard leading a riding horse complete with leather saddle and large saddlebags. He said his dad would loan the mare to me until things became normal again. Overwhelmed with Adam's generosity I thanked James and invited him for a drink. He said he had to get back. Holding him for a moment I said, "I hear your dad has signed the oath."

"Yes he has. Now that we own outright our farm he thought it would be prudent to go along with the revolutionary Committee and hope for the best."

"I value the loan of the horse, and your dad's generosity. Say thanks to him for me. By the way, does she have a name?"

"It's 'Myrtle.'"

When James rode out of our yard I prepared to go on the run. From Young Jacob's experience, I understood the danger I was about to face. Young Jacob was with a group that went off to join the British army and was captured by two rebels at the beginning of the year. In the guardhouse, he was treated harshly for some months. Later, the prisoners got a guard drunk and Young Jacob escaped and traveled to Ryn Beck. But three continental soldiers apprehended him in March and brought him back to the Albany guardhouse. Those soldiers were paid a bounty for their treachery, a paltry sum to deny a man his freedom. A few days later Young Jacob signed the oath and was released. Shortly after, he went into the woods with Gershom French and began causing trouble for the rebels.

That afternoon I took up my musket and skinning knife, packed some food, bid my family farewell, mounted my borrowed mare, and set out to find Gershom French in the woods. Jed had told me where he was, and shortly after nightfall, I found French and his band of outlaws, about twenty in all. I was told more men would be returning to camp from a foray for provisions. The men in camp were very rough. I did recognize four of my former neighbours, including Jed and Young Jacob both who expressed great pleasure at my presence. After an hour or two I understood the purpose of French's mission was to relieve any rebels they could find of their assets, mostly horses, which could easily be sold to the British army. At the same time, French was recruiting these men to be delivered to General Burgoyne on his march from Canada.

My mind was conflicted; I had gone to seek out Jed and Gershom because of a false accusation of stealing horses, and there I was in the midst of a gang of horse thieves. I was to become an outlaw and a soldier. At the time it seemed the only choice I had. My only hope was that the mess would soon be behind me and I could get back to my farm. But it was to be many years before I found a home in the northern wilderness far from Lena and most of my family.

After a week and some days, success was ours, having relieved several rebels of their mounts. French was very firm that we were to do no murder. I remember there was one encounter with an armed farmer on the road to Bennington who responded with hostility to our cause. He was not really a rebel but a Hampshire farmer who was having trouble with a New York lawyer and was trying to find Allen's Green Mountain Boys. To avoid bloodshed he was relieved of his musket but allowed to keep the horse, which, being old and lazy would have been of little use in any case.

Being at that time in the close vicinity to my farm, I left the loyalists that very night to see after the welfare of the children. The house showed no light, everyone being asleep, it being an hour when the moon was at the top of its bow. Banging on the door for several fearful minutes because of the noise I caused, Lena finally appeared in the opening, with Tom behind, carrying a gun. Once I was safely inside, her first words were, "The sheriff was here with a posse of men searching for you. He said he had a warrant for your arrest for horse stealing. Now you are in great trouble if they catch you. The sheriff was quick to say that stealing horses was a hanging offence." She was angry. "What is going to happen to your poor children?"

I knew that at that moment my future was set. I must go with the King and hope the English prevailed in this conflict. I said to Lena, "This will be over in a few weeks. The English have a large army on Lake Champlain coming toward this region and when it arrives here you will be safe. The horse-stealing charge will not apply once the colonial Government gets control again. The rebels will be defeated and things will be better than they have been since these outlaws took over."

This speech seemed to settle her, and she went off to prepare tea. My eyes followed her retreating back and I suddenly realized that she would survive her difficulties. She was a strong woman and some of her youthful spirit was noticeable again. I felt much better at leaving her. Tom was a strapping fellow and was able to do the heavy work that had to be done, and the girls were old enough to take most of the burden from Lena in the house, leaving her to care for Willem and the baby. I looked in at the sleeping children, blissfully ignorant of the tragic circumstances engulfing their young lives. I sent up a prayer to God for their safety while I was away. I consoled my grief with the conviction that it would be over soon. I told Tom that as young as he was he was now to look after the farm, the children, and their mother. I told him to go to Niclass if he needed help, and I tried to comfort him with the words, "God go with you as of a man," and told him I would be back home soon.

I left my family and possessions with a sad heart and set out for Bald Mountain. The Hoosick Road was crawling with men, mostly farmers, going off to fight the English. Some were moving west to join Schuyler at Fort Edward and others were moving east, no doubt to lend support to Allen's Boys, who were drifting back to Bennington after the recent defeat of the rebels by Burgoyne at Ticonderoga. Much of the fervour of revolution in the talk of the rebel farmers on the road meant little to me; I believed we would be less free if the rebels prevailed. It was not just the war with the English; evidence of future chaos was in the actions taken against my family and my neighbours by the Committee in Albany. What happened to my grandfather seemed to be happening to me. Grandfather used to talk about the desecration of Germany by the Swedes, who pillaged the countryside in the time of his ancestors Jörg and Hans. Another of grandfather's tales was about the war between the German tribes and the Roman legions. Riding toward my own future I could hear grandfather's reedy voice carried by the wind in my ears,

"...in the closing years of the reign of Augustus there was an uprising of the Rhineland peoples led by Arminius. He found that half the Legions' forces were on leave, and he incited the tribes to revolt. The river ran red with the blood of the slaughtered."

Grandfather said that in retribution for the slaughter of Augustus' Legions, "Germanicus marched his legions into the heartland of the tribes. The forest folk lay low and Germanicus, finding no one to kill, began a march back to his headquarters. The tribes fell upon his legions and slaughtered many Roman soldiers that day."

Grandfather said that the tribes were victorious in the end but only after they took on the mantle of Romanism. "Rome always wins, even when it loses." Recalling grandfather's words was perhaps an omen that in the end order would prevail.

All day I kept to the woods and hills, and traveling with great care reached French's camp on the mountain in the late afternoon. There were now more men than when I left, many that I did not know. We numbered in all, I believe, about three score recruits for the English.

The camp that Gershom favoured as his base was on a high ridge of rock, with a sheer rock face at its back and a screen of trees protecting the camp from being seen. The ridge was only possible by a narrow footpath favoured by the Indians, winding through the woods below. In past times a few families of savages had lived there.

Gershom grew up in Lansingburgh and knew of the secluded place on the mountain when the Indians lived there. He knew the mountain like the back of his hand, having climbed its rocks in his youth. In the cliff were three small caves, one reserved for French, who claimed it as his headquarters. His main recruiters, Jed being one of these, took up ownership of the others. The remainder of us recruits found our own resting places. I guess I wasn't surprised that Young Jacob was with those who came into camp with Jed. I took up a position near Young Jacob, who had laid claim to a spot under a narrow overhanging outcrop in the cliff, which afforded some shelter from inclement weather. I was anxious to hear of Young Jacob's time in the guardhouse, and that evening, somewhat removed from the men around the fire, he told me of the time he was in the hands of the rebels.

"We were thirty men of like mind who were meeting at different houses. I, and some ten others, were meeting in the house of Henry Balding when, about four o'clock, a large party of light horsemen burst through the door of the house with drawn swords. One of our men, I did not know his name, reached for a musket at his feet but was thereupon promptly seized and thrown to the floor. We were ordered to leave our guns and kits in the house and were pushed into the yard at gunpoint. The front yard seemed full of horsemen, at least a dozen, and they were herding and tethering those few horses that belonged to our party. Most of the men rode off, leaving four of their number to escort us. We were marched to the guardhouse with prodding from their guns as well as insults and taunts.

"The day following my confinement in the guardhouse I was taken before three men who said they were members of the Committee and threatened me with dire result, even hanging, if I did not confess and sign the oath. Confess what I knew not of, I told them. They threatened to tie me to the water wheel at the mill nearby and let God decide my fate if I did not expose honest farmers they claimed to be conspirators against liberty. Refusing their threat with a curse, I was roughly taken back to the guardhouse. Then, while I was sleeping, at about eleven o'clock at night, they took me from confinement. They stripped me of all clothing and tied me to a tree to be exposed to the bitter frost, for it was winter. I imagined every drop of blood to be frozen within my naked body, but then two of the Committee said that if I would tell them all I knew they would release me; if not, they would leave me to my fate.

"I told them I knew nothing that would save my life and I could not sign the oath, fearing God's banishment from his kingdom. They left me, but just as I felt there was no more life in me, the guard came and dragged my freezing form back to the guardhouse.

"Some days following, when I had fully recovered from the insult to my body, the guard, a rough fellow, addicted to drink we were told by the older prisoners, came to me with a cat-o'-nine-tails, drooping like an evil viper over one arm. At the sight of this terrible instrument of torture I felt weak, as if I would expire that very instant. The guard said he had been ordered to deliver one hundred stripes if I did not expose my farmer friends. "If that does not kill you, I am instructed to tell you hanging is your fate." Twenty stripes were then delivered with all the severity he could muster, which I forbore in great agony. I swear even one additional stripe would have forced me to tell all I knew, true or untrue. He left me to bear my agonies. From that day, no tory was allowed to speak to me and I was insulted and abused by all.

"Weeks later, our drunken guard was overcome by one of the prisoners, his keys taken, and we were free. I escaped to Ryn Beck, only to be apprehended by three traitorous fellows and brought back to stand in front of the Committee. My previous torture by these barbarous outlaws induced me to sign the oath. I was thereafter released."

Hearing of Young Jacob's treatment at the hands of the Committee convinced me of the rightness of the action I had taken. If these representatives of the Congress could be free to act in such a barbarous manner only God could help them prevail against the King.

The next day, Gershom, satisfied that he had a goodly body of recruits, announced to the assembled group that we would proceed upriver until we encountered the English force commanded by General Burgoyne. He urged great caution since the roads were crowded with rebels headed towards Fort Edward. We broke camp at one o'clock that afternoon. The woods were alive with vermin, rebels, and savages. Even the woodland pathways were crowded with rebels going to Fort Edward, where we understood General Schuyler was preparing take a stand against General Burgoyne. It was a period of the month when the moon was near full and the heavens without cloud, and although we mostly travelled by night it was a dangerous trek, particularly when we crossed over a large clearing.

During the day we made camp, at which time Gershom left our party and made forays into local settlements for recruits. We discussed the danger in this plan, believing that someone in the settlement would act in a traitorous manner and seize him, leaving us without a leader. Our fears aside, this did not happen and he was able to recruit some dozen men to our cause before we reached Burgoyne's army.

By now, Fort Ann was on our left hand, which we gave a wide berth for we had heard that there was a garrison of rebel soldiers there. On the third night from Bald Mountain we crossed a relatively open area that Gershom called the "pine plain" and as yet we had had no contact with the enemy, though we could hear the ringing of axes in the woods off to our left, across the river. French sent two men as scouts to see if this noise was from the rebel forces or from the British. They were gone for some four hours and worry grew that they had been taken and would be tortured to reveal our presence to the rebels. When they finally appeared they had news. "The rebels are cutting trees and clogging the creeks to delay the progress of the British. We saw no sign of Burgoyne's army but Jeremiah here with me thought he saw an Indian off in the distance that he believed to be an advance scout for the British. The army is surely not any distance from us."

That night we moved to the stream that I believed was called the "halfway point" and wondered from where it was half the way. The path we trod led to a fording place and, it being late summer, the stream was at low water. Two men were asked to test the fording, and on their return with a favourable report we crossed the stream that night without difficulty. About one mile into the woods we made our camp. When dawn broke there was both anxiety and excitement in camp, and about ten o'clock we could faintly hear the great British army moving toward our position. We gathered all our belongings, which were meagre, and attempted a dignified march into Burgoyne's headquarters. Our little party of recruits now numbered ninety-four souls dedicated to the preservation of a united British empire.

After a brief welcome by the general and the taking of the oath, we were assigned to a Lieutenant Colonel Francis von Pfister, who commanded a regiment called the Loyal Volunteers. We were told that we would eventually receive uniforms with a green coat. Even at my age, which was not young in comparison to most, I was moved to some emotion. But this brief elation soon fled, as our first duty in this grand army was to go forward to cut up the trees that hindered the army's advance and use the trunks to build bridges. It seemed even being a soldier in a famous army could not remove me from farm work. After the hardship and fear of the last many weeks, I did not begrudge the work.

The army was encamped on flat area with scattered pine trees, a relief from the deep woods. All was confusion. We were ordered to line up in front of a soldier in uniform who was shouting at us. As I approached the front of the line, he bellowed at me to go to the quartermaster's tent and get blankets and gear. Looking at a piece of paper, he roared, "You, Waeger, are billeted in tent number sixteen, over there, on your left about a hundred yards. Go there and come back here and line up over there," and he pointed to a spot where a stake had been driven in the ground with a green ribbon of cloth attached, which was fluttering in the slight breeze that had begun to blow across the clearing.

We lined up in front of the quartermaster's tent and were issued blankets and a kit that included a water flask, after which I found my home for the duration; tent number sixteen. Throwing down my blankets and bedroll on one of the bare cots, I dutifully lined up at the green flag. An axe was put in my hand and my musket examined for duty. The loud soldier, I found out later he was a sergeant, told us the reserve artillery had not yet made it to the front, "You must rely on whatever piece you have in your possession in case of a raid." He then sent us into the woods.

The rebels had cut many trees and broken all the bridges to hinder the British advance, so I spent my days clearing away fallen trees until at night my arms and shoulders seemed on fire. At dawn, we were rousted out, filled with beans, biscuits, and tea and sent out again to the woods. Some days I was relieved from chopping trees to repair or build a bridge, which was much easier than wielding the axe. Besides being sore all over, I was wet all day on most days since the country was swampy and swarming with mosquitos and other pests. We were fired upon, but with our superior numbers easily drove them off. Because of the difficulties, the army could only move about one mile each day. The slowness of our advance on the enemy was frustrating to the officers because the orders from the top were to, "Hurry! Every day the enemy is getting more numerous."

We cut our way to Fort Ann, expecting to meet resistance from enemy muskets but we found only burnt-out fortifications, except for a sawmill and blockhouse. The 9th Regiment had fought six times their number at Fort Ann and had repulsed the rebels. The enemy was now re-grouped at Fort Edward.

After clearing numerous trees, filling bogs and building some two score bridges, one of prodigious length, we finally reached Fort Edward in early August only to find it deserted. The rebels had only just gone.

The country we had recently penetrated was not good for foraging and the army was running out of provisions. Even beans were served up in smaller portions. We rested at Fort Edward to await provisions of food, artillery, and other supplies. Many Indians joined us, but when the general made it clear that looting was not permitted, they began to leave us again, some to attend their harvest at home. Not all the Indians were peaceful. One band massacred a settler family living on White Creek because they believed the father was helping a hated rival band. This incident brought a cloud of fear to the whole countryside and many settler families came into Fort Edward with their livestock for protection from the marauding Indians. They camped close to our camp and sold cows to the British. Some of the warriors joined Burgoyne for the campaign.

It was at Fort Edward that I became a fighting soldier. Colonel Pfister mustered those of the regiment who were not yet properly fitted out to get a fighting kit. I reported to the quartermaster stores with cousin Young Jacob, Jed and Gershom and others of our Bald Mountain group. The fighting kit was a Brown Bess musket with powder pan cover and sling, a cartouche, cartridge pouch, ramrod barrel scraper, and a French tomahawk. We were fitted for uniforms, but were told they had not yet arrived at the front. After my measurements were recorded I was given a piece of paper with a number and told to keep it safe. Thus was a simple, unlettered, untested farmer turned into a soldier! Little did I know that in a few days I would be tested to the limit of my mental and bodily strength.

Our next assignment was to haul bateaux and provisions from Fort George to the Hudson and transport army supplies to Fort Edward. That afternoon we set out across the carrying place between the Hudson and Fort George. The story surrounding the carrying place was already part of the folklore of the French and Indian war. It seems that Colonel Munro whose army had been under siege by General Montcalm and his Indians sent a message to General Web at Fort Edward for reinforcements. He was outnumbered four to one and needed help. The fort, then called Fort William Henry, was in desperate straits; Munro's cannon were disabled, there were three hundred casualties, the French had blown apart the walls of gravel and logs, and smallpox was raging in the crowded fort. On receiving the message for help, Web sent a return message by emissary to the effect that, "it was not prudent to assist you." The message never reached Munro and later the emissary was found scalped outside the fort still carrying the answer from General Web. Finally, Munro surrendered Fort William Henry to the French general.

Montcalm apparently trusted his Indians and agreed to escort Munro's garrison to Fort Edward on condition that his soldiers would no longer take part in the war. Not entirely trusting Montcalm's ability to control his Indians, Colonel Munro was prudent and ordered that all rum be wasted so as not to tempt the savages attached to the French army. Monro's strategy backfired. The Indians, looking for rum and not finding any, were furious and attacked the retreating column, many sick with smallpox. It was on the very road where we had to haul bateaux across country that some eight hundred staunch defenders of Fort William Henry, men, women, and children, had been slaughtered, scalped, or taken prisoner. Later, the Indians' savagery of spirit haunted their villages with disease for months to come because some of the scalps taken were from smallpox victims. In the fullness of time, the English built a new fort called Fort George, very close to the ruined Fort William Henry.

I tell this story here because the massacre of Munro's troops had already become a legend and our men were very fearful that Indians still hid in the woods ready to jump out and take their hair.

I was in a unit of eight soldiers ordered to haul a bateau from Fort George back to Fort Edward. It was exhausting work, only relieved when we found a clearing of grass, which, during the early morning, was wet with dew. Here the bateau was easily slid on the wet grass, but most of the time we had to drag or roll the beast on logs, sometimes over rocky ground. Once or twice we had to tip it over and hoist it on our shoulders. It was so hot and steamy that by mid-day I was worn out.

The spirits of the dead were still haunting the road two decades after the massacre. Even I caught the fear, so every sound from the woods made the hair rise on my neck and my scalp crawl. The younger members in my squad, seemed oblivious to the evil spirits surrounding us, and having found some rum in the fort were becoming quite merry by the time we reached the Hudson. It was late in the evening so we camped at the river's edge, along with other members of our unit who had trekked across the carrying place with provisions, artillery pieces, and ammunition.

We loaded the three bateaux that had made it to the landing place that day with the materiel from Fort George to be ferried down the river next morning.

Our task was accomplished by eleven o'clock the following day and after a mid-day meal of beans, potatoes, and corn we were ordered to set out that very afternoon to repeat the job until all useful materiel was transferred.

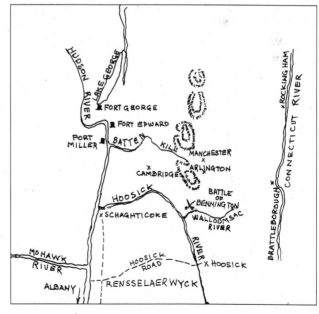

Altogether, I made three treks along that haunted road, and at no time did I not fear for my scalp.

Colonel Pfister mustered us for parade on the 9th and told the assembled regiment that we were going on a raid to Manchester to secure provisions for our hungry troops and horses for the dragoons.

Colonel Baum, a German mercenary with no knowledge of the English tongue or of the country, was to lead the raid. Our regiment was amalgamated with that of Colonel John Peters along with some Canadians and Indians. Lieutenant Edward Carscallen of Colonel Peter's corps posted the orders for the mission. Colonel Pfister mustered out the Loyal Volunteers and delivered the orders in the clipped tones of a Brunswicker.

"Men, we are to try the affections of the country, to disconcert the enemy councils, to get mounts for Reidesel's horseless dragoon, to finally complete Colonel Peters' corps and to capture large supplies of horses and carriages. You must travel as you are and carry no tents.

"From Batten Kill we are to proceed to Arlington and make a post there where some reinforcements will meet us. From Arlington, we march to Manchester and secure the pass over the mountains to Rockingham, and once accomplished, reconnoitre the activities of the enemy on the Connecticut River: from thence to Brattleborough, and then on to Albany, where we will again meet up with the main force.

"This is a major expedition of an estimated fortnight, so prepare accordingly. We are to be friendly but firm with the settlers, leaving them milch cows and other means for their subsistence. Your officers are instructed to pay specie for goods received, except to those who are known rebels. There is to be no plundering, on penalty of being shot.

"As Seth Warner, the man beaten back by our dragoons at Hubbardtown, is now at Manchester, we are told he will be in a mood for vengeance. So be prepared for some excitement there, although we anticipate he will fade away as we approach. Since many of you are still without proper uniforms, as are most of the enemy, it will be hard to tell friend from foe in a melee. In accordance with general Burgoyne's orders, you are to wear a white piece of paper in your hat to identify friend from enemy.

"I will be your field commander, but Colonel Peters has overall command for this expedition. We, along with his men, are to be the advance guard for the dragoons. Now, God bless you, and God save the King."

Having delivered the general's orders, he stalked off without taking questions.

We left Fort Edward bound for Fort Miller seven miles on, but just as we headed out, a change of orders came to Colonel Baum. He was to raid Bennington instead of Manchester because intelligence claimed it had a goodly supply of corn, flour, and cattle, as well as horses and artillery.

It was a diverse military force that set out that day to make history; un-mounted Brunswick dragoons, Captain Fraser's marksmen, a detachment of light German infantry. With Canadians, Indians, the Provincials, Colonel Pfister's Loyal Volunteers, Peter's Queen's Loyal Rangers, and Colonel Baum's dragoons we made up perhaps 650 men.

We left Fort Miller on the 11th and were encamped on the Batten Kill by late afternoon, where a company of light infantrymen that Burgoyne had sent as reinforcements caught up to Baum's troops. At dawn, we left the Batten Kill camp and marched to Cambridge. We captured a number of horses, cattle, wagons, and carts. There was some pride in our success so far, but it soon became known in the ranks that there were three times our numbers of rebels assembled at Bennington. On hearing the news that we were greatly outnumbered, General Burgoyne dispatched Colonel Breymann on the morning of the 13th with a large force of riflemen and a battalion of light infantry and grenadiers to follow. Afterwards we learned that they had trouble crossing the Batten Kill and did not reach Cambridge that night.

As we marched, our Indians were sent out in advance to capture cattle, but instead of herding the cattle to the army they slaughtered them for cowbells, leaving the beasts to rot. News soon spread throughout the countryside that Indians were on the warpath making it even more difficult for Colonel Baum's officers to procure supplies from the field. It was hard going. Rain and muddy roads hindered our progress. The countryside we were crossing was full of bogs and swamps, and it was a problem to stay dry. The swamps were cloudy with mosquitos. The horseless dragoons, with their heavy and cumbersome gear, were awkward without mounts, particularly in the swamps. Part of the reason for this expedition was to get them mounts.

During the three-day march, the men, brothers in misery, helped each other to endure the rough going. Before this march we had been working in the bush, isolated all day and too tired at night to pass along stories, news, or gossip, or to grouse about Sergeant Vetter, the lack of food, and the never-ending problem of being wet all the time. Now we had lots of time to grouse and those to grouse with.

It was on that march that I first ran into Jacob Huffman as we slogged toward Bennington to meet our fates. I guessed he was about twenty years old, a well-built lad with greenish-blue eyes and light brown hair just this side of red. After leaving Cambridge we ran into a swampy area with clouds of mosquitos. His light skin attracted great swarms of mosquitos and he was miserable, swatting at the beasts until I thought he might run away in an attempt to escape them.

"Goddamn these rotten beasts!"

He was so tormented he could hardly walk, so I offered him some of my mosquito dope.

"Here, rub some of this on your face and hands."

"What is it?"

"It's made from pine tar and castor oil. It works for me until I wash it off."

Jacob took the small bottle I gave him and did as I instructed. But after doing this he complained, "It don't work."

Give it time to dry I told him, and sure enough he quieted down some. He turned to me and asked, "How do you make this stuff?"

"Just mix equal parts pine tar and castor oil, simmer over a slow fire, bottle it, and there you are."

"Say, you from around here? Seems most of the men are."

"I live just off the Hoosick Road, pretty much where we are headed. Where you from?"

"Oh, I hail from over Arlington way."

We slogged silently through ankle-deep mud on a soft spot of the old Indian trail we were using. It was very tiring and not a time for a lot of talking. When we came to higher ground Jacob suddenly asked, "Say, how do you get rid of ticks? I sat on a log yesterday and two ticks got me in the back. I can't get them out."

"Spit tobacco juice on the little devils. A good healthy mouthful of tobacco juice makes them shrivel up and you can pick them off without losing their heads."

Jacob nodded, and then asked, "Say, what brought you into this mess?"

"Well, like you I guess, I refused to sign the oath and the Committee sent the sheriff for me. But I escaped and found Gershom French at Bald Mountain."

"Me, I didn't wait for the damn Committee. One day I was standing on the stoop holding the baby to give him some sun when a rebel snuck up and took a pot shot at me. The ball put a big gouge in the door, it was that close. So I handed the baby to its mother and said, 'Here Betty, hold the baby, I'm going to enlist.' I took the old long gun I used to killed squirrels, some food, and set out to find Ed Carscallen. He was a spy for the British who had escaped from a rebel jail. Word was that he was in the Arlington area, and I was pretty sure I knew where he was hiding. Anyway, I found him and he took me to join the British at St. Jean on the Richelieu River. That was in March. Burgoyne got there in June and the general put me in John Peters' Corps."

"How did you end up with Colonel Pfister?"

"I didn't like Peters, and when Pfister's regiment was formed I asked to go with him. Colonel Pfister thought I would be useful on this expedition because I know the Arlington area, where we were supposed to go in the first place."

After brooding silence he went on, "I think there is bad blood between Peters and Pfister."

"They don't get along, that's for sure. I think it's because Pfister is a Brunswicker by training and Peters American. It's like mixing castor oil and water."

Colonel Pfister was born in Germany, but he came to New York at age eighteen to serve as a skilled military engineer with the First Battalion of the Royal American Regiment. The British military had a scarcity of officers to conduct the French and Indian War in America so Pfister and other European trained officers were used. He was seen each day sighting through a theodolite when we camped, and it was rumoured that he carried a drawing of the Province of New York that he had made and that now served him well in helping Colonel Baum find his way across the country.

Colonel Peters had come into the British ranks in the fall of 1776 and was given permission to recruit Americans in Charlotte and Albany counties, a task at which he seemed very adept. He was assigned to the Royal Regiment of New York until he was given a uniform, made a colonel, and given his own regiment called the Queen's Loyal Rangers, which was the largest Provincial Regiment. While Pfister's regiment was the smallest with nowhere near a full complement, Peters seemed to want to muster a full regiment and was accused of trying to steal new recruits for his regiment. This is probably what made Pfister angry and frustrated.

I liked young Jacob Huffman for his spirit and I got to know his background on our three-day march to Bennington. Jacob was of Palatine origin. From Germany, his family went to England in 1709, but finding hostility there, his was one of the families sent to Ireland with other Palatines to help establish the Protestant religion. The Catholic Irish were also hostile, but a Lord Southwell took them in. There they were influenced by John Wesley and took to the Methodist religion. Jacob came to New York when he was four years old. According to Jacob's story, the people accompanying his parents to America tried to set up a weaving and linen manufacturing company in the Camden Valley near Arlington. One was a Methodist preacher and he established a Wesleyan church on land owned by a New York lawyer named Duane. Unbeknownst to their family, the land was contested by Ethan Allen and his brothers. He told me he thought it was one of the Allen boys that had tried to shoot him while he held his baby.

We ran into a detachment of rebels on the 13th and one of Justus Sherwood's men was wounded in the leg.

On the 14th we were on Walloomsac River where it seemed the enemy was prepared to take a stand. We met the enemy briefly at White Creek, and aside from a few balls coming our way no one was injured. The enemy destroyed the bridge across the creek and disappeared to the south but kept shooting from the woods. Under the sporadic enemy fire some Provincials managed to cross the creek and occupy a mill, recently abandoned. At nine o'clock it appeared that a decision had been made to take a stand on the high point beyond the river. Consequently, Colonel Baum occupied the hill north of the river and set his men to build fortifications.

It seemed the woods around us were alive with the sound of the enemy preparing for battle. A large force was gathering against us. At some urging from his officers, Colonel Baum sent a message to the general for re-enforcements.

Colonel Baum's engineer, dragoons and some Canadian Rangers built a breastwork composed of loose earth and logs on the very crest of the hill, with his line of defense spread roughly in a south-east direction from the hill crest, and across the river to a small hill that rose above the river. Our Indians held the road approaching the main breastwork. A number of paces down the hill towards the river was another corps of dragoons, at the foot of the hill near the river a body of light infantry, and to the south along the road defended by Grenadiers, Canadian Rangers, and Peters' Loyal Rangers. Our Loyal Volunteers of about one hundred, under the direct command of Colonel Pfister, was to defend the small hill across the river from the main army. We were the far right flank of the army and there was a lot of country behind us. Colonel Pfister led us, with some enthusiasm amongst the younger men for it was their first real battle, across the bridge to a small clearing on the escarpment, and set us to work building a breastwork of earth, logs, brush and hay. We worked feverishly in the hot sultry air, on into the night. All day an attack was expected. It was not until late that night, exhausted and unable to get rest that it came to me that we were in a very dangerous situation; isolated, with the river between the main force and us making retreat difficult if it came to that. I felt very lonely and isolated from the real world of civilized and God-fearing people until groups of local men started coming into camp ready to fight for their farms. Some of my neighbours from the Gilead church were among them.

A s dawn broke on that sleepless night in arms, it began to rain. The rain continued through the next day, and we again set to work completing our rough breastwork. It was not long into the new day that the rain turned the area to a sticky, gooey mess. I became more miserable as the day wore on, what with the mud, the physical exhaustion, and the mental agony of expecting to be killed by one of their sharp shooters hiding in a nearby tree. The fear of a major onslaught on our isolated position also wore heavily on the troops.

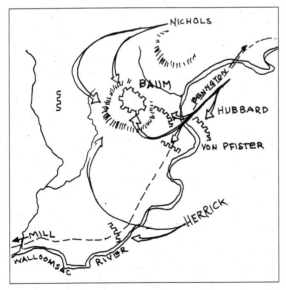

The second night in arms, with no hot food or shelter, was even more terrifying than the previous night. When the rain stopped and light was beginning to show in the east, everyone seemed to have accepted his fate and was anxious to end the misery, perhaps forever for some. I wondered if my hay would be cut that year.

On the morning of the 16th the sun came out and the tension in the air told me that the battle was on. Colonel Pfister walked up and down the two lines that we had formed behind the barricade. He was giving out pieces of paper and cornhusks to be put in our hats to distinguish us from the enemy who, like us, had no proper uniform. The action started with a great whoop from the woods and masses of men, some no doubt my neighbours, came screaming, "Liberty or death!" out of the woods. Colonel Pfister kept shouting, "Hold your fire! Hold your fire!" Suddenly, through all the noise, I heard the order, "Fire!" and let go at the man I could see directly in front. He grabbed his leg and collapsed. My thought was, "He's lost his hat." It was then I saw the white paper glint in the sun. Suddenly they were all over us in great numbers. They came from the side and from behind and over the barricade. It was impossible in the ensuing melee to tell friend from foe for everyone was wearing paper or a cornhusk in his hat. There was no time to reload before they were upon us. A youth with a fierce light in his eyes came charging at me with a long knife raised with the intention to send me to heaven. My musket being spent, I clutched for the tomahawk, my only other weapon, when a blast from behind me sent a ball straight into his heart. He lost the devilish light in his eyes to the blankness of death, and in his headlong rush skidded in the mud underfoot and took my feet out from under me. I remember the choking sensation that came to me as the mud of the battlefield filled my mouth and nose. The whole rebel army seemed to be kicking me and stamping on my back and head. After what seemed an eternity in hell the pounding of feet left me. They were running up the hill. I jumped up and out of the corner of my eye saw another column of rebels surging across the river and up the hill to attack Colonel Baum's redoubt. There was great confusion around me. Somebody was shouting, "The colonel's dead! The colonel's dead!" and at this shocking news a strange fierceness came over me.

A soldier suddenly appeared directly in front of me, intent on goring me with his long knife. I braced myself with the useless gun in one hand and the hatchet in the other. Fate intervened. He stumbled over a dying man and I slammed him in the face with my hatchet. As he went down, I was sure I saw a face that I knew. To this day I do not know if he was friend or foe; certainly he had been from this very area, and even today I swear he was familiar. That single instant, seeing his face disappear in a cloud of flesh and blood, took the very heart from my fighting career. I was not a soldier. Not yet. Not in this kind of war where you might be killing your own kin. The rebel soldiers did not linger near our redoubt, except a few who quickly looted the dead then followed their mates up the hill.

My fevered thoughts flashed to cousin Young Jacob. I thought I saw him running along the river toward the mill, but because of the gun smoke in the air, I was far from sure. I could see nothing but gun smoke at the redoubt occupied by Colonel Baum, but I quickly decided I could not help what looked like a lost cause, given all the rebels that were running toward the redoubt. Our battlement was littered with dead and dying farmers, men who were not soldiers and had no business dying on the battlefield. Two men were dragging the dying Colonel Pfister toward the river, where there would be some shelter from the battle.

In the dense smoke that still covered the battlefield I ran around to the south, crossing the track taken by the rebels who had now charged across the river and up the hill. I found a gully empty of water but bordered by bushes. It took me along the river towards the mill. As I ran I was aware of many other men headed toward the mill. A quick look assured me Young Jacob was not among them.

I ran along the gully until I came to a ditch, which seemed to lead to the river near the location of the mill. I arrived together with several Provincials, a few Canadians and Indians and we all clustered inside the door in much confusion as to what we should do. A man in uniform who said he was Colonel Skene began to organize some semblance of order. He posted a guard at the corner of the mill and we were instructed to find all openings, especially on the side facing the attacking enemy, and prepare our arms to defend the mill. I climbed to the second floor and discovered there were six windows, three facing Colonel Baum's redoubt on the hill. We waited. I was positioned at one of the east windows and through the dusty glass could just make out the scene of the final battle. The redoubt was completely surrounded by rebels, but the musket fire was not as intense as it had been. It looked as if Baum had run out of ammunition and was about to surrender. Rebel troops who were no longer being fired upon were looting the bodies on the field, friend and foe.

Suddenly I heard a great "Hurrah!" sung out by one of our lookout sentries. "Reinforcements! Reinforcements, we are saved." It was an advance corps of what I learned later was Colonel Breymann's regiment of six hundred men. A brigade of grenadiers with two cannon stormed the small hill where the enemy had hastily formed a line. The rebels were driven back, but a large number of reinforcements came out of the woods and it looked as though our troops were out of ammunition. They withdrew in an orderly fashion, only to surrender later. The tide had surely turned. We were ordered to defend the mill while the new troops swept past to storm the enemy. They were a magnificent sight with all the colour of a full parade, but before they had advanced very far the rebels seemed to come alive again. I could see a large wild looking man dressed in buckskin with a long rifle waving his firearm and shouting. He managed to assemble a fighting force and, to my unbelieving eyes, I saw our troops fall back and, after a brief skirmish, withdraw. This seemed to activate a wild melee with British redcoats and German Brunswickers retreating, and the rebels chasing them down, whooping like Indians. Alas, all was lost. It seemed the only out was to fade into the woods and await the outcome. Even in their fury for blood, the rebels did not approach the mill as darkness fell.

I found some men whom I knew to be with the Queen's Loyal Rangers and before that sad day closed, I had been assigned to Colonel Peters' Corps on cantonment. Colonel Peters survived, although his corps was badly mauled. Many of our Provincials had gotten caught in the surrender and we were sure they would be executed as traitors. It was then I learned that Colonel Baum had been killed.

As the remnants of Baum's expeditionary force straggled back the way it had come to find Burgoyne's main army, individuals and small groups of those who had managed to escape the tragedy came out of the woods to join our line. Colonel Peters took command of the small numbers of Colonel Pfister's corps who had survived and escaped. I was pleased to see that both my cousin Young Jacob and Jacob Hoffman were among those left, although there was no sign of Jed. Also, Lieutenant Carscallen, Jacob Huffman's friend, had lived to fight another day. Colonel Breymann, despite a wound in the leg, was able to bring some order and dignity in retreat.

We found the main army still at the Batten Kill, and I headed for my tent exhausted and weary of warfare. It was only next morning at roll call that I learned the extent of the disaster. The missing soldiers were too numerous to count. Jacob Huffman told his tent mates that Lieutenant Carscallen said Colonel Peters had lost over two hundred men, and altogether seven hundred were missing. No one seemed to know how many were dead, how many were prisoners, nor how many of the "missing" simply walked back to their farms and families, sick of war.

The nightmares started the second day back in camp. They were always the same, my face was buried in the mud and my shoulder was on fire. I was in a panic and about to stop breathing when suddenly I was free. Lying on my back I looked into the face of this unbelievably beautiful woman, all dressed in filmy white. This angel, for I am sure it was an angel, dragged me into the shade of a cool tree, where I fell into peaceful sleep. Zach, who slept in the next cot would shake my cot and wake me.

There being no rest for the private soldier, we were set to work building a new raft bridge spanning the Hudson, as the earlier bridge had been blown away in a great storm. I felt a tinge of satisfaction, even pride, at having nothing to do with constructing the earlier bridge.

Many Mohawks came into camp, escaping from rampaging rebels seeking vengeance for the Seneca massacre at Orinskany. Some farmers and a few farmer-soldiers who had abandoned St. Leger's siege of Fort Stanwix also arrived in camp. At the same time, we were losing our own farmer-soldiers, disappointed because of the setbacks at Bennington and Fort Stanwix. As each day folded into the next, the size of the enemy was growing, with men from all over the region sensing blood and massing against our sick and dwindling numbers. The British were becoming vastly outnumbered and Burgoyne was reluctant to engage the superior numbers arrayed against him. One morning a tent mate we called "Snorting Al" was not on his cot, and when he did not turn up at roll call, we knew he had left for home, having been one of those who were threatening to desert unless something happened soon to get "this thing over and done with."

When the new bridge was finished, it was close to mid-September. The army moved over the Hudson and encamped on General Schuyler's abandoned farm. Soon this large, attractive plantation was laid bare by the army's rapacious appetite for provisions. But, foraging in the open fields was a dangerous business and one day thirty of our men were killed or wounded in a potato patch by a rebel scouting party. They were given no chance to surrender. The conflict was getting increasingly

231

bitter on both sides. Still General Burgoyne hesitated to engage the enemy, which was getting more numerous every hour.

An incident happened during the hiatus that changed the whole course of my war. A group of men from the Arlington area who had joined Peters in June seemed to be unhappy with his leadership, so they petitioned the general to serve with Samuel McKay, a reduced line officer, instead of Peters. Peters told their emissary that, "the choice was his house or the guardhouse," but the general overruled him, citing the original agreement of their enlistment that they could choose whichever regiment suited them. Since McKay had been assigned Colonel Pfister's Loyal Volunteers, I too desired to be with my former friends, those that were left, and on August 22nd, along with several others, we moved our bed rolls to be with Samuel McKay. This, for me, turned out to be a fateful decision.

We were just a few miles above the enemy, which was encamped at Still Water. By Sept 18th the general was reluctantly preparing for battle, even against great odds. There was excitement in the ranks of the younger troops but gloom for some of us who had experienced more years of life and had been part of the horror of Bennington.

That the general had lost confidence in the venture became clear that very day when Mr. McKay mustered the Loyal Volunteers for a new duty: to prepare the roads and bridges for a retreat. Our work group was to be accompanied by Colonel Sutherland with General Fraser's riflemen. So again, I took up the axe and the means to protect myself and we set out to prepare a road to Canada. We were working within a short distance of Fort Edward when Colonel Sutherland was recalled because of an immediate threat of enemy attack on the main army. He left behind some two score men for protection while we were working. Shortly after his departure, some five hundred rebels appeared from upstream and more rebels cut off a return to the army. Trapped and greatly outnumbered, there seemed no way out except to try for the woods.

I was with about eight others working on clearing brush closest to the woods when the devils started shooting from the bush, as was their preferred method of warfare. When our men started running for the woods, without thinking I shouted to those near me, "Cover them! Get behind trees and keep moving while you reload." We ran behind the trees, and I found that firing, running to another tree, loading, and firing again we could keep up a screen of quite constant fire. In this way, the majority of our troops got safely to the woods although we lost about one quarter of our number.

We were now far distant from the army and cut off by a wood full of rebel troops when we finally, after two hours, rendezvoused. Forty-three men had been killed or captured in the skirmish. Given our losses, our low numbers and the impossibility of re-joining the main army, Mr. McKay decided to march to Fort

George, that he had heard St. Leger had reached on his march from Fort Stanwix with reinforcements for Burgoyne. But when we reached Fort George through the ghostly, haunted forest that evening we found that the battle of Freeman's Farm was over and Burgoyne had reached a stalemate with the enemy. Not only this bad news awaited us, but also a runner had brought word that General St. Leger had retreated to Canada.

It seemed to Mr. McKay that there was nothing we could do to help the general, even provided we could get past the enemy lines, so we left Fort George the next morning and began a long trek beside the lake to reconnoiter and clear the road to Fort Ticonderoga. There were five Indian scouts with us, who were sent ahead to warn of any large detachment of the enemy that might overwhelm our small numbers, as had happened in the vicinity of Fort Edward. We marched, with some discipline, I thought, on the old Indian trail beside the lake. Although it was narrow and muddy in spots, there were only a few trees down, which we cleared and deemed it passable by the retreating army with their guns and supply wagons. Apparently, there were a few bateaux at Diamond Island but unless the general could bring more from the Hudson there were insufficient numbers to lift the forces to Fort Ticonderoga. So, this road seemed the only practical means to get the army back to Ticonderoga.

As we marched, enemy soldiers from behind trees in the woods harassed the column, but a volley of return fire drove them away. The enemy seemed to be spread out in small groups in the woods. Mr. McKay believed the rebels were heading for Saratoga. About midway on the road to Fort Ticonderoga, a dirty man with greasy clothes stepped out of the woods waving a white rag tied to a stick. He said he was a friend of the King and wanted to trade information for, "A tot of rum." Mr. McKay questioned him at gunpoint for, "The truth, on pain of death," and thus, sufficiently frightened, he quickly spoke his piece. "John Brown and a detachment of rebels are decamped at the landing place at the foot of the lake and one of the Allen boys has captured the works at Mount Defiance. Brown is positioned at the old French lines and is bombarding the fort." At first, no one believed the man, but under prodding and threats he kept to his story. It came to me that the enemy we had met near Fort Edward might have been part of Brown's forces, and this thought I expressed to my seniors. They, I think, had also come to the same realization. We gave the man his tot of rum but took him with us under guard hoping to secure our men against treachery. Soon however, two of our scouts returned to the main body with the truth of the prisoner's tale.

By then we could hear the boom of guns. From the scout's report there seemed to be a considerable body of men in the vicinity of the fort. One of the scouts got sufficiently close to see evidence that there were several prisoners housed in a mill and a blockhouse, near the waterfall where the waters from Lake George dropped into Lake Champlain. Someone thought that if we could release these prisoners we might raise a large enough force to challenge the raiders, but they would be unarmed and useless. Another proposal was to make a wide circle to the west and gain the fort without being discovered. This seemed cowardly, but after some few other proposals to engage the enemy, which given our small numbers was impractical or suicidal, it was agreed to try to gain the fort, and help drive off the rebels. It was a risky strategy to move some ninety men and equipment through the woods full of rebel soldiers without being detected.

We had only four junior officers, and since my usefulness had been raised in the eye of Mr. McKay for my action near Fort Edward, I was part of the discussion as to how to proceed. Mr. McKay told us he had been at Fort Ticonderoga with Burgoyne, but they had left the area by Wood Creek, and although he knew the terrain around the fort itself, he was at a loss as to how to approach the fort from Lake George. Our situation was such, he said, that we could lie in arms until the bombardment stopped and the enemy either took the fort or retired, or to take the risky action of trying to gain entrance to the fort.

If the enemy withdrew, our presence would likely be discovered by the retreating troops. It was threatening rain and no one of us wished the prospect of lying in arms in the rain and wet for perhaps days or even weeks, so it was a unanimous position that we try to get inside the fort. "But how do we carry out such a plan? Does anyone know the approach from here to the fort?" No one spoke up.

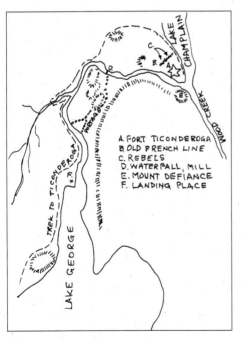

Foolishly, I ventured that I had read a letter from a relative that was with Abercrombie in '58. The correspondent included a rough sketch of the battlefield. I had also lived for the past two years with the Allen boys bragging endlessly about their capture of Fort Ticonderoga in '75. I did not really believe anything the Allen boys said, but if I could remember the details of the sketch I had seen, perhaps I could be of some help in describing the layout of the field ahead. McKay was quick to jump on this and said, "Waeger, you go with two scouts and two riflemen and lead us through the woods so that we get around the enemy without detection. Captain McDougal, you take ten men to protect the rear and I and Captain Sams will lead the main column. When we get within hailing distance of the fort, we reconnoiter the situation. We start at dawn."

I immediately regretted saying anything, but now I had no choice but to obey the order. To lead an advance party frightened me, and I think at that moment I gave myself up for dead. Desperately, I searched my memory for an image of the letter and sketch to fix in my mind the terrain between our location and the fort. I remembered that the failure of Abercrombie was partly due to his forces getting lost in the dense woods, so I ventured some advice to Mr. McKay to the effect that the most important thing for success in this strategy was to keep together and avoid getting lost. This being duly acknowledged by our leader, we marched toward the landing place and approaching within about one mile we found a small creek where we encamped for the night. A scout returning from observing the landing place reported that there were only a few men guarding a few bateaux. Somewhere ahead was a falls, making the bateaux useless to obtain the fort, so the only strategy was to go around the enemy. One of the letters I had read said the distance from the landing place to the fort was about seven miles, so our march the next day was quite possible. That night by the light of a candle stub I tried to recall the battlefield layout.

It started to rain during the night and it was difficult to get started the next morning, but start we did in the gloom of a wet and cold dawn. My plan, formed during the night, was to circle the men at the landing place and then to get back to the river that led to the fort to avoid getting lost in the woods. The river could be a point of reference until we ran into the enemy.

The sketch I gave to Mr. McKay the next morning was the expected distribution of the enemy positions and the route I proposed. He agreed it was a reasonable plan. I was full of excitement but the men were sluggish. Having no authority myself, they paid little attention to me. It took the orders of Captain Ward to get the troops out and prepared for the day's activity. With the enemy in numbers far exceeding ours, we left our camp as quietly as was possible with grumbling, hungry, and tired men. I set out with two of our Indians, two riflemen, and an axe man about two hundred yards in advance of the main body. Soon after we decamped, the guns started up, sending echoes down the shallow valley. The boom of the cannon was a noisy cover for own march.

Our Indian guide was able to pick a path through the heavy brush as we left the worn path along the lake and walked west, then north. Successfully circling the sentries at the landing place, we were able to get back to the river outlet from Lake George, where we again picked up the riverside pathway. My small advance party kept the main body of troops lead by Mr. McKay in sight or sound at all times. In about one hour, we were able to see through the rain and mist a landing place across the river. I called a halt and waited until Mr. McKay came up to us. We had a small conference. It seemed to me that the portage would lead to a point below the waterfall close to the fort but we would be on the wrong side of the river. Mr. McKay agreed with this reasoning and he supposed that the crossing of the river would be heavily guarded at that point because it would be an outer battery for an approach to the fort from the river. He decided we should keep to the original plan.

Proceeding, we soon came to a small creek, which, while getting our lower limbs soaked, was easily fordable. There was another small creek before we came upon a more substantial creek crossing, and again we stopped to reconnoiter with Mr. McKay. On his orders we turned west and pushed our way through wet bushes, moving upstream until we found a shallow crossing point. The stream was somewhat depleted because of the lateness of the season, so the crossing was accomplished without incident, and as far as I knew, without being heard. The noise from the cannon was in our favour.

The river took a sharp bend to the right and soon, during a lull in the noise from the guns, we could hear the sound of the waterfall. Our Indian guide told of a mill at the falls and a blockhouse nearby. Again, I waited for Mr. McKay, after which we left the riverbank and set upon a large circle movement behind the height of ground that we could see from a cleared area.

For about three hours we struggled through the trees and undergrowth. Then the rain mercifully stopped and the sun came out. The sunlight through the trees whose leaves were just beginning to colour, the noise from the small animals we disturbed on our way, and the soft moist air of a balmy afternoon heightened the spirits of everyone, even some of the more cantankerous of our troops. I felt young again and could pretend I was on a squirrel hunt instead of marching in the midst of an enemy who would shoot or torture me if caught. We came down off the height of land and I could see a body of sparkling blue water that was Lake Champlain. It was my first sight of the lake that had been in many stories that I had heard, but I had no time now to indulge in memories.

Suddenly we were in an open area, and off in the distance was the fort, its northern bastion reflecting rays of sunlight. It was a glorious sight, like the sight of heaven to a dying man. But getting inside would be the most difficult project in that so far successful day. Again, I halted my small advance detachment to allow Mr. McKay to join us. Getting across the cleared open space that gave the fort a prospect to the north without being seen was a problem. The clearing narrowed in the direction of the lake and to be safe from rebel eyes we headed toward the lake to go around the clearing. Having done so, there was a crude road through the deep woods leading to the south and presumably ending at the fort. It was here that Mr. McKay, saying he was familiar with the country, took the lead. He thanked me and the two Indian scouts for getting his very depleted regiment this far and I fell back with the rest of the men.

We kept to the road until it entered a clearing with two old redoubts from some former campaign, and again entered the woods. Here, tired and wet, but without the security to build fires, we lay in arms until dark. The bombardment had mostly stopped for the night with only an occasional cannon ball sent toward the fort. From the redoubts, we noticed the cannon balls mostly fell short, but nevertheless, being in the line of fire, it was an anxious few hours that we were huddled in the woods, within hailing distance of the fort.

The sky was clear of cloud and a weak moon appeared over the horizon, making our next foray more difficult. But about midnight, Mr. McKay, with a detachment of four of us and our ensign got ready to approach the fort by way of the gardens that lay just outside the walls on the east side of the ramparts. Our young ensign carried the Queen Anne flag and a staff with the regimental colours that Mr. McKay would show to identify us to the sentries. We crept through the corn stalks, heavy with unpicked ripe corn, then the potato and squash plants, until we were within a few yards of the gate. Breaking out the flag and colours we waited until we were seen. A challenge from a sentry and a response by Mr. McKay giving our regiment and our number was sufficient to have the gate opened to us. It seemed too easy, but unbeknownst to us, the fort had been plagued with refugees and deserters after Burgoyne's first battle at Saratoga and by now the sentries were used to errant parties knocking on their gates for security from a countryside full of marauding rebels.

We were safe without incident or loss of life, and forthwith reported for duty under the command of General Powell. It turned out that the guns of the rebels had no effect on breaching the ramparts. The bombardment lasted for two more days and then the enemy simply gave up the siege and left the area on September 24th.

While at Ticonderoga, Mr. McKay called me to his quarters and awarded me a non-commissioned status as sergeant, saying, "Sergeant Waeger, since the British Army does not recognize my commission this may not be recognized by the general, but you deserve it for your action back at Fort Edward. God save the King." Thinking that in this formal setting a salute was appropriate, I attempted such a gesture of respect and left. Two days later, I got my uniform coat.

I spent many pleasant days sheltered by the bastions and guns of Fort Ticonderoga, but after Burgoyne's convention with the enemy on October 17th, the people of the fort and the area prepared to leave and remove to Canada. The fort was to be burned. On the last day of this grand fortress' life, we loaded into bateaux and set out for Canada. As we sailed away, I looked back at the burning fort and wondered how could man be so stupid.

I know the sweat and tears and sometimes blood required to erect such a grand and beautiful edifice. I do not know, nor can I understand, the evil in men's minds that seeks to destroy such works of man and God. I carried that image of the burning fort the rest of my life.

9

JOURNEYMAN SOLDIER

That winter we were removed to the Montreal area and assigned garrison duty on the Chateauguay River near the village of Chateauguay. This seemed to be a temporary encampment so we lived in tents. It was horribly cold. Our fuel was firewood, mostly open fires, and retiring to a thin tent with the air so cold as to freeze one's very breath was Satan's revenge for our sins. The army did supply woollen blankets, but most of that winter we arose freezing cold and with three or four feet of snow on the ground. The Indians who were accustomed to this way of life showed us how to pile the snow around the tents to preserve the heat from our bodies and also how to build small smoke fires. As the winter wore on we were able to improve our sleeping quarters by building a low wall of logs and packed earth and snow on which the tent was pitched. The Indians, who seemed to be very friendly with the habitants, taught us how to live, as they had the original European settlers, in such a harsh and hostile country.

The only satisfaction during this time was that Young Jacob, who had also been made sergeant, as well as Peter Dedlor and Jim Perigo, was with me; all men with whom I had supped and jawed, back before Bennington. After a gruelling six months of privations of all kinds and moments of sheer terror, this small bit of home was a welcome relief.

That first winter, Mr. McKay died from wounds received doing his duty. He was his own man, a good leader in the eyes of his men, but not recognized for promotion by a hide-bound English military establishment. Such was the destiny of many of our good men.

When Mr. McKay died, the Loyal Volunteer regiment was given to Captain Robert Leake, but there was little activity by the army that winter. We were between generals. General Sir Guy had retired when General Burgoyne was given the command to invade the rebellious colonies. Sir Guy was in the bad books of the Colonial Secretary, being accused by some of not being aggressive enough in driving Arnold's rebel army out of Canada. The salt in Sir Guy's wound was that Burgoyne had been his second in command.

The impression left with me by those who loved to recount the foibles of others, while avoiding any talk of their own, was that General Sir Guy was too much an Englishman for successful service in Canada. For him, warfare was conceived to be the set-piece battles of the wars of Europe, and not the kill-or-be-killed, bushwhacking war of the kind that was being carried out in America by natives and whites alike. He also had no use for Canadian militia, which ironically got him out of trouble in 1775 when they killed General Montgomery, thereby eliminating one prong of the two-pronged attack on Quebec's Lower Town. On the other hand, the cold, brusque manner hid his humanity in insisting Indian allies must not kill women and children. He insisted the Indian campaigns could only be conducted under proper military management.

A new commander-in-chief was not yet in Canada. So strategic decisions for the next years were not taken, and without some strategy the army marks time. So it was that winter in Chateauguay; we marked time by keeping warm and fed, cutting cordwood, and hunting for meat.

I found that army life did not suit me. My life as a farmer was one of constant work, but work that enhanced the common nature of things; watching the crops ripen, nurturing new life of animals who grew and were sacrificed in the natural cycle of life, the arrival and departure of the seasons. A farmer is not a spectator but an actor in the grand scheme of nature. It seemed to me everything about wars and the armies that make wars a reality was unnatural. It was contrary to a nurturing role, and provoked violent, destructive action, even to the point where young men seemed bent on destroying themselves. Perhaps because I was somewhat older than my mates I found I could not, with any happiness, join in their revelry. I determined, in this winter of cutting firewood that seemed our major task, to try to understand the people that I was now living with.

E phriam was correct in his view of the people of this country. They were indeed warm and friendly as long as we did not steal from them. Stealing was a major crime among the Canadians, most of whom were poor and sometimes went without food, for the country was harsh and the climate very severe in winter. The Indians appeared to have sufficient food for they were good farmers, but they needed cattle for meat, and guns and horses for their wars. The people feared the Iroquois. There were many friendly Indians round about the countryside, but it was the fierce Iroquois that the villagers feared.

The people of the village, the habitants, were joyfully moral. Almost every week they gathered, danced, and sang their songs. Although there was drink, seldom did anyone become intoxicated beyond all reason. Disagreements were as likely to be settled by a laugh or a slap on the shoulder as by a fistfight, unlike the manner of Yankees. The younger women threw themselves into dancing with an abandon that belied their underlying moralistic behaviour. The older women fussed over the food, and in passing kept a keen eye on their daughters. Sometimes the house party would last until dawn, when everyone bundled up in wools or furs and head for home in a sled, tired but happy. Dances were held in the open air in the summer time.

In the village, men wore coloured shirts of linen or printed calico under a short waistcoat of wool in winter, linen in summer. Homespun pantaloons were richly woven with coloured stripes or made of doeskin. Covering the legs were soft leather leggings tied just below the knee with a colourful sash; in the woods, a long piece of cloth about a hands breadth wide that flaps around the legs and serves as a protection from poisonous snake bite. Over all was worn a knee-length coat with ties in the place of buttons to fasten it at the front. A major piece of adornment was a very colourful sash around the waist to keep the coat in place. In observing the dress of the male habitant, I could clearly see the Indian origin of the style involving colourful sashes and the use of leather. The villagers have learned much from the natives. An important and unusual item of dress was the wool cap, often of the colour red, sometimes blue. It was knitted in a conical shape with a tassel of wool or fur that hangs over one ear. In their language it was called a tuque. The tuque was worn proudly for all occasions by the habitant, being at once unique and colourful. In addition, it kept the ears from freezing in the winter.

The highlight of the autumn was the seigneur's supper and dance to celebrate the Yuletide season. Each year in October, well before the quiet family celebration of Christ's birth, the seigneur and his lady would host a supper and dance for the whole village. Everyone was invited, including those of the English army and Canadian militia that were living among the villagers. The women of the village spent much of the early autumn making fine clothes and preparing for the celebration. It was their chance to strut and impress their sisters. What was a surprise to me was how important this event seemed to my military unit. Hard and battle weary as they were, it seemed that they were desperate for any sign that the world around them was sane. There were a few loyalist women who had joined their husbands and contributed their skills to the festival. It was amazing how women of vastly different heritage, culture, and experience appeared to bond with each other in bringing civilized ways to a society. While competing with each other in fashion and status, they cooperated in advancing civil behaviour.

The event was held in the manor house. On the allotted day, the villagers wrapped themselves in their best wools and furs and walked or travelled by horse and sleigh along the river up the slight hill to the manor house. Being without family and not inclined to enjoy society, I had more or less decided to forego this social evening, but Elenora, the wife of my good friend, Conrad Dedlor, insisted I become part of their family and in very strong words told me I must go to the dance with her and Conrad as part of her family. How could I refuse?

I dressed in my best, trimmed my beard, and combed my hair. Passing my tent in late afternoon, Conrad gave me a great, "Hello," and with Elenora we trudged in the snow to the manor house. Already a large number of villagers had arrived, the men standing about while the women were off somewhere primping for the coming show.

The manor house was a very large structure built of fieldstone and partially faced with lime white wash. Massive chimneys adorned both ends of the building. The tile roof was steeply pitched to shed the snow. It had been built partly as a fortress, with gun slits at the windows to defend the house against the Iroquois. The living quarters were on one floor but the habitation boasted a loft with windows in the gables, again with gun slits. The loft area, approached by a wooden stair and trap door, was for children's sleeping area and for storage, except for times when under attack.

We were ushered into a grand hall where people were gathering, talking, and telling stories, a common pastime. Unlike the houses of the habitants where the family lived in one large room, kitchen at one end and the sleeping area at the other with the hearth in between, the seigneur's manor house had several rooms. Except for the grand hall, these were not to be entered. It was considered rude and in very bad taste to be curious about the intimate spaces of the family.

The furniture in the grand hall, which was probably a dining hall in the normal course of living, had been removed, or in the case of table and chairs, pushed against the walls. Suddenly, as I was looking around, the dancing began. Being unfamiliar with the mode of dance, I set my thoughts to the women present.

All ages were there. The younger girls were adorned with colourful ribbons sewn to their dresses and tied in their hair. The matrons were plainly dressed in a shift to the ankle. Most wore a jerkin that partially covered the shoulders, gathered tightly at the waist with a ribbon, and flared open at the hips. Some of the younger women exposed a large measure of white skin at the neck and bosom. Hair was either gathered at the back of the neck and tied with colourful ribbon or hidden by a simple bonnet.

Older people, mostly the old women of the parish sat in the chairs provided around the room. A row of benches was also available for tired dancers, although the actors on the floor seemed to emit tremendous energy without tiring. A supper of all sorts of meats and dishes of ingredients unknown to me was served at about one o'clock in the morning. The wine also flowed freely and some of the men became very intoxicated. At two o'clock I begged Conrad and Elenora to forgive me, and left them to find my way back to my tent and to bed.

Shortly after this celebration, I found Red Feathers.

I was returning to camp with two other men from a fortnight in the woods training recruits to build winter shelters. As we were returning to camp, we came upon a derelict cabin that was a familiar reference along the trail and a refuge from storms. It was late in the afternoon and the cabin lay in the deep shadow of the trees overhead, making it difficult to see more than the outlines of the old building, but a faint glow of fire through the open cracks between the bark pieces that formed its walls meant the cabin was occupied. I could hear moans and incantations as if someone was sick or dying. A few words of discussion with my mates led to further investigation in case someone was in a bad way.

Kicking brush away from the door, we pulled it open and peered into the gloomy interior of the cabin. In the middle of the floor a woman squatted on what appeared to be a bearskin. She had lifted her shift and fastened it to a beaded sash around her waist and was waving her arms and hands over some object on the bearskin between her knees. The indistinct object looked like an infant and I immediately concluded that she had just given birth. The newborn did not move or make any noise and it seemed to me that she had birthed a dead child. The woman was spreading her hands above the dead infant and singing what seemed to me a sort of prayer. Her hands did not touch the body on the bearskin, though she seemed to be willing her newborn from its lifeless state back into the womb. My mind flashed back to visions of the Salem witches and their incantations to Satan. It was not in my life's experiences to know what was happening. My instincts said I should leave the woman to her ritual; if the infant was dead we could do nothing to help her. Johann and Henry, the men with me, overwhelmed with fear and superstition, edged out of the cabin door muttering, "Let's leave here, it is not for us."

A dying fire glowed in the hearth showed only the outlines of the scene before us. In the general gloom of the interior of the cabin we could not see the nature of the woman but we all, I think, believed she was Indian. The circumstances of the birth and the incantations in a strange tongue seemed to point to this conclusion. That Johann and Henry wanted no responsibility in the situation seemed a natural reaction, but I, for some reason known only to God and nature, hesitated. It was to me a very unnatural circumstance, since I would have thought women of her clan would normally attend the Indian girl. Could it be that she had been banished from her tribe, perhaps because of the creation of the babe in her womb? I stood in silent indecision. Some long-buried spirit was urging me to stay with the woman. No such urge was pushing my mates so I bid them to leave and return to camp. They were much relieved, and after trying to persuade me to go with them, finally gave up their effort and trudged back to the camp on the Chateauguay.

Having decided to stay put, I proceeded to build up the fire with wood stacked beside the hearth. The new flames allowed a clearer vision of the cabin and the woman. There was a sleeping platform built into one wall so I sat there and silently waited for the woman to acknowledge my presence, which, so far, she had not done. She was still waving her hands and chanting her prayer, completely immersed in whatever ritual she was performing. In deference to her agony, I did not intrude into her mystical world.

I sat for an hour. Waiting, my thoughts turned to my own life. It was, for sure, an unnatural life. War had brought me to this strange place of different customs, different ways of speaking, and military ways I found difficult to accept. Some of the men seemed excited by the terror of meeting the enemy; others needed to dull their senses with rum. Either way they carried their fears into the night. I found killing an obscenity, a descent of mortal man into hell, but it was a job

242

that circumstances had thrown my way. The military is a world in which men lead an unnatural existence without women and children to keep their ambitions and violence earthbound. The seigneur's party had brought this home to me. The party, the women and children doing what women and children do, the music and dancing, and the joy of simply being alive was what I longed for after several months of living with men and seeing boys die in the mud, crying for their mother. Perhaps even worse was the fear of being maimed for life, and the loneliness of an unshared bed at night.

The rebellion of my countrymen had separated me from my heritage, my farm, my family, and from the woman for which I once had affection. My children were in rebel territory and with the disasters at Bennington and Saratoga I had little hope of ever seeing any of them again.

The fire in the cabin had diminished, so I rose and replenished it with more wood. As I was about to return to the sleeping platform, I looked toward the figure squatting over the bearskin. She was looking straight at me with a mixture of fear, shame, and embarrassment. She stood up and untied the laces holding the shift, and let it drop to cover her modesty. The flames from the blazing fire now revealed the features of the woman. She was surely Indian, her skin, her facial features, and her dress all bore the marks of her birth. Under my gaze she stepped away from her stillborn child and ran to a dark corner of the cabin where she stood and continued to stare at me. I took a step toward her and she pushed herself further into the darkness, cringing with fear. I was now at the edge of the bearskin and the fire revealed the details of the object at my feet. It was a doll. A leather doll stuffed with straw. Its eyes of blue beads shone in the firelight and seemed to mock me. It certainly deepened the mystery surrounding the Indian woman and the reason she was in the cabin performing a maternal ritual.

I made no further advances toward her and we continued for some minutes to stare at each other. Finally she said in good English, "Who are you?"

"I am Eberhardt, a soldier of the King, garrisoned in the village of Chateauguay." After another few minutes she said, "I am Red Feathers. My father calls me Moira."

After this short discourse, she seemed to recover somewhat. I could see that she was more relaxed, but neither of us made any move toward the other. I asked her why she was in this cabin, alone in the woods. I got no answer. To put her at ease, I retired to a corner of the cabin and sat on my heels.

She came out of the corner and as I watched she put on leather leggings and crept to the centre of the room, watching me as she did so. She picked up the doll, wrapped the bearskin over her decorated doeskin shift and, still watching me, backed out of the cabin. Stunned, it took me a minute to realize she had gone. I ran to the door, but she had disappeared with no trace.

On the hike back to camp I came to believe the woman was not real, but the soft and comfortable product of my war-weary mind. Illusion or not, I could not

243

put away her image for many days after. With the routine of camp's Spartan life-style, the Indian maid seemed more and more a product of my imagination. To satisfy my curiosity I asked Henry if he remembered the incident. He confirmed that indeed there was someone in that cabin that day.

O n a bright sunny morning, about two weeks after the incident, I received a message from the captain to come to his office. Thinking it was a new assignment I complied immediately. Military salutations over, the captain said to me, "Sergeant Waeger, there is an Indian squaw here to see you, I think. She came to my adjutant asking for a man called "Eberhardt" and I was told you might be that man. Is this the case?" I replied, "It may be. I did meet an Indian woman in the woods some time ago. Can I talk to her?"

Minutes later, behind headquarters, I stood before Red Feathers once again. She was not as young as I had thought in the shadows and strange circumstances of our first meeting. She was attractive with smooth brown skin unmarred by the pox and she looked at me out of very dark, perhaps black, eyes. In the bright sun-shine I could see that her silky black hair had a red tinge. This set me to wondering about her parentage, but not for long, as I had come to realize how pleasant I felt in her company.

She was dressed as she had been when she left the cabin in the woods. Neither of us said anything, I, because I did not have any words at hand. "I come to thank you." She said. "Thank me? I did nothing for you." I replied.

She said, "You did not beat me. You did not lie on me." What could I say to this? I thought you were a new mother? I said nothing.

She seemed to be preparing to leave.

I blurted, "Don't go yet. Tell me more about yourself."

She answered, "We will walk."

We started down the road towards her village that I knew as Kahnawake. Walking down that road with frozen ground crunching under foot and a woman by my side I felt very young again. She began her story.

"I am of the people of the flint. I am of the Turtle clan. In my tongue we are Kanienkehaka." She giggled, knowing that I would not know how to speak of her people in my language. "Many, many seasons ago my people left the far distant land of the setting sun and walked with their many clans toward the rising sun. They fought with the people of the Adirondacks. The great spirit of the west wind caused a storm to destroy the Adirondacks in their canoes and my people lived in peace on the river you call the Mohawk. We grew in numbers and lived on much land. Some came to Hochelaga which is an island "where the people divide." I grew up here in the village of Kahnawake. I live in the wigwam of my mother."

"You said at the cabin your father called you Moira."

"My father was Irish, from Belfast. He was a fur trader and went to the upper country many times. He drowned when the river upset his canoe. Now my father is Joseph."

"Are you married?"

A long pause, then she said, "I leave you now."

In a panic that I would lose her, I pleaded, "Can I see you again?"

Looking at me with those black eyes she said, "I will come to your tent."

We walked to the edge of the village where she stopped, and with a slight departing gesture of her hand, she continued down the road to the village. Elated and despondent at the same time I watched until she was out of sight over a rise and then walked back to my lonely tent. The sun was just going down, disappearing as quickly as Red Feathers had.

Two days later in the middle of the night, she came to my tent and crawled under my blanket. In the morning when I awoke, she was gone.

Alll the next day, and the next, and for many days, I held her warm body in my thoughts and her softness in my heart. Who was the mysterious woman who was practiced in the art of lovemaking but was so like the will-o-the-wisp that she became a shadow? For a week I waited for her in sweet anticipation but she did not come again to my tent. I began to doubt her reality. Was it all a dream? Did my torn emotions when I stumbled on Red Feathers in the cabin in the woods bring her spirit to my bed? Was any of it real?

Several times I walked to the edge of the village of Kahnawake to ask of her. But each time I stopped, fearful of her people and their treatment of enemies, but also fearful that my presence might in some way hurt her with her people. When I first encountered Red Feathers and her strange ritual with the doll I believed she had been banished from the village for sinful behaviour, but when I took her home that day she seemed to be comfortable going into the village. It was all very confusing and I swore to myself that if I ever saw her again I would find out the truth.

After a while, I gave up hope and tried to forget her. Then one day she silently came into my life again. I had walked to the Chateauguay River to spear fish and had found a promising spot where the riverbank was high off the stream and steeply sloped to the water. The river's current had, over the eons, created a pool of black water under two large cedar trees, a place where fish would feed off droppings and insects. Someone was keeping the gently swirling pool free of the ice. I sat on the outcropping rock with my spear poised for much of an hour and saw no fish. It was a world of silence broken only by a pair of noisy crows. A thin mist hung over the river and the bare trees across from the fishing hole rose through the mist like silent ghosts.

A soft voice from the high rock at my back whispered, "Hello." It was Red Feathers. Flustered, I sprang from my perch and scrambled up the rock to her. The crows flew away with final angry squawks.

She was so shy that again I doubted we had been intimate when she had crept into my bed. I greeted her as if nothing had happened between us, fearing she would fly away again like the crows. We walked into the silent woods bordering the river and out onto the road.

In the woods she walked behind me, carefully stepping in my tracks, but when we got to the road where horses and wagons had hardened the path I motioned to her to walk beside me. She did so, she in one track and I in the other. We had gone some distance from the woods when she finally spoke, and showed me her wrists, which bore scars from rope marks.

"My husband, he beat me. He put rope on my hands. He lie on Red Feathers with anger." Something I had suspected. My anger rose and I said without thinking, "I will kill him."

"No," she said. "He was killed at Oriskany by the rebels." God is merciful after all!

"My father Joseph, he puts me out of my mother's house. He say I have evil spirit." I kept silent, willing her to tell more.

"My mother, she is the only one who speaks for me."

After a period of silence, and knowing some little of Indian ways I asked, "Do you have no other husband? Do your brothers not speak for you?"

"I am taboo."

"Why are you taboo?"

"I have no man, no child. Joseph say it is evil in me."

Stopping and turning in front of Red Feathers, I could see in those black eyes the glistening light of tears. She was truly sad. I held her. There in the centre of a crude road in this strange country, caught by the power of those lovely wet eyes, my fate was sealed. I asked, "Will you come to my tent?"

She brushed her tears away with her fur and after a few moments said, "I see." And, with her composure and dignity restored, she walked from me in silence.

Greatly distraught at losing her once again, I was about to chase after her to demand an answer but then I stopped, forced by her show of dignity to think of my own. I had a wife with many children who would be scandalized by my behaviour. One of the crows dropped to the top of a nearby tree and with its raucous cry mocked me. So I let her go, praying I would see her again.

Three days later, Red Feathers appeared in front of my tent. She carried her clan blanket and wore a new feather in her hair, kept in place by a colourful headband. She handed over a small belt of wampum, and together we entered the tent. The next morning she went to the creek for water and washed my underwear. With this domestic action our union was complete.

In the euphoria of recent days I had put out of my mind any thought of the consequences of being with a woman, especially an Indian woman. Fortunately, I had my own tent due to my promotion, but it was not suitable for civilized living in this cold country. I decided I must report this new arrangement to the captain.

So, the next morning, I went to see him.

"Well Sergeant Waeger, it is not a good thing you have done. You know the women of the village and the English wives will spit on her."

"But sir, she is not all Indian. Her Christian name is Moira. Her father was Irish. He drowned upriver."

"You are a good soldier and I am pleased to have you in my regiment. We would not like to lose you, but you must keep your work here separate from your domestic problems. The military has no place for soft men. Do you understand?"

"Yes, sir. Is there a special allowance of provisions for married men?"

"We don't get enough now from London to feed those we have, let alone the flood of refugees that we are bound to look after. I will do what I can Sergeant Waeger. Come back in two days"

"Yes, sir."

So that very afternoon, I set out with my axe and sleigh to find timber and lumber to build a simple longhouse for Red Feathers. Later, the captain gave me a chit for a limited addition to my provisions, for which I was grateful. The rest we looked after together.

The next morning two angry braves appeared in front of the tent wielding hatchets. I thought I was going to lose my hair there and then when Red Feathers came rushing from the tent and shouted a stream of Mohawk words their way. With scowls and surly faces they quietly left, and I still had my hair. Red Feathers told me they came to rescue her from the "white man" but she told them to go back to the village and tell the elders and her mother that she did not wish to be rescued. I hoped her wishes to be with me settled the matter of our "marriage" with her people. I had had my hair a long time and I did not want to lose it.

But it did seem as if I had caused resentment among the young males in Red Feather's village. One day shortly after my encounter with the two braves I was ordered to visit one of our wilderness training camps. Setting out on snowshoes I was about halfway to the camp when one of the braves Red Feathers had driven away stepped out of the woods in front of me. He held a hatchet. Encumbered by the snowshoes I could do nothing but stand and wait to see the Indian's intentions. Without pointing my musket I drew back the cock and waited. We stood facing each other, he with a scowl. I tried to stay calm. After a few frozen moments he disappeared into the woods as silently as he had appeared. My only explanation of his retreat from this encounter, in which he had apparently planned to do me in, was that he finally calculated that if he had killed me the whole weight of the British army would descend on him and his village. In any case, Red Feather's villagers did not harass me again after that incident.

As the river was blasted with the full force of a Canadian winter we were expected to teach the new recruits, English redcoats and German mercenaries, in the use of snowshoes. The snowshoes used by the Canadians were patterned after the Algonquin style and were pointed and broad. Before that winter I had never donned snowshoes but an old man I saw almost every day on the route from my tent to the military stores had offered to teach me to use this strange footwear. It was not easy at first, but with my legs spread wide and toes pointed slightly inward I had finally became skilled enough to teach the new recruits. The footwear issued from the stores was the practical moccasin of the Indians, and with this flexible footwear tucked into the hole of the webbing it was easier to walk than with stiff European style boots.

The army unit spent the winter cutting cordwood, socializing with the villagers, learning to use snowshoes, and building huts in the woods and living in them for ten or twelve days,. Winter was said to be half the year, ending only at *Le premier mai*, when the villagers are invited to the manor house to plant the Maypole. I took Red Feathers to the planting and she was delighted with the dancing and the colourful antics of the villagers, but she made the other women uncomfortable. We left before the meal was served.

To the soldiers, village social life was tedious when they weren't drunk. The troops were longing for action. In the last months, some had become fighters and were excited with the thoughts of spring and a new campaign against the rebel enemy, even the French if that became necessary. Whatever way the future lay, I still saw my position in the army as just a job to do.

In spite of the wish for action, there was still a long period of inactivity and anticipation before much happened on the military front. The new commander-in-chief did not arrive until near the end of June and it was July before any evidence of his strategy came down to the lower ranks.

Red Feathers loved the winter. We spent hours walking in the deep snow on snowshoes; in the woods and along the river, and on the road that was lined with bare and silent birch trees standing like sentries against the grey, wintry sky. The white manor house on the hill was only visible through the trees by the dark outlines of shadow that framed it. It was a winter of wonder for me. Being with Red Feathers was like walking through a door into a world that had always been there, but which I had not seen lately; the whiteness of the unbroken snow, the yellow shadow of the ghostly birch trees, a silence so profound the ear swirled with noise. The flash of a small orange chipmunk scampering to its safe and warm hollow in a rotting log, the holes the rabbit punches in the snow as it leaps toward its den chased by the grey wolf, the fluffy softness of the new snow, and the hard crunch underfoot of the old snow; I had not enjoyed nature so much since a child sitting at Margaretha's feet in the sanctuary in her woods. Red Feathers listened intently to my new enthusiasms with a slight smile shining from those captivating black eyes. I had forgotten the trauma of the war.

She told me her people looked to winter with fear. It was a time of want. The elders taught the women how to preserve berries, corn, and pumpkin, how to keep vegetables underground, how to spear fish through the ice. Meat was scarce; the ducks and geese fled from the cold, and bears and many small animals hid in caves. Some years many old people died. Winter was a time of sewing for the women and playing games for the men. The Iroquois looked forward to spring and the renewal of life on the land. It seemed that the world of the Indian and that of the pioneer farmer were not much different after all.

When the ice left the rivers the regiment said goodbye to the people of Chateauguay and crossed the St. Lawrence to Lachine, where there were bateaux to carry us up the river. The bateaux had been raised, since they had been kept beneath the ice by rocks so the wood would draw up water during the winter, making them watertight. They were ready for use, but being waterlogged they were very heavy. We had also built some bateaux during the past winter, but they were made of greenish wood which was not yet drawn up and would likely sink if put to use without being seasoned by immersion in water for a period of time.

The typical bateau was made of three bottom planks bent upward slightly at the bow and stern, and three planks of wood nailed to oak frames for each side of the hull. Our bateaux were about thirty feet long with four banks of oars and a notch for a sweep at the stern. They were designed for ten men, eight oarsmen, a sweep, and a pole man at the bow to ward off rocks in the rapids.

Our detachment was assigned six bateaux and given orders to proceed up the

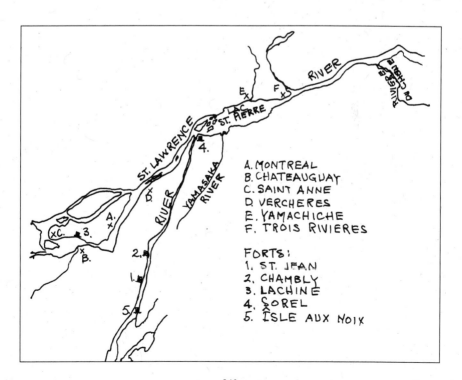

A. MONTREAL
B. CHATEAUGUAY
C. SAINT ANNE
D. VERCHERES
E. YAMACHICHE
F. TROIS RIVIERES

FORTS:
1. ST. JEAN
2. CHAMBLY
3. LACHINE
4. SOREL
5. ISLE AUX NOIX

river to Oswegatchie to repair the fortifications there. When the repairs were complete, we were to do garrison duty in case of an invasion by either the rebels or the French. We had a few women with us who were treated as baggage. Red Feathers sat at my feet.

All travel to the western country began at Lachine. Below there, the river narrowed and dropped several feet over a *sault,* or rapid, where the water became very turbulent and hardly passable paddling upstream, and very dangerous floating downstream, requiring great skill. We left Lachine early and the men, fresh and anxious for action, propelled the boats like bolts from the bow of the Iroquois. The paddlers found themselves in a race with some fur traders who were heading out to the upper country in four of their large canoes made from the bark of the birch tree. At the round stone windmill, which also served as a retreat from Indian raids, we parted company and the *coureurs de bois*, as the traders were called, went off towards St. Anne. At St. Anne they pulled their heavily loaded canoes ashore to attend mass at the small church that had been dedicated to them. After prayers for success and protection in the wild country, they rushed to an orgy of feasting, drinking, and whoring. Each canoe carried eight gallons of rum for the voyage and often it disappeared in one night of revelry at St. Anne.

Passing the windmill, we began the uphill battle to Lake St. Francis. The water from the lake came plunging down through a series of rapids and channels that seemed impossible for mere men and boats to overcome. The river current surged and rolled toward the bateau as if to swallow it and its crew. The most skilled navigators were in the bow and stern of the craft to keep the nose pointing always into danger. For many miles we worked the bateau up this mountain of water, sometimes standing deep in water pushing, sometimes pulling from the river bank by rope, and often we landed the boats and carried them and our provisions and tools around the most dangerous spots. In this manner, we worked the bateaux upstream past Les Cèdres.

I was wondered how the men would take to Red Feathers. Although Indian country wives were common, some men treated Indian women roughly. These men were themselves of a low social standing and they considered women, and especially Indian women, their inferiors in an attempt to elevate their low standing in the eyes of others. I had one such fellow in my squad and he went about with a surly attitude toward Red Feathers. But when she jumped from the bateau at the first rapids we encountered and helped push the vessel through the rocks against a heavy, fast stream, I could see that the men respected her efforts and from then on she melded with the squad as one of them. My friend, the surly one, was still at the bottom of the social heap in our boat. From that point onward, I accepted Red Feathers as a full partner.

At Coteau-du-Lac the river current was strong because of many islands, and the rapids were wild nature at its finest. It was here that General Amherst lost forty-six boats and no less than eighty-four of his men. Some time in the past, the residents of Coteau-du-Lac had built a dike creating a ditch for lightly loaded canoes, but our heavy flat-bottomed bateaux sat too deep in the water to navigate the primitive canal. I did not know then that I would spend many weeks there helping to build a canal for the army.

We landed the boats and dragged them over rocks and around fallen trees and shouldered the heavy bateaux a substantial distance around the rapids until we reached, at about three o'clock on the third day from Lachine, the upper landing place at a quiet point on the river above the rapids. We then had to trek back for the equipment and provisions. By the time we had forwarded all materiel it was very late in the day and the captain gave the order to camp for the night.

Orders were to carry no extra rum beyond our daily ration, but one boat had smuggled a small keg and it was not long after we had stopped for the night that evidence of the extra rum in camp could be seen in the behaviour of some the troops. However, it was not a sufficient quantity to do great damage to the mission and by eight o'clock the corps had become settled for the night.

There were a few Canadians attached to the corps and they gathered around a fire and made music with an old violin carried lovingly during the day by one of their number. The night was warm, the stars sparkled and soon a half moon ap-

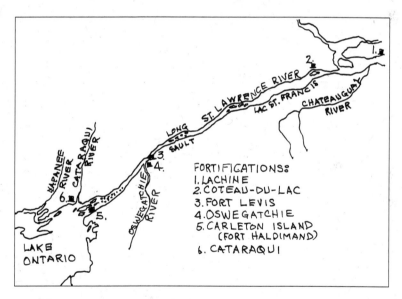

peared above the trees. With the sound of the rapids added to that of the gay fiddle music, happy men and wondrous nature made me feel that this was where I should be. My thoughts turned again to Margaretha. How mother loved nature! Her awe of the woods and river when we first settled on the Witaberger lands in America was profound. It now seemed an eternity since she had left this world.

The next morning before roll call and breakfast, I walked with Red Feathers through the trees to the river's edge to visit the rising sun. I placed my feet just where the river begins its descent to the ocean. The scene was like a mad witches' brew, bubbling and swirling then leaping up on the rocks. The sun's rays, just peeking over the broad river below gave many colours to the mist. Small rainbows hovered over those places where the roiling cauldron curled around a rock and plunged a few feet into a swirling pool of white water. It was an awesome display of the power of nature, roaring mightily in its show of force as the waters rushed from the primeval source above me to the restless sea below.

Finally, after days of struggling against rock and current, we were out on the open waters of Lake St. Francis. A competition sprung up among the boats. Much shouting and jeering got the blood up and the bateaux simply flew up the lake. I had a good crew of paddlers and we were the third bateau to reach the head of the lake. Here we again encountered many islands and rough currents. After navigating this part of the river we reached our encampment across the river from a village of the St. Regis Indians. Looking through the gaps formed by the islands we could see the fires of their village. All seemed peaceful, although when evening fell their drums were heard throbbing in the moist air. Our Indian scout, an Ojibwa, told me the drums were for the celebration of a wedding, not a rhythm to heat the blood of the braves for war. There was no sign of recent Indian occupation on our side of the river, but extra sentries were posted to secure our provisions.

Early the next day we could see the foot of the rapids called the Long Sault, a torrent of water flowing over rocks, and forming channels around many islands. The water leaped and then dropped, pouring into channels and forming whirlpools below the rocks and waterfalls. When the water ploughed into a rock a plume of spray went many feet into the air. Only a mad seaman would put his boat into such a fierce force of nature. Jim Perigo, who stood beside me, was telling a story, "It was here that the Frenchman Champlain, finding the woods full of fallen trees, gave up trying to drag his canoe through the woods and began to pull it through the water with a rope tied to his wrist while walking along the riverbank. The river caught his canoe, spun it around, and overturned it with all his instruments and supplies. Champlain caught his foot between two rocks and was saved from the river."

We beached the bateaux and unloaded them at a point of land in preparation for a long portage around those formidable rapids. Since Champlain's days a well-used carrying place had been cut through the woods, but it was still hard going. It took two days to bring the bateaux and our tools and provisions to relatively safe water above all the rocks and islands that made this passage against the stream impossible for our craft. Above the rapids, it was only a few hours to our destination.

We stopped at the ruin of old Fort Lévis, which was on a small island a short distance below where the Oswegatchie River enters the St. Lawrence. The French built Fort Lévis on the island they called Isle Royale to augment Fort de la Présentation, a short distance away at the confluence of the St. Lawrence River and the Oswegatchie River. The Englishman Amherst took Fort Lévis on his campaign to capture Montreal, bombarding the fort for several days, until it was virtually destroyed. Amherst re-named the ruined fort William Augustus. The day we arrived, the fortifications and primitive barracks were rotting away. It looked as if an Indian band had once used it as a camp, but it was now derelict.

Our destination was Fort de la Présentation, once a French mission with a small stone house and a picketed fort of one bastion. Before the French and Indian war, the French built a palisaded fort seventy feet square with four bastions. Our job, which we set to almost as soon as we arrived, was to repair the fortifications and garrison the fort against an attack by the French, or against Sullivan's force of rebels, which were assembling in Pennsylvania to march into the county of the Six Nations. Along with another trooper with an Indian wife, Red Feathers and I pitched our standard issue tent outside the palisade and at the edge of the trees. We felt quite safe because our wives were of the same nation as the local Indians. It was also what Red Feathers wanted, since she felt very uncomfortable with all the white men with which we were travelling.

It was hot, and the task given to us by the army was hard, especially without any social diversion except rum. About mid-summer four men got drunk, stole a bateau and paddled to the Indian village a few miles down river to find female company. They were not seen again. Their friends begged the captain to rescue them, but he, being worried about a full-scale Indian uprising against the corps, refused. It was not safe in that country to lose your head for fear that you would lose your scalp.

The matter was largely forgotten when, about a week later, an Indian trader came into the fort with a story told to him by people who lived in the village where our men had presumably disappeared. He said the St. Regis Indians had found two bodies floating in a backwater pool along the river's edge and an empty keg of rum caught in the bushes beside the pool. They rescued the rum barrel but did not touch the white men because it would bring evil spirits to the village. After some agitation from the lost men's close comrades, Captain Leake reluctantly sent out an expedition of six men to find the drowned men and bring them to the fort for a proper burial, or to find out from the Indians what had happened.

Two days later, the expedition returned without the bodies of the two men, and with very little information other than that told to us by the Indian trader. They had come to the conclusion that the four soldiers had gotten drunk, fought among themselves, and in midst of the quarrel run onto a rock and capsized the boat. The river had taken them in their drunken state and their inexperience. It was a lesson for us; the river could be a killer, as savage as the rebels or the Indian braves.

Sometime near the end of July, several companies of troops and some engineers under a Captain MacDonald stopped at Oswegatchie. We had new orders: to proceed to Deer Island and build a fort there.

The fortifications at Oswegatchie had been put in sufficient repair to defend the fort, although the barracks were not fully finished. A garrison was left at Oswegatchie. The men assigned to garrison the fort complained about their quarters, but Captain Leake told them the security of the Province was more important than their comfort.

We set out from Oswegatchie under a low grey and black sky. The rain began about mid-day. The river was wide and free of islands, and in spite of the rain and wet gear we made good distance before pulling the bateaux ashore on a point of land on the north side of the river. The rain continued during the night until dawn the next day. The sun came out and we looked forward to a good day after the misery of travelling and making camp in the rain. As soon as everyone was on the river the wind started to blow again. It kept getting stronger, stirring up the water and slowing our progress. It forced us to keep the boats pointed directly into the waves. During the height of the storm we began to encounter islands in that part of the river and the water flowing around the islands caused many crosscurrents. After two hours, I began to see that the wind and crosscurrents could put us in danger of capsizing. Suddenly someone shouted, "Man overboard!"

The boat directly behind had been hit by a huge wave from one side and by the current from another direction. The blow twisted the bateau and the sweep smacked into the ribs of the man in the stern, the long oar pushing him through the air and into the roiling water. He was rapidly being swept away from his comrades shouting curses and waving his arms, hoping that would make up for his inability to swim. The useless oar was following him in the current and someone was shouting, "Grab the oar!" over and over again. Without the steering oar, the bateau was not easily manoeuvrable and was spinning in circles. Being on the sweep, I pulled our boat around and we set out to the rescue. We caught the poor man about a mile down the river from where he had gone overboard and hauled him aboard our boat, nearly drowned and certainly at the end of his strength. There was an island nearby and we pulled in behind it. Here we found a cove with a very small beach, where we got the man dried out and the rest of us took some leisure from our recent adventure. The currents created a backwater in our little cove, and, lo and behold, the lost oar came floating onto the beach nice as you please. Soon we could see the others, finally organized in their paddling rhythm, using a spare oar as a sweep. When they drew their boat onto the beach we had a small celebration with a tot of rum for all. With renewed strength, we set out to catch the rest of the corps.

We came up to the others who were now in a labyrinth of islands. There were small islands strewn across the river creating narrow, swiftly running streams between them. Soon we learned by the swiftness of the stream where the main river course lay. At mid-morning on the sixth day out from Oswegatchie, according to the sketch drawn for us before leaving Lachine, we should be approaching Deer Island. As we came abreast of a large island that was surely Deer Island, we could hear the sounds of axes and see the smoke from fires of an Indian encampment that we had been told existed close by.

We landed in a bay on the southwest end of the island and were welcomed by a small contingent of the military. A cluster of Indians watched silently from a nearby knoll. We were to spend the rest of the summer on this island that the military was calling Carleton Island after the previous governor. Deer Island, also called Buck Island, lay in the St. Lawrence River just off Grande Isle. Carleton Island was some two miles in length by about one mile in breadth. It was home to a band of the Mississauga Indians. The probable reason the army chose it for a fortification was because of the attached peninsula on the southwest end of the island that was connected to the rest of the island by a narrow isthmus. This provided an outer defense and two bays to harbour ships.

The site of the fort was atop limestone cliffs about forty feet in height. It was to be named Fort Haldimand, after the present governor who had selected this place at the foot of Lake Ontario to be one of his major defensive positions. Here, at various times, I was destined to spend many months.

Captain MacDonald had brought together animals, wagons, and the larger tools needed to raise a fortification. He reviewed our small corps the morning after the day of our arrival and spoke to us about the overall plan of the fort. Displaying a drawing, he told us what had been done to date, which to my eye, seemed not a lot. Dismissed, we were assigned work squads and as I should have expected my squad were to be the woodchoppers. At least it was one up from the diggers.

We cut trees, trimmed them, and hauled the logs to the site by oxen. It was hot and tiring work and I was pleased to be able to return to my tent and to Red Feathers. Often though, she was not in the tent since she had begun to spend her days walking alone on the island, but always distant from the Mississauga village and landing place around the point from our camp. Red Feathers distrusted its people because of feuds between the Iroquois and the Ojibwa tribes north of the river. She said she would be kidnapped, although the Mississauga's were friendly, at least to the white army wives, and I told her that it was her superstitious Irish blood that made her fearful. Not knowing the depths of her culture or her feelings, for she was very quiet in those matters, I assured her my comment was truly in jest. But Red Feathers was finding it difficult to live in a place where everyone around her was a stranger. To make her feel more at home with her new, mostly white community, I began to refer to her as Moira.

Much work was done before the end of the season. The ditch had been dug and the ramparts thrown up. The trimming from the trees we cut down for timber made an *abatis*, which Captain Twiggs on inspection declared "almost" impenetrable. He wanted perfection in all things. The encircling parapet and banquettes were finished. Five bastions had been constructed for the guns that had not yet arrived from Niagara. With the logs my squad had cut and left on the site, the barracks, officer's quarters, magazine, and storehouse were begun. As well as a garrison, the fort was to serve as a storage place for Montreal traders, where goods would be changed from bateaux on the river to ships on the lake between Carleton Island and Niagara.

One day a two-masted snow-brig dropped anchor in the harbour to deliver its cargo of twenty cannon. Rafts were built to bring the guns to shore where they were hauled inside the fort on greased skids by oxen. The cannon were then levered on thick planks to the bastion platforms, four for each bastion. This task took two days but at the end of that time the fortification was capable of defending the island and the two harbours. Before autumn began to give way to winter, some ship building activity had begun.

The days were getting short and the air was getting cold. The squawking geese and ducks were overhead, headed for warmer climes. Man and beast began to hunker down and prepare for winter. Then one day our captain announced at morning parade that we were ordered to Sorel for inspection, which was to be headquarters for all the Provincial regiments. We would leave Carleton Island in two days, hopefully ahead of the freeze up. I think Moira looked forward to the change of homes because she enthusiastically ran about gathering together our few resources for the journey. At Sorel she would be closer to her own people, but I was not hopeful that she could go back to her village without causing great pain to her, and also to me.

Back on the river once more, we ran down the current and navigated through the Long Sault without mishap to the Coteau landing place where we encamped for the night.

The next day at Les Cèdres the paddlers lost control. My bateau was caught in a whirlpool, turned around across the current, and came up against a rock. Fearful the current would flip the immobile hull over the rock, I shouted at the paddlers to pull with all their might. After what seemed an eternity the paddlers and sweep got the boat turned into the rushing current and we slid around the slippery rock. I looked at Moira who seemed to be less fearful than some of the men. We came to the Lachine landing place tired and wet, but thankful for once again defeating the river. That very afternoon we set out for the journey to Sorel on an unfamiliar stretch of the river. As we were preparing to leave Lachine I noticed Red Feathers looking longingly across the river towards her ancestral village. She said nothing.

At Sorel I was able to get assigned to a very small habitation built for the refugees that were expected in the spring. Since it was uninhabited, I was able to acquire it with the argument that I could not take my country wife in barracks with the ordinary troops. It turns out the army does have a place for "soft men."

10

THE RESTLESS RIVER

B y the end of the year 1778, I had been in the service of the King for one year and six months. I had signed up for the duration, thinking it would be a short war and I would be free to get back to my farm, but the rebels were winning and I had to give up any thought of returning to my former home. I was anxious to see the end of the war and my service in the military so I could make a new start, if not in America then in the vast wilderness of Canada.

In winter we lived for rum and scuttlebutt. The Provincial regiments were at Sorel for inspection; comrades were together again and stories of past conquests and rumours of future adventures ran through the camp like a raging grass fire. Red Feathers and I were no more than settled when cousin Young Jacob appeared on our doorstep, having heard that I was living with an Indian woman. Red Feathers was not there at the time and perhaps because she was absent Young Jacob scolded me in a very rough manner. I told him to leave, which seemed to calm him down. "You're crazy, you know! What are you going to do about Lena and the girls? How are they going to take this foolishness of yours?" He paced in front of me, and before I could answer he continued his rebuke. "Her tribe will send braves to kill you. Her people do not like white men taking their women as country wives, and she will not be allowed in their village when you decide to leave her." My anger quickened, "This is none of your affair. Just leave me in peace. The village elders have already sent two braves with hatchets to scalp me but she told them this is what she wanted and sent them away. Besides, the braves don't want to bring the army down on their heads. She left her village for my tent because they did not want her in the first place. You can tell people she is a Christian and her name is Moira." I think this surprised him and he seemed a little less concerned about the situation. I said, "I really hope this is the end of the matter between you and me!"

I did say that I knew not what to do about my daughters Catharina, Rena, and Hanna, but could only pray that they would understand. "I believe Lena has no more interest in me, nor cares what I do or where I am. I have written letters but have had no reply. I think she has likely lost the house and farm to the rebels and gone to live with her kin in Backway. Even before I left, she was threatening to do this. I have lost everything; I have nothing to give so what use am I to her or to the children?"

Young Jacob had succeeded in making me despondent so I offered him some rum. After two drinks Young Jacob got angry again. "Why do you call me 'Young

Jacob'? I'm a sergeant in the King's army and you call me 'Young Jacob.' I don't like it!"

"Because you are over twenty years younger than me. Your father is not much older than me. You could be my son."

"Well I don't like it!" He was surly.

"If you hate it that much I will call you Sergeant Jacob. How's that?"

We got quite intoxicated and when Sergeant Jacob left we were cousins again. Afterward I sat by the hearth and let doubts creep into my heart, but when Red Feathers returned, excited by her excursions in the village outside the fort, I lost all doubts and embraced her brown body to mine.

The next morning we were mustered for roll call and service duty. The roll showed our company to be well past one hundred strong. My duty squad was assigned to the house construction detail, which was also to include volunteers from the countryside. The *habitations* were for refugee families that were forced to leave their former homes in New York Province.

Houses for the refugee families were small and simply built. Maple, ash, elm, or whatever logs were available from the cleared site were built up on a foundation of stones and chinked with lime and bar. A steeply sloped shed roof, covered with sawn lumber and bark kept most of the rain out of the *habitation*. A stone fireplace at one end of the single room finished the construction. These houses were sufficient until the family could build a better house with a gabled roof. The governor's men also looked around the parishes for vacant houses to which troops were sent to prepare for the refugees.

That winter was unusual. It was warm and rainy at first, but then turned bitterly cold. Working with wet timber in the rain and mud or with frozen timber and deep snow were equally undesirable, but I welcomed the cold air and deep snow since I was discovering more aches and pains from the dampness brought on by almost constant rain. It was a long winter, but one day I could smell spring in the soft warm air and each day the sun was riding higher in its daily arc. Birds were returning and looking for nesting spots to raise their young. Nature was preparing the earth for renewed life.

Soon the ice had mostly broken up and left the rivers, the snow was gone except for mounds still holding on in shady spots, water was running everywhere, and the air was warm and fragrant. The men were restless, speculating about where they would be sent next and grousing about their daily duties. Rumours were about that our depleted regiment, now not more than three or four companies, would be disbanded, causing even more anxiety among the troops. Mostly they liked and respected Captain Leake and wished to continue the war under his leadership.

The rumour turned out to be true. The Loyal Volunteers were no more. But a small cheer went up when Captain Leake announced that he was given permission to form his own company to be called Leake's Independent Company, which was to be our new home.

At the beginning of June, we were mustered for roll and duty orders. The captain called out names and asked those named to step forward. After more than half the company stood in the front line the captain said, "You in the front line are a combat company. You are to go to Lachine where you will report to Sir John Johnson and await orders. You are to take no women or children because a raid is planned and they would be in danger. We will arrange to look after your wives and children at the post. Be prepared to leave here in two days at dawn. Dismissed." Sergeant Jacob was in this group; I was not. The captain spoke to those of us who were still standing at attention. "You men," he said. "We have read your active service records and are much appreciative, I might say impressed, with your contribution and commitment to our cause. It has been said that you are useful with the axe but are not altogether to be depended on with the firelock. But the army could not fight without the work of engineers and artificers building roads, bridges, and fortifications and standing garrison duty. Some of you have been in the thick of the fighting at Hubbardtown, Bennington, Saratoga, and Ticonderoga, and based on some delegations to my office, are sick of war, especially this civil war where the enemy may be your brother. Some of you are quite sick in body and need a rest. I have here a list of those who have come to me asking for sick leave. I will post a list of those approved on the recommendation of the medical officer. The rest of you are assigned engineering duties, to be carried out here at Sorel or at Coteau-du-Lac. God save the King."

I was posted to Coteau-du-Lac under the command of Captain Twiss. Red Feathers was sad to leave since she had become friends with another of the country wives, but with good humour she began to prepare our meagre possessions for another fight with the river.

As was both custom and necessity, our company landed at Lachine and transferred to bateaux for our fight up stream. We reached the carrying place at Coteau-du-Lac without an incident of note. Curious about the name of the village, I accosted an old man with a long beard. He said in a curt, wheezy brogue, "It's the hill, laddie. We are at the end of the loch. Coteau-du-Lac: the hill at the bottom of the loch. Look out there, my boy, and see the killer stream. That's what we are here for, picking the dead bodies from the waters of doom. If ye need my services ask for the church sexton. G'bye ye!" I wasn't any wiser about the name of the place but I knew where to find the gravedigger. It was a morbid welcome to my new duties.

Not wishing to live in barracks with the men, Red Feathers and I set up our standard issue tent and I started to plan to build our own more substantial quarters. We thought our stay was at least for the winter since the canal was a major undertaking. Red Feathers wanted to live in an Iroquoian longhouse so, with her instruction and help I began the project soon after we arrived. I cut long branches from whatever source I could find nearby, as long as they were flexible and easily barked. Hickory is the traditional wood but willow and basswood were growing nearby. Gathering these and setting the long poles in the ground, we bowed them at the top and tied the poles together with hemp. Horizontal laths were tied to the upright poles. To form the roof members the horizontal saplings were set closer together than for the walls. Sheets of bark were used to cover the whole structure with an opening near the centre for smoke to escape. A door was fashioned on the long side. Our longhouse was very small. When we settled in, I felt I was living like an Indian. Lena, if she were here, would tell me the same thing with disgust in her words.

The task set before us was a substantial undertaking by the army. Captain Twiss told us it was the first canal in North America and he was about to honour us by helping to build it. He was hell-bent on completing this project as fast as he could get the materials and skilled men to carry out the task. I looked at our company of mostly uninterested men that had just put in a rough winter and which refused to get enthusiastic about anything. Captain Twiss would need great powers of persuasion and patient perseverance.

While the route and character of the canal was being planned and surveyed the troops were set to work tearing away obstructions to the current, making passage smoother and more navigable for bateaux being dragged upstream from the bank. Then the actual work began on the canal. It was to be built of timber at a water depth of two and one half feet, seven feet broad and nearly one thousand feet in length. The work never wavered or stopped. I found I liked the work of canal building.

When the company left for Fort St. Jean before freeze up I requested permission to stay on for the winter and help complete the canal project. Captain Leake and Captain Twiss agreed to this arrangement on the understanding I would re-join the regiment at Fort St. Jean in the spring in case of combat action on Lake Champlain during the next season. When freeze up came we started blasting rock as this could be accomplished with the earth frozen and covered with snow.

Red Feathers and I settled into our Indian home for the winter, but a peaceful winter it was not to be. In early January, Captain Twiss asked to see me. He had received instructions ordering me to go to St. Jean immediately for a court martial proceeding. John Peters had laid a complaint with the Board of Officers against the brothers French for theft from army stores and other acts. Gershom and Jeremiah were to be tried for selling flour to the citizens of St. John and Gershom had requested that I appear in his defense. We went back a long way since I had hidden out with him on Bald Mountain. How could I do otherwise than to go to his aid? I had strong silent words for the infinite wisdom of the army to call a court martial hearing in the dead of winter in a country where winter travel was very hard. When I told Red Feathers, she almost seemed pleased. Being spirited, she was bored with the sedentary life and welcomed the opportunity to be on the move, even in three feet of snow. Besides, she saw it as a chance to come into her own by helping me cope with the harsh conditions we would encounter.

Of late, Red Feathers had begun to fall into her old superstitious ways. She wanted a child so badly and was so active at night that I had begun to think that was all she wanted of me. Perhaps if I left her behind until I returned both of us would be the better for it, but I had to admit that the ordeal before me was not to my liking and Red Feathers could help us get to St. Jean. The new situation had changed things and I decided to take her with me. I also hoped the journey might dampen her ardour to be with child.

Two days later we packed dried meat, salt, tea, corn flour to make soup, and a small tent we had designed for travel in the woods. We put on our snowshoes and set out on the old portage route up the river until we found solid ice across the lake. There we made camp.

At daybreak the next morning, we began the trek over the ice. The dark clouds hung low in the heavens, heralding a dull, silent journey. Here the lake was some three miles across and once out on the ice it was impossible to distinguish the land from the ice in a world of unbroken whiteness and flat light. With Red Feathers leading, we made the south bank of the river at noon. Soon Red Feathers found an Indian trail and we headed downriver. The dark clouds, which had been with us all day, began to release high winds and to drop snow. About mid-afternoon, in a blinding snowstorm, we stumbled upon an Indian village. Since there was no activity in the village because of the storm and I was not sure if the band was friendly or hostile, I began to look for a suitable encampment in the woods adjacent to the longhouses. Red Feathers recognized the village as being Mohawk and urged me forward. With some fear, and knowing I was in her hands, we entered the village and were immediately accosted by two braves who stood before us with hostile faces. Red Feathers whispered, "St. Regis," and spoke a few words to the braves. She must have pleased the braves, because they motioned us to follow and escorted us to the lodge of the chief and his family; an old squaw, a man who had lost his youth, and a woman of a tender age and fresh beauty.

The village was small, with only five lodges, a few men and fewer braves. The villagers had recently been in the employ of the French against the English and I knew not what treatment to expect given this war, with the French supporting the republican rebels. However, the chief, a very old and wrinkled man, seemed very friendly towards my Mohawk companion and me and invited us to stay the night. This allayed my fears somewhat, and I was pleased not to be out in the storm for the night. I nodded my approval to Red Feathers and she passed this to the chief in his language. The young beauty's husband, for so I assumed him to be, made a fuss at this but the chief quieted him with a word. He went to the end of the lodge bearing a dark scowl. I anticipated trouble.

We sat for the pipe and a meal of samp; dried fish, and a sort of pancake made from maize flour. The chief, in honour of our visit, produced something that must have been precious to him, a jug of grape juice, with which he filled our drinking gourds. Full with food and drink and being very tired, I was shown to a platform built into the wall of the lodge while Red Feathers was to sleep on a mat beneath me. In the night she crept under my blanket.

The next morning we awoke to a bright, sunny, crisp day. Out on the trail once more I marvelled at the beauty of the winter landscape. The new snow was soft under foot and small puffs of powder flew off the tread of our snowshoes, glistening with rainbow colours where the sun caught them. The tall trees were layered with great towers of light snow that dropped like brilliant white clouds when a gust of wind blew through the branches. The woods were as silent as the grave, the birds and animals along the trail either gone for the winter or huddled in a den, dozing through the cold winter and living off the fat they had accumulated in better seasons.

We were walking an Indian trail that had been hacked through the wilderness, perhaps centuries ago. The small creeks were frozen to the bottom while the larger ones with open water either had an ice bridge across a quieter section or a makeshift bridge made of fallen trees. Sometimes beaver dams produced areas of quiet water that were frozen over with ice that looked thick enough to walk upon. Former travelers had made crude shelters about a day's distance apart, making the journey easier than it could have been. We came upon a fork in the trail. There were tracks in the fresh snow on the left branch, the one along the river, and this we followed. Soon it was apparent we were following a winter route across a frozen swale, which in the summer would be a swamp.

Occasionally we saw smoke rising in the still air from an Indian settlement. As we walked, the bird calls around us told of eyes in the trees following our movement, but no one appeared to challenge us. Near one village, a boy suddenly appeared on the trail. He was about twelve years old and from his facial deformation and his strange behaviour it was evident he was a lunatic. Red Feathers became very agitated and insisted we take to the woods and circle around the boy she said was full of evil spirits. I believe she was greatly relieved when he made no attempt to follow.

On the fifth day we found ourselves, as if some sort of spirit was guiding our trek, at the old derelict hut where we had met. The cabin was buried in snow. Only a thin line below the eaves was visible, with some five feet of snow piled along the walls and a deep drift of snow covering the roof. Using our snowshoes as shovels, we dug a hole in the snow where the doorway was located. After a few minutes of digging, we discovered there was no door in the entrance and snow had filled the opening and drifted some three feet onto the cabin floor. It was black as pitch inside, with only a small square of light filtering through the door opening. I could see nothing, but a pungent odour wafted from the dark interior that I instinctively sensed held danger. Behind me Red Feathers whispered, "Bear," and at the same time I heard a grunt from a far corner of the cabin. A bear had made it his winter den! My eyes had become used to the gloom in the cabin and I could see the beast rearing upright, about to charge. Fortunately, my powder was dry and the gun exploded with an ear-splitting roar caused by the closeness of the space within the cabin.

The bear, still almost hidden by the gloom, seemed to shudder as if surprised, and came bounding across the snow-covered floor heading for the lighted doorway. With Red Feathers directly behind me, I had to stop the beast. All I could see in front of my face was a gaping mouth, snarling and shaking, with blood from my gunshot flowing over the lower jaw. In desperation, I jammed my useless gun into its open mouth with such force that my feet were entirely clear of the floor. I let go of the musket and, losing contact with the hairy mass in front of me, I slipped and fell with the bear on top. Suddenly, Red Feathers was on its back with her arm flailing up and down, plunging her long knife repeatedly into the bear's neck and shoulders. Attention diverted, it tried to dislodge this pest on its back, allowing me to slip out from underneath. But the bear was finished. With the gunshot wound in his chest and the dead gun choking at its throat, the bear lay still with life slowly leaving its body. Red Feathers continued to pummel the animal, clearly excited and aroused. I had to drag her off the dead beast and hold her until she calmed down. With the killing of the bear we had become one person, more so than ever before.

I discovered the bear had been an old male after dragging the carcass out of the cabin into the snow. Red Feathers kneeled beside the dead animal and chanted over its body, asking for its forgiveness and wishing its spirit to abide in peace. Then we hung it from a tree and butchered it. Red Feathers believed the cabin now belonged to the bear and wished to move on for the night. But it was getting dark with no other prospects for the night so I persuaded her to spend the night in the cabin. That evening we feasted on bear meat.

The next morning Red Feathers left the cabin to visit her mother. She explained that she was going alone since she was afraid Joseph might kill me. She packed as much bear meat as she could carry and, without a further word, set out on the trail. With great sadness, believing I would not see her again I followed her with my eyes until she was hidden by trees.

Two days later, when I was finally getting enough courage to go to the village and rescue her from Joseph, she appeared at the cabin door, which I had repaired from the ravages of the bear. She told me her mother had wanted her to stay, but Joseph, as nasty as ever, had refused. Without a place in Joseph's longhouse she felt abandoned and once again left her mother and her village. I was humbled by the thought that she preferred to be with me, a rough old man compared to her youth and beauty.

We traveled to Laprairie, where Ethan Allen had met his defeat, and from that place caught an old Indian trail for some distance, and then the road south and east to Fort Chambly on the Richelieu River. This fort was hardly worth the name, being only a barracks surrounded by pickets easily subdued with cannon. Besides, the fort was surrounded on three sides by higher ground at less distance than a musket shot. A small garrison was quartered there and we were welcomed to stay the night. The commander was anxious for news from Coteau-de-Lac, which I duly supplied.

Fort St. Jean was twelve miles south of Fort Chambly, which we approached at noon the next day. This fort was also vulnerable to attack by cannon, being only a line of pickets, two old earth redoubts and a banquette where troops could stand and defend the fort. A deep ditch protected the barracks and storehouses from foot soldier attacks. This was why my former company, with its artificers, was garrisoned here.

I was pleased to see Jacob Hoffman and others that I had known at Bennington, but I was not sure they were happy to see me with a country wife. I was informed that Gershom was in the guardhouse and I may be able to see him on the morrow.

The guardhouse was in fact nothing more than a cellar dug under the barracks and entered through a trap door from outside the building. It was damp, but not cold. Gershom shared the cellar with a regular soldier, a lad really, who was sitting on a tree stump in the corner. He looked very despondent. Presuming this was not Jeremiah, whom I had never met, I enquired of Gershom the name of the lad and was told his name was Edward, a deserter being court-martialled for treason, as it was alleged that he had gone over to the enemy.

When I asked why Jeremiah was not with him, Gershom replied that the Board of Officers had left them both free on their promise not to attempt to leave the fort, but Gershom was so angry that he had refused to take the oath so here he was, "Locked up like a wild beast." He had been in custody for some time now and he did indeed carry the visage of a wild man, dirty, wild-eyed, and unshorn.

We talked about our times together, each carefully avoiding the reason he was here. I suspected he had indeed been selling flour from the army stores to citizens, but it not being dereliction of duty I wished not to know the truth of the charge against him. He was anxious to make certain my support would be forthcoming at his hearing, and assuring him positively, I prepared to leave. He grabbed my shoulder and much to my surprise, because he was normally a man in much control, he sobbed and uttered the single word, "Please." I said, "Don't worry, it's a minor charge." Gershom was a valuable asset to the British and I wondered about the reasons behind the claim. I shouted to the guard to let me out.

The Board met near the end of February. There were some witnesses against the French brothers, but none seemed to me to be truly convinced a serious crime had been committed. They likely knew of many similar cases. After all, it was winter and many people in the country were without adequate food.

When I was called in front of the Board I gave my statement to the effect that Gershom was a loyal man for the King, and that he had raised nearly one hundred men for service in the King's name. Accused of horse stealing in Albany County

I said, "I was with Gershom French in the woods, near Albany for a month or six weeks during the summer of 1777, and all that time never knew him to rob or plunder any friend of the government, but assisted him to disarm many of the rebels and take away their effects."

The Gershom brothers were reprimanded. Jeremiah was reduced in rank to lieutenant.

The young lad, Edward, the former career soldier who cowered in the guard-house, was found guilty of treason and taken out the next morning at dawn to one hundred lashes, and, if he survived the whip, banishment to foreign battlefields.

A t St. Jean I was back with my old regiment although I felt no more a part of the army than when I was with them in previous months. Living as a married man with Red Feathers put my heart at odds with the raucous life led by the encamped soldiers, although I did occasionally join them for rum and cards. But I was always somewhat relieved when I returned to the tent where Red Feathers was always waiting. Her dedication to my welfare was very humbling. Sometimes, when I was frustrated with her superstitious ways and I had had too much rum, I abused her. Even then, she brought me low with gratitude for her rescue from Joseph. It was mid-summer when she told me she had a child grow-ing inside her belly. For her, this was a happy fact. For me, it was a problem. I was living the life of a soldier and Indian, but the ways of my own Christian people weighed heavily on my heart. Seeing the happiness this child could bring to Red Feathers allowed my to bury my doubts and guilt. As usual, I found work the great peacemaker between my heart and my conscience.

My regiment was at St. Jean to repair and rebuild the fortifications and bar-racks to defend Canada from the rebels. That summer I was assigned, with a small squad of six, to build a blockhouse on the Lacolle River three miles north of St. Jean.

During the summer, a number of men stopped over at the blockhouse we were building, having been instructed to avoid the Richelieu forts. The men were on spy mission to the Mohawk forts to reconnoiter the situation there and to bring back recruits. They carried news from Carleton Island of scouts proceeding to the valley forts, prompting rumours that a raid was being planned. When the blockhouse was completed, my company was dispatched to Carleton Island for garrison duty.

W e did, however, rest for a day at Coteau-du-Lac. The canal was in use, and the time saved allowed a day's rest there. Red Feathers wanted to visit our former home. Time had not been kind to our construction, and the longhouse was in a very depressed state with the bark covering mostly gone and the interior full of debris. As with all of man's doing, nature had taken it back;

it was now a haven for mice and birds to nest in.

I went to examine my work on the canal and found it satisfactory to my eye, and on enquiry was told that Captain Twiss had invited the governor to the post to see his work. The whole garrison and townspeople turned out on the day of the governor's visit to examine the works. On that occasion, Capt. Twiss stated his determination to proceed with similar works at Les Cèdres and Pointe-des-Cascades. Governor Haldimand was pleased with Twiss' work and gave his support.

On leaving the next morning, the sky was overcast with dark heavy clouds and the wind had begun to blow up the river. A storm was brewing. The men were able to rig sails on the bateaux and with the strong wind at our backs seemed to fly on the surface of the lake. The elation quickly turned to concern when we reached the rapids and saw the chaos of the waters there. The wind pushing against the cataract raised the on-rushing stream as the water tried to escape the obstacles to its progress. The channels and hills grew ever deeper, higher, and heavier. The river, from bank to bank, was a mass of twisting, leaping, plunging white water. With awe and trepidation, we put into the landing place to begin the work of working the bateaux through this maelstrom of nature bent on halting our progress.

Working the loaded craft upstream, sometimes in the water to the waist or higher, sometimes pulling bateaux from the bank by means of ropes, was a daunting task. All morning the wind delivered fierce blasts although it was a warm day. The constant spray and submersion left us cold and some men started to falter. It was too much. The men complained and wanted to pull the bateaux to the bank and rest. But Lieutenant Furst kept shouting, "It will soon be over. Get to it chaps, we will win over this watery foe."

I was in charge of the lead bateau. There was a man on a rope pulling from the bank and a man on a stern rope keeping the craft in the current. The rest were in the high water trying to control the heavy vessel. As I watched, two of the men at the bow of the bateau disappeared beneath the surface. They had stepped into a deep hole in the river bottom. The current caught the bow and began to swing it further into the fast water, jerking the man on the bank into the water, who, to save himself from drowning, let go of the rope. The stern rope held and the boat swung broadside into the current. The men on the downstream gunwales, with poor footing and half underwater, were swept under the boat.

The heavy bateau was pushed onto a rock with such force the hull filled with water. It was now so heavy it was impossible to control. Red Feathers stood in the bateau with fear in her eyes, holding her swollen belly. I willed her to jump, but, perhaps thinking she could save herself and the bateau, she grabbed at a paddle. As I watched in horror, the man holding the rope attached to the stern was pulled into the water. Those of us still grasping the upstream gunwale of the bateau were unable to hold the heavy craft against the current and could only watch as the bateau was snatched away by the rushing stream. Red Feathers frantically tried to turn it as the gunwale was torn from my hands. I watched as the bateau slid around a rock and then crashed into another boat, throwing Red Feathers into the air in a spume of water. When she crashed into the stream the paddle was wrested from her hands and she plunged into the deep. Immediately, the rushing waters took her body and flung it over the rocks. Then she was drawn back under the waves. That is the last I saw of her. I stood in the waist deep water pounding the river with both fists in anger and frustration.

S lowly I became aware of men cursing and shouting. My men, those who were not swept down the river, were wading to the bank. I pushed through the racing water in great haste to reach Red Feathers, lost my footing, stumbled and almost fell but made the bank and scrambled up the steep rock face. Gaining high ground, I was faced with a tangle of bush and fallen trees. I fought the underbrush for a few minutes until, tripping on a root, I fell flat on my face. Stunned and devastated I wanted to linger in the wet and soggy earth until I became part if it. Life seemed unbearable without Red Feathers. As the cold earth seeped into my bones I came to my senses and realized Red Feathers was lost She could be two or three miles down the river by now with no hope of her survival. She had been so pleased to be a Mohawk once more with a warrior growing in her belly. I could not save her and her future warrior, no matter my actions now so I got up from the ground with a heavy heart and trudged back to find the others. The wind had died and it was raining hard.

The dull thud of axes directed my steps back to the rest of the company, who were cutting a clearing to make camp and dry out. Beside Red Feathers, two of my boatmen were lost, Nehr and Bruster. When a great fire was drying out the men, the captain spoke to Lieutenant Bryans, Sergeant Mathers, and myself, asking for a consultation. The captain revealed that a major raid was planned into the Mohawk Valley near the beginning of the month, and his orders were to move as quickly as possible to garrison Fort Haldimand. "It would be right to spend some time here looking for the men that are surely drowned, but my orders tell me we have to push on." I asked permission to stay behind and join the company later at Fort Haldimand. He said, "Permission granted to you, Sergeant Waeger because she was your wife, but I cannot leave anyone else. I believe it is hopeless for you. She could be anywhere by now, tangled in weeds on the opposite bank, or floated up on an island, or at the bottom of the lake. She might never be found." He added, "The same applies to Nehr, Bruster and our supplies. The bateau is likely broken up by now and our supplies and tools dispersed beyond recovery. We will leave them for the Indians.

"The question now is how we proceed from here. Do we send scouts to find the portage cutting, or do we continue dragging the remaining bateaux against the current? We are near the beginning of the rapids and with the rain falling the wind has died some, so the water will not be so rough. We can add four men to each of our other boats but if we lose another, some will have to walk to Cataraqui." After giving our opinion, which was not unanimous, his decision was to continue as we were.

I set about building a rock cairn under the cover of a great oak for Red Feather's spirit, much as her people would have done. I had nothing of hers to see her through the afterlife except the wampum belt she had given me as her marriage vow, which I wore under my shirt at all times. This I lay on a flat stone and covered with a mound of stones. I arranged them so that the wampum was encased in a small cave-like cavity. I did not believe I would desecrate her grave by erecting a crude cross at one end of the cairn so with my only possession left to me from the accident, my long knife, I carved into the crossbar the name, "Moira," and into the upright, "Red Feathers."

Taking my lead, others set about making crosses for Nehr and Bruster. We drove the crosses into the wet earth, marking the place as a small graveyard. Lieutenant Bryans, who had some religious training, said a few words over the graves we had fashioned. Standing in the rain, with the foliage beginning its cycle of reds, yellow, and oranges, dark emotions in my heart and the roar of the river in my ears, I said a silent prayer for her soul. To this I added a thanksgiving prayer for the pleasure she had brought into my barren life. A sad "Amen" brought her life to a close.

Having taken care of Red Feather's spirit, if not her body, there was no more I could do for her so I decided to carry on with the others as planned. Immediately following the ceremony for our dead comrades we crowded into our two remaining bateaux, and made Oswegatchie before darkness without further incident. By early evening of the next day, we were able to pull our battered bateaux onto the beach below the walls of Fort Haldimand. It was like coming home, but this time I was alone. Red Feathers no longer need fear her Mississauga enemies.

They say shocks come in threes. I got my second shock of that week the next day when I was called to Captain Crawford's office, "immediately." The tone of the message concerned me, and I went to see the captain with much trepidation, fearing I would be court-martialled for losing my boat and two men at the Long Sault. Imagine my shock then when I looked up to see young Tom, all decked out in a brand new uniform of the King's Royal Regiment of New York. Captain Crawford spoke.

"Waeger, here is a recruit who found us on the Mohawk. He claims he's your son. Is that so?"

I squeaked out the words, "Yes. He is Thomas, my eldest son. I am surprised to see him here, but yes, he is my son. I haven't seen him in over four years. He was a boy when I left."

"Good! You two are relieved of duty for today. Dismissed."

Thomas and I walked down to the beach where we sat on a rock and hurled stones into the water. In fits and starts, Tom told of home and the story of signing up with Crawford. "When you left they came to the house and ordered maw to leave. Uncle Niclass drove them off, but they came back and burnt the barn and all the hay, and drove off all our cattle and horses. So Uncle Niclass took us in his wagon to Backway where we lived with Grandma DeLange. I went to work in sawmills in Poughquag and Rhinebeck. I lived with Aunt Anna in Backway for a time. In '78 I went to Stoney Point to join up, but the British lost the battle before I got there. Some trouble came up at the sawmill and I had to leave, so I ended up in Claverack for a time. Things did not work out there, so I decided to try and find you."

I was afraid to ask what trouble Tom had been in, so I kept my silence while he went on talking.

"One night I was with two others in the local tavern when we got to talking about the war. Our minds being softened by the grape, we went out the next day to find the British. We left the manor and bought passage on a wagon loaded with farm implements bound for Albany. Bounty hunters were everywhere since a law had been passed requiring that parents of Tories caught going to the British lines be fined nine pence on the pound on the whole value of their estate. Tory or otherwise, the bounty hunters cared not as long as they could convince the governor and collect their bounty.

"Albany was a dangerous place to be so we trekked to Schenectady and hid out in the woods with others who were also looking for the British. Someone had heard of a man named Servos, a former rebel now spying for the British and giving false intelligence to the rebels. If we could find Servos we might be able to locate recruiters in the Valley. We trekked up the river towards Fort Stanwix asking those we met on the road if they knew of such a man. An Indian from Fort Hunter knew of Servos and soon he brought us to a Captain Crawford who was pillaging the area. With Crawford we fought a large body of militia, which retreated. We destroyed a mill and burnt barns and grain near Fort Herkimer and killed many cattle. Fort Stanwix had already been abandoned and burned. We came here with Captain Crawford only a few days ago. I am now in Crawford's company of the 2nd Battalion of the King's Royal Regiment of New York. I just got my uniform yesterday."

"When did you last see your mother?" I asked.

"I was in Backway in February. Maw never talked about you. Uncle Ari told me that she would never leave her home in Backway. She still has Catharina and Hanna with her, who help with caring for little Rena and the two boys. Willem is anxious to be old enough to fight. Hanna told me she would join you when she was older."

As we continued to toss pebbles into the river, I told him of Bennington and Fort Ticonderoga, and that I had been mostly cutting trees and building forts and a canal since being in the army. I said nothing about Red Feathers.

The days passed with drills and training. The fortification work, including bomb shelters that the new commander, Major Ross, had had built was complete. The inactivity brought thoughts of Red Feathers and I carried in my heart bereavement for a lost companion.

It was evident that a major raid was being planned. Messengers were moving between our fort, Fort Niagara, and Sorel. There was a large force of soldiers at the fort, obviously preparing for something before the winter closed the river and the lake. Being in a state of melancholy, I went to see Captain Leake to request assignment to a combat squad. The captain and I had been together since the beginning of my sojourn in Canada and I was reasonably hopeful he would look with favour on my request.

My last request to Captain Leake had been to be assigned to engineering duties, so he was surprised that I wished now to fight. He was not sure he could grant my request. He asked me my age and on being told, he frowned and asked, "Why do you want to do this?"

I had no answer, but I had to say something,

"I have been an artificer most of the time after Bennington, and sir, I need a change. There is only garrison duty here for me with, I believe, very little likelihood of the fort being attacked by the rebels. Besides, my son is here with Lieutenant Crawford and if we are going on a raid, Crawford has a company of young men and he lived in the Valley, so he will likely lead the expedition. I would like to be with my son in this."

"Sergeant," he said with a slight smile, "you are being insubordinate in telling me we are going on a raid. We are not in combat now, so I cannot assign you to a combat role. If what you say comes about, I will consider your request. But I tell you, you are not young anymore and I think your wishes are getting ahead of your bones. Take my advice and sit tight."

"Sir."

"Right! Now go back to your barracks and think it over. I might consider your request when the time comes if you still are of the same mind as of now. Dismissed."

"Yes, sir."

I left feeling pleased with what I took to be, "Permission granted."

It was a crisp morning, heavy with dew, an overnight frost stiffening the grass underfoot, when a body of regulars from the 34th Regiment, Provincials of the 2nd Battalion of the King's Royal Regiment of New York, and close to fifty men from Leake's company all under the command of Major Ross boarded the *Lake Queen*, a small barque, to take the force across the lake to Oswego. I was with them, as was Thomas. We were to meet similar numbers from Niagara at Oswego for a raid in the Valley. The Niagara detachment was late and did not reach Oswego until a week later. As soon as they arrived with a few Indians, we left for Lake Oneida. At Canasarago Creek, a depot was set up where four men and a small artillery piece were left to guard the provisions.

After a week of slogging in the rain and cold, with some snow, the detachment reached the Mohawk River. Two prisoners brought into camp revealed that the enemy was aware of our movements and were ready to do battle. On the upper reaches of the river all enemy targets had been destroyed either by previous raids or by abandonment. At Corrystown there were a few scattered inhabitants, and at our discovery the alarm guns were fired and runners set out to warn the militias at Fort Plain and Schenectady. Altogether, we were up against about two thousand militia and Continental troops.

Heavy rain, muddy roads, and enemy resistance took a toll on the troops and some were left behind as we marched during the night to Warrensborough, where a nest of rebels was holed up. We lay on our arms until daylight, and before noon the settlement was in flames for seven miles around. The inhabitants had fled in the night.

Although party to this sordid business, I was sickened by the destruction wrought. I found later that our troops destroyed close to one hundred farms. Crops were burned; cattle and livestock of all kinds were shot or axed. We were killing the bread and beasts of the countryside without yet engaging the enemy in a serious battle, although the rebel forces were on the march against us from every quarter, in far superior numbers to ours.

The river was swollen with rain, and enemy militia on its banks made crossing to Johnstown difficult and dangerous. The commander of Fort Johnstown came out with a party to reconnoiter. A skirmish developed and the commander was killed, but his party escaped and made it back to the fort. Pushed by the rebels advancing from our rear, we marched east to the woods, hoping to find the trail from the German Flats that would lead our force back to Carleton Island. We killed some cattle for food and took horses for transport, but our boots were not fit for the conditions, it was getting colder, and everyone was miserable.

By the late afternoon, we had advanced a small part of a mile into the woods with the rebels hot on our heels and the men were drawn up for action. The enemy advanced and when fired upon retreated, so seeing the inclination of the rebels, we were given the order to charge. Whooping and firing as fast as we could load we carried on a running battle to the edge of the wood, when suddenly the rebels broke ranks and fled. All but those on our left flank, where a field piece with a body of men kept up a brisk fire. As we turned on them, they gave way, leaving a brass three-pound cannon and ammunition behind. Our troops were tired but the battle was not over and another body on the right flank renewed their effort to kill us. We turned the cannon on them and would have destroyed them if night had not come, allowing them to escape. We retired to the woods for the night and resumed the march north the next morning. I was told later that we had been outnumbered by three to one.

Although worn out, cold, and wet, my spirits rose and I went searching for Tom. He was unhurt. His spirits were high, and he believed he had killed two rebels. Having seen many dead and mutilated men, I was not happy for him but said nothing to dampen his enthusiasm. He would learn disillusionment.

As we were crossing Canada Creek, the enemy attacked our men, killing Walter Butler. However, they did not seem inclined to pursue us further. Our losses were seventy-four men with some fifty missing. Many of the missing men gave themselves up to the rebels. Later that winter, a Loyalist came in and told us that the rebels lost forty-two men at the battle of Canada Creek.

It was a wet slog with little food, except horsemeat, on the march back to Carleton Island. No sooner had we returned than Leake's Independent Company was told it was to be disbanded. That winter, my son Tom was garrisoned at Oswego with his regiment, commissioned with the job of rebuilding the fort, and I spent many days suffering from lumbago that winter. A detachment of the 2nd Regiment of the King's Yorkers arrived in early December to replace those who went off to Oswego. In November, Captain Leake's company was disbanded and I was assigned to the Loyal Rangers of Major Edward Jessup, which, we were told, would be in charge of resettling refugees.

Word from Thomas at Oswego said the Indians there were not happy about the new orders to cease offensive activity and to prepare defenses only. Joseph Brant wanted to go on the warpath against those who had burned Mohawk villages, assaulted women, and claimed their hunting grounds for their own. The Indians were much divided, fleeing their villages and looking to the English at the fort for provisions and protection. Brant had set off with close to five hundred Indians and a detachment of light infantry under Captain Singleton before he was ordered to return to Oswego. Eight days earlier, they had attacked Fort Herkimer and captured cattle and horses, killing a few of the enemy. They went on to Fort Denton but alarm spread in the countryside and the cattle were driven into the fort for protection. They marched to German Town to round up cattle that were claimed by the Indians, who herded some off to Niagara. Thomas failed to say whether he had been with Singleton, so I believed he had fallen into my boots and was building fortifications.

I was sent to Verchères where I spent the winter helping to build houses for the refugees. They were a sick and sorry lot, often complaining about the lack of warm clothing and adequate food. It was not a pleasant experience until I learned to ignore the persistent demands put to me, since I could do nothing to improve their lot.

Looking from our barracks on the high bank, the river at Verchères was wide and gentle. Below was the old manor house of François Jarret de Verchères where his fourteen year-old daughter is said to have held off the Iroquois for a week. The manor house in her day was surrounded with a palisade, and on the day of the attack she ran to the fortified manor with two frightened soldiers and her younger brother. She is said to have taken charge, and the three of them kept up a constant fire which convinced the enemy that the fort was fully garrisoned, and in this way held off the Indians for a week until help arrived.

There was a hospital and the army was building houses to shelter those refugees from the war who were in increasing numbers coming into Canada for safety.

The people of the countryside were friendly and mostly full of life and joy. Some of them had expressed bitterness at the presence of *les anglais* and had considered themselves to be a conquered people since the end of the Seven Years' War. The habitants were mostly devoid of political interest, concerned with their homes and survival through another winter. They looked to the priest for spiritual peace and to the seigneurs for worldly sustenance. Unlike the Puritans of Massachusetts Bay, they found freedom in their hearts and had no ambition to force their ways on others.

Verchères, being midway between the trading post of Montreal and the military headquarters at Sorel, often had visitors who brought the scuttlebutt of the wider world to that small outpost.

Out of the mist of the river came the words of Lord North: "Oh God! It is all over." The ministry had resigned with the surrender of Cornwallis and word came from the new ministry to protect Canada from the French now that the thirteen colonies were essentially lost. A rumour spread of a large naval force being assembled in Brest to invade Canada. The order to the British forces in America was to cease offensive raids and to prepare the St. Lawrence ports against new aggressors. This made little difference for me, except that now that the war seemed lost, the Loyalists were dismayed, and those still left in rebel territory began to amass in large numbers to leave their homeland. The Loyal Rangers were charged with settling those who came to Canada via Lake Champlain and the Richelieu River.

Since the war was almost over, the troops were allowed to fraternize with the local people to an extent we could not have done before, due to our role as military occupiers. Being disenchanted with one another in the barracks and at meals, we were pleased to mix and mingle in the local tavern, which we could do as long as we carried on peacefully without fights or violent talk. After a few evenings at the tavern, I began to notice an old man who sat in a dark corner furthest away from the tavern keeper's scene of operations. One evening I carried my rum to the board where he was sitting and asked if I could sit. His eyes lifted from a keen examination of the floor and he muttered, "*Oui.*" I told my name and my reason for being at this place in English, hoping that he could speak either German or English. He responded in English, "I am Ulysse. I am from Acadie. Your enemy is my enemy but your friend is not my friend." With this confusing statement, he again looked at the floor and said no more.

To entice him to continue I said, "You seem to be like me, a man without a country. We are no different, my country is now taken from me by my former neighbours."

"My country," he said, "was taken from me by those same people. Mine was a land made fertile by the hands of an ancestor whose name I bear. Because we wished only peace and would not take up arms against either the English of Massachusetts Bay or the French of Quebec, we were exiled. For many years the English would not leave us in peace, but they would not let us go to other lands. Some families escaped to Isle St. Jean but I thought our family was safe. One day they came to our church and told us they were taking our lands and we were being taken away from our homes. At Grand Pré, they loaded us into ships and burned our farms. My family was taken from my bosom and dragged into one ship, and I into a different ship. The young men were separated and held hostage to keep the rest of the people under control. I have not seen my children since that awful day."

Ulysse was close to weeping. He buried his head in his hands and shook with deep sobs. I quietly removed myself from his presence, sad that I had provoked his remorse. His history sounded like mine. I had to learn more of it. Two nights later, my new friend Ulysse was in his old place in the dark corner of the tavern. Again, I sat with him hoping to hear more of his story. He greeted me with, "*Bonsoir,*" and then said, "Hello," in English. For a few minutes we talked about the very cold weather. Finally, curiosity getting the better of me, I said, "The last time we talked you were put on an English ship at Grand Pré."

"*Oui.* They pushed me down a hole into the bowels of the ship. It was dark and wet with only a grate above that let in light and air. We were kept below for several days with the ship rolling and jumping. People were sick and one old man died. The stink became unbearable. The smell of that dungeon is the thing I will remember all my life." Ulysse stopped talking and drew a breath as if to smell the air in the tavern and relive his horror.

"When they finally brought us up into the sunlight we were at anchor in a place called Norwich. Ships had brought a great number of Acadian souls to this port, and I had hope that this was where the rest of my family had been taken. A score of men with some wives and children were herded from the ship and taken ashore. This was to be our new home. The villagers, the 'French neutrals,' did what they could for us. They sent some to parishes in the vicinity and the church people tried to locate lost family members, especially children. The selectmen were not too pleased, fearing we would become a public charge.

"I was placed with an older parish couple, and a Mr. Bournes acquired a job in the shipyard for me. Soon, however, I shipped aboard a trading schooner plying the New England and the southern coasts as well as the West Indies, in the hope that I could find news of my family in the parts we visited. For two years I searched in port after port but found no word of my family. It was as if they had disappeared into thin air.

"By and by the Acadians of Norwich, New Haven, Boston, and New York began to be aware of each other's presence, and after ten years of knocking about I fell in with a group of families who were determined to return to Acadie. We trekked north as far as La Prairie only to find that our farms, farms that we literally made possible with bare hands, had been turned over to New England planters. My country is no more. It is now in the hands of Yankees but not in the soul of Yankees."

He became very upset at the loss of all that he, his father, and his grandfather before him had wrought. After a pause for a draught, he continued his story.

"I found here in Verchères a cousin. His wife agreed to take me in and I have been in this place for over one year now. I will die here. I will never see my family or my house in Acadie."

A cruel story. I went home with the thought that men in power had wrought cruelty on many. Red Feather's people had also suffered like those of old Ulysse, the man from Acadie.

An arrangement was made between General Haldimand and Monsieur Gugy, his friend from former days, to use the Machiche seigneury as a settlement for refugees, so the rest of the war for the Loyal Rangers consisted of building houses and performing garrison duties at blockhouses beside the Yamaska River. At Machiche that winter, I went through the ice on the river and came down with chills and the lung disease. For weeks, I suffered the indignity of a nurse slapping mustard plasters on my chest.

Army secrets soon became rumours, especially in the quiet of winter. Mid-February, troops were set out to practice snowshoeing, causing rumours of an attack on the posts of Lake Champlain. Thomas, at Oswego, wrote me that a large force of rebels attempted the fort but soon retreated. He was sent out with about two score men to encircle the enemy and harass them in their retreat. Not one of our troops was injured and the troops returned in eight days, proud of their victory. Thomas complained that the blockhouse where he was quartered had sprung leaks and made his nights very uncomfortable. Apparently, the attack on the Lake Champlain ports was an attempt at a feint, if indeed it was intended at all.

Britain had lost its thirteen colonies to the south of the St. Lawrence River, Lake Ontario, and Lake Erie; but there was no attack by the French Navy that the governor had been expecting. Peace proposals were being discussed at the highest levels, but life in the field had not changed much. The forts on Carleton Island and Oswego were likely to be abandoned, but the 2nd Regiment of the King's Royal Yorkers set to work rebuilding Fort Cataraqui. Carleton Island, it was believed, would be turned over to the rebels when peace was finally agreed upon. All my work there was for naught.

A tragedy and a waste had been visited upon the innocent people of America. Good and true men had been killed or crippled for life, families had been destroyed, homes and livelihoods lost. A people shattered in twain. A war brought on by men who used the mother country to expel the hated French from Acadie and Louisbourg and gain protection from the papist French of Canada; then rejected their king and the natural order of things. For this, I lost Red Feathers and her unborn child as well as my own wife and young children.

I was discharged from service at the end of the year. My war was over.

11

JOURNEY'S END

The last foray for me on that river of sadness began when the ice broke up in the spring of 1784. Discharged just before Yuletide, I was a refugee with no home, no farm, no wife, and missing four of my children. Red Feathers, my hope for a new life, was gone. Thomas had travelled south to the old homestead the summer before, after the shooting had stopped, to see what he could find out about my family. Thomas told me that young Willem had signed up but he knew not his whereabouts. He found Hanna who was anxious about my welfare and in the end decided to come to Canada with Thomas. Hanna was now old enough to fend for herself, and it pleased me very much that she had come to me. My life would have been very lonely indeed except for Hanna. She had always been my favourite of the girls. Thinking of Hanna bought a moment of sadness for the others, but I had hope that they would be safe once the war was over.

Thomas told me that the New York government was selling the farms confiscated during the war, and had passed a proclamation refusing residency to those who supported the Crown. Thomas, in defiance of the rebel government decree, had gone to our old home to see the situation for himself, and had found his way in and out without being caught. He told me that the people who had stayed behind were either indoctrinated with the cause of liberty, or living in fear of reprisals if they spoke the truth. Our former neighbours were hostile. He felt like an alien in his own country. He found our farm buildings burned, leaving only the house, which was not occupied. Angry at not being able to return to his former home, he set the house on fire one moonless night. From a hiding place in the woods, he watched it burn to the ground. He wanted no reward left for the rebels.

A ward of the military but no longer subject to its discipline, I was told by Captain Meyers at Rivière du Chêne to proceed to Machiche. Some forty-five men with wives and children, over two hundred souls in all, were herded into bateaux waiting at Machiche for the long journey to the lands promised us. Many of my old army mates were in the group. During my sojourn on the St. Lawrence I was thrown in with men from the New Hampshire Grants, who were now with the Rangers. Justus Sherwood was in charge of re-settling our group. He had been at Saratoga where he was taken prisoner and afterwards had become a spy. Edward Carscallen was also off somewhere spying for the English. Captain Jeptha Hawley, whose father was the founder of Arlington, a hotbed of Loyalists, was there, as was Isaac Briscoe, the former town clerk at Arlington and one of the richest men in the town. He married Jeptha's daughter, so they constituted a family. Peter Gilchrist and Conrad Sills from Butler's Rangers, along with Conrad's three sons who were with the Royal Yorkers, were in my party for the journey up the river to Cataraqui. Mrs. Hawley and her seven children added domesticity to our group.

Stopping over at Sorel and Verchères we arrived at Lachine the third night. Artificers were busy at Lachine constructing bateaux to carry refugees from the lower St. Lawrence and Richelieu Forts up the river to their new homes. One evening, shortly after we landed at Lachine, I was near Mrs. Hawley at supper. She was talking to a very handsome woman who had joined our party. They were comparing recipes for pine tar ointments for the protection of their faces from mosquitos and black flies. Mrs. Hawley was sure the best mixture was tar and castor oil, while the other woman swore by tar and sheep's tallow. I said nothing, but my thoughts were of Red Feather's concoction, which was a mixture of boiled cedar bark and lavender flowers.

While my thoughts were of Red Feathers, my eye was drawn to Mrs. Hawley's friend, whom she called Gabriella. Her face was flushed due to the heat from the fire and the passion of her discourse, but her skin was free from the ravages of the pox. She had a straight short nose over a fulsome mouth that showed straight white teeth as she talked. Sprigs of light hair crept from under the lace of her bonnet. Her eyes were dark blue and sparkled with good humour, glistening in the firelight like the reflection of a pool in a lush garden.

The discussion finished in favour of tar and castor oil, after which she rose and bid good evening to Mrs. Hawley. The light from the fire revealed that she was as high as a man and carried a straight lithe frame beneath the full costume she wore against the coolness of the evening. A very attractive woman indeed!

Our little band of discharged soldiers and Loyalist refugees set out from Lachine on the last day of May in a heavy, cold rainstorm. Although the ice had gone, the melting snow and swollen river made it a dangerous time to be pushing against the stream with the heavy loads of settler's goods. Avoiding portages meant manoeuvring the bateaux through swift, cold, and rocky rapids. A portage meant carrying the goods, provisions, and boats around the rougher parts in the rain and mud. Given the condition of the river, it was dangerous work.

The accident happened at a place where the bank was high and ran steeply from the river with a fast and powerful current. The women, children, and old men were walking on the trail above the river while the able-bodied men were working fully loaded bateaux against the stream by means of ropes from the river's edge. Suddenly, above the shouting and cursing from the haulers, a woman's scream pierced even the noise of the rapids. The scream came from the bank above and a little ahead. Looking up, I saw a young boy sprawled on the muddy slope, sliding towards the river with flailing arms and legs to try to stop his plunge into the water. I shouted to my bateau-men to hold the ropes tight and struck out over the slippery rocks to block his entry into the rushing stream, but I was afraid I would not reach the spot in time. The next time I was able to look up the bank, I saw he had been caught in a clump of willow bushes which arrested his fall about a dozen feet above the river's edge.

Then Hawley was beside me, scrambling up the slope, but the footing being wet and soft, he was not able to reach the boy. By giving him a boost, Jeptha was able to reach the bushes and pull himself to the boy. Grabbing him by one arm, the two of them slid to the river's edge. The boy was cut and bruised, but remarkably for his young age, he was very calm and showed no tears. A shout came from above: "Alexander, Alexander! Oh! Thank God!" I saw the face that I had admired at Lachine. Jeptha carried the boy along the river shore to a place where the bank was not high and delivered him to a very grateful and tearful mother. I was worried about the boats, so I rushed back and took my place on the towrope.

At Coteau-du-Lac we camped to rest and dry out before entering the lake. The next day I paid some attention to my appearance and went along the familiar path to the place where Red Feathers and I had spent many memorable weeks. At first, I could not find our former shelter, it being overcome with snow and fallen willow branches. In the three years away from this place, nature had taken back the clearing as if the hand of man had not been here. To me it was sacred, as sacred as the great church in Poppenweiler that my parents took me to when I was a very young boy. People might have considered Red Feathers a heathen, but for a short time she had filled my heart with joy. In my awkward way I said a prayer for her spirit.

Not seeing Alexander's mother in camp, nor the boy, I enquired of Mrs. Hawley of their whereabouts, with the excuse that I wished to seek the welfare of the boy. "Oh," she said, "Gabriella has come here to live with her son. He has property and is building a house. She has come to live with him as she is now a widow."

To the north of the barracks a large clearing had provided logs for a few cabins that were in different stages of construction. Mrs. Hawley had told me the site of the house where Gabriella was living, which I found with little difficulty. The house itself was finished and announced its completion by sprouts of plants beginning to emerge from the soft ground near the doorway. An outbuilding was in the beginning stages. No one was about.

She came to the door at my knock. I could see her beauty more completely in daylight than I had been able to by the light of the fire in Lachine.

"How is your son?"

"He has gone to stores to get flour. Oh! You mean Alexander. Are you not the one who saved him from drowning?"

"Well, I do not know if he would have drowned, I was concerned about his bones and bruises."

"Oh, but I am so thankful. Come in and have tea. Alexander is out back, searching for frogs."

The cabin was quite large with two rooms and a loft. The main room was sparse with no evidence of the woman's touch except the succulent smells wafting from the hearth. She went to capture Alexander for my inspection. Soon she returned and placed the boy in front of me.

"How are you Alexander?" I asked.

"Thank you, sir, for rescuing me. I slipped in the mud and fell."

"Do you hurt?"

"My arm is sore, see here. Goodbye, sir."

And, with boyhood reluctance to talk with adult males, preferring to talk to frogs, he left our presence. Meantime, Gabriella had been preparing tea and brought it to the board, which took up a large part of the main room.

"I take it you will be living here with your son from the army."

"Yes, until John, he's a captain in Montreal, gets young Alexander and me settled. John was my husband's brother." After a pause, which brought grief to her eyes, she continued, "My Simon was at Bennington. He was a good man. Did you know him?"

"Yes, he signed up with Burgoyne, but I did not know him well. I think he was lost at Bennington."

"The monsters took him captive to Albany and tortured the life from him. My son William went off with him and, thank God, he survived. This is his house."

"I knew William, he was in my regiment, the Loyal Volunteers. You lived, I think, over near Bennington from me. I had a farm on the Hoosick Road. It's all gone now, burned to the ground."

"In the fight between the Yankees and Yorkers over land title we lost almost half of our farm even before the war. My husband was very loyal to the Crown and joined Burgoyne. He lost his life for the King, leaving me a widow with young children to bring up. Alexander is the youngest."

"Well," I said. "He seems like a clever boy. He should do well."

"I am hoping John looks after his education. John thinks he can get him apprenticed with the North West Company. After all, it's in his family."

She was fidgeting on her chair and playing with her teacup. I sensed she wished to get on with her day's chores, so hoping to engage her longer I said, "He's a smart young lad, is Alexander, and I expect he will do well in the fur trade, may even become famous."

The tea was now cold. She rose and again thanked me profusely for, "saving my boy from a watery grave," but it was clear the discussion was at an end. Reluctantly, I got up from my seat and said, "I wanted to ask after your son. I see he has already put it out of his mind. I am pleased that he was not badly hurt." She said, "Thank you for your concern. I am sure he will forget about it soon." I bowed slightly, and left her presence. Another loss.

At the Long Sault, I asked to be put ashore to visit Red Feathers. The stone cairn that held her spirit was still complete, the stones being heavy enough not to be disturbed by wolves and bears, but there was some evidence of small animals living with her soul. This seemed fine, since she had been at one with all the creatures of the earth and sky. I took from my belt a turkey feather that I had found in Coteau-du-Lac and placed it between two stones. Straightening the weathered cross, I left her forever.

The flotilla of settlers put in at New Town and camped there, while a few regulars that were travelling with the settlers went on to Oswegatchie. At New Town, Justus Sherwood and Edward Jessup, who were organizing the settlement along the river, met us. Peter Gilchrist and others left us there to take up farms on that section of the river.

Tom and Hanna were not at Fort Haldimand as I had expected. His regiment had moved to Cataraqui to rebuild the fortifications of the ruined Fort Frontenac.

I spent some days on Carleton Island. The fort had both happy and sad memories; happy because of my time there with Red Feathers, and sad because she did not feel at home at the fort because of the Mississauga. One day I was introduced to Molly Brant, a handsome and a formidable presence because she and her brother Joseph had kept the Indians allied with the British in spite of their deep-seated feelings of betrayal by the King. She was the type to whom stories attach themselves. One story was that Molly, while at Niagara wanted Colonel Butler to give her a rebel prisoner's head to kick about the fort. Another story had her persuading Philip Schuyler's mistress to leave him, which she did, giving the English many rebel secrets. I felt it unfortunate that Molly Brant had not been at the fort to help Red Feathers fit in when she was there with me.

All was quiet at Carleton Island in the spring of 1784. Since the island was in the centre of the river, no one knew on which side of the border it would fall in the final peace treaty. General Haldimand, while refusing to accept that it would go to the enemy, reduced the garrison from over seven hundred men to one lieutenant and twenty-four men. The barracks and stores were kept intact.

Fort Cataraqui was to be the new post to deny the enemy access to the river. We arrived on June 26, 1784. Hanna, now seventeen was a young woman with the looks and grace of her grandmother Margaretha. A reunion with Hanna and Tom brought me news of their lives since I last saw them. Tom had been busy working on the fort, building a sawmill and gristmill, houses for Joseph and Molly Brant as well as finishing naval storage facilities. His regiment had been discharged earlier in June.

Some of the settlers were complaining of the wait, fearing they would not be able to get crops in that season. No turnip seed had yet arrived, and there was no wheat seed. More Loyalists were arriving, putting a great burden on the Post to provide food and clothing for both the settlers and the troops. Some had no blankets. Traders issued paper money and refused to redeem it in cash. The engineer paid the artificers in his own paper money, but the people who received it did not think it as valuable as cash. Only half the families had axes and hoes. General despair was rampant, and disputes were breaking out continually. Thieves abounded. By September, some settlers were being placed on the lower parts of the river and were able to transport sawn timber from the mill.

On the 17th of September lots were drawn. There was much confusion about assignment of lots. Some of Jessup's Rangers were assigned to lots in what were called the Royal townships down river beyond Carleton Island. The rest were to go to the Cataraqui townships that were strung along the north shore of the lake as far as a bay the French called *Lac du Kenté*. Captain Crawford had gone out the year before and made arrangements with the Mississauga chiefs for lands to settle Provincial regiments of the army. Cousin Sergeant Jacob and son Thomas were headed for township Cataraqui #3 and I was able to get permission to draw a lot in the same township.

Each family was given a short-handled axe, a hatchet, a tent, a spade, a hoe, a cow, a plough to be shared with another family, and a tool kit to be shared with four other families. When we finally left Cataraqui the air was crisp after a summer of high heat and humidity. The hardwoods were a blaze of colour against a backdrop of the dark green of the pine trees. I accompanied Thomas and Hanna, Sills, Hawley, Luke Carscallen and cousin Sergeant Jacob. Captain Crawford, who had bought the land from the Mississauga Indians, was the leader of our flotilla of several bateaux with soldiers, women, and children. Some of the men, who had gone through many dangers in the war, feared for their lives from the waves that sometimes splashed over the bow of the bateau. They kept a close eye on shore, no doubt judging the distance in case they were swamped and had to swim, although I suspect few could swim even if their lives depended on it. The St. Lawrence River, where I had lost Red Feathers, had taught me lessons about water travel, and after her drowning I had lost all fear for myself.

There was grumbling from some of the men that the cows that were coming behind on a barge would never arrive. But sink, swim, or starve in winter we had no choice in the matter, we were wards of the British military, and would have to survive the winter with whatever supplies delivered to us. The women were mostly stoic, gracefully accepting whatever fate brought their families. The young children were noisy and had to be watched so they did not bring disaster on themselves as well as the rest of us by their boisterousness.

After about two hours on the lake, hugging the shore, the initial excitement and grousing quieted and everyone turned his or her thoughts inward. Except for the occasional curse, there was little noise other than the splash of the paddles and a low murmur from the passengers. As we penetrated further into the wilderness, scouts familiar with what we called Indian country, were selected to keep a sharp eye on the woods. For fear of the Indians, Captain Crawford decided to paddle through the night, and this word was carried from bateau to bateau until everyone understood. He also decided we should move further offshore in case of an Indian attack by canoes. He felt safer there although this increased the fear of some, who found drowning more horrible than being killed with an arrow.

The anxious anticipation was for naught and about noon the next day Captain Crawford directed his bateau to the mouth of a small stream and waved the rest of the bateaux to stand off shore. His men pulled the bateau onto a very small beach, and the captain walked from the creek side to a cleared area. I could see that he was looking for something as we drifted in the direction in which we had come. After a few minutes of pacing he appeared to find what he was looking for and signalled the rest of the fleet into the mouth of the stream. The bateaux drew up on the left-hand side of the creek, which disappeared off into the trees to the north. When all were unshipped and the bateaux were secure, the captain, a lieutenant, and a sergeant gathered their charges around them in a circle and proceeded to tell us what to do. The captain spoke.

"Gentlemen, this is our new home. We have named it Cataraqui #3. Mr. Collins has laid out lots along the front and to the north around a bay where the soil is rich after the land is cleared. Just over there," he said, pointing towards the west, "Mr. Collins has laid out a town site that you will give a name in the fullness of time. Now earlier this past summer Major Rogers has allocated about two score lots along the front, a few of which are either not taken or abandoned. Some of you will have drawn lots along the front, but most will have back lots around the bay that is beyond the height of land to the north or along the *Appanee* River, which flows into a body of water the French called *Lac du Kenté*. It is said that somewhere in these lands there was once a Cayuga village whose members were massacred during the French Regime, but no one knows exactly where it was located. There is no worry now, the Indians are long gone and you will be safe here." Someone behind me said in a loud whisper, "So he says." Almost as if the captain had heard the remark, he continued. "We purchased this land fair and square from the Mississauga and they will not bother you.

"Now, I have scouted these woods, and those of you with back lots will find this stream will carry your goods inland to a rise of land where you will carry them across the rise until you find another stream, which will take you to large bay. It is an old Indian carrying place and well marked. Tomorrow I will lead you to the bay and beyond. But for tonight, there is a meadow just yonder behind that row of trees where you can pitch your tents. I expect you to be fit enough in the morning to get started on the trek to peace and permanence. Before the celebrations begin I invite you to my tent where I will have a paper showing the location of your lot. The boundary markers are numbered stakes held in place by a pile of rocks."

The next days were frustrating, confusing, and generally chaotic. Some soldiers had sold their drawn lot without informing the authorities, and so arguments broke out when someone claimed a lot that had been sold to him but the name on the paper on the captain's table did not match the claimant. Two or three had lost the paper with the lot number and had to wait until no one else claimed his drawn lot number. Cousin Sergeant Jacob had drawn lot three along the front, but Thomas and I drew back lots. There was bickering and trading all the next day and it was not until the following day that those of us on the back lots started the journey up the stream to claim a home in the Canadian wilderness.

EPILOGUE

Outside Eberhardt's cabin the leaves were falling from the trees and I could feel winter in the air when the old man finished his story. He was exhausted from his effort of the last few weeks, a task that had drained the enthusiasm he had had when he began chronicling his rough life. Eberhardt had left behind pillaged villages, men dead on the battlefield, animals slaughtered, homes burned, crops destroyed, women raped, families massacred, children set adrift, and all the terrors of hunger, cold, and fear of death that goes with war. His had been a life of action and the work of reflection had been very hard on the old man, and I feared he was near his last days.

Satisfied that I had garnered sufficient notes to make a story, and driven by the need to return to my own work after these many weeks away from the city, I prepared to leave my ancient grandfather to his ghosts. I roused him from his chair by the hearth where he had already fallen asleep and got him into his bed.

Before I left his bedside he spoke his final words to me, "Even though my eyes are dim I see my grandson that you have filled your book with my words just at the time I finish my story. Another winter is coming, which may be my last, and my wish is that you use the words to create my story so that I will not be a shadow."

Moved by the emotion expressed in his words I could only say, "I will do my best grandfather."

I waited for Mary, Tom's wife, who had taken it upon herself to keep an eye on the old man since he had refused to live with her and Tom. She visited him every day to look after his needs. When she arrived I gathered up my things, bid her a good day and left the cabin to put together a narrative that I hoped would satisfy his wishes.

A strong wind was blowing across the clearing, piling the fallen leaves against the snake rail fence. A black cloud to the west looked like snow was on its way. I looked back at the lonely cabin thankful that the old man's shadow had become my reality.

Some months passed, during which time I put down Eberhardt's story in my own words. Afterward I was anxious to see the old man with the hope of gaining his approval of what I had done. I wanted to please him, although he could be rough with me. But I did not hear his call. As much as I opened my mind and ears for some word from him, it did not come. So I set off to find him in order to relate the deliberations of my pen.

I stood on the road and looked for his cabin through the trees. But all I could see was a doe with her fawn nibbling at the grass in the clearing where I thought the cabin should be located. Thinking I was on the wrong road, I decided to investigate the site to be sure I was at the correct place. As I walked through the trees, the deer and her fawn bolted past me in flashes of white. With some difficulty I found the fallen chimney of the ruined cabin and a few rocks that had been part of the foundation. The cabin itself had collapsed into the hole that used to be a cellar and was reduced to a piled of charred and rotting logs, covered with moss and infested by ants that were gradually returning Eberhardt's labour back to nature. The fire that had consumed my grandfather's home had purged the site, which had become lush green grass and willowy bushes; fodder for the deer I had chased away.

I tramped around what used to be the crucible of Eberhardt's later life and found little evidence of his presence here. Even the cedar rails for the fences that he had spent many days building were no longer there; someone had stolen them.

Sadly, I prepared to go home. As I turned to leave, I spotted a flash of colour close to the back of the clearing. I could see a cross with what looked like red ribbons fluttering in a slight breeze that had just come up. Gingerly making my way through the grass to avoid hidden bogs, I approached the cross. Two red feathers were tied to a very old and weather-beaten stake with a drooping crossbar standing in a pile of stones that had been the anchor for a fence post. I had come to get reassurance for what I had written about Eberhardt, and here he was, but not able to re-assure me of the truthfulness of my efforts. I stood over the last corporeal remains of the man I sought, a man whose life had spanned the creation of three nations, lying in an unkempt grave in the woods alongside a ruined snake rail fence. The red feathers tied to the cross looked quite new. Someone still loved him.

ACKNOWLEDGEMENTS

O n these pages I explore the roots and historical context of a Canadian pioneer by speculating about the circumstances of his life and those of his ancestors. The story is both fact and fiction. Book one is Eberhardt Waeger's story before memory. Book two is what might have been as told in his own words. The primary characters were once real people, but I have attempted to give them a life that is fictional, but plausible. The places they lived and frequented are real places. The narrative, characterization and representation of behaviour are fiction.

For my story, I have stood on the shoulders of many people who have done primary research. More than half a century ago three men collaborated on exploring the roots of the Wagar family. Foremost is Howard Wagar who spent his retiring years wandering across Austria, Germany, the United States and Ontario, gathering material to put together a genealogy of his family before 1800. Howard's papers were generously donated to the Archives of the Lennox and Addington County Museum in Napanee, Ontario. Howard was aided in his research by Herr Egon Oertel, a German genealogist. Based on their work Mr. Paul W. Prindle produced a paper, referenced below as *Progenitors in the Württemberg Region, Germany, of the New York State Wagar-Wager-Weger Families,* compiled and produced by Paul W. Prindle, Darien, Connecticut, from data collected in Germany by Commander Howard Carlyle Wagar, USNR, Fairmont Minnesota, and by genealogist Herr Egon Oertel, Rymaunstr. 14, Oehringen, Germany. My copy of this paper was given to me by Howard Wagar and has no attribution, nor date. Mr. Prindle produced variations of the Württemberg material in 1961, 1962 and 1970. It was the work of Howard Wagar and his two collaborators, almost two generations ago that became the factual basis of Book one and part of Book two; namely Carinthia, Württemberg and Georg Waeger's life in America. I have used the artifice of a family Bible to reflect the genealogy of Eberhardt's story before memory.

My first knowledge of Eberhardt and son Thomas Wager's lives in Canada came from my father's cousin, Mrs. Rhea Allen in the form of notes prepared by C.E. Wagar, of Milwaukee, Wisconsin.

Mrs. Marilyn Stewart, a cousin who lives on the farm adjacent to the Thomas Wager grant in North Fredericksburg, Ontario, has compiled a most comprehensive genealogy of the Wager/Wagar family. Marilyn has also produced an excellent overview of Eberhardt's movements during his military service in Canada. My heartfelt thanks to Marilyn for her research results.

Having been privileged to have these documents before me, I took it to be my job to put some flesh on the bare bones of the family lineage. I alone must bear full responsibility for any miss-interpretation of the work of those people named above.

Several other people who have contributed to this project deserve my sincere thanks and appreciation: my daughter Susan who, faced with a high school project, first got me interested in finding my roots; Rebecca Fraser for her instruction on the rudiments of weaving techniques, and for providing several useful books from her personable library and that of the United Empire Loyalist's library; Jane Foster for her co-operation in allowing me access to the Archives of the Lennox and Addington museum at Napanee; Cora Reid for her help in many ways; Allen Brooks for passing on his mountain experience and his knowledge of Montreal; Linda Nygard for her always quick willingness to probe the mysteries of the Internet; Wendy Cosby for her copy of the Richard Montgomery letters; to Mrs. McChesney, Archivist for Center Brunswick, Albany County, New York for helping me get started on Eberhardt's history after spending a frustrating day in the area getting nowhere. Thanks also goes to Mrs. Nancy Kelly, Town Historian of Rhinebeck, New York; Dr. Prof. Wayne Kirk (now deceased) for his copies of letters and diaries; Aline Seywald for some translations from German; to Barbara and Wally Trotzki for insights into growing up in Germany; and to Duncan Hough who kindly took me in his tractor on a rainy afternoon, through overgrown fields to the grave site of William Wager, Eberhardt's son.

A special thanks goes to my wife Janet, who good-naturedly put up with my obsession over this project off and on for several years, and who typed some of the chapters. And to David and Ethel Bews for room and board while doing research in the Napanee area. Many thanks to Louise Oborne who reviewed an earlier manuscript; to Maya Merrick, who edited a very rough manuscript; and to Andy Brown of Conundrum Press; all for turning my scribbling's into something that might be of interest to others.

END NOTES

For those whose interest is the documented story I offer these background notes with references.

PROLOGUE

Cataraqui #3, the place where Eberhardt Waeger settled in 1784 was in the 17th Century the site of a Cayuga village whose exact location is unknown. We know that it existed because it became a mission and has been mentioned in various historical documents. The place at which the Ojibwa, and later the Iroquois pitched their wigwams was on the body of water the French called *Lac du Kenté*, and later, the English called the Bay of Quinte. These early people lived in two villages, Kenté and Ganneious, the location of both in doubt since no reliable archaeological evidence has, as yet, been found. (Herrington suggests that there may be traces of the foundation of a building erected by Father Fenlon near the entrance to the Napanee River on the North Fredericksburg side.) Historians have placed Ganneious at several locations; the site of the existing town or near Napanee;[1] on the north-western tip of the peninsula we now call North Fredericksburg;[2] at the head of Hay Bay;[3] just west of the planned townsite of Fredericksburg, now the village of Sandhurst.[4] Old maps locate the site of Ganeydoes/Gannejouts/Ganeous on a water passage from Lake Ontario, with a large body of water behind the village.[5,6,7] One interpretation of these maps is to assume that the site of Ganneious/Gannejouts was somewhere at the end of the Long Reach, perhaps on one of the coves near the present hamlet of Dorland–or on the site mentioned by Herrington–accessible through the Upper Gap, Adolphus Reach, and Long Reach, which could have seemed to the early explorers to be a large river. The lake indicated on the maps may be Hay Bay since there are no large bodies of water upstream of Napanee on the Napanee River. However Gannejouts may in fact be a village on Moira Lake or Beaver Lake or Varty Lake, depending on which river one ascends, the Moira, the Salmon or the Napanee River. But since there are no other Indian villages with a name that sounds close to Ganneious/Gannejouts, or any of the other names that are referred to in the references, I assume these references all refer to a unique village. The culture was a nomadic one, and perhaps one tribe lived at all these locations at different times. Whatever the actual location it seems clear that Ganneious was somewhere within the area that Governor Haldimand had had surveyed as Cataraqui #3 in the year 1783. By then the area had reverted to wilderness, with no white men and few, if any, native people occupying the land.

The place where Hehsot the Cayuga warrior beached his canoe is on the next lot east of St. Paul's Anglican Church, Sandhurst, Ontario. According to the research of Ruth M Wright this is where the settlers of the 2nd Battalion of the Kings

Royal Regiment of New York came ashore to claim their lots.[8] A sizable stream able to accommodate bateaux existed at the time of settlement and was used as an Indian portage from Lake Ontario to Hay Bay. Mrs. Wright states, "In 1687 the French used the same route to conquer the Cayuga village of Genneious on the north shore of Hay Bay." Today the stream is dry.

Although Margaretha's Bible is an artifice I understand an actual family Bible, written in German, does exist.

1. *Multicultural Canada Encyclopaedia*. www.multiculturalcanada.ca.

2. *History of the County of Lennox and Addington*. Walter S. Herrington, Mica Press, Belleville, 1972. p.7.

3. *Hans Waltermeyer*. Jane Bennett Goddard, Self-published, 1980. She gives several possible names for Ganneious: Gaungouts or Gunaroutes or Ganeydoes.

4. *Count Frontenac and New France under Louis XIV*. Francis Parkman, Beacon Press, Boston, 1966. p.140 (footnote 2)(Parkman gives an alternate name of Ganéyout.)

5. *Historical Atlas of Canada*. Derek Hayes, Douglas and McIntyre, Vancouver, 2002. (See Map 168 by John Mitchell dated 1775 on page 124. It gives the village name as Ganeydoes.)

6. *Historical Atlas of Canada*. (See, French Fur Trade Empire, by Henri Chatelain, dated 1719. Map p. 85.)(On this map the village is called Ganeous.)

7. *The Cartography of North America 1500-1800*. Pier Luigi Portiaro and Franco Knirsch, Crescent Books, New York, 1987. (See map, Carte du Theatre de la Guerre entre les Anglais et les Americains, by Brion de la Tour, Paris, 1777, on p.251.) (On this map the spelling is Gannejouts.)

8. *The Front of South Fredericksburgh*. Ruth M. Wright, The South Fredericksburgh Heritage Committee, 1999, p.4.

1: JÖRG: THE WARRIOR

Jörg and his son Hans of our story are hypothetical characters whose existence and life's experiences are based on the few facts I know from the official records of the state of Kärnten, Austria, as documented on two sheets of the Howard Wager papers housed at the Archives of the Lennox and Addington County museum, Napanee, Ontario.[1,2,3,4] It appears that a man called Jacobs gut des Unterweger lived near Radenthein between the years 1335 and 1414. Jacobs is followed by generations of a family or families called Unterweger or Weger, all living close to Radenthein, specifically in a farm area above Radenthein, on the slope of the Preidrof, called Schrott.

The genealogical record for the family line begins with a Georg or Jörg who is believed to have resided at Schrott in the year 1564. From Georg/Jörg comes Benedict and Kaspar. Kaspar and his wife Ursula have five boys and two girls; Eva, Gertrut, Erasmus, Florian, Balthauser, Thoman and Reupert. The Weger house located at Schrott No. 7 was apparently destroyed by fire in May 1971. It was "probably" 300 years old.[5] The Landhaus Archives in Klagenfurt give this site as the home of Thomas Weger and his father Kaspar Weger. The house was located

1.25 miles from St. Peter on the mountainside; above Radenthein and twelve miles from Spital am Drau. From what we know of the period that Kaspar and his sons lived, it is possible that one of Kaspar's sons (perhaps Thoman) could be a model for Jörg's adventures during the expulsion of Protestants from Upper Carinthia, and the Thirty Years War, which broke out in 1618.

The record[4] shows that Kaspar's son Thoman, who in 1647 was deceased, had a son Georg who was married in the year 1648 at Zell unter Aichelberg, which is in Württemberg. In the narrative I have created a story that speculates on the possible migration of Georg (Hans in my story) from Spital am Drau to Zell unter Aichelberg.[6]

The venue of the story of Jörg's family is Upper Carinthia, part of the Austrian state of Kärnten, which was in 1620 inhabited by farmers, miners, herdsmen, and woodsmen. They kept small herds but were not hunters. Families were self-sufficient, but did carry on trade, sometimes over long distances. They appeared to have few weapons implying a peaceful, democratic nature.[7] I have assumed this nature was carried through the generations, and was one of the reasons Eberhardt resisted the American experiment.

During the 16th century, Carinthia was caught in the struggle between emerging Protestantism and the Roman Church. In 1579 the archdukes of Tyrol and Styria meeting secretly with the duke of Bavaria decided to make no more concessions to the Protestants. In 1595 the young Ferdinand II returned to Styria from a Jesuit education, and in 1599 a special Reformation Commission began to close Lutheran institutions. About 2500 prominent Protestants were expelled, many of whom were exiled to Bohemia. Many brutal atrocities were committed.[8]

Even before his ascension, Ferdinand invaded Bohemia, a hot bed of Protestant revolt. This action started the ruthless violence of the Thirty Years' War in 1618.[9-16]

Our character Jörg was born during the Counter-Reformation period. As Jörg was reaching manhood many people were leaving the region. It is generally assumed that it was because of religious persecution, but probably the reasons are more complex. Jörg was adventurous. His brother, Erasmus was to inherit the farm[4]. His wife and the mother of his child had died. He realized he was not fit for domestic life. The Church was violently reclaiming its traditional authority. The soldier's life was both an escape and an opportunity.

The battles of White Mountain and Wimpfen[9] that Jörg finds himself, took place between the years 1620 and 1623 in the Thirty Years War, a succession of small wars throughout the Holy Roman Empire that eventually involved France and Sweden. Millions perished with the slaughter on the battlefields, and in the towns and villages the destruction was wanton and enormous. Besides the destruction wrought directly by the armies, the war exacerbated famine and disease. During the period of the war, plague ravaged town and country alike, crops and forage were burned, and combined with mother and infant mortality the lot of the citizen and peasant was unremittingly brutal. Germany lost a large part of its population dead and most of its villages and towns destroyed. There is still much controversy about the destruction caused by the war. Wedgwood writes, "In Germany the war was an unmitigated catastrophe. In Europe it was equally, although in a different way catastrophic."[9,p.18] A recent book by Helfferich speculates that "as much as a quarter of the Empire's population may have perished."[16, p.XIX] Wilson, in his monumental work on the war points out the difficulties of estimating the true destruction, suggesting that some accounts before 1900 describe the horrors of the war as a "Gothic atrocity narrative" that overstates the effects.[16,p.780] He found that some areas increased in population during the period spanning the war, such a Carinthia, while others such as the Bohemian lands had losses as high as thirty percent of the population.[16,p.788] Overall, recent estimates of population loss is 15-20%. But as Wilson points out: "Even a 15% decline would make The Thirty Years War the most destructive conflict in European history."[16,p.787] As a percentage of the European populations the First and Second Word War losses were 5.5% and 6.0%, respectively. The Soviet Union, suffering the highest casualties in the Second World War, lost less than 12% of its population.[16,p.787] But in truth statistics are abstractions of the horrors, brutality and suffering of the people affected. One must read the personal accounts of the time to get a true picture of the horrors of the War.[11,15]

The Peace of Westphalia (1648) brought the war to its end and ushered in a new, modern era for Europe.

1. *Die Kärntner Geschichtsquellen.* Herman Wiessner, 1335-1414.

2. *Kärntner Landesarchiv-Klangenfurt-Karnten-Austria.*

3. *Katalog der Allegemeinen Handschriften-Sammlung nach Orten u Herrschaften, Millstätt Section 61/1.*

4. *Records of Evangelical Church, Zell unter Aichelberg, Wüttemberg, Germany*

5. Letter to the author from Howard Wager dated June, 1980.

6. *Progenitors in the Württemberg Region, Germany, of the New York State Wagar-Wager-Weger Families.* Compiled and produced by Paul W. Prindle, Darien, Connecticut, from data collected in Germany by Commander Howard Carlyle Wagar, USNR, Fairmont Minnesota, and by Genealogist Herr Egon Oertel, Rymaunstr. 14, Oehringen, Germany.

7. *The Dawn of European Civilization.* V. Gordon Childe, Paladin, 1973.

8. *The Hapsburg and Hohenzollern Dynasties.* C A Macartney (ed.) Harper and Row, 1970.

9. *The Thirty Years War.* C.V. Wedgwood, Penguin Books, 1938. The battle of White Mountain, pp. 113-16; The battle of Wimpfen, pp.136-7. Wedgwood called the war "The Futile and Meaningless War" in an essay in *The Thirty Years War: Problems of Motive, Extent, and Effect.* Theodore K. Rabb (ed), D.C.Heath and Company, Boston, 1964 p.18.

10. *History of the Thirty Years War.* Vol.1 Anton Gindely, Richard Bentley and Son, 1885. (Excellent etchings of some of the battles.)

11. *Germany in the Thirty Years War.* Gerhard Benecke, Edward Arnold, 1978. (Some first hand accounts of the tragedies of the war.)

12. *The Thirty Years War.* Geoffrey Parker, Routledge and Kegan Paul, 1984. (Maps and chronology of the battles.)

13. *German Villages in Crisis; Rural life in Hesse-Kassel and the Thirty Years War.* John C. Theibault, (Domestic reports of tragic effects of the war.)

14. *The Thirty years War.* Charles Blitzer in "Age of Kings", Time-Life Books, New York, 1967, pp.50-53 (Graphic images of war called the "Miseries and Misfortunes of War", etchings by Jacques Callot, 1633.)

15. *The Thirty Years War: A Documentary History.* Trynte Helfferich (ed.), Hacket Publishing Company, 2009. (Contains a brief account of the war between 1618 and 1623 and the Battle of White Mountain. He translates first hand accounts of the tragedies befalling people during the war.)

16. *Europe's Tragedy; A History of The Thirty years War.* Peter H. Wilson, Belknap-Harvard University Press, 2009.

2: HANS: THE REFUGEE

The effects of the Counter-Reformation on the Protestants of Carinthia in the time of Ferdinand II, are described in a set of grievances written by an *Austrian Evangelicall Committee and Ambassadours* in 1620. The pamphlet lists such concerns as: teachers banished; church burying grounds dug up and coffins burned; holy books burned; many thousands of people tortured; families banished from the Country with short notice and without compensation for the property abandoned; and other "most terrible, inhumane, and barbarian tyrannies."[1] Hans re-lives this scene in his delirium in Munich.

In my story Hans is kidnapped by the military; escapes and becomes a salt miner.

The Celts and Romans developed the salt mines around Hallein, Hallstatt, Ishl, Aussee and generally in the larger region called Salzkammergut, in the eastern part of what was in the middle ages called the Bishopric of Salzburg. Close to the town of Salzburg there were large salt works exploiting the mines in the Dürnberg, Reichenhall, Berchtesgaden and Hallein. Etchings of early methods show miners bringing the salt in wheelbarrow-like carts out of the mine at Dürnberg. Kurlansky in his book on the history of salt gives a description of the salt mining methods in the area of Salzburg.[2]

Hans joins a salt train destined for Munich, where he falls in love, and contracts the plague. In 1634-35 Bubonic Plague killed about one-third of Munich's population.[3] A fictional description of the symptoms of the Bubonic Plague that appear accurate can be found in "Forever Amber."[4]

The Howard Wagar papers indicate that a man called Georg Waeger was married in Zell unter Aichelberg in the year 1648.[5] Church records there show that he was a son of "Thomas Waeger from Spital in Bishopric of Salzburg" I have created the fictional stories of Jörg (Thoman) and Hans (Georg) to tell how this connection might have come about. I have assumed that Georg Waeger came from Spital am Drau, married a local girl, Margaretha from Zell, in 1648. Georg and Margaretha's eighth child, Leonardt was born in 1665. He was Eberhardt Waeger's grandfather. Leonard married Anna Catherina and they had a son christened Hans Jörg who was called Georg, born in Zell in 1696. Think of him as Georg 2nd. He was Eberhardt's father.

1. Pamphlet in Bodleian Library, Oxford. Reprinted in *The Hapsburg and the Hohenzollern Dynasties in the Seventeenth and Eighteenth Centuries*. C. A. Macartney, (ed.) Harper, New York, 1970, pp.14-22.

2. *Salt: A World History*. Mark Kurlansky, Vintage, 2002, p.164.

3. *History*. Wikipedia website for Munich.

4. *Forever Amber*. Kathleen Windsor, Signet Books, 1944 and 1971, p. 368.

5. *Progenitors in the Württemberg Region, Germany, of the New York State Wagar-Wager-Weger Families*. Compiled and produced by Paul W. Prindle, Darien, Connecticut, from data collected in Germany by Commander Howard Carlyle Wagar, USNR, Fairmont Minnesota, and by Genealogist Herr Egon Oertel, Rymaunstr. 14, Oehringen, Germany.

3: GEORG: THE NOMAD

Sometime after the birth of Georg 2nd, Leonardt and Anna Catherina moved to Poppenweiler, where Leonardt was known as a citizen and tailor. Poppenweiler, a borough of Ludwigsburg, is an attractive village high above the Neckar River on the eastern side just south of Marbach. Poppenweiler sits on the edge of an agricultural plateau which stretches to the north and east of the village. To the west are vine covered slopes that end at the river. The Ludwigsburg area was becoming industrialized, particularly textiles and the production of Hock wines. Why the family moved to Poppenweiler is not clear, but we can surmise, since the family was involved in the cloth trades, that they moved at least in part for economic reasons.

Of the decendants of Georg Weger of Spital am Drau, Leonardt may have been the only one in the family to migrate to the Heilbronn/Marbach/Ludwigsburg region of Württemberg, although the next generation of Waegers inhabited many of the towns in Württemberg, and were successful in different trades. After moving to Poppenweiler Leonardt and Catherina had five more children. Beside Georg, Eberhardt's father, the story follows the life of his younger brother, Johann Leonardt who was born in 1705 and who goes to America with his older brother in 1738.

Georg and Leonardt and their two brothers Bernardt and Jacob were growing up in a time of great upheaval in Europe. Louis IV was trying to control the Spanish Hapsburgs and re-Catholicsize the peoples of the Rhineland. Louis' goal was to establish France's geographical boundaries to the Rhine and beyond, the Alps, the Pyrenees, and the Atlantic.[1] Between the end of the Thirty Years war and the birth of Georg in 1696 there were several wars, the Palatinate being a prime target of Louis. It was the War of the Spanish Succesion that brought the Duke of Marlborough at the head of an allied army that young Georg experienced while working in the vineyard. The Allied army marched across Württemberg to the battle of Blenheim.[2] Mundelsheim, where Marlborough encamped and met up with his Protestant allies, is some twelve miles from Poppenweiler along the riverbank. It is possible that this large army of British, Italian, and German troopers passed close by the village. If the army left the Neckar river it would involve ascending the escarpment at Marbach, so one could speculate that it kept as close to the river as possible.

Georg marries Maria Ernst in 1717, which ends in divorce.[3] The record indicates that Georg then married Sarah Bayhe of Smellenhof at Wüstenrot in 1724.[3] His second marriage to Sarah results in the survival of one child, and her death at age twenty-eight, shortly after the third child is born. The story of Georg as an itinerant weaver,[4,5] his time at Schmellenhof, and the circumstances leading to his marriage to Sarah is speculative fiction. The letter cited in the narrative by Jacob, Georg's brother, supposedly received from a relative who had gone to Pennsylvania consists of excerpts from an actual letter from Johann Jacob Weeger to his uncle dated at Albany County, New York, September 27, 1767.[3]

The attempt by Sarah to gain her inheritance was inspired by the story of Anna Buchler of Schwabish Hall who was illegally dis-inherited by her father in the early 1500's. The story of Anna is found in "The Bürgermeister's Daughter."[6] The letters Georg found amongst his deceased wife Sarah's effects to relatives in America are fictional letters based on concerns stated in actual letters given me by former classmate and friend Dr. Prof. Wayne Kirk, now deceased. These letters show that taxes for the support of troops, soldiers desecrating the countryside, poverty and debt were at least some of the reasons Protestant Germans migrated to America.[7] For example, the author of one letter complains about the number of heavy marches, and the great number of soldiers in the parish. This theme of supporting troops and the frightening consequence of war is a common one in the letters. Indeed, resistance to taxes, duties and church tithes by the peasants of Germany was a backdrop for several peasant revolts and the Reformation of the Church.[8,9]

Georg marries Margaretha Egermayer from Wangen, probably in 1731. Eberhardt is born in March 1732. Eberhardt's baptism ceremony is based on the modern Lutheran Book of Worship.[10]

A version of the legend of Bishop Hatto and the Mouse Tower can be found in *Germany: Myths and Legends*.[11]

Much of the description of landscape and the towns of Württemberg come from personal observation and etchings of Swabian towns as they were in mid-17th century by Mattheus Merian.[12]

---

1. *The Story of Civilization vol. VIII: The Age of Louis XIV.* Will and Ariel Durant, Simon and Schuster, New York, 1963.

2. *The Battles of Bleinheim.* Ch. 1 of "The Great Battles of all Nations", Archibald Wilberforce, Peter Fenelon Cooper, New York, 1898, pp. 386-402.

3. *Progenitors in the Württemberg Region, Germany, of the New York State Wagar-Wager-Weger Families.* Compiled and produced by Paul W. Prindle, Darien, Connecrticut, from data collected in Germany by Commander Howard Carlyle Wagar, USNR, Fairmont Minnissota, and by Genealogist Herr Egon Oertel, Rymaunstr. 14, Oehringen, Germany. n.d.

4. *The Magic of Linen: Flax seed to woven Cloth.* Linda Heinrich, Orca Books, Victoria, 1992.

5. *The Art of Weaving.* Else Regensteiner, Van Nostrand Reinhold, New York, 1970.

6. *The Burgemeister's Daughter.* Steven Ozment, Harper Collins, 1996.

7. *Voices in the Wilderness: Letters to Colonial New York From Germany (1726-1737).* Translated and Edited by F.J. Sypher, 1986, and housed at the New York State Historical Association, Cooperstown, New York. (The letters are dated at Flammersfield and Orffgen and are written by members of the Iskenius family to relatives in America.)

8. *The Germans.* Gordon A Craig, New American Library, New York, 1982. (See Ch.1, Historical Perspectives, pp. 15-34.)

9. *The German People and the Reformation.* R. Po-Chia Hsia (ed), Cornell University Press, London, 1988. (Case studies)

10. *Lutheran Book of Worship.* Augsburg Publishing House, Minneapolis, 1978.

11. *Germany: Myths and Legends.* Lewis Spence, Bracken Books, London, 1986.

12. *Topigraphia Sveviae.* Mattheus Merian, Theatrum Europeaeum, 1643.

4: MARGARETHA: CUTTING ROOTS

The fictional letter from Frieda Egermayer to Margaretha was based on an unpublished diary, compliments of Dr. Prof. Wayne Kirk of Kingston, Ontario[1].

A version of the Rhine legends that Margaretha relates to Eberhardt on the journey to Rotterdam can be found in Spence.[2]

I have used the name *Anne* for the ship that brought Eberhardt and his family to America, as documented as a possibility in "Progenitors…"[3] although I have not been able to authenticate that a ship called *Anne* could have been in service in 1738.

1. *Diary of Frederick Gottlob Mast, 1848.* Translated by Ruth Binhammer, Lauterwasser, 1968.

2. *Germany: Myths and Legends.* Lewis Spence, Bracken books, London, 1985.

3. *Progenitors in the Württemberg Region, Germany, of the New York State Wagar-Wager-Weger Families.* Compiled and produced by Paul W. Prindle, Darien, Connecrticut, from data collected in Germany by Commander Howard Carlyle Wagar, USNR, Fairmont Minnissota, and by Genealogist Herr Egon Oertel, Rymaunstr. 14, Oehringen, Germany.

5: THE SAVAGE SEA

Captain Hills' log for the voyage to America by the fictional barque *Anne* in 1738 is an adaptation of Captain James Cook's log on his first voyage to the Pacific.[1]

Description of the Azores is based largely on Joshua Slocan's single-handed circumnavigation in the late 19th century.[2]

My attempt to understand the myriad workings of an early 18th Century sailing ship comes from references.[3,4,5]

1. *The Journals of Captain James Cook on his Voyage of Discovery.* J.C.Beaglehole (ed), Hakluyt Society, series XXXVII, n.d.

2. *Sailing Alone Around the World.* Joshua Slocum, Rupert Hart-Davis, London, 1967.

3. *Square Rigged Sailing Ships.* David R MacGregor, Navasa Publications, North Vancouver, B. C., 1977.

4. *Sailing Ships of War, 1400-1860.* Frank Howard, Conway Maritime Press, Greenwich, 1979.

5. *The Arming and Fitting of English Ships of War, 1600-1815.* Brian Laverty, Conway Maritime Press, Greenwich, 1987.

6: EBERHARDT'S RHINELAND

The Esopus Indians, a tribe of the Mohegan nation, originally occupied the lands on the west side of the lower Hudson River. When the white settlers arrived, they supported the Mohegan in their wars against the Mohawks. Because of this liaison, the Mohegan's were friendly to the settlers. The Indians on the east side of the river, the place we are concerned with here, called themselves the Sepascos.[1,2]

Robert Livingston, a Scot, came to America with his father when he was nineteen. He settled in Albany, New York, and married the daughter of a Schuyler and the widow of a Van Rensselaer, two aristocratic landed families. In 1686 he received a very large grant of land confirmed by royal charter, an area that stretched twelve miles along the Hudson River and east to the Massachusetts border. The Monarch created the Livingston Manor and Robert Livingston lord of the Manor. Later his estates were confiscated, but he regained them in 1703, and in 1705 was re-instated to his many public offices.[3]

A few miles down the Hudson River the Sepascos sold over two thousand acres of land on the east side of the river to five partners, in exchange for "six buffaloes, four blankets, five kettles, four guns, five horns, five axes, ten cans of powder, eight shirts, eight pairs of stockings, forty fathoms of wampum or sewant, two drawing knives, two adzes, ten knives, half anker rum (an anker is about ten imperial gallons), one frying pan."[2, p.7] This sale was confirmed by a Royal patent in 1688 in the name of James II. The crown was to receive "forever, yearly, and every year, the quantity of eight bushels of good, sweet, merchantable winter wheat, as a quit rent, to be delivered at the city of New York, unto such officer or officers as shall from time to time be empowered to receive the same."[2, p.11]

Henry Beekman came to New Netherland in 1647 as an employee of the Dutch East India company.[2, p.10] His son, also Henry and a judge, in 1695 applied for a patent for land in Dutchess County lying opposite Esopus Creek, and known by the name of "Sespeskenot." In 1703 Queen Anne gave Henry Beekman a patent to extensive lands surrounding the land of the five partners, and in 1715 Henry Beekman Jr, his son, bought 5,541 acres adjoining his father's patent, and north of it. The Beekman's now owned the present town of Rhinebeck and part of Red Hook.[2, p.21]

It was to these lands along the Hudson River that Queen Anne brought Palatine Protestant refugees from the disease, wars and poverty that cursed the people of the German Rhineland. The story of the Palatine migration is well known and may be found in several references.[4,5,6]

Judge Henry Beekman, a friend of Robert Livingston, negotiated a deal with the Palatines to settle thirty-five families, consisting of one hundred and forty persons excluding widows and children, on his patent across the river from Kingston. They named the settlement Ryn Beck. The farms were small, some only twenty-five acres, most were fifty acres with a few of one hundred acres. The location had good soil. The tenant farmers, under life leases, were required to make all improvements and to pay an annual rent of a schepel (about ¾ bushel) of wheat to the acre, and to lose "the fruit of their toil" at the expiration of their leases. One of their first acts was to build a Church. It was a union church for both Lutherans and Calvinists and has since become known locally as the Old German Church.[1,2]

It was a generation after the Palatines arrived that Georg and his brother Leonardt with their families landed at New York destined for the now settled town of Rhinebeck. The document "Progenitors..."[7] cites the earliest court book in the archives of Poppenweiler, a borough of Ludwigsburg that contains the following statement dated February 13, 1738; "Leonhard Weger, former citizen and wine-gardener, told the court in Session that he and some other persons have the intention to emigrate to America, or to the New World." Leonard claims that he had "...paid his debts and discharged all other obligations from the proceeds of the sale of his home and other possessions...." His petition and renunciation of citizenship reads as follows, "Johan Leonhard Weger, former citizen-resident and vintner under the Poppenweiler-Marbach Administration, and his wife Catherina, nee Netherin, herewith renounce their citizenship, and that of their children, Paul and Eleanor, since they are moving into strange lands; and with them Barbara, nee Netherin, said Leonard Weeger's real sister (in-law)...."

Leonhard had sold his assets the previous year. The Taxes and Property book for Poppenweiler for the year 1737 list the transactions, "a small house and courtyard in the Rellingsgasse, 3 plots of acreage in Hochdorf, 2 plots of acreage in Erdmannhausen, 3 plots of acreage in Marbach, 4 wine-gardens, 4 meadow plots, and 1 grass and herb garden."[7] These properties were appraised at 267 Gulden, 40 Kreuzer.

The archives of the borough of Poppenweiler[7] also contain a renunciation stating that Johan Georg Weger, former citizen of Poppenweiler, has since April 18, 1737 been a citizen of Sternenfels. Georg's family at this time included his wife, Margaretha and their only surviving child, son Eberhardt.

It is not clear whether Georg had property, but since his second wife, Sarah left an estate worth 187 Florins, 16 Kreuzer at her death in 1730, it is reasonable to assume that the estate fell to her two surviving children or to Georg, or to both Georg and the children. The estate consisted of "a house and adjoining kitchen garden, away in the village between (the properties of) Hans Jerg Kolben and Jerg Fritzen, fronting the street, the rear reaching the church wall; a nearby wash and brook-house, meadows, mill acres, and carts and wagons.[7]

When the Waeger brothers arrived in New York in the fall of 1738 the community of Rhinebeck was a thriving settlement with several mills to produce flour, wool, lumber and paper. Hudson river sloops carried grain, lumber, pelts, herbs and farm produce to New York, and returned with hardware, groceries, household goods, brick, farm implements and even livestock. However, undoubtedly the biggest attraction for the Württembergers was the possibility of acquiring large land holdings. Letters flowing back to Germany at the time were full of superlatives and the beneficence of the Lord to bring them to America. The letters spoke proudly of land-holdings (largely leased at first, with quit rent paid to their landlords,) and also of their many livestock, and good crops. Many mention the abundance of wood. On the other hand, letters from Germany to America mention the imminence of another war, failing health of the elders, and a desire for freedom from taxes to support armies.

It appears Leonardt settled down and prospered on the Witaberger Lands and died there, whereas Georg seems to have lived at several locations in Dutchess County. Anna was baptized at Backway and Eberhardt was married there indicating that the family lived there for fifteen years at least. I have manufactured a farm life for Georg, although he may have been an itinerant labourer for several years after arriving in America.

The battle described in the letter Margaretha read to Niclass, from Henry to his sister, was an attempt by the English General Abercrombie to capture Fort Ticonderoga from the French General Montcalm. The battle took place during the Seven Years War, or as it was called by the English colonists the French and Indian War.[8,9] The war pitted the French and their Algonquin Indian allies against the British and her Indian allies.

A pivotal site for the French and Indian war was a place called "Tyeonderoga" by the Iroqouis, Fort Carillon by the French and Fort Ticonderoga by the British.[9] The fortification sits at the site where Lake George enters the south end of Lake Champlain. The English had pushed north as far as the south end of Lake George where they built Fort William Henry, and the French had pushed as far south as Fort St. Frédéric at Crown Point on Lake Champlain. That same year the French built a fort at the site where the restored Fort Ticonderoga now stands. It was called Fort Carillon from the sound of the falls dropping water from Lake George into Lake Champlain. The guns were removed from Fort William Henry, which Montcalm had taken in 1757 in defeating Monro, and that fort was burned to the ground, and left to decay. Fort George was built slightly east of the old fort by the English and from there in 1758 British General Abercrombie, with fifteen thousand men, more than half of these Provincials from New York, New Jersey, and New England attacked Fort Ticonderoga. Montcalm defeated Abercrombie by coming out of the fort, and meeting the British in the woods behind earthworks that his army of three thousand had constructed. The next year Jeffery Amherst with about six thousand regulars and the same number of Provincials attacked Fort Ticonderoga again for the British. This time the British took the fort, which had been much reduced from the year before.[9]

Having won the war against New France the British neglected Fort Ticonderoga, the garrison manned only by an officer and a few men. It was useful mainly for the storing of armaments, thus a prime target of Ethan Allen and Benedict Arnold in the first days of the Revolution.

The incident that Georg takes to his grave is based on the burning of New York in 1741.[10]

One of the land tenure problems for the settlers is illustrated by the Pendergrast affair, but it was only one of many similar uprisings. There were riots by farmers of North Carolina in the 1750's protesting the large grants given to speculators, who were in turn cheating the farmers with large fees. In Pennsylvania the "Paxton Boys" with about a thousand frontiersmen marched against the City of Philadelphia because they were not getting protection from the Indians. And, in New York, land speculators were evicting New Hampshire settlers causing Ethan Allen and his green mountain Boys to raise havoc along the contested border between New York and New Hampshire. There was much unhappiness in the backcountry of America because the people in the hinterland felt the towns of the Atlantic coast had taken most of the political power unto themselves.[11,12]

1. *Historic Old Rhinebeck: Echoes of Two Centuries.* Howard H. Morse, Published by the author, 1908. (Reprinted and Indexed by Arthur C.M.Kelly, 1977).

2. *History of Rhinebeck.* Edward M. Smith, Rhinebeck, New York, 1881. (Reprinted and Indexed by Arthur C.M. Kelly, 1977.) (An Appendix, p.225, describes pioneer house construction methods of the early 18th Century in the Rhinebeck area.)

3. *Robert Livingston (1654-1725).* The 20th Century Biographical Dictionary of Notable Americans, Vol. 6, p.458.

4. *An Address by Alexander Clark Caselman.* Read to the United Empire Loyalists Association of Canada, 1900. Reprint of Hamilton Branch, UELCA, 1984. (Caselman includes, in Appendix A, a list of Palatine heads of families who came to New York between June 1710 and to September 1714 compiled by Boyd Ehle, C.E. from the *Documentary History of New York, Vol. III.* (According to this reference the story about the Indian Chiefs inviting the Palatines to the Scholarie is likely a legend.) In addition, there are other lists of those Palatines from various places and different times. See also: *The Palatine families of New York: a study of the German Immigrants who arrived in Colonial New York in 1710.* Henry Z. Jones, Universal City, California, 1985. See also: *Early Eighteenth Century Palatine Emigration,* Walter Allen Kittle, Public Genealogical Publishing Co., Baltimore, 1979.) (Members of the Waeger family married at least two members of the families that came in 1709-10: the Barlemans (Parleman, Parliament) and the Hoffmans (Huffman)).

5. *To their Heirs Forever.* Eula C. Lapp, Mika Publishing Co., Belleville, 1977.

6. *The Palatine.* John Greenleaf Whittier, in *The Tent on the Beach and Other Poems,* Ticknor and Fields, Boston, 1868. pp. 90, 93,94,95,96,96. (See also *An Address by Alexander Clark Caselman* to the United Empire Loyalists Association of Canada, 1900, above.)

7. *Progenitors in the Württemberg Region, Germany, of the New York State Wagar-Wager-Weger Families.* Compiled and produced by Paul W. Prindle, Darien, Connecrticut, from data collected in

Germany by Commander Howard Carlyle Wagar, USNR, Fairmont Minnissota, and by Genealogist Herr Egon Oertel, Rymaunstr. 14, Oehringen, Germany. n.d.

8. *Montcalm and Wolfe.* Francis Parkman, Viking, 1984. (A "sweeping chronicle of the French and
Indian War", flyleaf)

9. *Fort Ticonderoga: A Short History.* S.H.P. Pell, Fort Ticonderoga Museum, 1978.

10. *The New York Conspiracy.* Daniel Horsmanden, Beacon Press, 1971.

11. *The American revolutionaries; A History in their own Words, 1750-1800.* Milton Meltzer, (ed.),
1987. (See "Seven hundred Levelers" pp.42-45. One wonders if Pendergrast's statement "if oppo-
sition to Government was deemed rebellion, no member of that court were entitled to set upon
this trial" was referring to the leaders of the coming Revolution.)

12. *The American Revolution: A General history, 1763-1790.* E James Ferguson, Dorsey press, 1979.
(The Pendergrast affair is told on pp.96-101.)

7: WAR DRUMS

The character Johann Leonard, Eberhardt's brother, is tentatively fictional, but may
in fact have existed. Supplement C of "Progenitors…"[1] mentions a Johann Leonard Waeger whose parentage is not known but "he was probably the brother of
Aberhardt and Niclass" born in the hiatus between 1738, the year the family landed
in America, and 1745 when Niclass was born. There was a Johann Leonard Wager
listed on the muster role of the 6th Regiment of the Albany County Militia at the
time of the Revolution, but it would be very coincidental if he was Eberhardt's
brother.[2]

I have also given Eberhardt a sister, Greta (Margaretha) that may or may not
have been his sister, possibly also born to Georg and Margaretha in the hiatus between 1738 and 1745.[1]

The original St. Paul's Lutheran Church on the Witaburger lands was built,
along with the graveyard, on land gifted by Col. Henry Beekman to Leonardt Wager and Michael Pultz. In a letter dated April 17, 1759 Beekman wrote to "Messrs.
Wager & Boltz:- Having received your letter of the 20th ult., concerning leave to
build church &c., which reasonable request I willingly grant,…."[3] Church records
show that the first Baptisms were in 1760, and included a "Margaretha, daughter
of Eberhard Wager."[4] Nothing more seems to be known of the circumstances of
this child's birth or what happened to her. My records indicate that Eberhardt was
married "ca. 1760" so this first child, named Margaretha possibly after her grandmother, two years before Thomas, is consistent with the conventions of that time,
and her existence, unless she died as an infant, is believable. However, a child called
Margaretha, was born on 22nd June 1760 to another Eberhardt, son of Bernard,
Georg's brother and our Eberhardt's uncle. It is likely the baptism record of St.
Paul's Church refers to this Margaretha.

The new war that was about to descend upon Eberhardt had antecedents that
went back to the previous century. The root cause of the American Revolution
was the same that caused the English Civil War of the mid 1600's, which led to

Cromwell's Commonwealth. Puritan ancestors who fought the King and Church for power sharing in the English Civil War planted the seeds of rebellion in the souls of the Puritan settlers of early America. In the decade between 1630 and 1640 one hundred and ninety-seven ships brought to America more than twenty thousand Puritans who established what was later called the Massachusetts Bay Colony. John Winthrop, one of these, wanted to create a "Bible Commonwealth" in America.[5,p.39] This earlier group was later followed by another wave of Puritans in the 1660's after the Restoration. Apparently, no less an American patriot than John Adams said the Revolution "began as early as the first Plantation of the country."[6] A further connection between the peoples of the Massachusetts Bay Colony and Cromwell's Commonwealth can be illustrated by the fact that Edward Winslow, a prominent member of the developing American aristocracy, a Governor of the Massachusetts Bay Colony and a *Mayflower* pioneer, was a consultant to Cromwell's Protectorate in the early days of its formation.[5,p.69] (Ironically, a descendent of Edward Winslow was a Loyalist and one of the founders of New Brunswick.)

Tax aversion that became the cause célèbre of the Revolution, was a natural response to the lack of representation in Parliament and its arrogant stubbornness, even for the German refugees who had left their homeland because of high taxes to support the grandiose ambitions of the aristocracy and the constant drain of the many wars. At the same time however, many New York Germans were resistant to the uprising and became Loyalists. Apparently they feared the rebels more than taxes. To them, the political situation must have seemed like anarchy.

Our interest here is with the backcountry people of the lower Hudson valley, which was at first settled by the Dutch, and after 1710 by many German Palatines. The newcomers to this wilderness were poor land hungry tenant farmers who depended upon a benign state and the large Crown-patronized landowners for their livelihood. It was a feudal existence; much like most of them had thought they had left for good. Talk of a tyrannical British King and philosophical ideas of Locke's rights of man must have seemed very abstract and otherworldly to the country people who in many cases had not yet mastered the language of their new country. They wanted their own farms, which as the talk of "life, liberty and property" in Boston became more virulent, their landlords more greedy, and their promised deeds mired in legalities, they must have seen their future at peril. One can surmise that many felt their future lay with a stable order that would allow them to evolve to a more prosperous life, which in a practical sense would be to own a piece of viable farmland. But, as had happened to their fathers and grandfathers in the countries they had left, peace-seeking lives were now about to explode into a thousand shards of violence.

So Eberhardt takes his family further into the wilderness. On the road to Claverack the troubadour's ditty is the first two stanzas, slightly altered, of a song named *American Taxation*.[7]

Eberhardt is able to lease two hundred acres of raw land and begins to build a farm. The precise location of Eberhardt's farm is not known. At the time Stephen Van Rensselaer was leasing Rensselaerwyck Manor land to settlers and it is recorded that Eberhardt leased land from him "near Pittstown."[1] Jacob Weeger, born in Germany seven years after Eberhardt and who lived in Nine Partners where he married Rosina and had a son Henrich, is also believed to have leased land from Van Rensselaer sometime between 1763 and 1765. A surveyor's map listing 133 settlers, dated 1767 of the east portion of Rensselaerwyck shows no settlers with the name Wager or its many derivatives.[8] Yet in 1790, after the Revolution, a map of the area "sometimes" called Feilstown drawn by John Van Allen from the survey books of Rensselaerwyck Manor indicates there were several Wager farms in the north and east parts of the Manor, including Nicholas, Jacob, John, Henry and Thomas.[9] In 1884, as today, there were many Wager families living in what is now called the town of Brunswick, especially in the north-eastern portion.[10]

After the Revolution Eberhardt made at least two claims for compensation for his losses. A memorial dated April 1786 gives his location as "Filstown, Albany Co. N.Y."[11] A second claim, made in February 1788 reads, "Evidence on the Claim of Everhart Wegar, late of Fitstown, Albany County, N.Y. Province."[12] Given the problems of language and spelling at the time I am left with the conclusion that Eberhardt's leased farm was probably somewhere between Brunswick Centre and Pittstown as they are called today.

Eberhardt clears forty acres, raises livestock, and with Lena is raising a family when politics and violence begins to threaten his life and livelihood. The politics of land ownership brings Ethan Allen into prominence with his attacks on the Yorkers. New Hampshire claimed its western boundary to be twenty miles east of the Hudson River. New York claimed its eastern boundary to be the Connecticut River. Before 1764 New Hampshire granted 117 patents. After 1765 New York granted 107 patents in the same, disputed area. Violence and sometimes bloodshed between New York officials and the Green Mountain Boys led by Ethan Allen was the result.[13, p.15] The Breakenridge affair is documented in Lapp.[14] The first shot to kill happened in April 1775. In May, Ethan Allen[15] and Benedict Arnold[16] captured Fort Ticonderoga, and took away its guns. In June the new Continental Congress approved an invasion of Canada. In August, Richard Montgomery mounted an invasion on the Richelieu River forts. And in September Benedict Arnold set out to meet Montgomery in Quebec by way of the Kennebec and Chaudière Rivers.[16,17,18]

It seems Montgomery considered his first foray to St. Jean not to attempt capture, but more of a reconnaissance mission as mentioned in a letter written to his wife Janet on the 5th of September, 1775. He left Fort Ticonderoga and marched to St. Jean, where, "We found the enemy's vessel (the Royal Savage), which mounts sixteen guns, almost ready to sail. We had but two pieces of artillery with carriages—by no means sufficient to undertake a siege, or to destroy the vessel, which is under the cannon of the fort."[19]

He expresses unhappiness with the rabble that he inherited to fight the English.

But it was on the 12th that he wrote a very long letter to Janet the contents being mostly an account of his frustration with the men under his command. He is wishing to resign, which he does after the capture of Montreal, but it is not accepted. "I am, my dear Janet, so exceedingly out of spirits and so chagrined with the behaviour of the troops, that I most heartily repent having undertaken to lead them." "Could I, with decency, leave the army in its present situation, I would not serve an hour longer."[19]

The Albany Commission for the Detection of Conspiracies was forcing the farmers to choose between loyalty to Congress or to the King. Eberhardt realizes he must make a decision. He visits his brother Johann Leonard who was with Montgomery to try to better understand his quandary.

The story told by Lodewick Beschler was inspired by Hawthorne.[20] Almost all colonies passed legislation making traitors of those who did not support the Revolution. In 1776 the New York State convention resolved "any person being an adherent to the King of Great Britain shall be guilty of treason and suffer death."[21, p.4,6]

Eberhardt's friend Jed wants him to join the rebels. Johann Leonard in his turn visits Eberhardt and he is chastised for sitting on the fence. When he listens to Fred's story of the seeds of mob rule he makes up his mind to support what he believes to be law and order over chaos.

1. *Progenitors in the Württemberg Region, Germany, of the New York State Wagar-Wager-Weger Families.* Compiled and produced by Paul W. Prindle, Darien, Connecrticut, from data collected in Germany by Commander Howard Carlyle Wagar, USNR, Fairmont Minnissota, and by Genealogist Herr Egon Oertel, Rymaunstr. 14, Oehringen, Germany.

2. *Report of Center Brunswick Historical Society.* Archives, Center Brunswick, Albany County N.Y. p.47.

3. *Historic Old Rhinebeck: Echoes of Two Centuries.* Howard H. Morse, Published by the author, 1908. (Reprinted and Indexed by Arthur C.M.Kelly, 1977). (Quote from Henry Beekman's letter p. 146)

4. *History of Rhinebeck.* Edward M. Smith, Rhinebeck, New York, 1881. (Reprinted and Indexed by Arthur C.M. Kelly, 1977). (Record of Margaretha Wager's baptism p.123.)

5. *The Trannicide Brief.* Geoffrey Robertson, Chatto and Windus, 2005, p.39 and p.69.

6. *The Loyalists of Massachusetts: and the other side of the American Revolution.* James H. Stark, W.B.Clarke Co. Boston 1910.

7. *Songs and Ballads of the American Revolution.* Henry L. Williams and Frank Moore, Hurst and Company, New York, 1905, pp.13-14.

8. *Map of the Portion East of the Hudson River of the Manor Renselaerwick.* Surveyed and laid down by JN° R. Bleeker, 1767.

9. *Brunswick in 1790.* Map adapted from a map of the eastern portion of the Manor of Rensselaerwyck drawn between 1787 and 1790 by John E. Van Allen and from the survey books of the manor compiled during the same time.

10. *1854 Map.* Reprinted by Burton F. Miller, 1975. Archives, Centre Brunswick.

11. *American Loyalist Claims.* Vol.7 Abstracted from the PRO Audit Office, Series 13, Bundles 1-3+37, National Genealogical Society, Washington, 1980.

12. *Second Report of the bureau of Archives, Ontario.* Claim 389. Toronto, 1905.

13. *Loyalism in the Hoosick Valley.* Bernard C. Young, self published, printed by Anything Printed, Woodstock, Vermont, 2008.

14. *To Their Heirs Forever.* Eula C. Lapp, Mica Publishing Co., Belleville, 1977.

15. *Revolution to Reconstruction:Biographies, The story of Ethan Allen.* Chapter II, text by Doug Robertson, 1994-2008.

16. *Benedict Arnold, Revolutionary Hero: An American Warrior Reconsidered.* James Kirby Martin, New York University press, 1997.

17. *Thrust for Quebec: The American Attempt on Quebec in 1775-1776.* Robert McConnell Hatch, Houghton-Mifflin, Boston, 1979.

18. *Canada Invaded, 1775-1776.* George F G Stanley, Canadian War Museum, publication # 8, 1973.

19. *Biographical Notes Concerning General Richard Montgomery Together with Unpublished Letters.* Louise Livingston Hunt, 1876. Reprint: Michican State library.

20. *The Scarlet Letter.* Nathaniel Hawthorne, Running Press, Philadelphia, 1991.

21. *Genesis of a Nation.* Laurier La Pierre, CBC Publications Branch, 1967. (La Pierre writes, "…practically every colony passed a Test Act, requiring each good citizen to carry on his person a certificate that he was free of the suspicion of loyalty to King George." To get a certificate one had to "…renounce allegiance to the king, and promise to support his state in its war upon him."

8: EBERHARDT'S WAR

Eberhardt's dream of the water monster and his grandfather's story of General Arminius are adaptations of Rhineland legends given in Spence.[1]

The character I call Young Jacob, son of Eberhardt (b. 1727 in Germany), was born near Rhinebeck in 1755. I believe he is the Jacob who was incarcerated, escaped, and subsequently ended up at first in Pfister's regiment and subsequently with Samuel McKay. Pfister was from the Hoosick area and I have assumed that Young Jacob was in that area before 1777. An account of Young Jacob's experience with the New York Committee of Safety is given in the minutes of the Committee and first Commission for Detecting Conspiracies, 1777-1778, as follows, "the following persons…were taken on their way to join the British Army taken at the houses of James Baldwin, John Craft and Henry Balding 1st January 1777…Jacob Wager."[2] Sometime between January 1st and March 16th Jacob escaped and was found in Rhinebeck. The minutes of the Committee dated March 17th contains the entry, "Mess[rs] Hoevenberg, Scott, & Lewis appeared (before the Committee) and informed (them) that they apprehended… Jacob Wager (and others) who lately escaped out of the Guard House & conveyed them from Rhinebeck to this place."[2] Sometime between March 17th and March 21st Jacob Wager took the oath of allegiance to the State of New York and was discharged. The three men who brought in Jacob Wager were paid £3, 5s and 4p for the "expenses of themselves & prisoners and Continental pay as privates each of them 4 Days."[2]

By the spring of 1777, the settlers were of split loyalties with some from the area joining up with the 6th Regiment of the Albany militia to fight against the British. Some stayed neutral and were subjected to harassment from the Albany

Commission for Detecting and Defeating Conspiracies but were not forced to take sides. Others of the settlers decided to resist. Eberhardt, his brother Niclass, and Young Jacob were among those who took active part in frustrating the rebels in their cause by aiding the British in any way they could. Raiding parties foraged up and down the Hudson valley. The roving bands of loyalists killed some innocent people, although the evidence indicates that Eberhardt was with Burgoyne before any one was killed. Eberhardt testified later, at the French brother's court martial at St. Jean, that during the summer of 1777 he "was with Mr. Gershom French in the woods near Albany, and all that time never plundered any friend of the Government, but assisted French in disarming many of the Rebels, and taking away some of their effects."[3] The effects he refers to here included horses, which brought a charge against him of horse stealing by the Albany Commission.

A story that has come down through the years is that Eberhardt was given a horse and saddle bags by a neighbour, and left his farm just before a posse came to lodge him in the guardhouse.

The historical record housed in the archives of Center Brunswick, New York State, reveals "that a company of Brunswick loyalists actually joined the British army, and may have even fought against their fellow Americans at the battles of Walloomsac (Bennington) and Saratoga." Included is the statement, "Number of men that joined Lieutenant Colonel John Peters...are the names Eberhardt Wager...."[3 p.47]

The activities of Eberhardt and the character I call Young Jacob (he gave his age as twenty when he enlisted with the Loyal Volunteers) during the summer of 1777 are highly speculative. The first edition of the Cruikshank and Watt book cites Jacob "As Sjt. In LV's, 15 Aug 77."[4 p.271] The Revised Edition has dropped that citation.[4 p.328.] During the two days before the Battle of Bennington men from the countryside were coming to Colonel Baum; Jacob, and even Eberhardt, may have been among these men.[4]

Evidence given in 1781 at the French brother's court martial at St Jean indicates that Eberhardt was with Gershom French in the woods in the summer of 1777, and therefore likely to have been brought in to Pfister or Peters by Gershom French. Whether Gershom French brought in Jacob to Pfister is speculative. Bernard Young in his excellent book, *Loyalism in the Hoosick Valley,* records that Jacob Wager was a signee to a document written in Chateauguay, dated April 1778, stating that the undersigned "Acknowledge to have been engaged in the Corps of Volunteers raised by the Late Colonel Francis Pfister of Hosack...."[5 p.68]

There was another Jacob Wager in Dutchess County, a Lieutenant in the New York State militia.[6]

I have assumed it was near the end of July 1777 that Eberhardt joined the British army. Burgoyne had captured Fort Ticonderoga on July 5th, and was moving south to engage the rebels. At the time of Eberhardt's assumed enlistment Burgoyne may still have been at Skenesboro where he was encamped waiting for provisions from Fort Ticonderoga, and for the way south to be cleared of trees cut by the rebels; and bridges repaired that had been destroyed to slow his advance. While camped at Skenesboro, Thomas Anburey records in July, 1777 that, "numbers have joined the army since we have penetrated into this place, professing themselves loyalists, …a third part of the number have arms, and till arms arrive for the remainder, they are employed in clearing the roads and repairing the bridges, in which the Americans are very expert."[7, p.152] It is possible that Eberhardt joined up with Burgoyne somewhere between Skenesboro and Fort Edward, or at Fort Edward, which the army reached on July 29th, after much difficulty due to the rough terrain. The situations at Fort Ann and Fort Edward were gleaned from Anburey [7, pp.148,154] and Lapp.[8, p.211]

The description of the massacre of Monro's retreating troops from Fort William henry is based on Rutledge.[9, p.442]

On Burgoyne's march to Albany, as loyalists joined his force he put them into three fledgling battalions: the "Kings Loyal Americans" under Lt. Col. Ebenezer Jessup; the "Queen's Loyal Rangers" led by Lt. Col. John Peters; and the "Loyal Volunteers" commanded by Lt. Col. Francis Pfister. A fourth unit was formed after Ticonderoga under Samuel McKay, a resident of St. Jean. Having been denied a commission by Guy Carleton he joined Burgoyne as a volunteer.

I have suggested in the narrative that Eberhardt was recruited by Gershom French, who brought in about ninety recruits to Burgoyne's campaign, which were assigned to Colonel Francis Van Pfister's Loyal Volunteers sometime near the end of July or the beginning of August, 1777. Cruikshank's history of the King's Royal Regiment of New York states that Pfister's Loyal Volunteers corps was raised on August 1st., 1777. He goes on to say; "The LV was in some fashion oddly amalgamated with the QLR (Queen's Loyal Rangers, under the command of Lieut-Col. John Peters) for a period in August, 1777 and fought…beside that corps in the Battle of Bennington, …where Van Pfister was killed. Command (was) transferred to Captain Samuel McKay.…"[4, p.159]

Eberhardt is listed in Peter's corps on August 16th, the day Pfister was killed.[8, p.196] Peter's corps was badly depleted in the battle losing 210 men killed and thirty taken prisoner. Since Pfister and Peters appeared to be commanding jointly it seems probable that Pfister's surviving men would go to Peters, and later to McKay. Assuming that Eberhardt was with Pfister at the battle at Walloomsac, and that Eberhardt is on the muster list of Peters corps on the same day as the battle it is very likely that he was involved in this battle. (The Battle of Bennington was fought within a few miles of the Waeger home, and given his local knowledge it is possible that he was with a scouting team of eleven men that were sent out on August 1st under Justus Sherwood to reconnoitre a supply of horses that were reported to be stocked at Bennington. However, I doubt this supposition because there is no evidence that Eberhardt was with Sherwood later in the war.)

The battle of Bennington was, arguably, the decisive battle for the Northern Department of the British military, as this humiliating defeat with seven hundred taken prisoner, brought more and more soldiers to the rebel side, and by the time Burgoyne got to Saratoga he was vastly outnumbered. For an account of the Battle of Bennington see,[10,11,12.]

It appears that the Loyal Volunteers was reformed under Lt. Col. John Peters with the loss of Van Pfister. Peter's papers names Everet Wager in his return of men as having joined his regiment on August 16th and leaving on August 22nd.[8, p.196] In the absence of reliable contrary evidence, I presume Eberhardt went with Samuel McKay shortly after August 22nd and remained with him during the retreat from Saratoga. I also presume that Eberhardt was mostly employed as an artificer, and again in the absence of contrary evidence presume he was with McKay when the latter was sent out to prepare a retreat route the day before the Battle of Freeman's Farm. Lapp recounts a story of McKay being sent out to reconnoitre a retreat and repair roads and build bridges, getting trapped by five hundred rebels and going on to Fort George to meet St. Leger's reinforcements after his defeat at Fort Stanwix.[8, p.209.]

The battles of Saratoga, fought on September 19, 1777 at a place now referred to as Freeman's Farm, and on October 7 at Bemis Heights, pitted General Burgoyne against General Horatio Gates.[11-14.] Thomas Anburey[7] gives a first hand account that is most useful for our purposes.

From the meagre evidence available, I have concluded that Eberhardt was with Samuel McKay building roads, and did not see action at the battles of Saratoga, but was with McKay when rebel forces attacked him near Fort George. General Lincoln, from Manchester took his detachment of militia across country in the rear of Burgoyne's army to try and capture Fort Ticonderoga and cut off the British. It was to be a three pronged attack: Seth Warner to take Mount Independence, Col. Woodbridge was sent against Skenesboro and Fort Ann, while Col. Brown and Col. Herrick were to cross Lake Champlain at the narrows, march through the woods and occupy the landing place at the bottom of Lake George and attack Fort Ticonderoga.[15, pp.130-132] These are likely the rebel soldiers Eula Lapp refers to when she quotes from a petition written by McKay to his ministry on July 20th, 1778; "shortly after (Colonel Sutherland's departure) about 500 rebels…crossed the river above us, where on consultation with my officers, it was thought impracticable to return to camp." McKay goes on to say "the number under my command was but 180, of which 43 were killed and (or) taken by the rebels on my attempt to return to the woods."[8, p.208]

The capture of the Lake George Landing Place and Mount Defiance and the old French Lines by the rebels is described in a letter by Col. John Brown to general Lincoln.[16] Brown lay siege to Fort Ticonderoga for four days, but his cannons having no effect, provisions running low and his fear of imminent British reinforcements convinced him he should withdraw. Afterwards, the houses and barracks were set afire by Gen. Powell who then retreated to Canada.[16, p.87]

1. *Germany, Myths and Legends.* Lewis Spence, Bracken Books, London, 1985. (The stories of Clo-dio's wife and Arminius from the legends of "The Merovingians", p. 24 and the "Rebellion of the Barbarians", p.21)

2. *Minutes of the Committee and First Commission for Detecting Conspiricies, 1776-1778, State of New York.* Vol.57, State of New York Historical Society, 1925. MPL 906 N556c pp.70,209,220 (The excerpts here are with the Howard Wagar folio of papers housed at the Lennox and Addington County Museum, Napanee, Ontario.)

3. *Report of Center Brunswick Historical Society.* Archives, Center Brunswick, Albany County N.Y. p.47.

4. *The Kings Royal Regiment of New York.* Ernest P. Cruikshank and Gavin K. Watt, Ontario Histori-cal Society, 1931, 1984, 2006.

5. *Loyalism in the Hoosick Valley.* Bernard C. Young, self-published. Printed by Anything Printed , Woodstock, Vermont, 2008

6. *Minutes of the Council of Appointment.* Poughkeepsie, New York, May 28th, 1778, N.Y. Historical Society, vol. 58, MPL 906 N556c, p.15.

7. *With Burgoyne from Quebec.* Thomas Anburey, MacMillan, Toronto, 1963. (Sidney Jackson, ed.). (A first hand account of Burgoyne's march to Saratoga, and a second hand account of the Battle of Bennington).

8. *To Their Heirs Forever.* Eula C Lapp, Mica Publishing Co., Belleville, 1977. (Return of men in Lt. Col, John Peters' Regiment as of August 16th on page 196 is taken from New York State library, Mss, 3580, Peters'Papers) (Lapp gives some insight as to what happened to MacKay's Loyal Volunteers at the battle of Saratoga, p.208. I have accepted her description of the events of the day before the battle as regards the Loyal Volunteers.)

9. *Century of Conflict.* Joseph Lister Rutledge, Vol., II, Doubleday, N.Y., 1956.

10. *The battle of Bennington in German Archives and Museums.* Thomas M. Barker and Waloomsac Battle Chapter, Empire State Society, National Society of the Sons of the American Revolution, Cambridge, New York, n.d.

11. *Decisive battles of the American Revolution.* Lt. Col. Joseph P Mitchell, Fawcett Premier, New York, 1962. (For the Battle of Bennington, the turning point of the War, see pp.107-113)

12. *The Centennial History of the Battle of Bennington.* Frank W Coburn, Littlefield, Boston, 1877. (An American view of the battle of Bennington.)

13. *American Battlefields.* Hubbard Cobb, MacMillan, New York, 1995. (See pp.49-52 for the Battle of Bennington.)

14. *Battles of the American Revolution.* Curt Johnson and Sampson Low, Roxby Press, 1975.

15. *History of Lake Champlain, 1609-1814.* (4th ed.) Peter S Palmer, Purple mountain press, 1992. (A good resource for the events at Ticonderoga, Crown Point and Valcour Island in 1775. Also gives details of the undertaking of Burgoyne's march to Albany).

16. *Fort Ticonderoga: A Short History.* SHP Pell, Fort Ticonderoga Museum, 1978.

17. *Rensselaer County Loyalist Soldiers: Loyalist Muster Roll of 1777.* Bernard C. Young, 2006. NAC WO28/10, Reel B-2867, pp.17-18. (The muster roll of Samuel McKay dated Dec. 20, 1777 lists Eberhardt Wager as a "Private under Convention in Cantonment")

9: JOURNEYMAN SOLDIER

Our story shifts to the confluence of the Chateauguay and the St. Lawrence Riv-ers, the scene of Eberhardt's military adventures after the burning of Ticonderoga and Burgoyne's surrender and retreat to Canada.

The upper reaches of the St. Lawrence River set the stage for the human drama that engulfed Eberhardt during the last years of his duty to the English king. It was during the time when the St. Lawrence was the bastion against the ambitions of General Washington and the Continental Congress, and his part was to help to provide fortifications against both the Americans and the French, who were allies of the rebels near the end of the war.

Following the Battle of Bennington Samuel McKay inherited the remnants of Van Pfister's Loyal Volunteers and got them safely to Montreal after the British defeat at Saratoga. His muster list of December 20th, 1777 named three hundred and sixty two men of which one hundred and ninety were, or had been, prisoners. (Many were paroled in late August of that year.) He named twenty-four dead. Some thirty percent of the men named for the Loyal Volunteers were members of the Gilead Lutheran Church of Center Brunswick, attesting to the fact that Eberhardt would likely have been acquainted with most of the men in his corps before the conflict. There were a substantial number also from Camden Valley that settled close to the Waegers on the Bay of Quinte after the war.[1]

In the book *Loyalists of Quebec* there is the statement that among those who McKay brought safely to Quebec were "...sergeants...Jacob and Everhart Weager."[2, p.41]

When Capt. McKay died the Loyal Volunteers were taken over by Captain Robert Leake and later many were placed with Major Edward Jessup and the Loyal Rangers, which was formed in 1781, when the shooting war was virtually over. The Loyal Rangers had no combat record.[3, pp.158-159]

For my very primitive (and shameful) knowledge of Quebec and the Iroquois culture I have had to rely on several sources.[4-10] The Indian woman Red Feathers did not exist. We know nothing about Eberhardt's domestic life during this period, specifically the relationship with his wife Lena. There is no evidence that she joined him, if still alive, at any time while he was in Canada. Some war widows from the Hoosick Valley whose husbands had joined the British were escorted to St. Jean. Farms were confiscated and re-sold. Apparently Lena was not one of them.

The fort the British called Oswegatchie was an old French mission fort called Fort La Présentation, built to convert the Iroquois to Christianity.[11] The fort was a base of operations by the French in the French and Indian War; in the defeat of Braddock and Washington in the Ohio Valley, in the destruction of Fort Bull on the Mohawk, in the capture of Oswego, and in Montcalm's siege of Fort William Henry. In 1759 the French abandoned Fort La Présentation and constructed Fort Levis on Chimney Island in the Saint Lawrence to defend the river against attacks on Montreal and Quebec.[12] In 1760, Amherst destroyed Fort Levis and went on to capture Montreal after losing many men and boats in the rapids at Coteau-du-Lac, west of Montreal.

1. *Role of the Officers, non-commissioned Officers & Privates of Royalists who served under General Burgoyne's Last Campaign.* Courtesy Bernard C. Young, Original Source; National Archives of Canada, WO 28/10, Reel B-2867, pp.17-18.

2. *Loyalists of Quebec, 1774-1825: A Forgotten History.* Heritage branch, United Empire Loyalist Association of Canada, Montreal, 1989. (What I learned about Capt. Samuel McKay I gleaned from several parts of this book. Eberhardt and Jacob Wager are listed here as Sergeants. p.41)

3. *The Kings Royal regiment of New York.* Ernest P. Cruikshank and Gavin K. Watt, Ontario Historical Society, 1931, 1984. Revised in 2006 as "The History and Muster Role of the Kings Royal Regiment of New York". (The latest edition lists Willem, Eberhardt's son as a drummer in the 2nd Battalion of the Regiment, enlisting in 1784.[p.328] Also included is the discharge certificate of Private Thomas Wagar, another of Aberhardt's sons.)[p.147]

4. *Sacred Life: A North American Ethnohistory Emphasizing the Iroquois of the Eastern Woodlands.* Daniel H. Page, Pine Tree Press, 1987. (Describes the ways and mores of the Iroquois.)

5. *The Parkman Reader.* Samuel Eliot Morrison (ed.), Little Brown and Co., Toronto, 1955. (A good description of the Huron and Iroquois by a renowned historian.)

6. *In Mohawk Country: Early narratives about a Native People.* Dean R. Snow, Charles T. Gehring, William A. Starna (eds.), Syracuse University Press, 1996. (First hand accounts of various travellers into Mohawk country between 1634 and 1810.)

7. *A Short History of Quebec.* 2nd ed., John A. Dickenson and Brian Young, McGill-Queen's University Press, Montreal and Kingston, 2000.

8. *Daily Life in Early Canada: From Champlain to Montcalm.* Raymond Douville and Jacques Casanova, George Allen and Unwin Ltd., 1968.

9. *La Nouvelle France: The Making of French Canada- A Cultural History.* Peter N. Moogk, Michigan State University Press, 2000. (Moogk points out that the natives viewed the white man as inferior, and especially repugnant if they had red hair. p.25)

10. *The Picture Gallery of Canadian History.* Vol. 1, Discovery to 1763, C.W.Jefferys, Ryerson press, Toronto, 1942. (Excellent illustrations and description of material aspects of life in early Canada. Excellent illustrations of aboriginal canoes and snowshoes.)

11. *History of Fort La Présentation.* www.fortpresentation.net/History. Html. (History of the French Fort that was renamed by the British "Oswegatchie.")

12. *Travel and Adventures in Canada and the Indian Territories, 1760-1776.* Alexander Henry, M. G. Hurtig Ltd., Edmonton, 1969. (A fur traders adventures on the St. Lawrence route to the west and the Ottawa route to the upper country. The story of Fort Levi and the loss of men and boats on the rapids of the St. Lawrence as he accompanied Amherst on his campaign against Montreal in 1760.)

10: THE RESTLESS RIVER

The river was called the *La Gr. Rivière du Canada ou de Saint Laurens* on an early map[1, p.60] now called The St. Lawrence River or Le Fleuve Saint Laurent. It is a great slash carved out by prehistory and separates the Pre-Cambrian Mountains to the north and the Appalachian Chain to the south. It was in Eberhardt's days a lively river hampering the European exploration of the southern great lakes. The fur traders found a more acceptable access to beaver country by way of the Ottawa

River, allowing the newly arrived Europeans to open the upper country of what would become confederated Canada a century later. An early road between Quebec and Fort Frontenac allowed armies to march up and down the river without perishing in the many rapids or "sault." La Grande Rivière du Canada, for the French, was truly the highway that took their empire in North America to its fullest extent. When the English surveyor Cook conquered the river in 1758 and in 1759-1760 by Wolfe and Amherst they were able to not only exploit habitants and the fur trade, but cut off the rebellious colonies to the south from westward expansion, which was a major factor in moving the Continental Congress to invade Canada. When the French teamed up with the American rebels after Burgoyne's defeat at Saratoga the war took a different tack for the British; one which was more directed to protecting Canada and the other British colonies left to them from the return of the French. The St. Lawrence River became the frontier for a much-reduced British North America and it was in this context that Eberhardt Waeger was part of its story.

Attached to the Provincial Line of the British army he spent several years sojourning up and down the river, and its tributary the Richelieu, doing I believe, mostly garrison duty and building barracks and fortifications to secure what was left of British North America. He may have gone on some raids into the Mohawk Valley, but it appears as if these raids were designed to scorch the earth rather than to re-conquer territory that seems to have been conceded to the new Republic early on in the long conflict. When the Mohawks realized that they were not going to be able to return to their homes, they were bitterly disappointed. When peace finally settled over the land the St. Lawrence River became the boundary between two new countries.

Haldimand, the new Governor of the colony of Canada was no remote "gentleman at his desk," a fresh face from the mother country, knowing nothing of the circumstances he was to control.[2] A Swiss national, who came to America to supplement scarce British officers there during the French and Indian Wars. General Haldimand, wounded at Ticonderoga when he was a colonel for Abercrombie, was later given the command of Fort Edward. He won a victory against Indians and Canadians at Oswego, and was with Amherst at the bombardment of Fort Levi and the capture of Montreal in 1760. He became the military governor of Canada for four years after the conquest, stationed at Trois Rivieres. He knew the ways of both the Habitants and the Indians. He had spent many years in the theatre where he was now expected to make both civilian and military judgments until peace could, hopefully, be accomplished. That he knew the imminent danger to Canada from the rebellious Americans, and a strategy to protect the colony by repairing old forts and establishing new ones is clear from his dispatches from Sorel to his Minister, Lord George Germaine at Westminster in Oct, 1778.[2, p.132]

Besides the forts on the Richelieu and St. Lawrence Rivers, Haldimand had started fortifying Carelton Island, improving the canal at Coteau-du-Lac and planning a fort at Oswego.

Haldimand brought all the stores from the Richelieu River forts to his military base at Sorel deeming the former to be not secure. He planned to make Sorel, being at the confluence of the St. Lawrence and the Richelieu and able to accommodate "ships of Burthens", a permanent fortified site. At first he estimated that he could only "erect some Temporary Redoubts, and to lodge but a part of the Body of Troops I mean to station there."[2, p.134] He went on to say the seigneury was offered for sale for £3000 and proposed the Government purchase it.

For Eberhardt's time at Sorel see,[3,4.] In July 1778 Robert Leake was given an official commission as a captain of the Provincial line. He was ordered to choose a company of fit men from the Loyal Volunteers. In May 1779 Haldimand ordered Sir John Johnson, commander of the 1st Battalion, KRRNY, to form a combat company from Leake's corps. This new company, named Leake's Independent Company, numbered 137 men in all and were divided for two separate functions; the combat detachment and engineering detachment. The combat company went on raids into the Mohawk Valley in 1780 and participated in the Duanesbourgh raid the next year. At the end of 1781 a second battalion of the KRRNY absorbed the majority of Leake's Independent Company. The balance joined the Loyal Rangers, led by Major Edward Jessup, and which had no combat record.[3, p.158]

At Coteau-du-Lac the "long house" Eberhardt and Red Feathers built came from various readings of Indian houses.[5, pp. 16, 56] The canal that Eberhardt worked on was the first canal built in North America.[2, p.184] His movements during this period are very vague, largely assumed from what I can deduce from the military records. His sojourn at Coteau- du-Lac is uncertain, but I think quite possible.

The description of the fort at St. Jean and Chambly came from[2, pp. 133,134].

The block-house at the Lacolle River built in 1781 still exists and is now a tourist attraction.[6]

1. *Historical Atlas of Canada.* Derek Hayes, Douglas and McIntyre, Vancouver, 2002. (The St. Lawrence River has had several names: "Riviere des Iroquois by Coronelli, 1685, p. 63 Hayes; "La Grande Riviere de Canada" by Du Val, 1653, p.56 and by d'Abbeville, 1656, p. 60. "The Grand River of Canada" contains a truth about the River that the more prosaic St. Lawrence does not.)
2. *Sir Frederick Haldimand.* Jean N. McIlwraith, Morang and Co., Toronto, 1906.
3. *The King's Royal regiment of New York.* Ernest A. Cruikshank, Gavin K. Watt (ed.) Ontario Historical Society, 1984.
4. *Building a House in New France.* Peter N. Moogk, Fitzhenry and Whiteside, 2002.
5. *The Picture Gallery of Canadian History.* C.W. Jefferys, vol. 1; "Discovery to 1763", Ryerson Press, Toronto, 1942.
6. *Michelin Touring Guide: Quebec.* Michelin Tires (Canada) Ltd., 1992

11: JOURNEY'S END

An order came from the War Office ordering the Provincial regiments be disbanded by December 25th, 1783. Due to the lateness of the season and the fact that the settlement lands were not yet surveyed the troops that had not already returned home were housed and fed into the next summer, and provisions continued after settlement.[1]

At the time of disbandment Eberhardt was with Captain John Meyers at Riviere du Chine.[2, p.510]

The discussion between Mrs. Hawley and Gabriella about the merits of mosquito dope is taken from[3, pp.242-250.] An astute reader may suspect the model for Gabriella to be Isabella Fraser, Simon's mother. In the narrative I have Mrs. Hawley and Gabriella traveling together. I have no evidence that Isabella Fraser and son Simon (Alexander) traveled with Eberhardt and the Hawleys from Lachine to Coteau-du-Lac but I think it possible. The Dictionary of Canadian Biography states, "Captain John Fraser, one of the brothers who had served in Fraser's Highlanders, had settled in Montreal and had been appointed a judge of the Court of Common Pleas. In 1784, with his help, Isabella and her younger children were able to join her son William, who had taken up land at Coteau-du-Lac."[4] Simon was Isabella's youngest child, and would have been eight years old at the time. Anecdotal evidence suggests that Mrs. Fraser travelled from her home in Mapleton, Hoosick Township to the Mohawk Valley, and from there, to Coteau-du-Lac. It is plausible that Eberhardt would have known both Simon Sr., who was taken prisoner at Bennington, and his son William who was also at the Battle of Bennington.

The life of Molly Brant is documented in[5.]

The exact place where Eberhardt stepped ashore is not certain. However, Redmond Crawford, Jacob Wager, members of the Sills, Hawley and Carscallen families, all comrades of Eberhardt, came ashore at an old Indian portage to Hay Bay from Lake Ontario. It is reasonable to suggest that Eberhardt, his son Thomas, and cousin Jacob came ashore at this point, just east of the Anglican Church at Sandhurst. Jacob's drawn lot #3 was here. Ruth M. Wright writes that in 1615 Champlain, returning with Huron warriors from an expedition into Iroquois territories came "through the Upper gap, landed on the shore in the area of what is now Conway-Sandhurst and carried their boats and gear about half a league across land to the south shore of Hay Bay, about where Sillsville now stands."[6, p.3] She writes, "In 1687 the French used the same route to conquer the Cayuga village of Genneious on the north shore of Hay Bay."[6, p.4] A sizable creek, able to accommodate bateaux existed at this location in those days.[6, p.4] Today it is dry.

---

1. *The King's Royal Regiment of New York*. Ernest A. Cruikshank and Gavin K. Watt (ed.) Ontario Historical Society, 1984.
2. *Hans Waltimeyer*. Jane Bennett Goddard, Self-published, 1980. (Lists Everheart Wager in John

Meyer's Company of the Loyal Rangers). See also, *Marilyn Stewart Papers*. Marilyn Stewart, Napanee, Unpublished, n.d.

3. *Camping and Woodcraft*. Vol. I, Horace Kephart, 1917.

4. *Fraser, Simon*. Dictionary of Canadian Biography, Library and Archives Canada, 2005.

5. *Three Faces of Molly Brant*. Earle Thomas, Quarry Press, 1996.

6. *The Front of South Fredericksburgh*. Ruth M. Wright, The South Fredericksburgh Heritage Committee, 1999.